RETOLD

The Story of Jesus

Steve Lipscomb

THE
CiderHouse
PRESS

Retold: The Story of Jesus. © Copyright 2015 by Steve Lipscomb.
All rights reserved.
Printed in the United States of America on acid free paper

www.theciderhousepress.com

For correspondence with the author, contact:
SteveLipscomb@SteveLipscomb.us

For ordering books, scheduling interviews or appearances, permissions, and other information, contact:

The CiderHouse Press
Topeka, Kansas
info@theciderhousepress.com

First edition published 2015.

Cover and interior design by Rob Peters www.rob.peters.com

LCCN 2015900119
ISBN 978-0-9864078-4-0 (pbk)
ISBN 978-0-9864078-3-3 (hardcover)
ISBN 978-0-9864078-0-2 (ebook)

10 9 8 7 6 5 4 3 2 1

RETOLD: The Story of Jesus is a work of fiction. Although the story written here follows many of the events as they are reported in both the canonical and the so-called gnostic gospels, it is, for the most part, a creative work of my own imagination.

If you are unable to read or think or imagine anything about Jesus that is not contained in the Bible, then you will not enjoy this book and should not buy it.

For those who feel compelled to write and tell me of the book's inaccuracies as they relate to holy scripture or historical record, there is no need to do so. I already know this. Again, I have taken creative license to produce this work of fiction and am aware of the inconsistencies contained herein.

To borrow a phrase from Jesus: Blessed are those who take no offense at me.

—Steve Lipscomb+

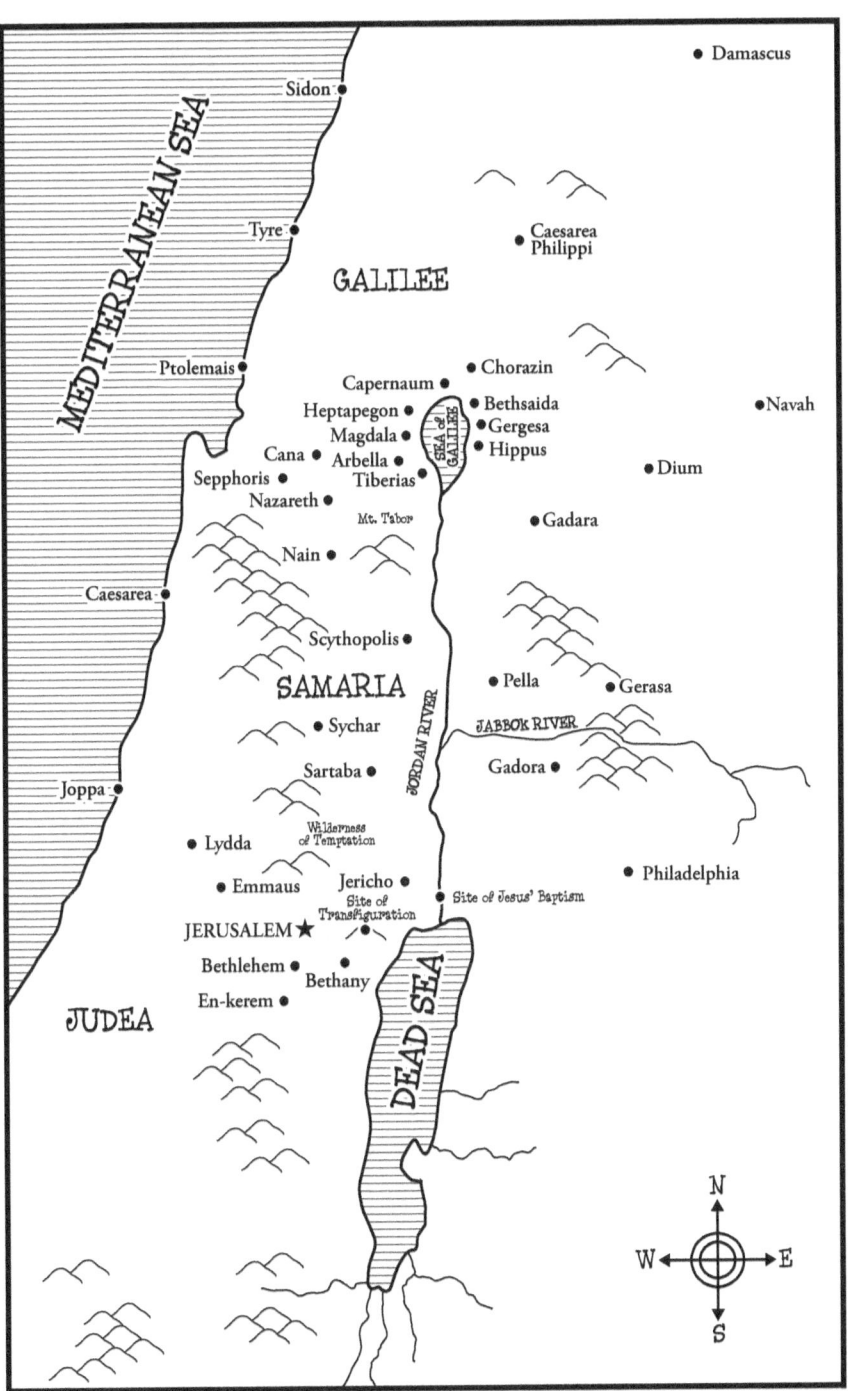

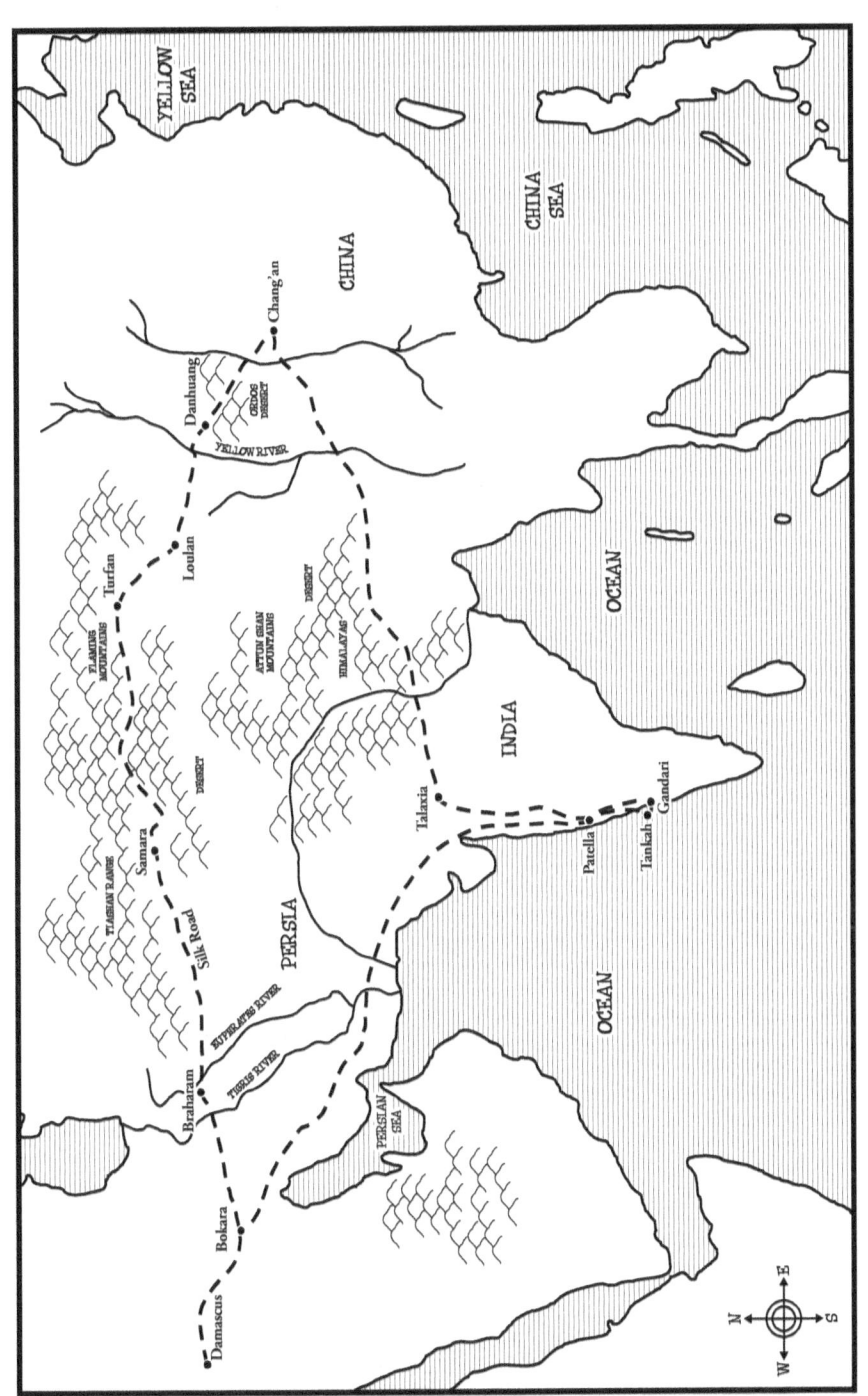

And the Word became flesh and lived among us . . .
—John 1.14

Prologue

Nazareth, 5:00 a.m.

In the early hours before sunrise, young Mary lay awake in bed, daydreaming about her future life as a wife and mother. She had recently been betrothed to a man from Bethlehem named Joseph. It was a marriage that had been arranged by her father years before. Her fiancé was of good stock, connected even to the House of David. He was a carpenter by trade, not rich but not poor. He was a kind man, thoughtful, and not half bad-looking. Mary's father had done well in procuring such an arrangement—for her and for her family. She had been a girl and a daughter for fourteen years. It was now time for her to become a woman and a wife.

> *Mary was uncommonly beautiful. Her skin was olive but darker than most, and her eyes were blue, rare among her people. She was tall and slim and her teeth as white as alabaster. She had adopted blue as her favorite color and all her clothes reflected this preference. Her laughter was infectious, and her mere presence enough to generate pleasure and joy in those around her. Her heart and soul were pure. She loved God and was, herself, beloved by all.*

Mary sat up on the side of her bed. It was still dark and the others in the house were fast asleep. Just as she was beginning to replace her daydreams with the realities of the day, it happened. First, there was a blinding flash of light and then the figure of an eight-foot-tall angel standing in the corner of her room. Mary was too surprised and frightened to scream. And Gabriel, the angel, was speechless, too, at first, struck by the incredible beauty of this earthly creature. He could sense her innocence and faithfulness. *God has chosen well,* he thought.

Sensing Mary's fear, Gabriel regained his own composure and cleared his throat. "Do not be afraid, Mary," he said, "for you have found favor with God."

As the angel relayed God's plan to her—that she would conceive and bear a child who would be God's Son—Mary sat quietly, troubled and unconvinced.

"Is there a problem?" he asked.

"Uh, yeah, a couple of problems, actually," Mary said. "Number one, I'm a virgin. How does that work? And number two, if God does manage to pull this thing off, what's going to happen to me—my future? What am I going to tell my parents? My friends? The townspeople? What am I going to say to Joseph? 'Oh by the way, I'm pregnant, but not to worry, it's God's baby inside me.'"

"I understand your concern," Gabriel said, "but this is God's will, God's plan, and it isn't really our place to question it. I can tell you this, though. Your cousin Elizabeth, who was barren, is now three months pregnant herself, and I suspect her pregnancy has something to do with yours. Maybe you two should talk."

Again, Mary quietly considered her future life and the potential that this plan had for shattering all of it. Then, suddenly, strangely, her heart was filled with peace and joy. Her hopes, her dreams, her future were all overshadowed by the present reality of this one moment of opportunity and service, of what God was doing through her and in her. She felt blessed. And remembering God's faithfulness, Mary, in her own faithfulness, responded. "Here I am, a willing servant of the Lord. Let it be with me according to his word."

"Your acceptance has made it so," Gabriel announced. He took in one last, long look at Mary. *How incredibly beautiful she is,* he thought to himself, *and how trusting she is in God.*

And then, in another brilliant flash of light, the angel departed from her.

Part I
B.G.

Chapter 1

The Announcement

With every step, mushroom clouds formed above Anna's feet, like tiny bombs exploding. It was just after daybreak, but the sun was already hot as Anna made her way back along the road that led from the village well. Her bare feet burned and her brow furrowed as she kicked up the dust that seemed to sear her lungs with every breath. Anna was confused, angry, worried. The night before, her daughter Mary had confessed that she was pregnant. In hindsight, Anna should have suspected. The signs were obvious: morning sickness, the complaint of tender breasts, a couple of fainting episodes. But she was the mother of a fourteen-year-old child, a good girl, the daughter every mother dreamed of—beautiful, intelligent, pleasant, and happy—and betrothed to a respectable and honorable man.

Anna was troubled, too, about how she would break this news to Joachim. He was a proud man. He loved Mary. Indeed, she was the favorite among all his children. He didn't let on about this, never openly displayed his partiality. But Anna knew, and so did the other children, and so did Mary. Nevertheless, there were rules among men about women—promiscuous women.

As Anna reached the door, she took a deep breath. She went through the scene again in her mind, rehearsed the words she would say one more time. She dreaded the thought of it: the look on Joachim's face as she told him, the inevitable broken heart and the tears that would follow, and then, quite possibly, the rage. The response to Mary's tragic misstep was what troubled Anna most.

Would Joachim expose his eldest daughter's sin to the community or would he leave that to Mary's growing belly? Either way, pregnancy out of wedlock was a serious offense and, possibly, a capital one. She would be ostracized and likely banished from Nazareth at best, stoned to death at worst.

Anna was perspiring heavily and felt faint. She set the water jug on the floor just inside the front door, walked through the house and back outside to the kitchen. She removed the freshly baked bread from the oven and brought it to the table, where she collapsed on a stool opposite Joachim. And then she began to cry.

Joachim said nothing, confused about the state of his wife, whose usual morning joviality often irritated him. While he spent an hour or more in the mornings trying to will himself awake and into a better mood before heading off to his shop, Anna was always singing or humming or ranting on about all the news she had gathered from the other women at the well. What had caused this sudden change? What tragedy had befallen her or what sad news had she heard from one of the other women? He waited.

When Anna had composed herself, she explained the situation to Joachim. He reacted as expected. The tears came. He hid his face in his hands. Then, suddenly, he banged his fist on the table so hard that it sent cups flying into the air and onto the stone floor where they broke into shards. The only word Joachim spoke aloud was, "Joseph!" but Anna noticed he mumbled much more under his breath.

The noise of Joachim's anger awakened the children. They dressed quickly and, one by one, entered the main room for breakfast. As they took their seats at the table, neither Joachim nor Anna spoke. The children, sensing something was amiss, sat quietly as well, waiting for parental instruction. It came from Joachim.

"Wash, then take your bread and eat it outside." This he said in a calm but solemn voice.

They did as they were told without conversation. As they headed out the door, Joachim spoke again.

"Except you, Mary."

Mary stopped, as did her older brother Joshua, who looked toward his father for some meaning of what was going on. He sensed that this was not the time to question. He moved on out the door behind his younger brother and sister.

"Sit down," Joachim said to Mary.

The conversation lasted more than an hour. There were tears. There were loud, almost violent moments, and, thankfully, there were calm and quiet moments too. Anna served as a masterful communicator between the girl and the man. Mary explained to her father, just as she had to her mother, about the angel and all that had taken place just as he told her it would. She also explained that, until a day ago, she had been frightened to tell the story to anyone. Besides, even she wasn't certain it was true. Maybe she had dreamed it. Or maybe she really had been visited by an angel, but maybe the angel hadn't gotten it quite right, or maybe he was playing some mischievous trick on her! But none of that was so. The angel had been right. Three months later, the tiny bump in her belly proved it, and Mary couldn't keep the secret any longer. The tale she had been dying to share with someone, especially her parents, could now be shared, *must* now be shared. She had tested the story on her mother; it didn't go as well as she had hoped. Still Anna had insisted on being the one to tell Joachim.

"Then we can sit down and talk about it together," her mother had said.

And, now, here they were, sitting down to talk about it together. Once again, it was not going well.

Anna hadn't believed Mary, and neither did Joachim. "It's ridiculous," he said. "Why on Earth would God impregnate a human woman? And of all women, a barely-of-age, unmarried woman? And of all barely-of-age, unmarried women, a peasant woman like you? And why would you blame this thing you have done on God? It is blasphemy!

Sin upon sin! You have broken your chastity. You and Joseph have done this unspeakable act. And *you* will pay the price, Mary. Not Joseph, but *you*! And us! You have disgraced your family! And, by God, I will see that Joseph *does* pay! He will pay me, if I don't kill him!"

Mary burst into tears. "But what I have told you is true, Abba. This is not Joseph's doing, nor mine. It is God's doing. I swear I haven't been with Joseph."

The blood that had turned Joachim's face beet red in anger and humiliation suddenly drained and was replaced by dizziness. He felt sick. Sicker. "Are you telling me that Joseph has no part in this? That this isn't Joseph's child? That Joseph doesn't know?"

"I have told no one of this, except Mama," Mary said. "Not until today."

Joachim studied Mary's face. This time he did believe her. He believed that Mary believed the story she was telling, and now he had to consider the possibility that Mary, lovely Mary, his favorite child, had gone mad. Perhaps that was the reason she had allowed herself to lie with a man. Or perhaps a man had forced himself on her, and the trauma of that event had driven Mary mad. Perhaps, to compensate for whatever terrible thing had happened, and to repair the damage done, her mind had concocted the idea that her seducer—or attacker—had been an angel sent by God. Such stories had been told before in the pagan religions. Their gods had descended to Earth to lure and persuade human women into amorous affairs. He doubted whether Mary had even heard of these stories.

However, there was one story in the Pentateuch with which he knew Mary was familiar: It was the time of Father Noah, when wayward angels came down from heaven to take for themselves human wives. *Yes, that must be it!* Poor Mary. Her outrageous tale was not a covering for sin but, rather, a trick of the mind—a mental block to protect her from remembering the truth of what had happened. Never would his darling Mary have participated in the event willingly. It was forced upon her. And what better way to block out a heinous event than to try and turn it to a holy one?

Suddenly, all the anger in Joachim turned to compassion, the rage to sympathy. He took his daughter in his arms and held her tight. She sobbed into his shoulder. "There, there, my dear. We will help you figure this out. We will help you remember."

Mary wouldn't remember differently. She would not change her story of the angel and the promise that her child was from God. She professed to Joachim, again and again, that she was with no man. Joachim oscillated from frustration to desperation, from concern for Mary's sanity to concern for his own. He wanted to believe his daughter but simply could not. *How can this be?*

Time was running out for Joachim. Joseph would be making his bimonthly visit to Nazareth soon. Each time he came to visit his betrothed, he brought Joachim money as well as other gifts—as much as a donkey could carry—as a part of the bridal price: dates, goat cheese, barley, and wine; blankets, thread, frankincense, and myrrh. Some of this Joachim kept for his household, and some of it he sold from his market shop.

When he could no longer wait for Mary to be brought around gently, Joachim reluctantly sent Anna, along with a neighbor woman as an honest witness—one he felt would not betray their confidence—to examine Mary to see if she was still a virgin. It was a humiliation for Mary, he knew, both to expose her nakedness before another and to acknowledge the distrust of her father in ordering the examination. But what else could he do to prove to Mary, and himself, that there was no angel and no supernatural act—no *immaculate* conception? Joachim already knew, of course. Mary was delusional, maybe due to some defense mechanism for a horrible act committed against her or, maybe, God forbid, for an act in which she was complicit. Either way, Joachim had to get to the bottom of this and quickly. Whoever had done this to Mary, whether as a participant lover or a despicable thief, would pay a penalty of reparation to Joachim. And, of course, Joachim would have his own reparations to pay to Joseph. This was not his greatest concern, though. What of Mary? Was she raped? Could she be guilty of fornication or, perhaps, even adultery? Would she ever come back to her senses completely or would she continue to keep an addled mind because of whatever had happened to her? And what would the community demand? He believed he could save her emotionally and physically, if he could get her out of town in time, before they knew about her. But time was running out. Joseph was coming, and once Joseph knew, everyone would know.

Anna and the neighbor came out of Mary's room. Their faces looked troubled.

"She isn't a virgin," Joachim sighed.

"She *is* a virgin," said the neighbor.

"Thank God," Joachim almost shouted, as he bowed his head and covered his face with his hands. "She isn't pregnant."

"But she *is* pregnant." Anna mumbled. "She is most certainly pregnant and most certainly a virgin!"

Joachim lifted his head slowly and looked at Anna. "Holy crap."

The next day, Joachim sent his son Joshua to Bethlehem with instructions to tell Joseph not to come. "Tell him that Mary went to En-kerem to care for her cousin Elizabeth, who is with child. Tell him she will be gone for at least three months until Elizabeth delivers."

As soon as Joshua left, Joachim took Mary and bought her passage on a caravan carrying goods to Jericho, Jerusalem, Bethany, and Bethlehem. Between Bethany and Bethlehem, they would take Mary to En-kerem and the home of Zechariah and Elizabeth.

This would give Joachim time to think, to ponder. *How can this be?*

Chapter 2

The Visitation

I t was springtime when Mary arrived in the hill country of En-kerem. Warm days and breezy, cool nights. The change of location put Mary somewhat at ease. Here, the pressure of constant interrogation, of questions and accusation were gone. In the end, though, Joachim had assured her of his unconditional love for her. Nothing would change that. Still, even after the examination, she wasn't sure if Joachim, or anyone else, for that matter, believed her story. She was even beginning to have doubts herself. That is, until she arrived at the door of Elizabeth's house.

Mary had no sooner said hello than Elizabeth was overcome with emotion.

"The moment I saw you," she said to Mary, "the child in my womb leaped for joy!" Then Elizabeth told her that the spirit of God had revealed to her that Mary was with child, and that the child was from God and the fulfillment of God's promise of a savior for Israel.

Mary was overjoyed, and relieved to know that everything she thought had happened to her, indeed, *had* happened, and someone else knew it! Someone else believed her and rejoiced with her! And Mary sang this song:

My soul praises God; my spirit rejoices in God;
For the Lord has looked favorably upon me and blessed me.
Surely, now everyone will know the great thing that has happened
to me.
Holy is the One who shows mercy and strength to all generations,
Who lifts up the lowly to high places;

Who fills the hungry with blessings.
He has kept his promise to Israel and, in mercy, has sent a savior.
My soul praises God; my spirit rejoices in God.

Elizabeth and Mary joined hands and danced in circles. They laughed and cried tears of joy and sang the song again. Then they walked together, and Elizabeth explained to Mary all that had taken place with her and Zechariah and how she herself had become pregnant by an announcement from God.

When Zechariah was serving in the Temple, an angel had appeared to him and told him that God would bless him and his wife with a child. Because Zechariah was old and Elizabeth past her childbearing years, Zechariah had questioned the angel and asked how such a thing could be. Apparently, this did not sit well with the angel, who told Zechariah that it *could* be because God said it *would* be.

"I have been sent by God to tell you this news," the angel said. "But because you have questioned God's word, you will be mute and will not speak again until this thing has taken place."

"Wait a minute!" said Zechariah. "It's not that I question God, but how do I know *you* are *from* God?"

The angel's silver aura turned to gray. "Not that I have to explain this to you," the angel said, "but, first of all, this is the Lord's Temple, the inner sanctuary. It's *his* place. When something supernatural happens here, that should be a clue that it's his doing. Second," the angel continued, "I'm a freaking angel! I'm a messenger of God. That's what I do. When God says, 'Go,' I go. When God says 'Take this message,' I take the message. And here I am bringing God's message to you. That's how you know I am from God!"

"But..." And that was the last word that came from Zechariah's lips. With a wave of the angel's hand, Zechariah was struck mute. And the angel disappeared from his sight.

When Zechariah came out of the sanctuary into the Temple and the other priests saw that he couldn't speak, they were perplexed but suspected he had experienced some kind of holy encounter. After counseling with one another for some time, they decided to send Zechariah home. Once there, he took a tablet and reported the entire episode to Elizabeth. Two months later, it was clear that Elizabeth was indeed pregnant. What the angel had said had come to pass or at least was in the process of being fulfilled.

Now, because Joseph was from Bethlehem, only a short distance from En-kerem, he visited Mary there. Although it was Joachim's place to bring the matter to Joseph, he had not yet done so, and Mary saw no reason to keep it from him any longer. Elizabeth had validated Mary's experience as being from God, and with her cousin sitting at her side, she broke the news to Joseph. Just like Joachim and Anna, he did not receive it well. Joseph, who was ten years older than Mary, didn't react in anger, but he did not believe her story. He listened, shocked and brokenhearted, trying to wrap his dizzying mind around what he was hearing. He loved Mary deeply. But, in the end, he couldn't make any of it fit together. It was too fantastic—absurd, really.

When Mary was finished, and after Elizabeth had relayed her story to him as well, Joseph sat quietly for a long time. They all did. He asked Mary if they could go for a walk alone. He professed his love for her. They wept together as they embraced one another. He asked her to tell the story again, interrupting her along the way with specific questions: What did the angel look like? What exactly did he say? Did he physically touch her? Did anyone else see him? He tried with all that was in him to believe her. But he couldn't.

He walked her back to Elizabeth's house, clasped both his hands around hers, then, without another word, turned and walked away. She didn't see him again while she was there, nor did she expect to see him again, ever. She assumed the wedding was off and that Joseph would make that known to Joachim. She didn't know that Joseph was thinking on all these things—contemplating all these things in his heart.

Mary stayed with Elizabeth through her third trimester and the birth of her son. When the baby was born, the midwife went to Zechariah, who was still unable to speak, and asked what the child's name was to be. He took a tablet and wrote,

He is to be called John.

Mary was six months pregnant and beginning to show when she left En-kerem and returned home to Nazareth.

Chapter 3
The Best-Laid Plans

When Mary arrived back home, she spent her first hours getting reacquainted with her family. She listened excitedly to her brothers and sister as they caught her up with all the happenings in Nazareth since she had been away. She shared with them and her mom and dad about Elizabeth and Zechariah and the birth of their child, though she left out the part about Zechariah's visitation from the angel and his subsequent loss of speech. (She thought they had had enough of angels for now and would save that part of the story for a more prudent time.) Anna and Joachim remarked about what a miracle it was for Elizabeth to give birth in her old age. *If they only knew!*

After the others had gone to bed, Mary stayed behind at the table with Joachim. She told him of her visit with Joseph. He wrapped his arms around her and told her everything would be all right, though he was not at all sure that would be the case.

The days that followed were pleasant ones for Mary. Troublesome for Joachim. Mary was barely showing, and her loose-fitting tunic helped disguise the baby she carried, so she was allowed to come and go as she pleased. Her juvenile naiveté as well as her certainty that God's plan was at work in her kept Mary from worry. Joachim, on the other hand, worried much and set about collecting various wares from his store and other items he hoped would satisfy Joseph as repayment for the bridal price he had paid to Joachim. If he played his cards right and returned to Joseph more than he had been given, if he called on Joseph's sense of decency and showed the proper contrition and, on his knees, lamented the offense perpetrated on Joseph by his daughter and himself—and if he did all this in time—then perhaps Joseph would kindly and discreetly break off the engagement and let the matter drop. Otherwise, disgrace would surely befall Joachim's family, particularly Mary, and there could be dire civil actions taken against her. Joachim and his sons would set out for Bethlehem tomorrow and take with them four donkeys loaded with supplies for Joseph. He prayed it would be enough.

Joseph had been praying as well about what he would do in regards to Mary and the entire situation. He was a good man, and he didn't relish the idea of exposing Mary to the disgrace and abuse she would surely face if he publicly denounced her. In fact, he had already decided he wouldn't do this. Instead, he would quietly dismiss her, informing only Joachim and, through him, Mary, that the marriage was off and the obvious reason why. He didn't intend to tell even his own family the truth of the matter. Instead, he would say that because of cold feet and a lack of desire for the young maiden, he had decided not to pursue the arrangement. This, no doubt, would be an embarrassment to his family. They would see it as a shameful act on his part. They would fear reprisals from Joachim. But he would tell them that he and Joachim had reached an agreement: that Joachim would keep the bridal price in exchange for Joseph's withdrawal from the contract. Surely, Joachim would agree to this in order to keep things quiet and protect his own. It was the only thing Joseph could do to protect Mary from a fate he didn't want for her. He knew she still had such a hard journey ahead, but this was all he could do. In spite of everything, he still loved her. But he couldn't marry her.

He had said nothing of this to his family since returning from En-kerem. He planned to leave for Nazareth tomorrow for his regular bimonthly visit with Mary. When he returned, he would spin the tale about an argument and his loss of feelings for Mary, and, hopefully, that would be that, except for the grieving that would surely continue for a long, long time.

It was not yet daylight when Joachim, Joshua, and Jacob set out from Nazareth for the four-day trip to Bethlehem. They traveled south through Nain, then east, avoiding Samaria and stopping just outside Scythopolis for the night. They pitched a tent and ate some of the barley loaves and figs they had brought for the journey, as Joachim told stories about the Patriarchs—Abraham, Isaac, and Jacob. The night was warm, but they made a fire, anyway, for light and to ward off the lions and, hopefully, the snakes and scorpions. It was not to be so. They hadn't been sleeping long when young Jacob's scream awakened them. An adder, no doubt looking for smaller game, had slithered into the camp and onto the young boy's mat. Jacob had probably moved in his sleep, threatening the snake, which sank its deadly fangs into the boy's ankle. The reptile was coiled and ready to strike again when Joshua spotted it from the light of his torch. He picked up a rock and smashed the serpent's head, then took out his knife and decapitated the venomous intruder to finish the job.

Meanwhile, Joachim attended to his younger son. He knew in an instant that Jacob's chances weren't good. They were ten miles from Scythopolis, and even if they were there and could find the herbs used to combat snakebite, it really would do little more than ease the excruciating pain as the venom passed through Jacob's bloodstream and into the nerves and muscle tissue of his body. They took wine and poured it on the boy's wound and forced as much as they could down his throat, hoping the effect would provide him some relief. Jacob was writhing in pain, but the panic, then shock, caused him to gradually settle into a trance-like state. Within ten minutes, he was barely conscious, except for an occasional moan. His ankle looked like a huge pink melon.

They didn't wait till morning. Joachim ordered Joshua to break camp and pack the animals. They would have to risk the snakes and wild animals in the dark in order to get Jacob medical attention without delay.

At first, they had made a bed for Jacob and placed it and him on one of the donkeys. When it was clear that the animal's gait was too rough for Jacob, Joachim took the boy down, and he and Joshua took turns carrying him. They were exhausted, but adrenaline kept them going.

It was just daylight when they came to Nain. Jacob's breathing was so shallow that Joachim could barely feel the boy's chest move. They found the town's apothecary shop, took Jacob inside, and placed him in the owner's bed. For the rest of the day, Joachim sat by his son's side, applied and reapplied the herb-soaked bandages, and prayed. All day long, he prayed for Jacob, and he continued his prayers for Mary. Earlier, he had sent Joshua on to Nazareth to inform Anna of the trouble. Jacob had not regained consciousness.

When morning came, Joachim was awakened by Jacob gently rubbing his hand across the sparsely spaced hairs on Joachim's balding head. The boy smiled at Joachim and Joachim smiled back. He reciprocated Jacob's gesture by running his own hand through the lad's dark curly locks and then bent over him and kissed his chest.

"Somehow, he made it," the apothecary said to Joachim. "He may lose his leg and he may die from that, but the poison won't kill him."

"I need to get him home," Joachim said. "We'll deal with the rest of it there."

Joachim paid his bill and bought new bandages and medicine for the road. He sat Jacob on one of the two donkeys that Joshua had left behind, and they set out for Nazareth.

Chapter 4
The Meeting

Within two days of Jacob's return home, with the help of the local doctor and the love and care of his family, he felt almost well. The swelling in his ankle had reduced to almost normal size. The color of his leg had turned to a curious and unattractive rainbow of purple and blue and yellow. The pain was gone, but the leg was sore and itched uncontrollably. Still, it was blessed relief for Jacob, and everyone else as well.

The mood changed in Joachim's house. Nothing seemed as dire as it once had. There was laughter and playfulness and loving embraces freely shared. There was still concern for Mary's situation, for sure, but Joachim was confident they would see it through, and he had told them that very thing last night. With Jacob's health improving, Joachim would start for Bethlehem again tomorrow to settle the matter with Joseph. Only this time, he would travel in the safety of a caravan and without Joshua, who would stay and keep the shop open.

The next morning, Joachim was just leaving home for the store and to ready his supplies for the trip, when he stopped in his tracks. The man was still thirty feet away, but Joachim recognized the crimson cloak and headdress, the thick jet-black beard and handsome face. There would be no trip to Bethlehem. Joseph was here. And the meeting Joachim was so anxious to have was about to take place.

Joachim didn't walk down the street to meet Joseph (not knowing the reaction he would receive), nor did he retreat. He simply stood outside the door of his home and waited for Joseph to come to him. It was not a gregarious greeting, nor was it cold. Joseph smiled, called Joachim's name and embraced him, kissing his cheek. Joachim reciprocated. The two men went inside where Joseph greeted Anna, who, after a short exchange of conversation, excused herself and retreated to the outside kitchen where she began baking for her unexpected guest. All the children were out except for Jacob, who was resting in the children's bedchamber. Joachim invited Joseph to sit and, at the same time, moved to close the bedchamber door. There was an awkward moment of silence. Eye contact was fleeting. Then both men began to talk at the same time. There was a brief pause. Then Joachim began, again.

"Joseph, I had intended to come and see you. In fact, I was on my way, just outside Scythopolis, when Jacob was bitten by an adder."

"My God! Is he all right?" asked Joseph.

"Amazingly well, yes. We thought we were going to lose him, but, thanks be to God, our prayers were answered, and he is almost fully recovered."

"That is good news." Joseph paused. "And how is Mary?"

"She is well."

"Joshua and Miriam?"

"Well, too. Joseph, Mary told me the two of you have talked. I know you are not the father of this child. I also know that she told you the same story she had told us. I assume you do not believe this story is true."

"I do not. Do you?"

"Of course not! I don't *know* if I believe her. At first, I thought her story might be some kind of mental deception—a defense mechanism—to cover or block some traumatic event that happened to her: a rape or, God forbid, a moment of temptation and unrestraint. But after questioning her again and again, she wouldn't budge from her account. Finally, to force her into the reality of the situation, I ordered Anna and a witness to examine her. Joseph, she hasn't been touched! Frankly, I don't know what to think. The question is what do you think?"

"I think I cannot go through with this marriage." Joseph dropped his head and sighed.

"I understand," said Joachim. "I have supplies, new ones. All the things you've given me and more. I simply ask, Joseph, that you show mercy on my daughter and my family. Please, do not publicly accuse her."

Joseph didn't look up. "I don't want repayment of the bridal price, Joachim, and I have no intention of accusing her. I plan to dismiss her quietly today and begin the journey back to Bethlehem tomorrow." He then told Joachim of how he planned to deceive his own family by the report he would make to them.

"Thank you, Joseph. You're a good and kind man. You've shown mercy to us, and I am forever in your debt."

"I still love her, Joachim, but I cannot marry her."

"Of course not."

"I long to see her face again but dread the thought of turning from it for the last time. I fear the hurt I will cause her."

"Of course." Joachim could think of nothing else to say. He was amazed to see Joseph's compassion for Mary, his love for her, his broken-heartedness. Still, Joachim couldn't help but breathe a sigh of relief. The catastrophe had been averted. But Mary was still pregnant. That wouldn't change. And there was still the community to deal with.

When Mary and Joshua had closed Joachim's store for the day, they began the walk home. Anna, Joachim, and Joseph were in conversation at the table, but Anna knew it was time for her children to return, and she had been listening carefully for them. When she heard their voices and laughter coming from down the street, she excused herself and went outside to meet them. She wasn't about to let Mary walk into a situation for which she wasn't fully braced.

Anna's stomach had been in knots all day, and now as she went to meet Mary, the butterflies fluttering restlessly inside her threatened to make their escape. Her mouth became salty and just to be sure she got her words out before she became sick, she stopped, still twenty feet away, and said, "Mary, Joseph is here."

Suddenly, sickness was the last thing on Anna's mind. To her surprise, she watched Mary dart past her in a dead run and into the open door of the house. She ran to Joseph and, smiling ear to ear, wanted to embrace him. Instead, she maintained proper decorum for public displays of affection. She clasped her hands together in a praying posture and bowed before Joseph. At first, startled by Mary's abrupt entrance, Joseph calmed and his eyes settled in on her beautiful face. He returned her smile and bow.

She grabbed his hand and led him outside and around the corner of the house. They were both laughing as they ran. Once they were in the alley between her house and the neighbor's, she stopped, turned toward Joseph and, wrapping her arms around his neck, hugged him tightly. He couldn't believe how his heart raced as he returned her hug. How he had missed her! How he did love her! How heartbreaking it all was.

The scene lasted only for a moment. They went back into the street and began walking slowly toward the marketplace. She asked about the last two months since they'd seen each other, his family, and his work. He responded to each question briefly. There were long moments of silence in between. They both knew the conversation they were trying to avoid had to take place, but neither was eager to bring it up. When they reached the market, they turned around and walked back toward Mary's house.

After supper and additional small talk about Joseph's family, Joachim's business, Jacob's recovery, and little sister Miriam's growth spurt since Joseph had last seen her, Joachim excused the other three children who went to the bedchamber and closed the door behind them. Anna began to clear the last remnants of supper from the table and Mary moved to help her. It was an effort to delay, at least for another moment, the discussion she knew was coming. Earlier in the day, she'd hoped that something in Joseph might have caused him to see things differently than he had at En-kerem: that he had come to reclaim his love for her and his place as her betrothed. But she had sensed all evening by his quietness and mood that this was not the case.

As Mary began to move away from the table to help her mother, Joachim took her hand. "Sit down, Mary," he said gently.

She sat, her eyes pointed downward.

They didn't wait for Anna to return to the table.

Joachim was the first to speak. "Joseph has come to tell us that he is breaking off the engagement. It is understandable. He has offered to do this discreetly. He will do so, asking no penalty or repayment from us, and we are grateful to him for his charity."

Neither Mary nor Joseph looked up.

Joachim continued. "In fact, Joseph is going to tell his family that he initiated the dissolution of the engagement. He will, no doubt, suffer some consequence among his own for this. It is a noble gesture on his part, a kind and caring act toward you, Mary, and toward us all."

Mary began to sob, as did Joseph, as did Joachim.

Anna had been standing at the door. She moved to Joseph and placed a hand on his bowed head. Then she sat down beside Mary and took her in her arms. She didn't cry. She rocked Mary back and forth and whispered softly in her ear.

Nothing more was said. Mary had tried to speak once but couldn't. Nothing could travel past the sobs that had gathered as a giant lump at the base of her throat. Joseph wanted to say something to try and comfort Mary, and himself, but no words would come. They all sat quietly, grieving.

Then Anna helped her daughter to her feet. "I'll sleep with Mary tonight," she said. And the two went off to Mary's bed.

A sleeping mat had already been made for Joseph on the roof terrace. The two men sat for a minute more at the table and then said good night.

Chapter 5
Joseph's Dream

A mazingly, mercifully, Joseph's body and mind didn't fight sleep. He thought of Mary, of her heartache and pain, and of his own. He thought of her loveliness and of what a wonderful life they could have had together: a home and children. Many children. And then, he drifted away.

There was a light in Joseph's eyes that roused him from sleep, and then a voice.

"Joseph, get up."

Could it be morning already? Joseph opened his eyes and saw in front of him a glowing giant! Using one hand to push himself away, and the other to shield his face from the light, Joseph crouched against the corner of the terrace wall. He said nothing because his speech had left him. He was terrified and, yet, entranced by the figure before him.

"Do not be afraid, Joseph, and do not put Mary away. For the child she carries is from God, as she says. Take her as your wife and accept the child she will bear as your own. But never forget this is a child of the Holy Spirit. He is sent to save God's people, to fulfill what has been spoken by the prophet: 'A virgin shall conceive and bear a son and his name will be Emmanuel, which means, "God is with us."' But you, Joseph, are to name him Jesus."

"But..." Joseph began.

Then the angel was gone and Joseph awoke.

"Holy crap!" Joseph said out loud. "Was that a dream or did it really happen?"

Whatever it was, it was enough to convince Joseph, who needed only a reason to claim his lovely Mary again. This was reason enough! He quickly dressed and went downstairs. Only Anna was awake and outside at the oven. He grabbed her and spun her around and around. He was singing a song that Anna had never heard but one she would never forget:

> *God is great and blesses his people,*
> *But God has blessed me among all men!*
> *No greater gift can a man receive than the true love of a wife.*
> *Mary is my betrothed, and I will cherish her above all things.*
> *She will be my wife,*
> *Because God is great and blesses his people*
> *And has blessed me above all men!*

Anna cried and then laughed out loud. Joseph kissed her on the forehead, then picked her up above his head and spun her around again. He danced a jig, then turned and ran for the house and Mary's room.

"Wait!" Anna called after him, fearing that Mary might not be decent.

"What the hell is going on!" shouted a sleepy-eyed Joachim, as he met Joseph head-on just inside the doorway. Joseph kissed him on the forehead as he passed by. Joachim did *not* laugh.

When Joseph had awakened the whole family, he explained his dream or vision or visitation or whatever it was and told them the wedding was on, and the sooner the better. With Joachim's and Mary's permission, he would inform his family to come to Nazareth immediately. They wouldn't like it; they expected the wedding to take place in Bethlehem. But they would come.

Joachim listened to all of this, slightly confused. But the sooner the better for him too. His daughter was six months pregnant! People would still talk. The baby would come too soon. They would know that Joseph and Mary had been intimate before they were married. But nothing would be done about it. Things like this had certainly happened before. A late marriage was unseemly but not illegal. Mary was off the hook, and Joachim's household would not be disgraced.

As they sat at the table and planned the wedding feast, everyone was happy again. It seemed like such a long time since worries hadn't clouded their days. As they discussed the banquet, the food and flowers and music and wedding garments, Mary told all of them about Zechariah's angel.

"For God's sake!" Joachim mumbled. "Has everyone had a visit from a freaking angel but me? Anna, have you been visited by an angel?"

"I think so," Anna said, smiling. She was looking at Joseph.

T he wedding took place two weeks later at Mary's uncle's house. Anna's brother owned a farm just outside of town. With its pastures and gardens and streams, it was a lovely place, and the site of many Nazareth weddings. The entire village was invited, as was Joseph's family and many others from Bethlehem. The affair lasted for four days, with the Nazareth residents going back and forth from their homes, while the out-of-town guests stayed with Mary's relatives or in tents at the farm. When the feast finally came to an end, Joseph announced to his family that he would not be returning to Bethlehem, but that he and Mary would make their home in Nazareth.

"But you were to take over my carpentry business, Joseph!" protested his father, Yeshua.

"My brothers will do well enough with that, Abba," Joseph said. "My place is here."

"Your place is at home in Bethlehem. You are my eldest. The family business is your birthright. Your brothers can work for you."

"Thank you, Abba, but no. I can start my own carpenter's shop in Nazareth. My brothers can share yours. They will do well by you."

"I suppose, but none of them knows the lathe and saw like you do. No one knows the trade as well as you, including me."

"I know only what you taught me, Abba."

"You know far more than I taught you, Joseph. Much more. God has given you a great gift."

"Indeed, he has. And I love her."

Yeshua smiled through his disappointment. "I was speaking of your skill."

"I know." Joseph returned his father's smile. "But, as I said, I will make my home and my trade here in Nazareth. Who knows? Maybe, one day, I'll have a business as successful as yours."

When Yeshua was sure Joseph wouldn't change his mind, he kissed his son and blessed him, then gathered his family and began the journey back to Bethlehem.

When everyone had gone home, Joseph and Mary, at her uncle's invitation, remained at the farm. They spent the next two days honeymooning in a small guest house. Then they returned to the village where Joseph had rented a one-room house with a stable attached. He used the stable space to open his very own carpenter's shop where he spent his days making furniture, farm implements, windows and doors and, occasionally, toys, which he would give to the children in the village.

He and Mary lived there, among their Nazareth neighbors, happy and content, and eagerly awaiting the birth of their first child.

Part II
THE STORY OF JESUS

Chapter 1
Jesus' Birth

Now in those days, a decree went out from Caesar Augustus that every person in the region was to be registered in a census. It was also a requirement that the head of each household be registered in his city of birth and that every member of the household be present and counted in person by the census takers. This was not good news for Joseph and Mary. She was now nine months pregnant and ready to deliver. With no choice, Joseph gathered up what was needed for the journey, packed it onto one of Joachim's donkeys, and he and Mary started out for Bethlehem.

It was early winter in Israel, cold but not freezing. Mary made the first day of the journey without incident or complaint. It wasn't easy for her but not terribly uncomfortable, and Joseph constantly checked to be sure she was okay. In the evening, the baby protested only slightly, kicking more than usual at the inside of her belly.

The next morning, Mary's feet were badly swollen. She managed to get her sandals on and quickly hid them from Joseph under her tunic. She was determined to make at least one more day before she had to trouble her husband with another worry. By noon, she could barely walk. Joseph, noticing that her pace had slowed considerably, had been asking about her condition all morning. Finally, he made her sit down, and she showed him her feet. They were red and raw, and the sandal straps had virtually disappeared beneath the swelling flesh that overlapped them.

"My God, Mary! Why didn't you say something?" Joseph said, with great concern.

He was finally able to remove her shoes, much to Mary's discomfort and groans, and he poured aloe oil over her wounded feet. He then lightly wrapped them with strips of cloth cut from an extra change of clothing.

Although Mary and Joseph had started from Nazareth alone, as they followed the road that led to Nain and on to Scythopolis, they had been joined by fellow travelers heading to various destinations for the same purpose of registration. The small caravan had stopped while Joseph attended to Mary. It was lunchtime, anyway, so each household gathered in its own group to share a meal. After eating and repacking their camels and donkeys, the men gathered together to discuss the route they would take from Scythopolis.

Two roads led out of Scythopolis. One went through Samaria, an area that most Jews preferred to avoid, as the Samaritans were a foreign and apostate people. There were more villages along this route, but the terrain was rougher—desert and hills. Nevertheless, by taking the Samarian route, several hours could be saved for those traveling to Jerusalem and beyond. This was the case for most of the travelers.

The other road went southeast to Pella and followed the Jordan River to Jericho and then west to Jerusalem. There were virtually no villages between Pella and Jericho, but the route along the river was gentler and interspersed with oases and shade. A few in the group had to take this route as their destinations were east along the way. The majority, however, decided to take the Samarian road.

Joseph weighed the options, thinking solely of Mary. Was the shorter distance or the easier road the best option? He believed the latter would be the wisest choice, but most of those going in this direction would veer east to Gadora and Philadelphia along the way. The few others would stop in Jericho, their destination town, and he and Mary would be left alone for the twenty-mile trip from there to Jerusalem or Bethany unless they could join up with other travelers along the way. That seemed a distinct possibility. From either of those towns, they could make the short trip to Bethlehem on their own. In the end, Joseph thought the easier route the best. If the baby was born along the way, he thought, its best chance for survival would be in this

more fertile, less rugged land. After bidding farewell to those traveling
through Samaria, Joseph lifted Mary onto his donkey and joined the
smaller group along the road toward the Jordan.

The trip along the river was uneventful and would've even been
quite pleasant had it not been for Joseph's constant concern for Mary.
Her feet were healing and the swelling was less, but it was clear that she
was uncomfortable. The donkey was not comfortable either. It wasn't
built to carry the full load, plus Mary, and every morning Joseph left
behind some things he thought they could do without in order to
lighten the creature's burden. There were times when he'd have to coax
the donkey out of a stubborn stall, as it refused to cooperate with its
task. There were other times when he had to argue with Mary. Because
of her sympathy for the beast, he could hardly convince her to stay
on the donkey's back. But he would allow her to walk only when her
tailbone could no longer take the pressure of the lumbering animal's
gait. As a result of all this, they had fallen far behind the rest of the
group. They were still in sight, but barely. They would catch up each
evening before stopping but the next day fall slowly behind again.

The day before, a family had exited the group for Gadora. Today,
three more households bade them farewell and departed the tiny caravan
on their way to Philadelphia. They had picked up no new travelers along
the way. Only Joseph and Mary and two more households—a family
of four and another of six—headed for Jericho, the final destination
for the remainder of the couple's fellow travelers. Joseph had decided
they would spend the night there. They would find a room where Mary
could get a proper rest, while he searched the town for a caravan or
another family leaving for Jerusalem or Bethany.

Joseph and Mary had fallen behind once more on the day they
arrived at Jericho. By the time they entered the city, their traveling
companions had already disappeared into the crowd. Joseph looked
for a room to rent, but because of the registration, there was nothing

available. As he worked his way back to the city's entrance where he had left Mary, Joseph felt depressed. He looked at his wife sitting against the city wall, exhausted and listless. One of her hands was covering her face to block the sun, the other was underneath her belly, pressing up to relieve the weight.

There was nothing he could do. He had been away from her for hours. He had inquired at dozens of boarding houses, asked hundreds of people about where he and Mary might stay. He would have to attend to her as best he could, care for her as much as possible, with the remaining supplies they had available. They went outside the wall, and Joseph pitched a tent for them beside several others. They apparently weren't the only ones in this predicament. But, as Joseph looked around, he saw no other pregnant women. For him, and he was sure for Mary, it certainly *felt* as though they were the only ones.

The next day, Joseph loaded the donkey, set his tired wife on the animal's back, and began the last leg of their journey. There were a few others leaving along the same road, so he set pace with them. Bethany was a slightly shorter distance than Jerusalem, and others were headed in that direction, so Joseph followed south bypassing the great city.

When they arrived at Bethany, Joseph helped Mary dismount and sat her in the shade of a tree while he searched for lodging. Once he found a house willing to take them in, he returned for Mary. He placed her in bed and then secured the donkey in their host's stable, putting some hay in a manger and a bucket of water on the floor of the stall. He paid the owner of the house for a night's lodging, said good night, and collapsed in the floor beside Mary. He had brought food for her, but she was already asleep. In minutes, he was sleeping too.

Joseph awoke with new energy. Mary was still sleeping, so he left her while he made preparations for the five-mile trip to Bethlehem. He ate at the table with his hosts and took bread, dates, and milk to Mary. She was awake and greeted him with a smile.

"Good morning," she said, as she stretched her arms above her head. Her sun- and wind-burned face contrasted with her white forehead that had been protected by her headdress.

"Good morning," Joseph replied. "Did you sleep well?"

"Heavenly," said Mary. "I'm starving!"

"I brought you food last night, but you were already asleep."

"I needed the sleep more than food."

"So did I. Sit up and eat. I still have a few things to do before we leave. We're almost there, Mary. We'll be at my father's house before noon."

"Heavenly," Mary repeated.

He left her alone.

When he returned from packing the donkey, Mary was in the main room, enjoying the company of her hosts and thanking them for their kindness. They said their goodbyes, thanked the family again, and were on their way. They traveled the five miles to Bethlehem alone. It was a gloriously cool day. They arrived at Joseph's family's home just before noon.

Mary had known from the time she arose that this would be the day she would give birth. The baby was not acting up so much today, but she could tell that his position had definitely shifted, and there was pressure at the base of her womb. When they arrived at Joseph's family's house, there was a great show of affection toward them. There were hugs and kisses from everyone. Mary felt very welcomed. She had anticipated some coolness toward her due to her pre-wedding pregnancy and the fact that they had made their home in Nazareth rather than with Joseph's family in Bethlehem. But there was none of that. The family could not have been warmer toward her. She felt at home and a real member of the family.

"Tell us how you're feeling, Mary," inquired Joseph's mother, Salome.

"I feel better now that we're here."

"When are you due? Will you have the baby here?" his sister asked, excitedly.

"Surely, I will. Maybe today! I certainly can't make another trip like we've just done in this condition!"

They all laughed.

"Joseph's intentions were for us to be here until the baby is able to travel well, perhaps a month or so."

They all clapped.

"Yes, you must stay," Salome insisted. "We must all have time to get to know our newest family member. And we want to get to know you too, Mary, and you us!"

Mary smiled. "Yes, I would like that."

The main bedchamber of the house was for Joseph's father and mother. In the rather large house, there was another bedchamber where all the children slept. Now, however, since there were only two unmarried children still living with Yeshua and Salome, there was plenty of room for visiting relatives. In addition to this, there was a small upstairs bedchamber, built exclusively for guests; in addition to that, each of Joseph's two married brothers had built a room onto their parents' house, where they lived with their wives. Both the brothers were younger than Joseph, and neither of them had yet fathered children.

Because of the registration, the house was full—aunts, uncles, and cousins—and every bedchamber had several families sleeping there. Even the brothers' rooms had people sleeping on the floor. There were no available boarding rooms in all of Bethlehem. It was as if every person ever born in Bethlehem, and still living, had decided to descend on the city the very same week, even though the census was to be conducted over an eight-week period.

"It's ridiculous!" Yeshua complained to Salome and Joseph. "Everyone thought if they arrived early, they could register without waiting in long lines. Now, the whole world has arrived at once, and people stand in line all day and never even get close to the registrar's table. Of course, in our family's case, everyone thought if they arrived early, they could stay longer to eat my food and drink my wine and take advantage of my hospitality!"

"Shush!" said Salome. "We're happy to have all our family here for such a wonderful reunion."

"Humpf!" puffed Yeshua.

"There's a matter at hand we need to talk about," said Joseph. "Mary is to deliver her baby any time now. Where is she to do that? On the living room floor? Ordinarily, I would seek out a room for us at an inn, but there isn't a rented room available in all of Bethlehem. So, what are we to do?"

"Well, ordinarily," said Yeshua, "there would be plenty of room and private space here, but these are not ordinary times. Suppose we have the boys build a partition for you upstairs. I know we're wall-to-wall people up there, but that would give you a sense of privacy."

"Well...," considered Joseph.

"Forget it," said Mary, who just happened to be passing through the room and past the strategy session that was taking place on her behalf. "Do I really need to sit here to make sure you two gentlemen come up with a better plan than that?"

"Don't worry, dear," said Salome. "I'll be here to talk them through a suitable solution. You go rest."

Mary smiled, gave her mother-in-law a thumbs up, and disappeared through the doorway.

"There really isn't a suitable solution for this house, Mama," said Joseph. "Like Abba said, the place is wall-to-wall people. What are we going to do?"

"We'll figure something out," Yeshua said in a dismissive tone.

Joseph responded in a more serious one. "Well, we'd better figure it out quickly! We're running out of time."

After a moment of thoughtful silence, Yeshua spoke. "Joseph, go get your brothers at the shop and meet me around back at the stable. Tell them to bring hammers, nails, and a cart with all the boards it can carry."

Joseph watched his father walk out of the room and then, confused but obedient, got up and started for the family's carpenter shop just down the street.

When he returned with the tools and supplies his father had requested, and two equally confused brothers in tow, his father was moving all the livestock out of the stable and tying them to posts outside.

"Get some pitchforks and get all the old hay and manure out," Yeshua said, directing his sons. "I want this place as clean as a pin."

"Abba, what are we doing here?" Joseph asked.

"You want privacy. I'll give you privacy. We'll clean this place up, build a wall across the front, and you and Mary can have your own private little love nest to deliver your baby. By the time we're through with it, it'll be as nice as any room in the house, especially with all those freeloaders inside!"

"Uh...Abba, no," Joseph said.

"Nonsense! Just get a pitchfork and get to work. You said yourself, we're out of time."

Joseph's brothers began doing as they were told. Joseph stood still for a minute, thinking of what Mary would have to say about this idea. But, at least, it was an idea, and he couldn't think of a better one, so he grabbed a pitchfork and followed his brothers inside.

By the time they were finished, it was well past dark. But the moon was full and gave them plenty of light to admire their handiwork. The stable had been thoroughly cleaned. The smell was tolerable, a musty combination of animal musk, manure, and new strewn hay. They had built a wall across the front of the stable, which was really just a cave dug into the hillside, and fitted it with a door. In one of the larger stalls in the back, they'd built a raised wooden platform and covered it with hay. A small manger had been placed in the corner of the stall to serve as the baby's crib. Finally, two lanterns had been hung on posts to give the new family light throughout the night.

The women hadn't noticed at first, but once the hammering began, it was clear, at least to Salome, what the men had in mind. She had started to protest, but because she couldn't think of a better idea either, she said nothing, including to Mary, who was oblivious to the plan for her future living arrangements.

When Joseph came inside, he dodged Mary's gaze as he passed through the room. He gathered their things from upstairs and dodged her again as he took their belongings to the stall. Then he returned, helped Mary to her feet, and took her outside. As they passed through the stable door, Joseph waved his hand in front of them to display his and the others' completed work. Mary didn't say it, but she thought it: *Holy crap!*

Joseph sat Mary down on a blanket. She was still speechless, but she smiled at him and pretended to be pleasantly surprised. Joseph went back to the house, kissed his mom and sister good night, and grabbed some bread, dates, and goat's milk to take back for supper. Mary had to admit that it was good to be out of the busy house and away from all her new relatives. The privacy and quiet were welcome and soothing. The place was starting to grow on her. After they finished their meal, they trimmed the lanterns down to a low glow and were asleep in no time. Until a few hours later, when Mary was awakened by the rush of warm wetness on her sleeping clothes. Her water had broken. It was time for the baby to come.

Joseph ran to wake his mother. All eight of the aunts and female cousins sleeping in Salome's room came with her. The stall wasn't big enough for everyone, though, at first, a valiant effort was made by all the women to squeeze in. Finally, at Salome's command, they all backed away and decided, after some ridiculous arguing, that only Salome and her oldest sister, who had some experience at midwifery, would stay with Mary to assist. A couple of the older women were also allowed to stay inside but stationed well out of the way. Most of the other women waited in the yard just outside the stable, while the girls were sent back to bed. Some of the women, miffed because they had been banished from a closer view, returned to bed too, though some graciously busied themselves heating water and cutting up bands of cloth for wrapping the baby.

Mary was in labor for less than two hours. The delivery went well. After the baby was wrapped, and Mary cleaned up and dressed in a new sleeping gown, Salome ran to the house and announced to every room that the baby was born.

Yeshua dressed himself and, along with the company of several others who were more curious than sleepy, made his way to the stable. It was his first grandchild, and he was much more excited than he thought he would be. He waited impatiently as the women, already crowded in the stable, took turns viewing the newborn babe. Finally, when it was his turn, he entered, took a seat on a milking stool and watched in awe as the child lay sleeping. He hugged Joseph and kissed him on both cheeks. He gently stroked the top of Mary's head, congratulated her, and told her how happy he was to have her for a daughter-in-law. Mary smiled. She couldn't take her eyes off her son.

Someone had built a fire outside. Men and women and boys and girls were standing around joyfully discussing the new birth. It was almost dawn. A flute began to play, then a drum, then a tambourine. People began to sing.

Yeshua came out of the stable. "The boy has been named Jesus!" he announced.

Everyone cheered.

Then Yeshua began to dance around the fire, singing,

Glory to God! Glory to God!
A child has been born in Bethlehem!
Jesus, son of Joseph, the son of Yeshua;
A child has been born in Bethlehem.
Glory to God! Glory to God in the highest!

They all began to sing and dance with him. It seemed as though there were many more voices singing than just those around the fire.

Now, in the fields around Bethlehem, there were shepherds keeping their flocks. They thought they heard singing too. Suddenly, above them, angels appeared, and the night sky turned bright around them. The shepherds were afraid and hid their faces.

Then one of the angels said to them, "Friends, do not be afraid, for we have come to bring you news of a great thing that has taken place in Bethlehem. A Savior has been born, a deliverer for the whole world.

Now, get up and go see! You will find him in a stable, wrapped in cloth and lying in a manger."

After the angel had finished speaking, the multitude of angels with him began singing.

> *Glory to God! Glory to God!*
> *A child has been born in Bethlehem!*
> *Glory to God! Glory to God in the highest!*

When the angels left them and returned to heaven, the shepherds said to one another, "Holy crap!" Then they arose and left their sheep and went to Bethlehem, where they found the child wrapped and lying in a manger, just as the angels had told them.

After eight days, as was the custom, Mary and Joseph took Jesus to the Temple in Jerusalem to be circumcised. As a first born male child, Jesus was dedicated to the Lord, according to Jewish law. At that time, there was a man named Simeon living in Jerusalem. Because he was a righteous and devout man, God had spoken to Simeon and told him that he would not die before he saw the Messiah. Simeon was old and was beginning to question whether this could be so. On the very day, at the very time, when Jesus was at the Temple, the Holy Spirit guided Simeon there. When Simeon saw the child, he asked if he could hold him. Mary placed Jesus in his arms, and the old man knew that God had kept his promise. He praised God and said,

> *Lord, you now have set your servant free*
> *To die in peace as you have promised:*
> *For these eyes of mine have seen*
> *The salvation of all peoples,*
> *A light to the Gentiles*
> *And the glory of your people Israel.*

With tears of joy running down his cheeks, he handed the child back to Mary and said to her, "Blessed are you among women," and to Joseph, "Blessed are you among men." As he walked away, he kept praising God.

Mary and Joseph looked at each other amazed, and Mary treasured all this in her heart.

After the circumcision, they stayed the night in Jerusalem. When they arose the next morning, they began their journey back to Nazareth, where the child grew healthy and strong.

Joseph had a dream. The angel appeared before him.

"You, again," Joseph said in his sleep.

"Yes," replied the angel.

"Is Mary pregnant?"

"No. This is serious, Joseph."

"I expected as much. What is it?"

"Herod is freaking out. Some astrologers from the East came to him and told him they had seen a star that predicted a new king had been born. They told him the star had led them to this region, and they had come to ask if he had information that would direct them to the newborn. Fearful of a rival, Herod told the astrologers to come back to him if they found the child, so that he could go and pay homage to him as well."

"Yes," said Joseph. "I remember those guys. They showed up here about a month ago. They brought gifts and fell down on their knees in front of Jesus. They stayed for two days, camped right outside our door. It was a little embarrassing. The other villagers were starting to get upset with the fuss they were making. So, finally, we told them they should go, and they packed up and left on the road to Caesarea."

"Well, they didn't go back to Herod," the angel said, slightly gloating. "With my help, they figured out what he was up to."

"Let me guess. A dream, right?"

The angel ignored the remark. "So, as I said, Herod is freaked out. He's ordered the execution of every male child two years and younger. That's because of what the astrologers told him: that they had first seen the star almost two years ago. He's covering his bases. He's going to kill every male child in Nazareth and the surrounding cities just to be sure he gets the right one."

"You have to stop this!" Joseph said, horrified. "God has to stop this!"

"Herod won't listen to God. And God can affect only those who will listen to him. God won't stop the free will and designs of humans, Joseph. God won't stop the evil that they do, but God will overcome it and God will rectify it."

The reality hit Joseph. "Jesus. They'll be coming for Jesus!"

"Yes. That is why you must take the child and Mary and flee from Israel to Egypt."

"But..."

"Joseph! Do not question me. The Lord will reveal his plan to you when it is time. Now, rise up. Do not tarry. Pack your things, take Mary and Jesus, and go!"

Joseph awoke from the dream and did as the angel had told him.

The news of the terrible thing Herod had done made its way even to Egypt. Every ruler of every country that heard about Herod's murderous act could scarcely believe he would resort to such extreme tactics, even to secure his kingship. They all held him in disdain. Everyone except Caesar. He did not condone the act. He saw it as only another dogfight within the kennel called Israel.

They were an obstinate and fanatical people, impossible to control without resorting to brutal measures. He abhorred Herod, even before this incident, but the man did a fairly good job of keeping his people in line. He would leave internal matters alone, as long as they didn't disturb the peace of Rome.

Joseph plied his trade in Egypt. Beginning as a laborer for a building contractor, Joseph's skills quickly propelled him to the position of foreman, and he oversaw the building of several upper-middle class homes. He was paid well, and the family lived well during their time in Egypt, but there was never a day when they didn't long for home. In the three years they were there, Mary gave birth to two more children, James and Marion.

When Herod died, the angel appeared to Joseph in another dream and told him to return to Nazareth. They left for home the very next day.

I t had been a week since the holy family arrived back in Nazareth. They had moved in temporarily with Joachim and Anna, and, with Jacob and Miriam still at home, the living arrangements were tight. Mary, Joseph, and their children were in one bedchamber; Joachim, Anna, and Miriam in the other. Jacob slept on the roof terrace or in his parents' room when the weather was not agreeable. During the day, everyone stayed out of each other's way as much as possible. Still, it was good to have the family together again. Joachim and Anna made over their grandchildren, two of whom they had not seen before, and remarked at how much Jesus had grown.

Joseph managed to save much of the money he had made in Egypt. The plan was to rent a place for a while and then to build rather than buy an already existing house for their permanent home. For the most part, however, the only affordable apartments available for rent were of the one-room variety. This was the case with Mary's uncle's guest house as well. Joachim and Anna assured them that staying with them was not a problem and that they should wait until a suitable house became available.

A few weeks later, on the occasion of Jesus' fifth birthday, a party was planned. Several of the neighborhood children Jesus' age were invited. This, Mary thought, would give Jesus a chance to make some new friends. There were adult guests, too, mostly mothers of the children, but Joachim and Joseph were there, as were Anna, Jacob, Miriam, and Jesus' brother and sister.

When the time came for Jesus to blow out the candles on the cake, Mary coaxed him on. "Go ahead, dear. Make a wish and blow out your candles."

Jesus stared straight ahead, a slight but studied smile on his face.

"Do it!" urged Jacob, almost ready to take over the task himself.

Jesus continued to stare, his smile still determined but gradually growing.

Mary began to be concerned that something might be wrong with her son. Then, suddenly, the candles extinguished themselves. Jesus had neither moved nor exhaled toward the cake. Mary shot a quick glance at Jacob, thinking he might have been unable to resist taking the guest of honor's privilege. But Jacob had his own look of concern as he stared at the cake, then at Jesus. The chatter and various conversations that were circulating around the room suddenly hushed. Mary looked at Joseph, who was looking at her, and then at her father who was looking…well, not good at all!

Mothers began grabbing their children by the arms and taking them out of the house. Some were leading them in a brisk walk back to their homes, others picking their children up and running. Within seconds, it seemed, the room was completely empty of guests, and the others sat speechless, every eye fixed on the boy who now diverted his interest to a small wooden camel that Joseph had made for him.

"There must have been a breeze," said Joseph.

"There was no breeze," said Mary.

Joachim stood, his worried eyes locked on the boy. "So…um… Joseph, how's the house hunting going?"

This was only the first of many incidents that showed Jesus' "special giftedness." It was a great concern for Mary and Joseph, and not well received by their neighbors.

A few months after this, Jesus was playing outside after a rain. At the end of the street, where the cobblestones ended, Jesus was with several other small children making mud pies from the sloppy ingredients of the wet dirt road. Jesus noticed that some of the children had begun molding crude but recognizable animal shapes. He wasn't sure whether they were sheep or donkeys or camels or cows, but they were definitely of the four-legged variety. This gave Jesus a *better* idea. With the tip of his tongue protruding slightly from the corner of his mouth, he set about molding a ball of mud into a bird. It was a sparrow, he decided, and a quite nice one at that.

When he finished his work, he stood and, holding the object between his hands, said, "Watch this." He threw the form into the air. In an instant, it sprouted wings, feathers, eyes, and feet. It hovered for a second, looking down at Jesus, and then flew away.

"Holy crap!" the other children said. "Do it again!"

And he did, again and again, to much applause.

The next day, the fathers of the other children came to see Joseph at his shop.

"Your kid is at it again, Joseph," one of the men said.

"He has a demon!" said another.

"What has he done?" Joseph questioned.

"He turned mud into birds! Breathing, flying birds!"

"This sounds like the imaginations of your children," Joseph argued, fearing it wasn't. "What proof do you have that this is so?"

"They were birds, Joseph. Birds! How can we gather evidence for proof of things that fly away?"

"I will hear no more of this!" Joseph said. "You cannot bring an accusation based on the testimony of children. You'll be laughed out of court."

"Not in this town, Joseph," said one of the men. "Everyone knows of the strangeness of your child."

"No one said anything about court, Joseph," said one of the more reasonable accusers. "We're just asking you to talk to the boy. Get him under control. Whether this is magic or miracle, it's too much power in the hands of a child."

"It's a demon!" shouted another.

"It isn't a demon," the other man continued, now in defense of Jesus. "He isn't mad; he doesn't have fits, as possessed people do. He goes to synagogue and prays and worships the Lord. One with a demon can't do these things. He's a good boy, most of the time. You know this."

The mumbling and shouting from the crowd ceased.

"Just talk to him, Joseph."

"I'll talk to him," said Joseph.

Joseph did have a long talk with Jesus, with Mary and Joachim listening. "You may not do these things, Jesus. I forbid it. How many times must you be told?"

"But birds are God's creatures, and God loves all that he has made."

"They weren't birds until *you* made them, Jesus! God didn't make them; you did."

"Same thing," said Jesus.

"No, it is *not* the same thing!" Joseph said, frustrated. He took a few breaths to calm himself. "Look. We know you are special, Jesus. You're a chosen vessel of God. You've been given special gifts for God's purposes and, in time, God will put those to use in you. But you must wait for that time. You must wait until you've come of age and have the quick mind of an adult to discern the path God has for you and how to use the gifts he has given you. Do you understand?"

"No."

"Do you understand?" Joseph repeated, slowly and loudly.

"Yes!"

"I think you need to spend the next hour in your room, thinking about these things."

Jesus got up and started toward the bedchamber.

"No more birds out of mud!" Joachim interjected, as the boy walked away. He couldn't prevent a little smile on his lips as he thought back to all that surrounded Jesus' birth. This was, indeed, a special child.

After several months of living with Joachim and Anna, Joseph finally found a house to rent. It was small, only two rooms and an outside kitchen, but they wouldn't be there for long. Joseph had begun building their house soon after they arrived in Nazareth. He had purchased land from Mary's uncle, so it connected to the larger farm. It was a small tract but large enough for a four-room house, with a terrace and a separate building for the kitchen. A wall, eight feet high, surrounded the back of the house, and this enclosed the terrace and kitchen hut.

The building of his own house had to come between Joseph's other jobs. He now had a successful construction company that specialized in building high-end homes for the well-to-do, mostly Romans and other foreign agents working in the area but some Jewish clients too. Many of his jobs were in surrounding towns, and Joseph spent much of his time traveling from project to project to oversee the work. His reputation as a builder was growing, and he employed several crews of his own, as well as subcontractors and architects.

When the family finally moved into their new home, Jesus was eight and had three siblings. Mary was just pregnant with her fifth child.

One day, when Jesus was walking home from school with his brother James, they were accosted by several older boys. They were making fun of Jesus because of the bird thing and a couple of similar incidents. They called him the devil's son and began to throw rocks at the brothers, one striking James in the face. He was bloody and crying, and the other boys were laughing and dancing around them.

"Stop it!" Jesus shouted.

"Why don't you just sprout wings and fly away, son of Satan," one of them shouted back.

"Can you turn these rocks into birds?" one asked, sarcastically.

"Or bread," said another. "Then they won't hurt as much."

They continued to laugh and ridicule their prey.

Jesus' temper was rising. "If you won't stop, then I will stop you!"

One of the boys reached down for another rock but suddenly went limp and collapsed on the ground. The laughing stopped, and the boys all stooped to check on their friend.

"What did you do to him, you little shit?" yelled one of the boys. He stood and charged Jesus with a rock in his hand. Jesus lifted his hand and extended his forefinger toward the boy, who suddenly lurched back in the other direction. He fell on his back and didn't move. The other boys dropped their rocks and ran away.

Jesus went to his brother, who was kneeling with his face in his hands. "James, let me see."

James removed his hands from his face and looked up at Jesus. The rock had clearly broken his nose and blood was pouring from the corner of James's left eye. With his hand open wide, Jesus placed his palm over James's entire face, and when he removed it, James was perfectly healed.

"Holy crap!" said James, and he ran home ahead of Jesus.

Luckily, Joseph was working nearby that day, so as soon as James came and explained to Mary all that had happened, she sent him to Joseph's worksite to tell him to come home. Jesus walked slower than usual the rest of the way. He knew James would've given his mother a full report, and he knew what was coming. He'd done a pretty good job of restraining himself and his "special gifts" over the years, but this one had gotten away from him. As soon as he walked in, Mary was waiting.

"Sit!" she said to Jesus.

He sat.

"What were you thinking?" Mary asked.

"I tried to get them to leave us alone, but they wouldn't. They said I was the devil. When they hit James in the face with a rock, I lost it."

"James said you killed them. Jesus, did you kill those boys?"

"Kind of."

Mary placed her face in her hands. She shook her head back and forth. In a moment, she looked up at Jesus and said, "You sit there, and don't move until your father gets home." Then she went to the kitchen and began to cry.

Half an hour later, James and Joseph came in the front door. "Well, Jesus, I think I've heard everything from James. Is there anything you'd like to add?"

"I doubt it," said Jesus. "But if James told you the story, there are probably a couple things I could subtract."

"That's enough of your sass, Jesus! Yes, James has told me the story. Now you tell it to me. All of it!"

Jesus recounted the story to Joseph as Mary and James listened. Marion had been asked to take the other children outside and attend to supper. Jesus told about the taunting, the rock throwing, the two boys he had zapped, and how the others ran away. When he said nothing more, James jumped in.

"And then, he healed me! Put his hand over my face, and just like that: No more blood, no more pain. It was awesome!"

Jesus was thinking it might have been a good idea to strike James mute at the same time.

"Jesus, are those boys dead?" Joseph asked, wringing his hands, anticipating the worst.

"I think so."

"You think so?"

"I'm pretty sure."

There was the sound of someone calling from far away. "Joseph! Joseph!" It was Joachim. He was walking at a fast pace and almost out of breath.

Joseph went outside to meet him.

Joachim took a moment to collect himself. Then he spoke, "Joseph, there is wailing in town. Two boys are dead. They say Jesus killed them. Is this true?"

Joseph couldn't speak.

"Is this true?" Joachim repeated louder.

"I believe it is true," Joseph mumbled despondently.

"They'll be coming for him, Joseph. They'll stone him."

Joseph pressed his fingers to his forehead and began to pace back and forth, wondering what he could possibly do to avert his son's execution. Suddenly, he had a thought. He walked back in the house and sank down on one knee in front of where Jesus was sitting, so they were face-to-face. "Jesus, can you bring those boys back to life?"

"No."

"What?"

"They don't deserve to be brought back to life. They deserve what they got," Jesus said smugly.

"You listen to me. I don't think we want to talk about people getting what they deserve, right now. Do you?"

"You're not my real father, you know."

Joseph's face turned blood red. "Today, I am."

They waited.

At dusk, Joseph saw the crowd coming. He stepped out the front door to meet them but not too far. He hadn't gone into town to talk with them because he knew the mob would have likely killed him when they saw him coming. And then, they would have come for Jesus. This way, he could at least make his case before they demanded the boy.

They arrived with the two dead boys on biers. The women were wailing. The men were carrying sticks and torches, and many of them carried leather pouches filled with rocks they'd gathered along the way. It was clear what they'd come to do.

"Give us the boy, Joseph," one of them said. "Give us your murderous son."

The others jeered in agreement.

"We knew it would come to this!" said another. "The boy has a demon!"

The noise of the crowd rose up again.

Joseph raised his hands and pleaded. "Does he not deserve a hearing? He claims self-defense. His brother, James, is his witness."

"We have witnesses as well, and we've already heard them. These boys here say Jesus committed murder!"

They pushed the three surviving bullies forward, but they quickly shrank back into the crowd, afraid of a similar fate from Jesus.

"There have been no murders," Joseph countered. "These boys are only sleeping." (He said this hoping against hope that Jesus would do—could do—as he had asked.)

The crowd responded to the fantastic claim with sardonic laughter. Joseph saw that a few of the men were reaching into their pouches for stones. If one rock was thrown, it was over. The others would quickly follow suit. He was losing the crowd. It was now or never.

"Bring the biers and place them here." Joseph motioned to the ground in front of him.

The crowd silenced. They were curious about what Joseph was planning to do. One of the leaders motioned for the dead boys to be brought forward. They laid the biers where Joseph had instructed. He swallowed hard, in an effort to push his heart back down into his chest.

"These boys are alive," Joseph said. "I'm bringing Jesus out. Don't hurt him. He will show you." He went to the door and motioned for Jesus to come. He noticed the boy shaking. His color was pale. If Jesus had not properly assessed the gravity of the situation before, he surely realized it now. He stepped out the door.

"Murderer!" someone shouted.

The mob enlivened again, but Joseph held up his hand. A leader of the group did the same, and the crowd hushed. Jesus stepped to where the boys were lying. He looked at their expressionless faces and had great pity for them. A tear came to his eye.

Just then, a woman ran forward and fell before her son at Jesus' feet. "Jesus!" she pleaded, "Have mercy on me! Heal my son!"

With great compassion for the woman, and the boys, Jesus said in a voice no louder than a whisper, "Get up."

The boys opened their eyes, saw Jesus, and, as quickly as they could get to their feet, ran away to the back of the crowd.

No one spoke for a full moment. The mothers embraced their sons. The men with rocks slipped them back into their pouches. Finally, someone in the crowd said, "Didn't anyone check to see if they were dead?" There were other mumblings. The three bullies were being scolded by their parents for false reporting. The parents of the two supposedly deceased boys were questioned about how they ever had thought the boys were dead. There were even a couple of people who claimed they knew the boys weren't dead.

"I swear I saw one of them move when we were still in town," one said.

"I tried to convince you all the way here that this was a farce," another said to his wife. "I know a dead person when I see one."

The mother who had thrown herself before Jesus ran to him and hugged him. "God bless you!" she said.

"Ridiculous!" said a bystander. "Does she actually think the kid can raise the dead?"

The crowd was dispersing. Joseph, trying to gather himself, was fighting back the urge to cry.

"You know, Joseph," said a man standing beside him, "you dodged a dagger on this one, but it doesn't change the fact that something is wrong with the boy. You've got to do something or this isn't over."

"I know," Joseph said, wiping his brow.

He watched as the crowd and their torches disappeared into the night. Then he went in the house, into the bedchamber, and closed the door.

The next morning, Joseph talked to Mary about moving to Capernaum. Most of his work was there and he could be home most nights. She agreed that it was in the best interest of everyone that they move on from Nazareth. Later in the day, Joseph had a long talk with Jesus. After yesterday's near catastrophe, he listened to his father more attentively than he ever had. They sold their home to Mary's uncle, who would use the place to house his foreman. Within a month, they were in Capernaum in a rented villa overlooking the Sea of Galilee.

Jesus loved Capernaum. When he wasn't in school or working with Joseph, he spent his time watching the boats come and go and helping the fishermen clean their nets. They often gave him fish as compensation, and these he took home to Mary.

Jesus thought fishing might be his trade. When he spoke of this to Joseph, his father told him he should do what his heart called him to do, but that he hoped Jesus might consider joining him in the family business. "I suspect, though, that God may have something special in store for you," Joseph said.

Jesus suspected this, too, but it was not a topic of great conversation.

Jesus excelled in school, studying the Torah and the Psalms and learning the different languages. He spoke Hebrew, Greek, and Latin fluently, as well as the different Aramaic dialects of the region.

When he was twelve years old, Jesus was invited to travel with his parents to Jerusalem for Passover. This was his first trip to the great city, at least that he could remember, so he was quite excited about the journey and the destination. It was, he thought, the mark of adulthood to go to Passover and to worship in the great Temple.

When they came within first sight of David's City, it was almost more than his eyes could take in. Still far away, it was the most magnificent place he had ever seen. Rising above the great wall that surrounded the city was building after building after building, and there, at the very pinnacle of the grand metropolis, was the Temple, the largest building of all. As he stood on the Mount of Olives and looked down into the valley that led to the east gate of the city, he could see streams of pilgrims, thousands of them, all headed for the same place. He wanted to run ahead, but Joseph kept calling him back.

"Stay close, son. We'll get there."

And they did. They stayed for a week, and it was glorious, Jesus thought. Every offering, every ritual, every celebration seemed the greatest experience of his life.

When the week had ended, Joseph and Mary and all the others that had traveled with them from Capernaum made ready to leave. They took a headcount, and all the children were accounted for. Both Mary and Joseph had seen Jesus walking with his friends as they left through the north gate. They traveled throughout the day, and when evening came, the group made camp. Mary built a fire and began preparing dinner for the three of them, while Joseph fed and watered the donkey and pitched the tent.

"Where is Jesus?" he called to Mary. "He can be gathering sticks for the fire."

Mary looked at Joseph. "I thought he was with you. He's around. Please go and find him."

An hour later, Joseph came back. "I can't find him. I've checked with every adult and every child. No one has seen him since we left Jerusalem. I think he may still be there."

Mary panicked. "Oh, my Lord! We've left him! Joseph, we have to go back now!"

"Mary, we can't go back in the dark. Let's continue to look in the camp. If we don't find him, we'll go back at first light."

"But what will he do for the night? Where will he stay? Who will feed him?"

"Mary," Joseph said, "he's twelve years old. He can take care of himself. He'll be okay for one night." He said this calmly, but he was just as troubled as Mary.

They searched the camp again but didn't find Jesus. Neither of them slept.

The next morning, just before dawn, Mary and Joseph began their trek back to Jerusalem.

When they arrived, around noon, Mary was sick from hunger and worry. Joseph forced her to sit down, and he bought falafels for both of them. They ate quickly and began their search. It was like looking for a needle in a haystack. The city was still filled to the brim with pilgrims.

"Have you seen a boy? Dark curly hair?"

Of course they had. Hundreds of them.

They searched the markets and street after street. Suddenly, Joseph said, "I know where he is."

They went to the Temple and, in the courtyard, saw a small crowd gathered.

They worked their way through the crush of onlookers and, there, sitting on the steps of the Temple, was Jesus. He was with a dozen Pharisees and scribes vigorously discussing the scriptures. Some of the men looked rather flustered—irritated—flailing their hands about, as they tried to make their points and defend their views. Others sat studying Jesus, rubbing their chins and considering his arguments. Jesus was animated but perfectly calm, speaking with the same shrewd half-smile on his face that Joseph had seen many times, just before the boy got himself into trouble.

Before Joseph could react, Mary broke through the line of people in front of her, grabbed Jesus by the wrist, and started dragging him away.

"Leave the lad alone," said one of the Pharisees.

"You leave him alone!" snapped Mary.

The men were indignant. Such brashness from a woman!

"Stop it, Mama! What are you doing?" Jesus protested, as Mary continued to pull him by his arm.

When they reached the corner of the courtyard, and everyone else had returned to their business, Mary turned and put her face directly in front of his. "Jesus, what were you thinking? Your father and I have been searching for you all day, worried sick!"

Jesus looked at her with genuine surprise. "Why were you looking for me? Did you not know I would be here, in my Father's house?"

"Uhhhh!" cried an exasperated Mary. As she turned, leading him away, tears of relief were flowing down her face.

When they had returned to Capernaum, Jesus told his brothers and sisters all about his pilgrimage to Jerusalem. They all longed for the day when they would be of age to make the trip themselves. For many nights, Jesus dreamed of Jerusalem. Some of the dreams troubled him greatly.

That same year, the family—which now included six children, and Mary expecting another—moved into the new house Joseph had built for them. It certainly wasn't as grand as some of the homes Joseph built for his clients, but it was larger than anything they'd lived in before. It was a two-story dwelling, with separate living and dining areas downstairs and a bedchamber for Joseph, Mary, and the three smallest children. Upstairs was a large room for Jesus, James, and Marion and, eventually, the other children as they grew older.

A wall surrounded the whole compound with a front gate that led to the street. In back, there was a kitchen, a large terrace and garden area for growing flowers and vegetables, already mature fruit trees, and, best of all, a stairwell leading to the top of the house and a roof terrace that boasted a 180 degree view of the sea. Jesus spent much of his free time here, watching the boats and gazing at the great brown hills on the western shore and the cool and mountainous Golans to the east.

At age fourteen, Jesus finished his studies at the synagogue. Because of his brilliance and an unusual aptitude for learning, he was invited to continue his work there as a kind of student-teacher. Joseph wanted Jesus to work with him, at least for a while. Jesus still contemplated the fishing trade and was very much in favor of continuing his education. But ever since the debacle in Nazareth, when Joseph had saved his life, he mostly wanted to please his father. He'd learned to love and respect him greatly, and he knew Joseph loved him too. He had been, for the most part, an obedient son since that day, and he would continue to be. He would do as Joseph had asked and join him in his work.

Not long into his apprenticeship with Joseph, Jesus met a man for whom Joseph was building a part-time home in Caesarea. The man was an emissary from Greece and a resident in Caesarea about six months each year. He was impressed by Jesus' knowledge and skills, and he went to Joseph to ask if Jesus might accompany him on a tour of the Mediterranean, acting as a companion and tutor to his son who was a few years younger. Knowing he would jump at such an opportunity, Joseph took the invitation to Jesus, who, with Joseph's blessing, excitedly accepted the job. The next day, Jesus left the work site at Caesarea and traveled back to Capernaum to say goodbye to his mother and siblings and to collect his things for the trip.

Jesus traveled with the man back to his home in Athens. From there, they would sail to Crete, then to Tunis, then to Rome. They would stay a week or so in each of those locations and then return, stopping at Alexandria and other African ports along the way. Finally, they would sail to Joppa, where Jesus would disembark and return to Capernaum by land. In all, the trip would take about seven months.

Jesus was fifteen when the trip began; Joseph, forty-one; Mary, thirty.

The trip was a grand adventure for Jesus. He delighted in the sights of each place visited and the different cultures experienced along the way. At every stop, at his generous host's expense, he purchased books, sampled new foods, and collected souvenirs for himself and his family. When the ship was under sail, Jesus instructed his protégé in math and measurement, languages (Greek and Latin), and history. At night, by lantern light, he devoured his newly acquired books.

In Alexandria, their last stop before returning to Israel, the Greek decided they would take a land trip by camel to Giza and the Great Pyramids. This would delay their homecoming by two weeks, but Jesus was excited about the opportunity to see the place where the Hebrew people had been enslaved for centuries, where Father Joseph had once governed, and where Moses had challenged the mighty Pharaoh and set God's people free. Never had he seen such wonders of workmanship and building skill, not even in Athens or Rome. It was said that the Hebrews themselves had constructed the pyramids, and he thought he would like to bring Joseph here some day. He would be impressed.

They took a boat trip down the Nile. It was the biggest and most beautiful river Jesus had ever seen, perhaps half a mile wide with waters as blue as the sky. The land was fertile and lush, and palaces dotted the riverbank, alongside archaic and architecturally unique monuments to various gods. The river wildlife was a marvel as well: crocodiles, hippopotamuses, flamingoes, and huge rainbow-colored fish, said to be man-eaters.

The next day, they mounted their camels for the trip back to Alexandria and the ship. As they rode, Jesus and the Greek man discussed future journeys. He told Jesus he was thinking, after his retirement next year, of a trip along the Silk Road to India. The round trip would take about two years, and the man's entire family would be accompanying them, including a daughter, who was "quite beautiful" and whom Jesus "might like to marry." Jesus had read about India. He was excited about the idea of the trip—but not the idea of marriage.

"I would consider this," Jesus said. "The trip, that is. I understand the religions of Hinduism and Buddhism are practiced there." Jesus had a great interest in the ancient religions of the world.

"Those and others," the man said. "There is much you could learn on such a trip, and I would teach you the merchant trade. I will be buying many things to bring back to Greece."

"I've also heard that the Ark of the Covenant is there, in a monastery temple somewhere near Gandari."

"I do not know of these things," said the man, disinterested in the tales of religion.

"It should be in Israel," Jesus said. "If I went with you, and if I located it, would you help me get it?"

"Am I to buy this for you?" asked the Greek. "I know nothing of this Ark, but if it is a religious artifact of some significance, I should think it would demand a hefty price."

Jesus was not thinking of buying the Ark. If it really was there, it did not belong to those of another religion. It was the Ark of God, and its rightful caretakers were the People of the Covenant. It wouldn't be stealing any more than the Israelites stole it away from the Philistines. It was more like *returning*, Jesus thought. But realizing this wasn't a proper conversation to have with his present and, possibly, future employer— and the wrong ally for the endeavor anyway—he let the matter drop.

"I'll think about this journey, Jesus said.

"Good," said the Greek. "I will think on it too."

By the time the trip ended, Jesus was almost halfway through his sixteenth year. At Joppa, the Greek presented Jesus with thirty denarii as a parting bonus. They said their farewells.

"My house must be finished by now," the Greek said to Jesus. "When I arrive there, you and your father must come and be my guests. In the meantime, you talk to Joseph, and, if he agrees, we'll discuss the matter of the trip then."

Jesus shook his hand again and boarded the rowboat that took him to shore. As much as he had enjoyed the trip, he would be glad to be back in Capernaum and to see Mary and Joseph and his brothers and sisters.

When Jesus arrived at Capernaum and was near the house, his mother saw him and ran to meet him.

"Jesus! Jesus!" she cried, and threw her arms around him. She was sobbing, he thought, because of her joy in seeing him, but as soon as she caught her breath, she said, "Your father is dead!"

Jesus heard her well enough, but he wanted to believe he had misunderstood.

"What?"

"Joseph was killed in an accident a month ago," Mary said between shaky, shallow breaths. "He was working in Bethsaida, and a stone wall collapsed on him and two other workers. "They all died, Jesus!"

He held her as she cried. He cried too. He kept repeating, "Abba. Abba. My beloved abba."

They were there in the street for a long time. Jesus' brothers and sisters came and put their arms around Jesus and Mary. They grieved together. They grieved for Joseph and for each other.

Because Joseph had been a relatively wealthy man, his estate was required by law to make reparations for the other victims' families. Each received one-quarter of the estate. Mary was able to keep the house and about six hundred denarii. Eventually, she sold the house, and the family moved into smaller quarters.

Jesus knew nothing about his father's construction business, but he did have some carpentry skills, so they bought a small shop where

Jesus made furniture and small boats, and the occasional ox yoke. He was now the bread winner for the family—a mother and six younger siblings. His fate was sealed. He didn't think of journeys anymore.

Chapter 3
Jesus, the Carpenter

Jesus was seventeen years old. The period of mourning for Joseph had just ended. Today, Mary could remove her veil and stop wearing the dark clothes required of grieving widows. This morning, as she entered from the kitchen with breakfast, Jesus was glad to see her still lovely face—the first time he had seen it in six months—and the return of her blue tunic, the color she almost exclusively preferred in dress. When she met Jesus' eyes, she returned his smile.

She put the plate of fresh-baked bread on the table beside the goat cheese and dates and bowed her head as a sign that she was ready. Jesus said the blessing and took the first piece of bread before passing it on to his mother and siblings. James was now fourteen. He had just finished his studies and, today, would join Jesus in the carpenter shop as a full-time assistant. Marion, Anna, and Salome would help Mary with chores at home, and Jacob and Simon would walk to school at the synagogue.

Jesus was making a living at the shop. They occasionally had to dip into the family's inheritance to make ends meet, but, for the most part, their savings were still intact. Jesus had resigned himself to the fact that he would probably never leave Capernaum. He was okay with that. He liked the town and especially the lake, where he sometimes hired out to his fisherman friends on Sundays. Also, he wanted to be there for his mother and family.

Every Sabbath, he went to synagogue. He listened to his old teachers as they taught. Sometimes, he would be invited to read from the Torah and to give the homily that followed; other times, he would simply sit and listen to the wise ones and contemplate what they read and said. Jesus was quite popular with the younger worshipers, but many of the elderly in the congregation found him arrogant and brash. After all, he was only a carpenter. How was it that he would be a teacher to them?

There was a young man named Peter who lived in Capernaum. He had attended school with Jesus but, in those days, at least, was of lower class. In fact, they didn't have much in common at all. When school ended each day, Jesus had been free to do as he pleased. Peter, on the other hand, was required to go immediately to his father's fishing business, where he washed and mended nets and helped unload the boats as they docked at the end of the day. Peter was not the religious sort, nor was his family. They seldom darkened the door of the synagogue on the Sabbath, and Peter hadn't been there since the day his studies ended. Conversely, Jesus and his family were in the congregation every Sabbath day. He never missed any occasion for a synagogue gathering and, often, closed his shop to be present for daily prayers or just to talk with his former teachers. Peter was, in many ways, jealous of Jesus and his seemingly unhurried lifestyle, but he also disliked Jesus for this same carefree demeanor and saw him as being irresponsible for his age.

Peter had been saving money for a long time. His dream was to own his own boat. He hoped to continue to work with his father, as his brothers did, but being his own boss and having his own business was attractive too. Either way, his share of the fishing trade would be much more lucrative if he could captain his own ship and crew. Working as a deckhand and net-mender was all he would ever be able to do without a boat of his own, and he was determined to do more with his life than be a laborer for others.

James actually had more of his father's carpenter genes than Jesus. Already skilled to some degree, he took to his new occupation with a passion. He could do the work that Jesus did in half the time, and, while this pleased Jesus, they were suddenly producing much more than they could sell. Not only that, but the extra materials required for the work of two carpenters (or three, if you counted the extraordinary production abilities of James) was causing the shop's expense to exceed its income. Jesus praised James's work but encouraged him to slow down, just a little, so that sales could catch up with inventory.

It was James who had the idea of expanding the business to include larger boats. Those they had been making were simple flat-bottomed boats that held one or two men. These were for individuals who were not fishermen by trade but simply wanted a boat to get to deeper water and bigger fish for the family table. The larger and much more intricate and expensive fishing boats were made in Bethsaida. They were made by a single company that had the tools and knowledge to bend long wooden planks and then cure them in a way that caused them to retain their shape after they had taken to water. But it was a small operation—father and son—producing only two or three boats a year, depending on their size. There was no other competition.

"Why," James asked Jesus, "don't we invest in some equipment and start making ships? You can continue to do what you've always done, and I will be the ship builder. I can do much of the work alone and when I need help, I can use Jacob or one of the girls."

Jesus thought of two things: He liked the idea of getting James out of the shop and into the yard, but he worried about the huge outlay of funds required to buy equipment and the massive amount of materials it would take to build a single boat. He also knew that he'd likely be much more involved in the boatbuilding than James let on, but that would be okay. He thought he'd be interested in learning to build big boats. In the end, they agreed this would be a good move for the shop and good industry for Capernaum. There would be demand. Tonight, over supper, they would discuss the matter with Mary and see about borrowing funds from her savings.

The cost of equipment would be expensive, for sure. They didn't know how much exactly, but James had an idea of what was needed. Several large vises would be required, along with various-sized clamps. These would all have to be new, either made in the shop or purchased, since the clamps they already owned would still be used in their other ongoing projects. They would have to have a furnace, a boiler, a steam box, and several different sized molds. They would need some new wood chisels, and they would need saws with smaller, more intricate blades to make kerfs in the wood they were bending. Finally, of course, they would need an ample supply of materials: wood, glue, nails, tar. All totaled, the start-up cost would be around three hundred denarii, perhaps a little more. Counting labor, their first two, maybe three, boats would get them back only to even, but eventually they would see profit. If they built just two boats per year, they could double their shop's income. But James was already dreaming bigger.

The Sea of Galilee was really just a large lake. Eventually, no more than a few large boats each year would meet its demand. But Capernaum was not that far from the Mediterranean and the seaport cities of Ptolemais and Tyre, Sidon, and Caesarea where there was ample demand for even bigger ships. In time, the business could move exclusively to boat-making and maybe even relocate to the coast. They could be as successful as Joseph had been and restore their mother to the lifestyle she once knew. Jesus liked the idea of James's success but didn't want to spend his life building ships or, now that he thought of it, furniture, either. As Jesus listened to James's dreams, he began to dream again too—of travel to faraway lands to learn of new people and things, and to search for that undeniable but still unknown "special thing" he was destined to do, a calling by his heavenly Father to pursue and accomplish.

After supper and family conversation about how each person's day had gone, Jesus, James, and Mary remained at the table, while everyone else went to bed. James revealed his plan to Mary, who listened but continuously glanced toward Jesus to try and get a read of what he thought of the venture. Jesus sat quietly through the whole presentation, sometimes listening, sometimes not.

Honestly, this evening his thoughts were a thousand miles away. He was remembering the great voyage with the Greek and his son: the exotic destinations, the endless ocean, especially at night when he was alone on deck. He remembered how big the sky was and how bright the moon and its reflection on the water. He could feel the sea spray in his face. He thought about the Greek's proposed journey along the Silk Road to India. He wondered if their caravan was already on the road, on its way. Oh, how he longed to be there, somewhere other than home. He loved his family, he loved Capernaum, but he needed something more. He had a calling to more, and he wanted so badly to find out what that was.

"Jesus? Jesus?" James was looking for an affirmation from his older brother.

"What?"

"You agree with me about the plan to expand the business, to build boats?"

"Yes, Jesus," said Mary. "I'd like to know your thoughts on this. You've been very quiet."

"It's James's plan, "Jesus said. "He believes we can do it, and so do I. James is the real builder between the two of us. I'm just a carpenter, and an average one at that. James is the one with the expertise. He's a natural just like Abba was. If he says we can do this, I believe him."

"It's a lot of money, boys, but it's not just my money. It's yours as well. If you both agree, then tell me what you need, and I'll see that you have it."

James was grinning from ear to ear. He reached his hand across the table toward Jesus, who took it and smiled back.

Mary placed her hands on top of theirs. "Well," she said, "I guess we're in the boatbuilding business!"

A few days later, James was leaving for Joppa, then on to Jerusalem. He'd order the needed supplies in those cities and make arrangements to have them delivered to Capernaum. Then he'd return home for a day before heading north to the forest areas around Caesarea Philippi to order the needed lumber.

In the meantime, Jesus, in James's absence, continued to run the carpenter shop, actually relishing these last days of working in solitude, at his own pace, in his own way. Within a month, everything would change and never be the same again. A part of Jesus grieved in anticipation of this loss, but a part of him welcomed the new direction that might actually open some options for him. Perhaps he could, once again, consider his quest for whatever it was he was looking for. To seek out that "special thing," as Joseph often said, that God had in store for him.

Perhaps it was God, and perhaps it was just Jesus' restless nature—his passion to see more, feel more, know more, do more. Maybe it was both. He did sense that God was in it, somehow, and that, for God's sake and his own, he was destined for a life other than a carpenter's in Capernaum.

A month after James returned from his buying trips, the Jerusalem materials arrived, a week after that the Capernaum supplies, and a few days after that the first shipment of lumber from Caesarea Philippi. It took about a week to set up the furnace and steam box. The first of the lumber was used to construct a second building detached from the shop. Underneath this three-sided shed were the vises and forms used to shape the boat's wood as well as the barrels of tar, glue, and nails. Pegs on the walls held the saws, clamps, chisels, hammers, and other tools needed for the new work. All around the two buildings were stacks of lumber, grouped according to length and thickness. Within two months of James's first mention of the idea, the brothers were building their first boat. This one had not been ordered—no payment had been made—but why wait, they decided. The materials were sitting in the yard. Start now and, hopefully, they'd find a buyer before it was finished. There was only room for one boat in the yard, so it was necessary that the finished boat be sold and moved before another could be started.

True to his word, James focused on the boatbuilding while Jesus filled the orders for tables and chairs, beds and cabinets, ox yokes and other farm implements. If extra help was needed, Jacob or Marion was brought in to assist. Occasionally, even Mary herself, curious about the whole boat-building endeavor, would come and lend a hand.

One of the other things Jesus often crafted from his shop, for businesses and residences, was signs. There was one outside his old shop that honored his dad. It read JOSEPH'S CARPENTER SHOP. Now, with his newest sign finished, he presented it to James:

BAR-JOSEPHS' BOAT YARD

THE BEST BOATS AT THE BEST PRICES

LIKE WALKING ON WATER

James beamed, though he was puzzled about the last line. He immediately got a hammer and nails and secured it to the side of the new building, facing the street. BAR-JOSEPHS' BOAT YARD had an official name and was officially in business.

Silas and Barnabas were two brothers, similar in age to Jesus and James. They were the third and fourth sons of a farmer, whose first two sons had pretty much claimed any share in the family business the father was able to give. So, the younger brothers had come to Capernaum, where they had gone to work for Peter's father in the fishing business. They had befriended first Jesus and then James and spent many evenings at Mary's table, enjoying suppers and the company of their adopted family. Marion was clearly taken with Silas, which didn't sit well with Mary. She liked the young man, but he was uneducated and poor, and, while Mary's family didn't enjoy the social status they once had, she wanted more for Marion. Silas had never given any indication his intentions for Marion were anything other than platonic, but Mary knew how quickly that could change, especially when a young woman as fair as Marion was sending signals of interest.

"So what are your plans for the future, Silas?" Mary inquired one evening, as they were finishing up a feast of tilapia prepared by her and supplied by the fisherman brothers. "What is it you aspire to?"

"I don't know," answered Silas. "I'll continue to work as a fisherman, I guess. Maybe one day own my own boat."

"Maybe a whole fleet of boats," interjected Barnabas. "We may even move to the coast and fish the Mediterranean! That's where the real money is!"

"Barney has big plans for us," Silas grinned, referring to his brother by the nickname he had carried since childhood. "His dreams exceed his means, I'm afraid."

"Everyone begins poor," protested Barney, "at least everyone from our station. Dreams are the beginning of means!" He looked hurt that his brother made light of his remarks.

"Of course, Barney," Mary replied. "There is nothing wrong with dreaming of a better future."

"I think there's a future for us here in Capernaum," said Silas.

"There are plenty of fish. We have good friends here. Our family is nearby. We do need our own boat someday, but there's a living to be made as fishermen on the lake."

Both Mary and Barnabas looked down at the table with no further comment.

"We have a boat," said James.

"What?" Silas questioned.

"Well, not yet, but we're building a boat at the shop, Jesus and I. If you're interested in buying a boat, we'll have one to sell."

Barnabas looked up excitedly, first at James, then at Silas. Both were silent.

"I think what Silas meant was that he would like to buy a boat *in time*," said Jesus.

"Yes," replied Silas, concerned with the turn the conversation had taken. "We can't afford a boat now but in time. *Someday*," he emphasized.

"I'm just saying," concluded James.

There was no more conversation about boats that evening. In fact, there wasn't much more conversation at all. Silas, almost frightened by the mere suggestion of such an expense, never really regained his wits. Barnabas, at first, excited by James's idea and then frustrated by his brother's inability to even consider the possibility, sulked in silence the rest of their visit.

Mary ended the evening by announcing it was time for bed. They all said their farewells, and the brothers left for their home. As Jesus and James were getting into their beds, Jesus admonished James for raising the subject.

"I didn't bring up the subject of boats," James said defensively. "I was just joining in the conversation."

"Those boys can't buy the kind of boat you're building, James," scolded Jesus. "Don't try and talk people into things they can't afford. You don't have to be that kind of pushy salesman."

"I was just saying," James said, as he retreated into sleep.

When Silas and Barnabas told Peter about the boat under construction, he was indignant. "What does Jesus know about building boats?" Peter's resentment of Jesus resurfaced, as he considered the carpenter's new trade. Nevertheless, he listened as Silas and Barnabas recalled their conversation with James and the proposition he'd posed to them.

"Actually, I think James is the boat builder," Silas said. "Jesus pretty much does what he's always done. James is the one that expanded the business to boats. According to him, he's about halfway finished with this first one, and it has to be sold before he can begin another. Maybe your father would be interested."

"Let someone else buy their first boat," Peter scoffed. "We'll see if it floats before we think about buying boats from Nazarenes." Peter liked to remind himself and others that Jesus and his family originated in Nazareth. It was a dirty little place, made up mostly of indigent farmers, and wouldn't be a city at all except for its ample water supply. The high water table allowed for an abundance of springs and wells, ergo the farming community. The village was there to support the farmers, and it attracted shop owners who were as uneducated as they were unscrupulous. Not that Capernaum was far above Nazareth in wealth or sophistication, but most there liked to think of themselves as vastly superior to their Nazorean counterparts. Certainly Peter did when it came to Jesus.

Peter found the idea of the Capernaum shipbuilders hard to shake, especially when news of the new venture began to circulate around the docks. Finally, at the end of the day, after his nets were clean and put away, his curiosity caused him to walk the mile or so to Jesus and James's shop. They had already closed for the day, but the stone and board fence that surrounded the yard was more to mark boundaries than for security, so Peter opened the gate and walked over to where the boat was set, braced by supporting timbers. Its exterior was almost complete, and it was impressive. Thirty-six feet long and fourteen feet wide, it was bigger than any boat his father owned: as big, in fact, as any boat on the lake. *What temerity,* Peter thought. *Leave it to Jesus to make such an arrogant statement on his first attempt.* He ran his hand along the side of the boat, feeling for unevenness at the joints. There was none. The curves were smooth and fluid, the joints tightly sealed, the cap rails thick and rounded.

A ladder was leaning against the side of the boat, and Peter climbed it to have a look inside. Here, there was still some work to be done. The floor of the boat had not been built, so this afforded him a look at the hull. Again, impressive. Huge joists, each one beveled carefully at the ends, fit precisely against the shape of the hull. He didn't see one inch where the trusses didn't meet the exterior boards of the ship perfectly. He examined each place where the timbers joined with exact dovetail notches. It was the finest boat he'd ever seen, and he wanted it! He'd been saving his money for this very purpose, and now the opportunity was here. Maybe. Could he negotiate an affordable price? Could he swallow his pride and allow himself to deal with Jesus? As he walked home, he considered the possibilities. If he couldn't afford the boat himself, perhaps he could take on a partner, although a partnership was not what he'd hoped for. As for his aversion to Jesus, that could be assuaged by dealing with James. After all, it was James's boat, not Jesus'.

Peter didn't sleep that night. All he could think about was the boat and the gamble he was about to take. It was a decision that would change his life, for good or for ill. Everything he had, or ever hoped to have, would depend on its success. His father would not be happy about losing a deckhand and gaining a competitor, and he wouldn't take Peter back if his venture was a failure. Still, the moment of truth—the moment to act—had come, and Peter wasn't about to shrink from the opportunity before him.

After the morning's run of fishing, Peter helped load the fish onto the dock and clean the nets. Then he took the bread he'd brought for lunch and ate as he walked toward the carpenter's shop. He'd brought money—one hundred denarii—for a deposit, in case he was able to make a deal with James for the boat. When he arrived, he saw no one in the yard, so he walked around to the door of the shop. Jesus was there, planing a long wide board that looked like the side piece of a cabinet. He didn't see James.

Jesus looked up. "Peter!"

"Jesus."

"It's been a long time, my friend."

"Too long," Peter lied.

"How's your family?"

"Everyone's well. I trust all is well with yours."

"We are well," Jesus responded. "What brings you to the shop?"

Peter avoided the question. "Uh...Is James around?"

"He's gone home to get lunch for us. He should be back any time."

As much as it pained Peter, he made small talk with Jesus for about ten minutes, and just as the conversation reached an awkward silence, James walked in with a basket containing lunch.

"James, you remember Peter," said Jesus.

"Of course. How are you, Peter?"

"I'm well."

"And your family?"

Here we go again, Peter thought, and, at the same time, tried to think of how he might get James away from Jesus so they could talk about the boat alone. Jesus solved the problem.

"James, Peter's come to speak with you. Why don't the two of you go out in the yard while I finish up here? Then we can have lunch together. Peter, will you join us for lunch?"

"Already ate," Peter said, patting his stomach.

Jesus nodded and turned back to his work, as Peter followed James out the door.

"I've come to ask about the boat," Peter said, pointing at the ship.

James grinned. "It's beautiful, isn't it?"

"It looks fine," Peter agreed, trying not to give away his enthusiasm.

"Come, let me show you some detail." James motioned as he walked toward the boat.

Peter followed.

They walked all the way around the exterior as James talked. Then he had Peter climb the ladder to take a look inside. From the ground, James called attention to the fit and finish of everything Peter was looking at—everything he'd already seen the day before when James wasn't there. When Peter climbed down, James was still going on about the quality of the wood and the seaworthiness of the large vessel. Peter knew this better than James, and it was time for him to get back to the docks for the late afternoon catch. As soon as he could get a word in between James's, he said, "How much?"

"Five hundred and fifty denarii," James said. He had gone over the numbers again and again, so he knew exactly what he was going ask for this eight-month project.

Jesus winced as he listened through the window. He thought this was exorbitant, but he had an idea of the price from ongoing conversations with James. He'd warned that such a boat was too expensive for the lake fishermen, and he had implored James from the start to consider downsizing his plans. James had refused, arguing that this was the boat of the future for the Sea of Galilee and one that would last a lifetime. While the other boats on the lake were smaller and certainly less expensive, they were also of lesser quality and more susceptible to the storms that could come so suddenly. The Sea of Galilee was notorious for this. One minute the skies were clear and the water calm, and the next the boats were tossed about like toys on waves ten feet high. Three or four boats were lost every year, and many more were damaged beyond repair. In the long run, James argued, this would be an investment worth the extra expense. Over time, the cost would be far less than constantly replacing or repairing the more crude vessels.

Peter bristled, too, when he heard the price. He expected it to be an expensive craft but had hoped the inexperience of James might cause him to undervalue the boat and sell it to him for a bargain, though still at a cost higher than he wanted to pay. He also knew from the beginning that such a boat would likely be beyond his means. Still, he'd hoped that there would be some way. Now that Peter had seen the boat, he would never be satisfied with anything else.

"I only have four hundred," Peter said, almost pleading. This was true. There was no use countering with anything less than every cent he had.

James shook his head. They were too far apart to haggle. "I can cut the price to five hundred. That's the best I can do. This was true too. It would leave James a profit of two hundred and twenty denarii, about a denarius a day for his labor, less than his wages for making furniture.

Both men were disappointed, but there was nothing left to say. Peter had to get back to the docks. They both looked at the ground for a moment, avoiding any further eye contact. Then Peter turned and walked away. As he was walking home, he couldn't help but think that, somehow, Jesus was to blame.

By road, ten miles south of Capernaum (five miles by sea), on the western shore of the Sea of Galilee, was the village of Magdala. An exclusive community, it consisted mostly of summer homes owned by the very wealthy. While a few of the homes were occupied full-time, the majority were vacation retreats for government officials, traders, and the "old money" absentee owners of huge farms leased to sharecroppers. Most of Magdala's year-round residents were the servants of homeowners, who kept their employers' properties pristine and ready for their return.

There were no patrolled gates at Magdala, nor any sanctions to keep the residents of other nearby villages from intruding on the elite neighborhood. The exclusivity was self-imposed. There was simply no reason, and no desire among the common folk, to mix with their part-time neighbors. The "visitors" would come and go and, when they were here, would create a bit of extra business for the lake's year-round entrepreneurs.

There were docks at Magdala, and in the summer, six days a week, a small market was set up from mid-morning till late afternoon. Fish, lamb, grain, fruits, and vegetables were available to the house cook for the preparation of daily meals; cloth, bags, jewelry, woodcarvings, and pottery for the shopping amusement of the homeowners; furniture and other items for general housekeeping.

Mary was the daughter and only child of one of the servant families. She was fifteen and for the past three years had carried a full share of her family's household duties, including the care of their employers, a wealthy couple from Damascus. Mary cooked, though not as well as her mother, and helped with meal preparation some of the time. She also helped her father with keeping the master's home clean: dusting, sweeping, washing, making beds, and scrubbing the Italian tile floors. Most of her time, though, when the estate owners were in residence, she attended to the needs of the mistress and avoided, as much as possible, the forward advances of her employer, an overweight, pompous ass whose opinion of himself far exceeded anyone else's. He had never worked a day in his life. All his wealth came from his father, who had inherited it from his father.

Mary spent as much time as possible at the docks and the market. Every day, her mother would send her with a list of needed supplies, so she knew many of the fishermen and merchants well. She enjoyed their company. As she talked with them about their homes and villages, Mary longed to see the other towns that surrounded the lake and meet the people who lived there. She wondered what it would be like to live in a place with neighbors rather than masters. In her entire life, she had never been outside of Magdala.

The people at the market enjoyed Mary, too, especially the young fishermen. Her personality was pleasant, her beauty incomparable. In fact, Peter believed she could be the most beautiful woman in all of Galilee. Perhaps, in all of Israel! He was quite taken with her and would always volunteer, between morning and evening fishing hauls, to take a part of the catch to the Magdala market, hoping to see her.

Mary's natural beauty was enhanced by the make-up her mistress would supply for her and insist that she wear. She taught Mary how to line her eyes with indigo and apply henna along her eyelids, cheeks, and lips. Her parents detested the make-up and expressed their displeasure to Mary, but they didn't dare raise their objections to the benefactors of their livelihood. Mary, on the other hand, didn't object to her exotic looks at all and, recognizing her parents' dilemma, continued to receive her mistress's attention and supplies.

One afternoon, as Mary was cleaning the bedchamber of her employers, the Damascus fat man walked into the room. As usual, he made his not-too-subtle advances toward Mary, and, as usual, she dodged him by scurrying to another part of the room and another supposed chore. This time, he didn't back off. He cornered her and placed his arms against the wall on either side of her. He pressed himself against her and tried to put his lips on hers. She turned her head quickly to avoid the kiss.

"You've been tempting me, Mary. Trying to make yourself up like my wife to get my attention. Well, you've got it."

He moved himself around toward her face, and she quickly turned it again, the other way. With his mouth, he dove into her neck and began licking her. She stiffened, too frightened to move or make a sound. She tried to push him back, but he met her resistance with his own, crushing her against the wall. One of his arms was an inch from her mouth and, with no other defense, she bit him hard. He yelped and jumped back. His expression was a mixture of fear, pain, and anger.

"You little bitch!" He slapped her across the face.

She could taste blood. She tried to run, but he grabbed her by the arm and threw her on the bed.

"Lie there! Do not move!"

She didn't.

"I will have you, you little whore." He raised his gown and climbed on top of her, then began raising hers. Suddenly, there were the sounds of voices downstairs. *No one was supposed to be home!* It was the mistress and someone else. He got up quickly and adjusted his clothes. "Get out! And say nothing of this to anyone!"

Mary rolled to the opposite side of the bed and bolted for the door.

"This isn't over," she heard him say as she was leaving.

Avoiding the room where the mistress was entertaining, Mary hurried to her own house next door. Too afraid to cry before, the tears were now streaming down her face, and she used them to try and wipe away what she could of the make-up. Most of it had stained her skin and wouldn't budge. Still, she washed and scrubbed until her face was almost raw.

The fat man didn't speak to Mary after that, but each time they passed one another, his stare was constant and his expression sinister.

One morning, near the end of the summer, Mary was returning from the market and saw a wagon and donkeys at the front of the house. Slaves were loading the wagon with trunks and packing bags and supplies onto the animals.

Thank God! They're leaving!

The mistress appeared at the door and saw her. "Oh, Mary," she said, smiling. "Come quickly."

Mary walked to where the mistress was standing and placed the basket carrying her market goods on the ground.

"I have talked with your parents about you coming with me to Damascus and being a servant in my house there. Would you like that?"

I would not like that at all, Mary thought. The little defense she had from the bastard that was her master was her parents and their quarters separate from the main house. With that gone, she had little chance of avoiding the eventual rape he had promised to perpetrate on her. She said nothing.

"Mary," said the mistress, slightly perturbed at the girl's apparent ungratefulness, "you can come back with us every summer and visit your parents. Every girl must leave home sometime. Now go and pack your things. We're leaving in an hour."

Mary swallowed the lump in her throat, picked up her basket, and did as she was told.

Her mother helped her pack her bags as she tried to comfort her speechless daughter. "This is a wonderful opportunity for you, Mary," she said, trying to calm her own broken heart. "You'll be in a real city. You'll have a chance to meet new people. Maybe you'll even meet a young man you'll want to marry. There was never much chance of your father arranging a marriage here. Not in Magdala. We're too isolated from the rest of the world here. You should be happy to get away."

Mary made no response until they were at the door, where she gave her mother and father a tearful hug goodbye and headed for the main house.

When she got to the wagon, the driver took her bag and set it on one of the donkeys. He offered his hand to help her into the wagon. She ignored it and stared at nothing, far away, as she waited.

Finally, the mistress appeared, followed by her sickening husband. When he saw Mary, he stopped. "Wait a minute. Where is she going?"

"I'm taking Mary back with me," the mistress said, not bothering to look back. "Eunice is getting old and can use the help, and eventually, Mary will take her position as my chambermaid. I've promised her she can travel back and forth with us to see her parents, so she'll be with us year-round now."

He considered this, as thoughtfully as a stupid man could: Yes. He wanted her and intended to have her, but would this complicate or simplify things? Having her in Damascus would present more opportunity, but it could also increase his risk of getting caught. As his wife's main chambermaid, she would also have her confidence, even her friendship. She might become bold enough to expose any untoward advances on his part, and this could mean serious trouble for him. There were already plenty of servant girls at home to molest, ones he already knew wouldn't talk. Perhaps, he would prefer his conquest of Mary as an annual summer event. His vacation dalliance. Still, it seemed his wife had already decided. What could he do? His original plan had been to get his wife on the road and, once she was gone, to lie in wait for Mary when she was attending to her cleaning duties. She would not be so resistant to him next time, he thought, and if she was, another slap across the face would settle her down. If she wanted discipline as foreplay, he would accommodate her. Then he would have her without the hindrance and worry of possible interruption. If he could just keep her here.

"Just a minute," he repeated. "Leave Mary here with me. I still have two weeks before returning home. I may have need of her. You go home. Tell Eunice of your plans and make ready for our arrival. I'll bring her with me when I come."

The mistress studied her husband for a moment, then turned and took the hand of the driver who helped her up the steps and into the wagon. "I suppose that makes sense," she said. "Be sure you bring the lamps and tables I bought. I'll see you back in Damascus." And, without so much as a goodbye, she motioned to the driver, and the wagon rolled away.

Mary was staring at the ground during the entire conversation, and she didn't raise her eyes now. But she could feel the master staring at her. She picked up her bag that the driver had taken down from the donkey and started toward her parents' house. She glanced out of the corner of her eye to see if he was still there, still staring. He wasn't. He'd gone back into the house.

The fat man was in the living room, sitting in a chair and smiling. He had done it! His plan had worked! He became aroused just thinking about Mary and what he would do to her tomorrow, and maybe the next day, and the day after that. Once he had had her, she would come around. *After all,* he thought to himself, *what's not to like?* When they were on the road to Damascus, he would remind her about keeping her mouth shut and the consequences if she didn't. He would enjoy having Mary's company on the trip home. She would provide some fun recreation along the way.

That night, Mary lay in bed thinking about what she would do tomorrow. Should she tell her father about the unwanted advances the master had made on her? Would he do anything about it, and if he did, would he be out of a job—would they be out of a house—with no prospects for any kind of work? Could she feign sickness and avoid the housecleaning, and the man, for at least one day? Could she kill the asshole and figure some way to escape being stoned? It would be impossible to win a claim of self-defense, arguing that the man attacked her. People might believe it, since it happened all the time between masters and servants, but peasants winning judgments against the wealthy *never* happened. In the end, she had only one option: stay and accept her fate or run away. She decided she had no option.

Mary rose before sunrise. She couldn't sleep. She dressed and sat at the table until her mother awakened and started preparing breakfast for the three of them. (She wouldn't cook for the fat man until much later when he finally roused from his drunken slumber.)

"Mary, why don't you go to the well and get water? Breakfast will be ready when you get back."

Mary took a two-gallon pottery jar and two one-gallon water pouches attached to straps that fit over her shoulders. By the time she was out the door, it was just light enough to see.

An hour later, Mary's parents were beginning to be concerned about her delay. They had gone ahead with breakfast, finished, and Mary's father was about to go and look for her when there was a knock on the door. It was a child, a ten-year-old girl, carrying the jar and water pouches.

"Mary asked me to bring these to you," the girl said. She was breathing heavily, the load almost unbearable.

"Where is Mary?" her father asked, as he helped the girl with the water containers.

"I don't know," the girl replied.

"Where did you see her?"

"She was just coming from the well."

"The well isn't fifteen minutes from here. Mary left an hour ago."

"She told me to wait until the sun was in the sky before delivering your water."

Mary's father was puzzled. "Why?"

"I don't know why," the girl said.

"Where was she going?"

"I don't know."

Confused, Mary's father thought for a moment and came up with only one last, seemingly trivial, question: "Which way did she go?"

"She was walking toward Capernaum."

He put the water containers inside, gave the girl a coin, and closed the door. "What's going on?" he said to Mary's mother. "She isn't hurt, thank God. But she obviously has no intentions of coming back soon. Otherwise, she wouldn't have sent the girl with the water. It appears our daughter has other plans for the day. What do you know of this?"

"I know nothing," said her mother. "She was up. I sent her for water."

They looked at each other for a long time. Then her father put on a head covering, grabbed his walking stick, and went out the door.

By the time he had walked to the edge of town on the Capernaum road, back to the docks and market, and down every side street between there and home, it was late morning. He washed himself, had a drink of water, and then proceeded to the rich man's house to begin his cleaning duties. The man had already finished his late breakfast and was back in his bedroom, waiting. When Mary's father entered, the man was surprised.

"Where is Mary?"

"Mary isn't feeling well today, master."

He should have expected as much. The little whore was trying to delay the inevitable. "Nothing serious, I hope."

"No, sir. I expect she'll be fine by tomorrow."

"I hope so," said the rich man. "You know the mistress insists that Mary clean the upstairs and bedrooms."

"I know that's true when the mistress is here, for reasons of modesty and because she enjoys Mary's company."

"She does not *enjoy* a peasant's company, you stupid little man, any more than I enjoy yours! The mistress tolerates Mary, as I do you. She pities her, so she has shared beauty secrets to try and improve her attractiveness. It has helped, somewhat, but it was a poor canvas to begin with. The mistress is a kind woman to treat your daughter with such care. See that you show her respect! Mary will clean these rooms tomorrow."

"Yes, master, of course. A thousand pardons."

"Now, go! I do not wish these rooms cleaned today."

Mary's father turned to leave the room, and, suddenly, the fat man realized his mistake.

"Except the bed. Come back and change the bed." He liked clean sheets because they didn't smell so much like him. He also wanted the cleanest and freshest bed linens for his anticipated rendezvous and conquest of the sweet virgin Mary. Once again, he was aroused by the very thought of it.

After cleaning downstairs and outside around the rich man's home, Mary's father tended the garden in back of his own small dwelling, all the while keeping an eye on the gate, waiting on Mary. At the end of the day, he got his walking stick and began combing the streets again looking for her. No one had seen her, not in the street, not at the dock markets, not at the well. It was getting dark and his concern was turning to worry.

When he arrived back home, his wife was waiting. He explained that there was no sign of Mary. No one had seen her all day. They talked for a while, trying to piece together an idea of where she might be. They came up with nothing. Forlorn, Mary's mother walked to Mary's room and stood at the door, gazing. She knew something was terribly wrong. Then she saw a small piece of folded paper on the bed. Apparently, she had missed it this morning, but she wasn't particularly looking, either. She sat on the bed, and opened and read the note.

"Simon, come here!" Mary's mother called out in distress. She read the note to Simon. It told of the attack of the fat man and Mary's fear that he would try again. She promised she would come home after the master had returned to Damascus. She begged her father not to do anything that would jeopardize his job, or worse. They would sort things out together when she came home. She didn't say where she was going or with whom she was staying. But, at least, they knew—they hoped—she was safe.

"That animal attacked Mary!" her mother said through clenched teeth.

Simon didn't speak. He rose from the bed, walked to the table, and sat silently. He was thinking. After several minutes, he said to his wife, "Let's eat."

The next day, Simon worked in the garden until mid-morning and then began his house duties. He cleared the table and mess from the master's breakfast, hung the rugs and beat them clean, and then began dusting and straightening the downstairs.

About noon, the fat man descended the stairs, his housecoat half opened.

"Simon!" he yelled. "Where is Mary?"

"She isn't here, sir. She's gone to visit an aunt near Jerusalem."

"What?" he roared, his face turning red. "Who gave her permission to go?"

"I did, sir. Her aunt is...uh...ill."

He looked at Simon in disbelief. "*She* is under *my* employ! YOU are under my employ! How dare you send her away without consulting me! When I am here, I expect to be served by my servants!" He was angry. His blood was boiling. His plans had been foiled. "Send for her! Go get her! I don't care if her aunt is ill! If she is not back here in two days, I will replace you. You and your whole family can find another place to live. Someone else to work for."

"Please, sir. She's been gone for two days. By the time I travel two days, she will have traveled four. I can't possibly catch up to her and be back in two days!"

The fat man was confused. "I thought you said Mary was sick yesterday."

"I didn't tell you the truth, master. I don't know why." Simon lowered his head.

"I know why, you little worm. You know something. She has told you something. Well, regardless of what she told you, your whore daughter tried to seduce me. You listen to me. You get her back here by the time I'm ready to leave for Damascus. The mistress is expecting her. If she isn't back by then, you can start looking for new employment. Is that understood?"

"I understand, sir," Simon said, resisting the urge to slit the man's throat.

"Good," said the fat man, feeling infinitely superior. "And as soon as she arrives, send her to me." He couldn't suppress a sick grin, as he thought, again, of his plans for Mary.

Simon didn't reply. He didn't look up. He turned and walked away, seething, scheming of how he would kill this putrid pig.

With the exception of a couple of rest stops in the shade, Mary had walked all day to reach Capernaum. She'd thought along the way and decided Peter was her best bet. She knew lots of the fisherman but none better than Peter. She was aware that Peter fancied her—nothing could be more obvious—and she liked him too. It wouldn't be hard to find him. She would find the docks and wait on him until he returned from fishing in the early evening.

Mary was starved. She'd had nothing to eat since the night before, and nothing to drink, either. All day, she wished she had kept one of the water pouches she sent home. She had resisted drinking from the lake. Most people didn't anymore. For those who did, sickness wasn't unusual.

Capernaum was a city of wells. She didn't have to walk far to find one. She could smell the sweet water, not ten feet from her nose. She could look into the well and see it. But she couldn't reach it. She didn't wait long before a woman came with jars to replenish her home supply. Mary asked, and the woman obliged. Tying a rope to one of the jars, she lowered it into the well then lifted it full and spilling over. As the woman filled her other jug, Mary drank and drank. They talked for a while, the woman asking Mary about where she was from and what she was doing in Capernaum. Mary explained, giving as much information as possible, and as little as necessary, to avoid suspicion.

She told the woman she was from "Um...Arbela" (thinking it best not to use the name of her real hometown), that she was a friend of Peter (true) and his family (never met them), and that she had just come for a brief friendly visit (half-truth). The woman seemed satisfied with Mary's story, though it did seem strange that a girl would be traveling alone. She didn't approve of Mary's make-up, some of which was still there as stain, but the woman surmised that this would be the type of girl Peter would be attracted to, and would attract. However, the more she talked to Mary, the more she saw what a beautiful girl she was, and sweet. By the time they parted company, the woman was asking herself why such a girl would have any interest in Peter. Maybe it *was* true; maybe they *were* just friends. She hoped.

With directions to the docks, Mary made her way there and waited for Peter to return from the afternoon catch. It was just getting dark when the boats began coming in from the lake. She watched eight or ten of them dock and unload, but she didn't see Peter. Finally, a smaller boat arrived. It didn't pull up to the dock like the others but landed on the shore just to the west. Three men jumped out of the boat and into water about knee deep. They used ropes to pull the boat to shore and then secure it to some nearby trees. She recognized one of the men as Peter and began walking toward him. He was unloading the baskets of fish; the two others were in the water removing the lake-bottom weeds and other debris entangled in the nets.

"Peter!" she called out, smiling as she walked toward him.

He didn't recognize her at first, here in Capernaum, out of her element. But, as she came closer, there was no mistaking her beautiful face, then the smile.

"Mary!" He smiled back, but, a bit confused at her presence, he said no more. When she was standing right in front of him, he continued. "What are you doing here?"

"I wanted to see Capernaum," she said, "and visit you." (She said this because she hadn't thought her story through and had nothing else at the moment.)

Peter, though excited, was still confused. "You came to visit me? Why?"

Good question. Mary was at a loss. "Uh, because you're my friend, Peter. Do you have anything to eat?"

Peter ignored her question. "I'm glad you're here," he said. "Why don't we walk? As they started toward the village, he called back to his brother. "Andrew, you and Zeke take care of the fish. I have something to do."

His brother gave him an objectionable look but said nothing.

"I'm glad you've come, Mary. I've wanted to talk to you for some time now. Just the two of us alone." He stopped, took Mary by the hand, and looked into her eyes. She collapsed right in front of him.

When Mary regained consciousness, she was on a bed in Peter's house. As her vision came into focus, she was surprised to see at least six unfamiliar faces looking down at her. Suddenly, her stomach growled, and she remembered why she had fainted.

"Can I have some water, please, and something to eat?"

Peter's mother scowled but moved immediately to fulfill Mary's request. She didn't know the young woman Peter had brought home in his arms. In fact, she'd never seen her before, and she knew virtually everyone in Capernaum. She didn't like her painted face, either. She brought Mary a cup of water and some bread and cheese. Mary set the water aside and began devouring the bread and cheese. Instantly, she felt better.

No one asked her any questions for a while, but everyone in the house was staring at her, watching her eat.

Finally, Peter's mother spoke. "Are you feeling all right, dear? Is there anything else we can get you?"

"No, thank you," said Mary. "You've been very kind. I walked here from Mag...Arb..." *What's the point?* she thought. *I might as well be honest with these people.* "I walked all the way from Magdala without any food or water. I guess it was just too much for me, but I'm fine now. Thank you for your kindness."

"Why did you walk here from Magdala?" asked Peter's father. "And why did you carry no food or water?" There were servants in Magdala, and there were slaves. He was becoming suspicious that Mary might be running from something, or someone, and there were serious penalties for harboring slaves.

Before Mary could compose a reply, the front door opened. Andrew and another of Peter's brothers entered the house, still aggravated by Peter's sudden departure, leaving them to finish the day's work alone. They didn't see their houseguest.

"Where did you go, Peter?" Andrew pouted. "And who was that girl?"

Their father raised his hand to interrupt the argument. "We're talking with the girl now," he said.

Andrew saw and recognized her. "Mary?"

"Hello, Andrew," she said.

"Well, you all seem to know each other," his father said, addressing no one in particular. "Why don't we sit down and someone can introduce the rest of us. Then you can tell me what's going on here."

No one spoke. Everyone looked at each other.

"Well?" said their father.

"This...is Mary...of Magdala," Peter began. "She is the servant girl for one of the families that summers there. We know her from the market, when we take fish to sell there." Peter was out of information, so Mary began.

"Yes, I know Peter and Andrew. I know Peter best. He's told me so much about Capernaum, and I wanted to come for a visit to see for myself."

"A rather unprepared visit," the father interjected. "Why did you leave home without food and water, child?"

"I wasn't thinking. I've never been out of Magdala before. I didn't think the distance would be so far."

Peter's father looked at her suspiciously. "Mary, are you a servant or are you a slave?"

"Oh, I'm a servant," she answered. "My parents and I live in Magdala year-round. We have our own quarters and keep the master's house when he and the mistress are at home in Damascus. When they're in Magdala for the summer, we serve them as they wish. They seldom bring any servants or slaves to stay with them. Their servants there bring them and then return to Damascus. When the summer is over, they return to take them home."

"And your parents know you're here?"

"Of course. I'll be here for a week or ten days and then will return home."

"And your master knows you're here?"

"Of course. The mistress has already returned to Damascus, so there's really no need of three servants for the master only."

Peter's father considered Mary's story. He doubted the parents of a young woman would allow her to travel alone and without food. But these were servants. He knew little of the ways of servants, so he decided to let the matter drop.

"I have one more question, Mary," he said. "Where are you planning to stay?"

Clearly, Mary hadn't thought this through, or anything else about the trip. She had left in a hurry, with no thought other than escaping her master's intentions for her. "I...I..."

"She will stay with us," said Peter's mother. "She can sleep with the girls, and she can help me with chores. I could use another set of hands around here." She still didn't trust Mary fully or her story but had sympathy for the girl and wanted to support her in her need. Besides, she thought Peter could do worse.

Before Mary's arrival, Peter could think of little else than the boat sitting in James's shop yard. Now, he could think of nothing but Mary. Every morning, he hated to leave her; every evening, he couldn't wait to get back to her. After supper, they would sit on the roof terrace and talk until long after the rest of the family had gone to bed. He loved her and wanted to marry her. This was all the more reason to buy his own boat and begin working for himself. He could buy something less than what James was building. Or, he could buy something used, but how long would it last, and how much farther along would he be when the worn-out wreck was used up and he had to buy another?

He contemplated a partnership with Andrew, but Andrew didn't have the same aspirations as Peter and had saved little toward the goal of boat ownership and his own business. Thinking of Mary and a life with her forced him to think of boats. That would have to come first.

The next day was the Sabbath. There was no work for Peter, and he knew James would be at the synagogue with his family. After breakfast, he announced that he planned to attend worship, which brought inquisitive looks from the others at the table. No one commented on Peter's sudden interest in religion, except for Mary, who said she would like to go with him. Her suggestion both pleased and displeased Peter. He wanted to be with her but wondered how he might continue his entrepreneurial discussion with James with Mary along. In the end, he decided it couldn't hurt. It might even impress Mary to hear of his future plans of being his own man with his own business. He would just have to be sure that Mary understood this discussion was to be kept quiet from his family and everyone else, until he was ready to act.

The synagogue wasn't far from Peter's house, just down the street. When they arrived, Mary went to sit with the women, while Peter walked toward the front to join the men. He saw James, who wasn't looking his way. Then he saw Jesus, who was staring straight at him, waving and grinning.

"Peter!" Jesus said. "It's good to see you here, my friend! Come and sit with me."

Peter begrudgingly returned a half-smile but said nothing.

They sat down and the service was called to order. A hymn was sung. A passage was read from the Book of the Prophet Isaiah, and then one of the elders stood and gave the homily. Peter rather enjoyed the service, and, when he wasn't preoccupied with the conversation he would have with James afterward, he considered thoughtfully what the elder had to say. After prayers and another hymn, an elder dismissed the congregation.

"So, how have you been, Peter? How is your family? How's business? Why don't you come and have lunch with us?" Jesus peppered him with question after question, trying to make conversation, but Peter gave only short answers, trying to break away and get to James. As they reached the door, Mary joined them. Peter looked at her and then at Jesus, who was obviously waiting for an introduction.

He sighed. "Mary, this is Jesus. Jesus, Mary."

As the two exchanged greetings with one another, Peter's focus returned to locating James. He spotted him just outside and waited as James finished his conversation with another man. Then he said, "Mary, I have to see someone. I'll be right over there." He pointed in James's direction.

Mary and Jesus continued to talk, as Peter made his way through the crowd toward James.

"James!" he called out.

James looked for the voice. "Peter! How are you? Still looking for a boat?"

"Shhhh!" Peter said out loud, without meaning to. "Please, I need to keep the boat business quiet until I'm sure I can make the purchase. But, yes, I'm still looking and I'm still interested in yours."

"Sorry," said James. "I didn't realize it was a secret."

"It's not a secret. I just don't want anyone to know about it yet."

"There's a difference?"

"Never mind. I don't suppose you've considered reducing the price?"

James looked disturbed. "No, Peter. I've given you my best price."

"Would you consider a payment of half now and half in a year?"

James did consider it, for a moment. He needed to sell the boat and he'd had no other interest. "I can't, Peter. Half would barely cover the materials. I can't carry the debt for a year."

"Then promise me you won't sell it to anyone else until I talk to you again. I have to consider my options."

"Look, Peter, if someone comes to me with the money, I can't ask them to wait until I talk to you. I can't even start another boat until that one is out of the yard."

"Just give me a week."

James looked up at the sky and sighed. "All right, I'll give you a week."

"Thanks," said Peter. He turned and walked back toward Mary and Jesus.

In the five minutes they were together, something between Mary and Jesus clicked. Jesus had inherited from his mother a rare trait among Semitic people, piercing blue eyes, and they mesmerized Mary. She also saw in him a goodness that captured her very soul. She felt he knew her in a way that no one else did. It allured and frightened her. The attraction was mutual. Jesus found her uncommon beauty to be both enchanting and disturbing. His heart stirred. He had never felt this way about a woman before. It was a relief for both Jesus and Mary when Peter returned to break the spell between them.

"Let's go, Mary," Peter said, avoiding eye contact or conversation with Jesus. He took her hand and led her away.

Ten days passed and Mary had not returned home. Her parents were concerned about her absence but not desperately so, as she had stated in her note that she would come back as soon as the master had departed. The fat man was very concerned. He wanted to make good on his promise to remove Simon and his family and replace them with new caretakers. But that would take time he didn't have and an effort he didn't wish to make. He would go back to Damascus and dispatch one of his managers to take care of the Magdala business. Because he would miss the pleasure of putting Simon out on the street himself, he was careful to remind Simon every day of his fate.

His larger concern, however, was explaining to his wife why he had not returned with Mary, as he had promised. She was quite fond of the girl and would not be happy. He could tell her the truth, that Mary had simply run away, and when she asked why, he could feign ignorance and say he didn't know. But would she put two and two together and guess why? He had been caught and reprimanded for his improper advances on young servant girls before. In fact, the last time, the mistress had presented him with an ultimatum should it happen again. It was not a pleasant one. In any case, it wasn't something he could deal with now, so he simply turned his focus on his own disappointment. He wouldn't have the pleasure of Mary's company on his way home. He wouldn't get to know her intimately, or she him. He was sure that once he had raped her, she would be overcome with affection for him—a co-conspirator in the affair—unlike the other girls who somehow seemed ungrateful for his attention. He was aroused again.

When the servants and slaves from Damascus arrived the next day, they packed the master's things on the wagon for the trip home. Just before leaving, he said a last hateful goodbye to Mary's parents, swearing to ruin them for their disobedience and lack of loyalty.

Once all was ready, he climbed aboard the covered wagon and they drove away. Simon watched until the wagon was out of sight, then he turned and spat on the ground, not giving a second thought to what he had done.

There was nothing for Peter to do except approach his brother about a partnership. He and Andrew had been in the same boat all day. As they were coming in from the evening run, Peter said, "Andrew, have you seen the boat James bar Joseph is building?"

"The carpenter? No. Is there something special about the boat he's building?"

"Yes, indeed. This is not one of their small boats. It is a thirty-six foot, state-of-the-art vessel."

"Sweet Jehovah! That's bigger than anything on the lake! When did Jesus and James start building big boats?"

"It's not Jesus' boat. It's James's!" snapped Peter.

"Whatever," said Andrew. "What of it?"

"I want to buy it. Start my own business."

"Abba will not like it. He won't like losing you, and he won't like the competition."

"If he doesn't like it, then he can talk to me about an equal partnership."

"Yeah, that's going to happen."

"That's what I think too. So what about you and me? How would you like to be my partner?"

"I like having a bed to sleep in at night. I like having food on the table. We get that at Abba's house."

"Andrew, if we have our own boat, we can make more money in a day than we make in a week working for Abba. We can get our own place. Hell, we can each get our own place! I'm thinking of getting married, anyway."

"You? To whom? Mary?" Andrew laughed.

"Yes! To Mary!" Peter didn't laugh.

Andrew was quiet for a moment. "So how do we get this boat?"

"How much money do you have?"

"I don't know. Forty, maybe fifty denarii."

Peter closed his eyes and sighed. "Do you blow every cent you earn?"

"No, I said I had forty or fifty denarii."

Peter sighed again. They were at the shore.

As they unloaded their haul and cleaned their nets, Peter and Andrew continued the conversation. In the end, they decided they would approach James again with what they had and a promise to fund the balance within two months. If James wasn't agreeable to this, then they would try and borrow the difference. From whom, they didn't have a clue.

Thursday was payday. Andrew and Peter collected their wages from their father. With that and their savings, they had a total of four hundred and sixty denarii. When they arrived at the carpenter shop, James and Jesus had already gone home. Andrew marveled at the boat, which appeared to be finished, as Peter pointed out the various quality features of the vessel. They then hurried on to James's house, hoping to find him there.

Marion answered the door and invited them in.

"Thank you," Peter said, "but we have business with James. If you could send him out, we won't disturb you."

She disappeared back into the house. A few seconds later, it was Jesus, not James, who came out to greet them. "Peter!" he smiled, extending a hand which Peter was forced to accept. "It was great to see you at synagogue. I hope you'll come back this week."

Peter said nothing.

"Andrew!" Jesus turned toward the brother, offering his hand. "It's good to see you as well. So, what brings you boys here? Please, come in!"

"We're here to see James…about the boat," Peter said, not moving.

"Ah, yes, the boat," said Jesus.

Just then, James walked out of the house to where the men were standing. Before he could speak, Peter immediately took his arm and pulled him away from Jesus and Andrew.

"I want the boat," Peter said, as he was still leading James away. "I have four-sixty, and I can have the rest in two months, maybe sooner.

"Peter," James said, "I've already told you. I have to have cash."

"And I have cash, just not all of it. James, do this for me. I want the boat. I *need* the boat! You need a buyer. It may take you a while to find another, maybe two months, maybe even longer. Take what I have now— right now—and take the rest in two months. We both get what we want."

James thought about this. "If I sell you the boat with a balance to pay, then I have to have the original asking price. Five-fifty: four-sixty now; ninety in two months."

Peter was taken aback. Now, instead of being forty short, a manageable amount over two months, he was ninety short. Not manageable. He didn't care. He had his boat. He would figure it out later.

"Deal!" he said. They shook hands. "Let's go, Andrew." Peter was walking away.

Andrew looked at Jesus. Then he looked at James. "Bye," he said weakly and hurried to catch up with his brother.

On Fridays, they fished in the morning only, as all work ceased at dusk, the beginning of the Sabbath. By the time they unloaded the boats and cleaned and mended the nets, it was four in the afternoon. Peter and Andrew gathered all their money together and headed back to the carpenter shop. James wasn't there; Jesus was.

"Hello, Peter. Andrew. James told me about your deal. He's gone to borrow a wagon and recruit some help to get the boat to the water. We're going to move it first thing Monday morning. We appreciate the business!"

As much as he hated making the transaction with Jesus, Peter shoved the pouch containing four hundred and sixty denarii into Jesus' hand.

"Here it is," he said, "four-sixty now, ninety in two months."

Jesus read the excitement *and the anxiety* on Peter's face.

"Peter, I'm sorry you had to pay the full price for the boat. I thought five hundred was a fair price."

"Then take five hundred," Peter pleaded.

Jesus shrugged. "It's James's boat. It's your and James's deal."

"Then stay out of it!" Peter scowled. He turned to walk away.

"Peter," said Jesus, "what if I made you a loan? You can pay me back when you can."

"That would be great!" said Andrew, already feeling overwhelmed with the deal his brother had gotten them into.

"Shut up, Andrew!" Peter turned and looked at Jesus. "I don't need your money, Jesus. I told you, stay out of this! You've always thought yourself better than me. Well, that's about to change! Soon, you may be asking to borrow money from me!"

Jesus was shocked and hurt by Peter's reaction. "Peter, I didn't mean to…"

Peter raised his hand to silence Jesus. "We'll be back as soon as it's in the water. Send us word."

He walked away, with Andrew following behind.

On Sunday morning, James was hard at work building a cradle around the boat to support it during the move. Two large beams at the bottom of the cradle were attached to three wagons, one at each end and one in the middle. On these, the boat would be transported—slowly, gently—from the yard to the water about seventy yards away. James had carelessly overlooked the path the boat would have to take to get to the lake. As a result, the furnace and steam box had been assembled directly in the way. There was no turning the boat, so the equipment would have to be taken apart and moved. Jesus scolded James for not having the forethought to realize this, but James reminded Jesus that he'd been there the whole time and never thought of this himself. Neither man had much defense, so they let the matter drop. By dark, all the work was done.

The next morning, twenty men and boys, and many spectators, gathered to help guide the boat to the water. The back of the fence was dropped and moved out of the way. Some of the men had ropes and pulled. Others began to push at the back, and slowly the boat began to creep forward. The wheels of the wagons creaked and wobbled under the weight of the great load. James was standing to the side of the boat, calling directions to each man.

"Easy, easy. We need to go right. Everybody on the left side push harder!"

As they moved out of the yard, the ground sloped gently, then more steeply. By the time they were halfway to the water, the ropes in front began to go slack. James realized they should have attached ropes to the rear of the boat as well, to pull back as they picked up speed. He called to the men in front, "You guys bring your ropes around to the side! Pull back!"

The men in the rear were clinging to the sides of the boat, digging in their heels and trying to slow the thing down, but it was too late. Some were falling away or giving up and letting go. Others were hanging on, being dragged along.

Finally, when the boat was still thirty yards from shore, and moving faster than they could run, James yelled, "Everybody get out of the way!"

There was nothing they could do but watch. The boat raced down the hill, the wheels leaving the ground as they bounced over rocks half the size of sheep. One of the wheels on the middle wagon broke in two, and the wagon spun to the left and out from under the boat. Fortunately, the two other wagons held the weight. The boat hit the water with such force that James was sure it had cracked the hull. When the ship came to rest, only the last four or five feet of it was still grounded on shore. After a moment of anxious silence, the crowd at the top of the hill erupted in celebratory cheers. They appreciated the entertainment. James remembered to breathe, and then climbed aboard to inspect for damage. There was none. He built it to withstand storms. It had just come through its first, unscathed!

The only loss: three wagons—two belonging to the carpenter shop, the other borrowed. Dozens of people ran down the hill and, under James's supervision, helped push the boat the rest of the way into the water.

No message had come to Peter and Andrew concerning the boat, so after finishing their workday, they decided to walk over and see if it was ready. They saw the boat in the water long before they reached the carpenter shop (or, as they now preferred to think of it, the boatyard). It looked even bigger and more majestic in the lake. They practically ran to the shore, but it was moored too deep to wade out to, so they ran up the hill to the shop. Jesus and James had decided on a new location for the furnace and steam box and were reassembling them when the two fishermen walked up.

"Is the boat ready?" Peter asked excitedly.

"It's ready," said James.

"Well, are we supposed to swim to it?"

"We're just finishing up here," said Jesus. "I'll row you out."

"We'll swim," said Peter.

"Oh, for God's sake, Peter!" said a frustrated Jesus. "James, row them out!"

"Peter, we can't take the boat home tonight," Andrew reminded him. "Remember, we talked about this on the way over."

In his excitement, Peter had forgotten their conversation and their situation. They had decided that, if the boat was ready, they would return home, break the news to their father together, and then return first thing in the morning to begin their new business venture.

"Yes, we won't need to go aboard tonight," Peter said, correcting himself. "Will you be here early in the morning to row us out?"

"Yes," said James.

"We'll both be here!" Jesus barked, still frustrated with Peter's attitude toward him.

"Does it have a sail?" Peter asked.

"No," James replied.

"For that kind of money, it should have a sail."

"No sail, but a spar and mast," James said proudly. "You furnish the sail and the nets."

"We have nets. We can get a sail that'll work for tomorrow, and make one to fit in a day or two. We'll see you in the morning, first light."

"I'll be here," James said.

As the fishermen were walking away, James heard Peter say to Andrew, "For that kind of money, it should have a sail."

When they spoke with their father that evening, things went better than they had expected. There was no yelling, no reviling; nobody got angry or kicked out of the house. They described the boat in all its majesty, taking turns to point out its exceptional features and workmanship. When they had finished, they waited for the question they knew would come.

"And how much would such a boat cost?" asked their father.

Peter swallowed hard before announcing the price.

His father almost fell out of his chair. He scoffed at the expense. "Not one of my boats cost even half as much! (Which was true, but even his best boat was crude compared to this one.) And at the end of the day, I make a profit. You'll just be making a payment to the carpenters!"

He rose from the table and started for his bedchamber. "I wish you both luck," he said. "You'll need it. I hope your big boat catches you lots of fish." He waved his hand above his head as he walked away.

Peter and Andrew rose early. It was still dark when they left the house for the boat. They had borrowed an extra sail from their father's supplies and rolled it onto a long oar to keep it stiff so that each of them could get under it with a shoulder. Around the sail they wrapped two large nets, all the weight they could carry. The plan was to fish back toward the docks this morning, where they would pick up two more nets to fully outfit the boat for the afternoon run. The sail was too small for their boat, but it would catch enough wind to move them about. Working nights, late, the two of them could have their custom sail sewn in two days.

James wasn't there when they arrived at the shop, but they weren't surprised. It was still not quite dawn. They allowed the heavy load to roll off their shoulders and onto the ground. Andrew found a large rock and took a seat. Peter continued to stand. They watched the silhouette of the boat as it rocked gently on the calm water.

"Why don't we just swim for it?" Andrew asked.

"With a hundred pounds of sail and nets?" Peter replied. "James will be here soon enough. And we'll stay dry."

It was just after daylight when James and Jesus arrived. They waved at the men on the shore, then Jesus went into the shop, and James went down to meet them.

"Are you ready?" James asked.

"Ready," the fishermen said in unison.

They loaded up the rowboat, and all three pushed it away from shore before jumping aboard. James manned the oars and rowed the short distance to where the larger boat was moored. Andrew climbed aboard, and Peter lifted up the sail, then the nets.

"Good fishing, boys!" James called out, as he turned the rowboat back toward the shore.

If there was a reply, James didn't hear it.

The two men busied themselves attaching the sail to the mast. It looked tiny and out of place on the big ship, which it was. There was just enough wind to fill the sail but hardly enough to push the boat along. They attached two of the boat's six oars to the rowlocks, and both the men strained against the weight to help move the boat farther out on the lake. By the time they reached deeper water, they were drenched with sweat. It was going to be a hot day and, apparently, a windless one.

"Just our luck," Andrew said. "Our first day out and we're stranded. We can't fish if we can't move."

"I knew the sail would be too small, but it's all we've got." said Peter. "Still, if we get a wind, it will move us, and we'll get wind later in the day. We always do. In the meantime, let's set the nets and get ready."

The wind came about ten o'clock. The sail stretched out full, and the boat began to move at a slow but steady pace. They set a course for the docks at the northern end of the lake and dropped the nets.

Fifteen minutes later, the boat stalled. The wind had actually picked up, and the sail was full and tight.

"What's wrong?" Andrew asked.

"I'm not sure," Peter replied.

"Did we drop anchor?"

To be sure, Peter glanced at the stern. The anchor was there, sitting atop the long length of rope attached to it. "Something isn't right," he said to himself. He looked around searching for the answer. "The nets! Pull in the nets!"

They both ran to the back of the boat and heaved at the ropes holding the submerged nets. They couldn't move them. One of the features of the boat was a pulley system attached to the spar. (It had been Jesus' idea to include this for just such an occasion: too many fish, too few hands.) They quickly tied a length of heavy rope to the main rope holding one of the nets and began leaning their weight into the large wheel on the side of the pulley. It was working. The rope began wrapping around the pulley wheel. The spar strained, and the boat actually leaned toward the water where the net was being lifted.

When the net hit the surface of the water, the men couldn't believe their eyes. There were so many fish that the net couldn't close around them. Many were spilling out of the top and back into the lake. *Spears!* They had no spears with them to stab the fish and haul them aboard, lightening the load. If they tried to lift the nets any farther out of the water, they would surely burst, allowing all the fish to escape.

"Quick!" Peter shouted. "Grab a bucket." *Crap! There were no buckets aboard!*

"Andrew, take off your clothes! Get down there and use your tunic to hand the fish up to me!"

Andrew followed the instruction. He quickly disrobed and stepped down onto the net full of flopping fish. He filled his tunic with as many fish as he could lift and handed it up to Peter, who dumped the fish onto the boat's floor and handed the tunic back to Andrew. They did this again and again until the net was light enough to haul on board. Then, they did the same with the other net. When they were finished, they collapsed on the floor, exhausted, trying to catch their breath.

From the shore, Jesus could barely make out the boat. It was far away, and there was a haze in the late morning air. Still, he knew exactly what had happened. (It was why he had insisted on installing the winch.) He smiled and walked back toward the shop.

Peter and Andrew didn't drop their nets again. They were afraid the same good fortune might befall them, and they were too tired for a repeat episode. The wind never lifted to more than a soft breeze, so it was near evening when they limped into the Capernaum docks. All the other boats were in, and the fishermen were doing their end-of-day work before heading home. Due to the lack of wind, it had been a lousy fishing day for everyone, and the mood was sullen. Once the giant boat was spotted, every eye watched as it made its slow approach. Finally, some of the fishermen already finished with their work, and seeing that Peter and Andrew could use some help getting in, decided to man small rowboats and help the larger boat to the dock. When they reached them, they threw ropes up to the brothers, who tied them off, and rowed them the rest of the way to shore.

Everyone was greatly impressed by the boat's size as well as its fit and finish. They hadn't seen anything like it on the lake before. They were even more impressed by the boat's ability to catch fish. While everyone else had had their worst day in months, Peter and Andrew had hauled in a record catch! After tours of the boat were done, they all assisted the brothers in salting and laying out the fish to dry. Then they all went home.

At supper, Peter and Andrew recounted their tale to the family. Peter's father began to think more highly of the boat and considered asking the boys about a partnership between the three of them. But anyone can have a good day, he thought, and they would need many more days like this one to pay off their massive investment. Besides, boats don't catch fish, do they? He let it pass.

The wind returned the next day, and the day after that, and the day after that. And every day, twice a day, Peter and Andrew had successful catches, though none to equal their haul on that first morning. Peter's boat now had a sail fit to size, and it could move with exceptional speed up and down the lake. More distance traveled meant more fish caught. The brothers had agreed to pay themselves only laborers' wages until their debt to James was settled. As a result, if they kept up their pace, they would have enough saved to pay James in full by the end of the month. Then Peter could turn his thoughts to Mary and marriage.

On the day that the fat man left Magdala for Damascus, Simon had brought two baskets to the wagon. "This one has bread for your servants," he said. "And this one is for you: bread, dates, dried fish."

The fat man took them and bade a final farewell, "Enjoy your last days here, Simon," he said and closed the curtain on the wagon.

They had lunch on the move that afternoon. The man gave each of the servants and slaves a piece of bread to eat as they walked, while he ate in the wagon from the servants' basket. He would save his own food for a couple of evening feasts.

Once they had stopped for the night, the glutton rationed out meager amounts of food for each of his men and then settled into his own meal. He poured the poisoned wine into a silver chalice and began eating a piece of fish, also laced with oleander. By the time he had finished, his stomach was already beginning to cramp. Then the wagon began to spin. He fell over on the bed, hoping to calm the storm inside his head and belly. He called for help. Two of the servants helped him to his feet and got him outside just before he began vomiting. He couldn't breathe, but he could think. He knew exactly what was happening to him. He knew what Simon had done.

"Bring me the slaves!" he commanded between gags. The two slaves were brought to the evil man, who pulled his knife and slit their throats. "Now you!" he said to the driver and the other servant. "Kneel before me!" He was going to die. He knew this. And if he was going to die, everyone with him would die too. The servants backed away.

"Come here!" screamed the fat man. He was on his knees now, writhing in pain. "You ungrateful bastards! Die...with...your... master." There was no more breath left in him. His heart was pounding slowly...slower. His vision darkened...darker. He fell to the ground; sand covered his thickened tongue.

"Tell...the...mis...tress...Si...mon...." He convulsed several times and then went limp. The fat man was dead.

"What should we do?" the driver asked.

"Load him in the wagon and take him home, I guess," said the other servant.

"They'll know he was poisoned. I mean, look at him." (His tongue was protruding from his mouth, swollen and black.) "And we have two slaves with their throats cut. They'll think we did this, the master and the slaves too."

"So what, then?"

"I'm going to Tyre. It's just a couple of days west of here. We can get on with a ship's crew there."

"If we run, we'll look guilty for sure. They'll hunt us down."

"Not if none of us returns. They'll think we were ambushed by robbers or killed by lions. We'll burn the wagon and bury the remains along with the slaves. We'll leave that son of a bitch to the wild animals. It's a big desert. If we cover our tracks, they won't even know where to begin to look for us. They'll search, find nothing, and assume we all met the same tragic end."

"Fine. Let's go," said the other. "But first, I'm having some of the master's wine."

"Are you crazy!" said the driver. "The fool just died from poisoning. We don't know if it was the wine or the food."

"Oh shit! What if it was the food?"

"We've eaten our food and we're fine," said the driver. "Whoever did this, Simon or his wife, they wanted only the master to die, not us. We'll take *our* food and the water. Nothing else."

The two servants stood there, silent for a minute. Then the driver said, "You get a shovel and start digging. I'll start the fire."

He took a lantern from the side of the wagon and gathered everything they would need for the journey. Then he removed the globe from the lantern and threw it inside.

Mary had great affection for Peter, but she didn't love him, not like he loved her. Since her brief encounter with Jesus, Mary could think of no one else in that way. Her heart and soul belonged to him.

One evening after supper, Peter invited Mary to go for a walk. They went the short distance to the docks and sat under a full moon, looking out over the lake.

"Mary," said Peter, "I've been thinking a lot about us lately. Things have gone well for Andrew and me. Business is good. We've saved almost enough money to pay James for the boat, and, after that, my income will be sufficient to support a wife and family. We can live well, Mary, you and I. I can give you the kind of life that will make you happy. I would like to ask your father for your hand in marriage."

Mary swallowed hard. This was not a conversation she wanted to have with Peter, and she tried to bring it to a graceful close. "Peter, I'll be returning home soon. I never intended to stay in Capernaum. My parents need me. I have a job there, keeping the master's house."

"But I can give you your own house, Mary. And a better one, and children. You won't have to work for anyone."

Mary struggled for a response that would remove her from the awkward moment, without hurting Peter's feelings. She could think of nothing.

"My parents need me," she repeated. "I can't leave them just yet."

"*I* need you, Mary," Peter pleaded. "You're fifteen years old, for God's sake. You can't live with your parents forever."

Mary was silent, trying again to think of something to end the conversation. "Isn't the sky beautiful tonight?" she said, to change the subject. She started to get up.

Peter grabbed her by both shoulders and sat her back down, hard.

"Mary! Listen to me! I love you! And you *will* marry me!" He kissed her on the lips.

Mary was startled, and momentarily stunned, by his physical treatment of her, and the kiss. When she didn't pull away, Peter tried to push her down and reached for her breast. The groping immediately reminded her of the fat man's attack, and she fought violently at Peter's advances. Peter, suddenly shocked at his own behavior, released her. She quickly stood and backed away. Even in the dark, Peter could see the expression of fear and outrage on her face.

"Mary, I…"

"I do not love you, Peter! I do not want to marry you! How dare you touch me!"

"Please, Mary…I'm sorry."

She turned and ran away.

Mary considered walking all the way back to Magdala in the dark. She didn't want to return to Peter's house, although she knew, once there, she would be safe. Peter's parents would protect her from him, and he wouldn't try anything in front of them, anyway. She even knew Peter wouldn't display such poor judgment again. He was not that kind of person. Still, she didn't want to face him, not now. How could he have gotten so carried away? How could he have done that to her? They were friends, she thought. Apparently, Peter thought they were something more.

When she got back to Peter's house, she went straight to bed, but she didn't sleep. Instead, she made her plans. She would leave for Magdala first thing in the morning. Surely, the master was gone by now. She would see if her father could help her find servant's work in another house. If so, then she wouldn't care if she ever left Magdala again. But she would not work in the master's house. If she couldn't find work in another house, then she would find another town. A larger town where there were many households in need of servants. As she was thinking on all these things, she drifted into sleep.

The next morning, Mary helped Peter's mother with breakfast and told her she would be leaving for home. At the table, she said her goodbyes to the family, and the men headed off for work. Peter said nothing. There was no use. He knew the irreparable damage he'd done to their relationship.

Mary helped with clearing the table and washing the dishes. She gave hugs to Peter's mother and sisters and started on her way.

When she was passing the carpenter shop, she decided to stop in and say goodbye to Jesus. She noticed James had already begun a new boat, but she didn't see him in the yard. She stepped into the shop and saw Jesus putting the finishing touches on a large storage cabinet. He noticed her in the doorway.

"Mary! Come. Please." He motioned her to a new set of benches in the corner.

"These are nice," she said, sitting, running her hand along the smooth surface of the bench. "So is the cabinet."

"It's all for the same customer," Jesus said, taking a seat beside her. "I'll deliver them today. Mary, I'm glad you came by. I've wanted to talk to you since our first meeting. Tell me, what is your…um…relationship with Peter?"

Mary sighed. "We're friends, that's all. I know the family and have been staying with them while in Capernaum. But my visit is over. I'm heading back home just now."

"I'm glad to hear that," Jesus said, smiling. "Oh, not that you're leaving Capernaum but that your relationship with Peter isn't romantic."

"Certainly not!" Mary insisted.

"I don't even know where you're from. Where are you going home to?"

"Magdala."

"Ah, Mary Magdalene." Jesus lifted his eyes toward the ceiling as he spoke the words with such emphasis, it sounded like a song.

They both laughed.

"Well, Magdala is too far for a young woman to be traveling alone. If you would allow me, I'd like to walk you there."

"But I'd be taking you from your work. And it's far enough that it would be night by the time you got back."

"Don't worry about that. My boss, the master James, isn't here today or tomorrow. He's gone to Caesarea Philippi to order lumber supplies. And, as for walking back, perhaps I could impose on your family to let me stay overnight and walk back in the morning."

"My family would love to have you and, trust me, we have plenty of extra room." (They had used the master's house before to house guests when he was away, and no one had ever been the wiser.) "So, yes. I'd very much like to have you walk me home."

"Good!" Jesus said. "It's settled! We'll stop by my house and let my family know. Then we'll be on our way."

When they got to Jesus' house, his mother Mary insisted that they stay and have lunch, but Jesus protested.

"Her parents are expecting her, and, besides, I was thinking a picnic on the way would be fun."

Both of the women smiled at the idea. The younger Mary, of course, thought any idea Jesus had was a wonderful one. Just the two of them having lunch together along the road would be cozy and intimate, and it would give them a chance to talk face to face, rather than while walking side by side. It would also give her another opportunity to look into those deep blue, penetrating eyes that held her spellbound and caused her to wonder just how deeply he could see into her soul. The older Mary liked the idea as well. Jesus had never mentioned this girl, but she could tell he cared for her, and this pleased her.

"I'll pack you a lunch," she said.

They walked for a couple of hours before stopping for lunch. Along the road, the conversation had been pleasant but nothing more than small talk. They were both a bit nervous with their new relationship. As they ate, they continued to laugh and enjoy one another's company, but they also began to probe deeper into each other's lives. Mary marveled at all the places Jesus had been and the things he'd seen. He told her about Greece and Rome, Tunis and Alexandria, and Jerusalem. He told her all about his family and the tragic loss of his beloved abba. She shared with him about her cloistered life in Magdala, her mother and father, the affection she held for her mistress and the disdain she held for her master. She didn't mean to tell him more, but his eyes guided her deeper, and she recounted the advances of the fat man, the attack, and her subsequent flight to Capernaum.

"I left my parents a note," Mary said. "They don't know where I am, but they know why I left. I don't know how the master reacted toward them because of me. I don't know what kind of reception I'll receive when I get home. I don't even know if I have a home anymore."

Jesus smiled and patted her hand. "Whether they're at your master's estate or not, they wouldn't have left Magdala without you. We'll find your parents there. And it sounds like we'll have quite a lot to talk about!"

Mary smiled back and wiped her tears.

An hour passed since they had stopped for lunch. It was five o'clock, and they still had three hours journey ahead of them.

The sun had set when they passed through the south gate at Magdala. Most of the summer sojourners had already departed for their permanent homes, so many of the houses were dark. It was ghostly quiet and seemed to Jesus to be a deserted village.

Actually, this was Mary's favorite time of year. Not only was the master gone, but the town belonged to its real residents again. There was plenty of leisure time for everyone, and, for at least seven months, everyone was happy.

They came to the gate that led into the master's courtyard. "This is it," Mary said, and she pushed open one of the two iron picket doors.

They stepped onto a cobblestone yard, bordered by a variety of flowering shrubs and trees. Straight ahead was a huge two-story mansion constructed of giant blocks of pink and gray marble. To the left was a small mud-block cottage. This was Mary's parents' home. Through the windows, they saw the flickering reflection of lamp light. When they got to the entrance, Jesus noticed Mary taking a deep breath. Then, without knocking, she pushed open the door.

Her parents were at the table, eating, her father facing away from the door. Her mother, at the other end of the table, looked up and saw her.

"Mary!" she gasped. She jumped up and ran to her.

Her father turned in his seat. "Mary," he said, echoing his wife. He rose and went to her, and the three of them embraced—kissing and hugging, laughing and crying. They ignored Jesus.

Finally, Mary broke out of the circle and said, "Abba, Mama, this is Jesus, from Capernaum."

"Thank you for bringing our daughter home," said Simon.

Jesus nodded but said nothing. He wasn't certain if he had brought her, or she him.

"Where have you been, child?" said her mother. Then remembering her hospitality, she said, "Oh, Jesus, please sit down and eat."

"Let's all sit down," said Simon, beaming. His daughter was home, his happiness restored.

Mary told them all about her journey, about her staying with the family of a fisherman she knew from the docks, and about Jesus offering to see her home. She apologized for leaving home so abruptly and causing them pain. She didn't mention the reason, or the note. In fact, to everyone's relief, there was no mention of the reason or the master at all. Everyone knew. Simon knew the master wouldn't be coming back. Nothing else needed to be said.

"Of course!" Simon said, upon Mary's request. "We would be honored to have Jesus stay with us tonight. We'll make up a bed for him in the fat man's quarters."

"Simon!" said his wife. "You should not speak of the master in such a way."

Simon was determined never again to refer to the scum he had murdered as his master. Not even if they came for him. He thought the chances of that were unlikely. He calculated two scenarios: Upon their master's death, the servants and slaves would bolt, fearing reprisals for allowing him to die on their watch; or they would risk returning the dead man to his home but, along the way, help themselves to the man's food (not realizing his cause of death) and make Simon a mass murderer. He prayed for the former, but either way, only the wagon would be found. The desert animals would consume the body (or bodies) and the tainted food. There would be no evidence of Simon's involvement. He had even made provision for disposing of the poison wine by carving several holes in the wineskin and sealing them with gum that the wine would dissolve in a matter of days. Once the wine had leaked out, evaporation would do the rest. Simon was not proud of what he had done, but he had no regrets. He truly did hope he was responsible for only one murder.

At the end of the evening, Simon took Jesus to an upstairs bedroom in the main house. "I hope you sleep well, Jesus. You're welcome to stay with us as long as you like."

"Thank you, Simon. But I'm expected back tomorrow. I'll leave after breakfast."

Simon set the lamp on a table and started toward the door. Then he stopped, turned, and said, "Thank you, Jesus, for bringing my daughter home. I assume she told you why she left."

"She did. What do you plan to do about him?"

"I'll talk to him," he lied.

"Do you think that will be enough?"

"It will if I threaten to tell his wife about his indiscretions."

"I hope so, Simon. Mary is afraid. You cannot allow this animal to abuse her again, not physically, not even emotionally."

"He will not."

"Good."

"You care for her, don't you?" Simon asked.

"Yes, very much," Jesus replied.

"And what are your intentions toward her?"

Jesus hesitated. "Honorable, sir." He could think of nothing else to say. He did not want to say more.

It was enough for Simon. He let the matter drop. He smiled and then took his leave, closing the door behind him.

The next morning, the four had breakfast together. There was much conversation and laughter. It was as if all the troubles and concerns of the previous days were over: dead, as it were. Jesus thanked his hosts and promised to return for a visit soon. Mary walked him to the street gate. She thanked him again. They clasped hands for a moment. She looked into his eyes again and he returned her stare. Something moved, deep inside each of them.

"Goodbye, Mary. I'll see you soon."

"Goodbye, Jesus. I..." She didn't finish.

He turned and walked away, down the road toward Capernaum.

All the way home, Jesus tried to sort out his feelings. There was a stirring inside him he had never felt before. He loved her, he knew, but did he love her enough to consider marriage? Marriage had never really been a consideration for Jesus. It meant settling down for a lifetime, raising children. Of course, he'd done that in a way already, resigning himself to a life in Capernaum, being the head of his mother's household, a father figure to his youngest brothers and sisters, a partner with James in the carpenter shop.

But deep in the recesses of his mind, he still saw himself leaving Capernaum one day to see the rest of the world, or at least a portion of it. He still held out hope that James would assume the place as head of the family, or that something would happen to release him from the responsibilities that weighed heavier and heavier on him as the days and weeks and months passed. He still believed that God had some yet-to-unfold special purpose for his life. Marriage would forsake all of that. But, then, what if none of his visions or hopes or beliefs came to fruition? What if he woke up one morning and found himself an old carpenter, alone, without his beloved Mary, childless, regretting every decision he had made to follow a pipedream that never came to pass?

He was three hours into his journey and a little more than halfway home when he came to a grove of trees by the side of the road. It was the same place he and Mary had stopped for lunch on the way. It was just past ten and too early for him to eat, but he stopped anyway, to think. And to pray.

It was Saturday, the Sabbath, and no work was done on this holy day of the Jewish week. Even non-practicing Jews, like Peter and his family, were bound to abide by this community, indeed, this national rule.

Two weeks passed since Mary had left Capernaum. Peter missed her, and he couldn't release the feelings he had for her. Neither could he erase the memory of his colossal misstep at the docks the last night he was with her. His inappropriate advances and his angry tone haunted him. He had to see her and apologize for his behavior. Such disrespect was not like him. He held no hope of marriage. She didn't love him. She had made that clear, but he did need to try and set things right between them, to ask for her forgiveness and, hopefully, to restore their relationship as friends.

Peter and Andrew had had tremendous success with their new boat. In just over a month, they had caught and sold enough fish, and saved enough money, to pay James the remaining ninety denarii they owed for the boat. Today, with the entire day free, Peter would walk to the synagogue and find James. After paying off his debt, he would go to Magdala, find Mary, and beg her forgiveness. With those two things accomplished, if she forgave him, he could begin his week with a sense of relief and peace, and get his life back on course toward a happy end.

He wanted to time his arrival at the synagogue just right: too early, and he would have to fight off countless invitations to come in and worship; too late, and he would miss James at the door and have to wait until services were over to catch him. He decided his best course of action was simply to walk up and down the street in front of the synagogue. He would walk far enough in either direction so as to not attract attention, but not so far that he couldn't keep his eye on the front of the synagogue and the people that were coming.

James arrived with his entire family in tow, including Jesus. He *really* didn't want to talk to Jesus. Peter walked closer. Eventually, the family began to split up as they exchanged greetings with others. When James was alone, he made his move, catching him on the steps just before entering the synagogue.

"James!" he called.

James turned around. "Peter. You've come to synagogue?"

"No. I've come to see you." He pulled out a pouch and handed it to James.

"Here's the remaining ninety denarii. We're paid in full."

James looked shocked and pushed the pouch back toward Peter. "Peter, this is highly inappropriate. It's the Sabbath. We shouldn't be conducting business transactions. And here, at the synagogue, of all places!"

"For God's sake, James, just take it and we're done."

James raised both his palms toward Peter, shook his head, and walked through the synagogue door."

"Damn it!" Peter said, receiving some unfavorable looks from those passing by.

What was he to do? The money was burning a hole in his pocket. He couldn't wait another day to get it to James, nor did he have the time to waste. Tomorrow was a work day. He wanted—and needed—to own his boat, free and clear, *today*!

He looked up at the sun. He couldn't wait around to reason with James. He had to leave for Magdala now. As he walked, he decided that this would all work out fine. At a brisk pace, it would take less than four hours to get to Magdala. A couple of hours there with Mary, then back. By that time it would be after dusk; the Sabbath would be over, and he could stop by James's house and pay him off. Perfect. He breathed a sigh of relief.

Peter had no idea where Mary lived, nor did he know her master's name. Because of the Sabbath, there was virtually no traffic on the streets, so he made his way to the dock, looking for someone to give him direction. Two young boys were there, skipping stones on the water.

"Hi," Peter said to the youngsters.

They looked at the stranger warily, giving no reply.

"I wonder if you can help me find someone."

Again, no reply.

"I'm looking for Mary, daughter of Simon."

One of the boys walked over to him. "Who are you, sir?"

"My name is Peter. I'm from Capernaum. I bring fish to the market here. My friend is Mary. She lives somewhere in Magdala, but I don't know where, exactly. If I can find her house, I'd like to pay her a visit."

"She is the daughter of Simon, you say?"

"Yes."

The other boy came up to them. "I'll take you," he said.

"No, I'll take him!" the other countered sharply.

Sensing some unexpected tension he didn't have time for, Peter said, "Okay, why don't you both take me."

The two boys stared at each other for a minute, then they both started running toward the village.

"Wait!" Peter shouted.

"Follow us," one of them called back.

By the time he caught up to them at the cross-street, the boys were arguing and beginning to shove each other. Peter got it.

"Look," he said. "Both of you take me to Mary's house, and I'll give you each a copper coin."

They looked at each other, weighing the fairness of the compromise, and then both boys presented their palms to Peter. He sighed and pushed a coin into each one's hand. They took off down the street again.

"Wait!" Peter yelled again and began to run behind them.

When they reached the gate of the estate, one of the boys stopped (the other didn't). He looked at Peter, pointed at the gate, and then hurried after his friend. Peter went through the gate and closed it behind him. He didn't have to guess which house was Mary's. He walked to the front door and, with some trepidation, gave a light knock. He suddenly realized that after two weeks of thinking of little else than this, he didn't have a clue as to what he was going to say, or at least, how he would begin the conversation.

Mary's mother answered the door. She looked at him inquisitively but said nothing.

What does she know? What has Mary told her?

"May I help you?" she finally asked.

Peter panicked. "Mary?" he said.

"No, I'm Mary's mother."

What? His mind was spinning. "Oh, of course you are. I...uh... I'm... Is Mary here?" he finally managed to blurt out.

"She is. And who is calling?"

"My name is Peter, from Capernaum." *Okay. That's it*, he thought. *Now she knows.* He winced, waiting for a verbal—or physical—beating. Nothing happened. "I'm...uh...a friend of Mary's."

She studied him up and down. "Just a minute," she said and closed the door. She smiled as she went to the bedchamber where her daughter was resting. "Mary," she whispered, "a young man is here to see you. He says his name is Peter, from Capernaum. Another gentleman caller?"

Mary sat up straight. *What is Peter doing here? What does he want?* Surely, he hadn't come to ask for her hand in marriage. She should have known he would come, that he wouldn't take no for an answer. She hadn't discussed this with her father. She didn't need to discuss it with him. She would turn Peter around where he stood and send him on his way.

Mary hurried through the house, stepped outside, and closed the door after her. She grabbed Peter by the hand and dragged him back to the gate. Then, she whirled around, looking directly into his eyes. "Peter," she said sternly, "you listen to me. I don't love you. I don't want to marry you. Now you go right out that gate and back to Capernaum. You'll only make matters worse if you upset my parents. And they will be upset!"

"They know, then, what I did to you?"

"No one knows anything about that except you and me. And no one needs to know. But I'm warning you: If you don't go right now, I will tell my father. Believe me, you don't want that!"

"I'll go! I'll go! But, first, please listen to me. I didn't come here to ask for a marriage. I came to ask for forgiveness. I know you don't love me. I know you don't want to marry me. But you need to know how sorry I am for my behavior that night, how sorry I am that I disrespected you in that way. That's not who I am, Mary. I was upset that you turned down my proposal and that you didn't feel the same love for me that I felt for you. But I understand now, and I make no excuse. I beg for your forgiveness, and I hope that somehow we can be friends again. I value our relationship, Mary—as friends. I would be happy to get that back, but, if not, *please*, at least forgive me."

Mary sighed, both from relief and compassion. She dropped her head toward the ground and then returned her gaze to his eyes. He was sincere. She saw his pain, and she saw that his love for her was still there, unremitting. "I forgive you, Peter. Of course, I forgive you." He had made everything all right between them. She had grieved so at the loss of this special friendship, and now it was restored. She wanted to hug him, but she didn't dare. He was still lovesick and would need time to heal, but this mending would help the process. "It was wonderful and brave of you to come. It shows me how much you care."

Peter felt a huge weight lift from him. He did still love her, but it was going to be all right now. He had his friend back. Life was worth living again. He felt tears welling up in his eyes, so he sped his exit. There was nothing else to say, anyway. "Thank you, Mary." He smiled. "So, I guess I'll see you at the dock?"

She laughed. "I'll see you at the dock."

He stepped through the gate and onto the street. They smiled at each other again. Then she waved and disappeared back into the courtyard, latching the gate behind her.

When Mary came back inside, her mother was waiting. "He's a nice looking man, Mary," she said. "Not as good-looking as Jesus and a bit awkward with his speech, but..."

"He's just a friend, Mama," Mary interrupted, smiling.

"And Jesus?"

Mary's smile unintentionally widened. She winked at her mother and went back into the bedchamber.

It was just dusk, and Peter was three miles outside of Capernaum, when three men stepped out of a grove of trees and onto the road.

"Ho, friend!" one of them called. "Do you have water?"

"Only a little, but you're welcome to it." Peter immediately felt troubled by the encounter. He remembered his money pouch in the pocket of his tunic. As the men approached, one flanked around behind while another moved to the center of the road about ten feet in front of him. The other man, the one who had spoken, came beside him, and Peter offered him the waterskin. He drank and then threw the skin to his partner in front.

"What else you got?" he asked, flashing a single rotten tooth and sinister grin.

"I'm afraid that's all," Peter said. "I had some bread, but I ate it on the way."

"That's too bad," the man said. "I think we'll need more than just water to let you pass." The other two men chuckled.

"Look," Peter said, "Water is all I have. I've offered you that. If you want to come home with me, I'll see that you're fed. But there's nothing else to take. Keep the skin and follow me or let me pass."

"If you don't mind," the spokesman said, "we'll decide if there's nothing else to take."

The man in front of them pulled a club from behind his back. Peter pushed the man beside him and turned to run the opposite way. Before he could gain a step, a blow struck him from behind. The pain exploded in his head. He felt himself falling to the ground, but he didn't remember reaching his destination.

When Peter awoke, it was dark. He rolled onto his back, and pain rushed through his head again. As he looked up at the stars, his vision cleared. Then he started to remember. He quickly grabbed for his money pouch. It was gone! After a moment of despair, he sat up. The pain returned along with the dizziness. When it had subsided, he got to his feet, waited out the whole head-clearing process again, and then began to finish his walk home. With every step, his head pounded. He felt the warm trickle of blood coursing down his back. *That's what I smell! That's what I taste!* He put his hand to his face. His beard was drenching wet.

When he got to the village, he was exhausted. He knew he couldn't make it to his own house, so he staggered to the nearest place where he knew he would be taken in. Once he got to Jesus' door, he had just enough strength to pound his fist against it. The door opened, and he collapsed.

Jesus and James carried Peter inside and put him on a bed. Mary took a bowl of water and began washing the blood away. They couldn't see how he could have any blood left in him. His clothes were soaked. They removed these and put one of Jesus' bed gowns on him. There were two gashes on his head: one on the back left side of his upper face and skull (the original blow), and another just back of center on the top of the head (likely administered as a death blow when he was unconscious and on the ground). Mary had plenty of experience with sewing the nasty wounds of construction accidents. While Peter was still unconscious, she threaded a large needle, pinched the skin together, and began her work.

James was dispatched to Peter's house to let his family know.

"Tell them what has happened," Mary said. "Tell them he is alive, but tell them no more." She wasn't sure if Peter would survive.

It was four in the morning when James returned with Peter's father and his brother Andrew. They sat with him through the night, and when morning came, they were joined by his mother and sisters. The two younger brothers had stayed behind to run the boats. At dusk, Peter's father instructed Andrew to remain with his brother while the rest of the family returned home. Mary, seeing the anguish on Peter's mother's face, invited her to stay as well, but her husband insisted that they all had duties at home. Andrew would be sufficient and could retrieve them all in a hurry if they were needed.

"He will recover," Peter's father announced. "Then Andrew can bring him home. He can convalesce there." And with that he left, taking the rest of his obedient family with him.

After three days, Peter was still unconscious. He had eaten no food, drunk no water. The situation was dire. Mary couldn't understand how a mother could leave her dying son's side—why she hadn't returned to see about him.

"Don't judge her harshly, Mama," Jesus said. "Women are bound to obey their husbands. He feels her place is at home with the rest of the family."

"I swear on all that is holy, Jesus, if you were dying, I would not leave you. Soldiers couldn't pull me away."

At her words, a strange grief suddenly swept through Jesus. He didn't know why. It must be poor Peter's state, he thought.

Jesus went to the bedroom where Andrew was asleep in a chair. He'd been at Peter's bedside the entire time. "Andrew," he said, gently touching his friend's shoulder. "Please, let me relieve you. Go and eat something. Step outside and breathe in some fresh air. I won't leave him."

"I can eat here," Andrew said, "If he wakes up, I want him to see me and know that I'm here."

"If he wakes up, I'll come for you immediately. Now, please go. Take just a minute."

Andrew stood, and his knees almost buckled beneath him. His back ached, protesting as he tried to straighten himself. He'd been in the chair for hours without moving. When he had regained control of his body, he slowly dragged his feet toward the bedroom door and into the living room.

Jesus looked at his friend Peter. He cared for him deeply. He knew the feeling was not reciprocal. Why should it be? They didn't know each other that well. Still, he'd always felt there was something very special between Peter and himself, and that their lives were somehow inextricably linked.

Jesus questioned whether what he was about to do was right. As he had grown older, he'd come to realize that Joseph was right. The powers he had were a gift from God, but they were to be used only at the time and purpose for which God intended them. Perhaps this was the time. Perhaps it was not. He didn't know. What he did know was that Peter was dying. He wouldn't last another day. He looked over his shoulder. There was no one. He placed his hand on Peter's head and prayed.

Peter slowly opened his eyes. It took him a moment to focus on the face in front of him. Jesus. *Great,* he thought to himself. *Just the person I wanted to see. But, why is he here? Why am I here? Why am I in bed? What happened?* He tried to wrap his head around all these thoughts.

It bothered him greatly that Jesus was staring down at him with weepy eyes and a goofy grin! He sat up.

"Where am I, Jesus? And why am I here?"

"You had an accident on the road. We don't know what happened. It appears you were attacked."

Suddenly, it all came back to him. He reached for his side. The money pouch was gone. He reached his hand up and felt his bandaged head. Then he lay back down, closed his eyes, and sighed.

"There's someone here who would like to see you," Jesus said. Peter didn't open his eyes or respond. Jesus left to get Andrew.

When Andrew entered the room, Jesus stayed outside and closed the door to afford them some privacy.

"Peter, how are you feeling? We thought we had lost you!"

"It's gone, Andrew. They took it."

"Who took what?"

"The money, the balance we owed James for the boat. I had it with me. I was going to give it to James this morning at synagogue, but he refused to do business on the Sabbath. So I went to see Mary in Magdala and was going to wait until I got back, at dusk, to pay James. When I was almost home, three men—three thieves—attacked me and took the money."

"Why did you do that, Peter?" Andrew lamented. "Why would you take our money on a journey like that alone?"

"I'm sorry, Andrew, I wasn't thinking. I'm so sorry!"

Andrew sighed. "It's all right. The important thing is you're okay. We'll make the money back."

"I'll make it back, Andrew, out of my share of the business. I'll make it all back!"

Everyone in the house was thrilled with Peter's "miraculous" recovery. Mary came in to change Peter's bandages and examine his wounds. She was followed by Marion who brought bread and soup and water.

"After you've eaten," Mary said, "we'll take a look at that head of yours and see how quickly you can travel."

Peter ate, and with gusto. He felt remarkably well. There was no soreness or stiffness. Except for his apparent unconsciousness, he hardly wondered why he'd been put to bed at all. He listened in disbelief as they told him he had been there for three days, on the brink of death.

When he finished his meal, Mary began to unwind the bandage around his head. The more she unwrapped, the more startled she became. She ran her fingers across his head where the wounds had been. They were gone. Even the stitches had disappeared!

"I...I...don't..."

"Well!" Jesus quickly interrupted. "It looks like you're good as new!"

"I thought you said he had gashes," Andrew said. "Really bad gashes."

"I...I..." Mary repeated.

"Let's get you up!" Jesus interrupted again. "See if you can walk."

Peter threw the sheets off and almost bounded out of bed. "My clothes. I need my clothes."

"I'm afraid your clothes are ruined," said Jesus. "You can borrow some of mine. You can return them later."

"That's fine," Peter said, "But if I've been here for three days, Andrew and I have to get back to work."

"I know you want to get back home," Mary said, "but you might want to rest a couple of days before you return to work." She said this, questioning her own statement, and sanity. He seemed perfectly well, like he'd never been hurt at all.

They all left the room to allow Peter to dress. Then he and Andrew thanked them for their hospitality and left for home.

For the rest of the day, Mary carefully considered Peter's remarkable recovery. She was surprised and thankful for it, but she had seen this sort of thing before. She knew what Jesus had done. But she said nothing.

On the following Sabbath, Jesus announced to Mary that he would be making a trip to Magdala. After synagogue, the family returned home for lunch, and Jesus ate quickly.

"I want you to stay overnight," Mary said. "It will be too late for you to start home after your visit. Remember what happened to Peter. In fact, I would feel better if you took one of your brothers with you."

"I'll stay overnight. They have room for me. But I'm not taking anyone with me. That would be intruding on their hospitality. Besides, there's plenty of traffic on the road during the day. I'll just fall in with some other travelers and make my way back with them. I'll be fine."

"But what about the trip there? There will be few on the road on the Sabbath."

"I'll be fine, Mama. I think we both know that, don't we?" He smiled at her.

Mary pursed her lips. She knew what he meant, but she did not find it funny, although she did find it comforting if worse came to worse.

Jesus stood and started to help clear the table.

"Leave it," Mary said. "You need to be on your way."

Jesus leaned over and gave her a kiss. "I'll be back in the morning."

"Jesus," interrupted James, "I'm going to need some help on the boat tomorrow. There's some heavy lifting to do. Too heavy for the other boys."

"I'll be back in the morning!" Jesus repeated, as he walked out the door.

It was about six in the evening when Jesus arrived at Mary's house. Simon answered the door. "Jesus!" he said, smiling. "It's good to see you. Welcome! Please come in. We're just about to sit down for supper."

Mary was surprised and overjoyed to see Jesus. The butterflies in her stomach suppressed her appetite, but she filled herself with Jesus' presence, as he told them about all that had happened since he'd last seen them. Simon, in turn, reported to Jesus about the goings-on in Magdala. Mary barely heard his words. She was focused on Jesus. She couldn't take her eyes off him and, aware of this, had to force herself to look, occasionally, at her mother or father just to prevent being caught up in a hypnotic stare. It didn't work, completely.

"Mary. Mary? Mary!"

Her mother's voice suddenly jolted her back to reality. She turned to her mother's concerned, slightly aggravated face. She noticed everyone had stopped talking and was looking at her. "Yes, ma'am?"

"I said, would you please get the wine cruet and bring it to the table?"

"Yes, ma'am," she said, embarrassed. She could feel her face turning red and warm.

When she left the room, her mother smiled at Jesus. "Apparently, our daughter is quite taken with you."

Now, Jesus was embarrassed. He looked at Simon who wasn't smiling but raised his eyebrows as if to say: *Well?*

"Honorable, sir."

"What?" Simon asked, puzzled by the remark.

"My intentions, sir. As I told you before, they are honorable. I like your daughter very much."

Simon was internally amused but responded in a serious tone. "That's good, son. That's very good."

Mary returned with the wine and still red cheeks. She had brought new cups and went around the table, filling them. Jesus had intended to tell them about Peter, but the timing never seemed quite right. Now, with the sudden silence that enveloped the room, he blurted it out.

"My God, that's terrible!" said Simon. "He seemed like such a nice young man. A little strange but very nice."

"Yes, a little unkempt but *very* nice!" agreed his wife.

"Is he going to be all right?" asked Mary, concerned.

"He's fine," said Jesus. "Good as new, now, but he was very badly beaten."

"There are too many thieves on the road," complained Simon. "You'd think the Romans or Herod would dispatch more patrols. I know neither cares about the common people, but there are enough wealthy folks traveling back and forth on these roads nowadays to merit some attention out this way. One of Herod's sisters even has a house in Magdala."

"Well, we're thankful Peter is all right," said Mary's mother.

"Yes, indeed," said Simon.

"Most thankful," said Mary.

After they finished their wine, the women began to clear the table, and Simon invited Jesus outside. "Tobacco?" Simon asked, as he loaded a small pipe.

"No, thank you," said Jesus.

"So tell me about these 'honorable intentions' you have for my daughter, Jesus. Do you want her? Because I think Peter does. You know he's been here, and Mary has spent time with his family in Capernaum. If you want to ask me for her hand, you'd better hurry. I have a feeling Peter is going to ask on his next visit."

Jesus was taken aback. He didn't know what to say, and he didn't know there was a courtship occurring between Mary and Peter. Jesus knew he had feelings for Mary, strong ones, but he wasn't sure he was ready for an engagement. On the other hand, he didn't want Mary engaged to Peter, either!

"So you have no thoughts on the matter?" asked Simon.

"I have thoughts," said Jesus. "I'm just trying to put them together."

They walked on to the master's house and upstairs to the bedchambers.

"These are silk sheets," Simon said, as he spread them on the bed, slightly perturbed by Jesus' silence. "The jackass will have nothing else." He was determined to keep his promise never to refer to the man as 'master' again.

Jesus didn't hear him at first, still trying to compose a response to Simon's inquiry. Then he said, "I don't want her here when he returns."

Simon said nothing, knowing the fat man would never return.

After a moment, Jesus continued, "I think I love your daughter, Simon, but I'm not ready to ask for her hand."

Simon looked disappointed. "I see," he said. He continued with his bed-making.

"Do you think she loves Peter?" Jesus asked.

"No. I think she loves you."

Nothing else was said until Simon started out the door. "Good night, Jesus. I think *you* have some thinking to do. I will see you in the morning."

It was not a good night for Jesus. He thought about his destiny and call, the still unknown plan God had for his life. As much as he wanted that, if he even did want it, he did not see it as being a carpenter in

Capernaum, with a wife and kids and grandkids, eventually growing old, having accomplished nothing of significance in the world.

Mary's destiny, he thought, was different. Like any woman, she would want a marriage and children and a home—stability and roots. He didn't want to stand in the way of her happiness. Or Peter's. Peter could give her those things; he could not.

The next morning, after saying goodbye to Mary and her mother, Jesus asked Simon to walk him to the gate. "I cannot offer your daughter what Peter can offer," he said. "If he asks you, and if Mary agrees, you should accept. I don't expect that I will ever marry, but please know that I hold your daughter in the highest respect."

"You have spoken your words, and I have heard them," said Simon, disappointed. He walked Jesus through the gate and out to the street, where the two men embraced and shook hands. Then he watched, as Jesus walked away toward Capernaum.

All the way home, Jesus thought and rethought. Several times, he almost turned back to make a proposal to Simon but he didn't. He walked on to Capernaum and past his house to the carpenter shop where he worked until dusk. He didn't eat supper, nor had he eaten lunch. He had no appetite. When everyone else had gone to bed, Mary went up to the roof terrace where Jesus was sitting alone.

"I really like her, Jesus."

"Who?" he said, as if he didn't know.

"Mary. Who else? She's a very attractive young woman, and nice. You should marry her."

Jesus rolled his eyes and sighed. "Mama, please! Don't be ridiculous."

Mary laughed. "You're the one being ridiculous, Jesus. You're clearly pining for her, after just a day apart. You're clearly thinking about asking her father for her hand. So do it!"

"I'm thinking no such thing!" Jesus growled. "Look, I love her. I'll admit it. But you know as well I do, I can't take a wife! You know that God has something planned for me, something special that I must do, away from here. You know it, Abba knew it, and I know it! I just wish to God I knew what *it* is!"

"I believe there is something special about you, Jesus. God has gifted you in a special way, and there *is* a special purpose he has for you. But I don't know that it is away from here. God can use people in Capernaum as well as anywhere else. But if it is not to be here, then you can take your wife and family with you. You know, your father and I did a bit of traveling with you and your brothers and sisters before we settled here. It's easier if you have a partner."

"It won't be easier, Mama. I don't know what God has in store for me, but whatever it is, it will be hard. Very hard. I can sense that."

Mary's heart hurt when she heard these words. She didn't know why.

Jesus looked up at the stars and sighed. "Besides," he continued, "even if I'm wrong, even if my destiny is to remain in Capernaum and grow old, my place is here with you. As the oldest son, I am the head of this household. The others will grow up and get married and have families. That is their destiny. If I stay, my responsibility is to provide for you."

"No, it isn't, Jesus. And don't try to put this on me! I have a house. I have savings. Your father left adequate provision for me. James will be here. He isn't leaving his business. The others will probably remain in Capernaum too. If you stay, and if you marry, you can build a room right onto this house. So don't play the martyr with me. And don't make me, or God, responsible for your indecision and fear. Marry her or don't marry her, but that is all on you!" She stood up to leave. "You could teach in the synagogue, you know. You know more than any of those old goats that take our offerings. Maybe that is God's plan for you, right here in Capernaum. Did you ever think about that?" She left.

"Holy crap!' Jesus said, feeling thoroughly chastised.

Jesus spent the next several days in fervent thought and prayer, receiving absolutely nothing in the way of a reply from his heavenly Father. His earthly mother wasn't very receptive to him either. He tried to ease the tension with playful banter and pleasant conversation, but he had dashed her hopes of a daughter-in-law and grandchildren, and, at present, he was definitely not her favorite child.

Finally, filled with anxiety, pain, and consternation over the matter, Jesus prayed one last time, "If you don't tell me what I'm supposed to do, maybe I'll decide myself! I offer myself to you. Show me your will. Show me the way you would have me go and I will follow."

Nothing. Not then. Not in an hour. Not the next day. Not the next week.

Jesus was now truly confused and a little pissed. All his life, he was sure that God had a special purpose for him and would reveal that purpose and direct him at the proper time. It's what the angels had told his father and mother: that Jesus would be a major player in the restoration of Israel as a great nation and in the inauguration of the kingdom of God. Now he had reached adulthood without any indication that this would come to pass. And how was he to do all that from Capernaum, anyway? His mother seemed to have forgotten the angel's prophecy. Maybe he should forget it too.

Maybe it had never happened at all, or maybe God had just changed his mind.

Yet, in all his disappointment, Jesus felt a twinge of happiness and relief as well. Now he could pursue his relationship with Mary. He could resign himself to a lifetime in Capernaum, a place he really *did* love. He could spend the rest of his days in the carpenter shop, be near his family, watch his nieces and nephews and his own children grow up and have children of their own. He could take care of his mother and grow old with his beloved Mary. He should be content with that. He *could be* content with that. He *would be* content with that. Shouldn't he? Couldn't he? Wouldn't he? His stomach and his heart ached.

Simon was torn as to whether he should tell his daughter about his conversation with Jesus. He was all she talked about, day and night.

To her mother: "Did you see his blue eyes? Did you hear how he talks?"

To her father: "Did he say anything about me? Did he say when he was coming back?"

Simon could not bear to break her heart. But it would have to break sometime. Sooner or later, she would have to know.

After two weeks with no communication from God or angel, and little more with his mother, and after some considerable "sorting out" on his own, Jesus announced to James at the supper table that he would be taking the following day off.

"Ridiculous!" snorted James (a bit of a workaholic). "You just had a day off two weeks ago."

"I'm aware," replied Jesus, "and I'll be taking another one tomorrow."

"Why?"

"James, and MOTHER," he emphasized, "I'll be traveling to Magdala tomorrow to contract with Simon for Mary's hand in marriage." Jesus glanced at Mary, who was smiling, then at James, who wasn't.

"That's great, Jesus. I'm happy for you," James said. "That'll be one more mouth to feed, you know. And with you working only part-time, we…"

At that second, a wooden spoon struck James directly in the center of his forehead.

"Mama! What the hell?" He dodged her second utensil.

"Watch your language in this house! And be respectful of your older brother. Jesus, this is wonderful news! GO! With my blessings and Godspeed!"

"And my blessings, too, Jesus," James said, rubbing the sore spot on his head. "I'm sorry. Congratulations. We'll welcome her with open arms. Let me know when you want to start, and I'll help you with adding a room to the house."

"Thank you, James. There will be plenty of time for that, but I'll appreciate the help. Now I think it's time for bed. I want to get an early start in the morning."

As Jesus walked the road to Magdala, he gained confidence in his decision. He was happy, contented, even excited about his future. His only regret was in thinking about how this might hurt Peter. Of course, he loved her. How could he not? But it would all work itself out, Jesus thought. After all, this must be in God's plan—for all of them. He hoped.

When Jesus entered the gate of the estate, he immediately saw Simon, working on his knees in the vegetable garden. He raised his hand and waved but Simon wasn't looking, so he called out.

Simon looked up, his eyes squinting in the sun, trying to recognize the visitor. He stood. Both men moved toward each other. "Jesus?"

"Simon. Peace."

"Peace to you, Jesus," Simon said warily. "Why are you here?"

"Simon, I have come to discuss Mary with you."

They exchanged a handshake. Then Simon said more defensively, "What do you have to tell me about my own daughter? What is it that we have to discuss?"

"I would like to discuss…uh…a marriage proposal," Jesus said nervously.

""Ahhh…A marriage proposal," Simon said, in a studied voice. "I thought you said you weren't ready for marriage. Are you ready now?"

"I am."

"And, tell me, what has changed?"

Jesus thought the temperature had suddenly become warmer. He was sweating. "I've had time to think about it, to consider it, and… uh…I think it seems right."

Simon nodded, slowly. "So, you *think* it seems right. I see."

Both men were silent. Jesus sweated some more. Finally, Simon spoke, "Jesus, do you *think* you love my daughter?"

Jesus smiled. "I love her, Simon. I know this!"

Simon smiled back. "And I know she loves you. So let's discuss a marriage proposal."

They walked to the master's house and sat in the living room while they fleshed out an agreement for Mary's hand. The bridal price was more than fair. Simon had no need for *things* at least as long as he had his job. He had no place for animals, and Jesus had none to offer; there was no room in his small cottage for extra furniture or anything else that Jesus made in his shop. It was finally decided that Jesus would pay Simon one hundred and fifty denarii, about a half a year's salary. Should Simon lose his job before the marriage was consummated, Jesus would pay another one hundred and fifty to support Simon during his search for new work. Finally, as incentive, if Simon should become a grandfather within one year after the marriage, he would give fifty denarii back in thanksgiving and appreciation. The engagement would be for one year.

Jesus was concerned about this. "I don't want her here when your master returns."

"He's not my master," Simon said, sharply, reiterating his vow, "and don't worry about him. I'll handle him."

"I'd like to run all of this by Mary," said Jesus, "to be sure she agrees to the marriage."

"Are you kidding? You're all she talks about, all she thinks about. She'll be delighted. Trust me."

Mary was delighted. And so was her mother. The four of them sat at the table, discussing and making plans for the nuptial event. Jesus offered his great uncle's farm near Nazareth, the site of many of his family's weddings. There was some brief mention of Magdala, but in the end, it was decided the wedding should be at Capernaum. Jesus would be in charge of securing the site and finding lodging for out-of-town guests. Mary and the two mothers would plan the festival of four or five days. Simon suggested that the costs be shared equally by the two families, but Jesus (with his mother's advance instruction) insisted on his family footing the total bill.

Though the invitation was extended, Jesus did not stay overnight. In fact, he was anxious to get away. He was happy, but the whole episode had left him a bit overwhelmed. He thought it would be good to have some time alone on the road, away from the excitement and commotion, before facing the same thing again once he was home.

Peter went back to work the very next day after he had returned home. There was no need for recovery time since his miraculous healing was, at once, complete. He and Andrew had discussed many times the matter of the stolen money. Peter was adamant about making up the loss himself, but Andrew was just as insistent that they recoup the funds together.

"It's my loss," Peter said, again. "It was my stupidity—my impetuousness—that caused me to take off on the road alone with all that money. *Our* money. I will make it up. It isn't your responsibility."

"Look, Peter," Andrew replied, "I've told you, we're partners in this business, and I'm much more interested in getting the boat paid off than I am in padding my savings. Once the boat is ours, free and clear, we'll both be better off."

Paying the boat off as soon as possible was important to both of them. In fact, just paying down the debt was important and made them that much closer to being the sole owners and stakeholders in their business. So, today, they decided that, between the morning and afternoon fishing trips, Peter would walk to the carpenter shop and present James with a partial payment of the debt owed. Peter had saved thirty denarii and Andrew twenty-five. This would take care of more than half the balance, and leave them owing only thirty-five more before James was paid in full.

Taking the money from Andrew was hard, not only as a matter of principle and pride, but also because it revived the memory of the last time he had taken money from his brother for the same purpose. He didn't realize how still shaken and traumatized he was from his encounter with the thieves, not until Andrew dropped the money bag in his hand. His palms were sweating and his heart was racing. He thought of asking Andrew to walk with him or to take the payment himself. But all that was silly, or he was sure it would seem so to Andrew. Besides, he didn't want to ask any more of his brother. He was a grown man. He could walk a mile by himself, in his own town, to conduct his own business.

When Peter walked into the carpenter shop, Jesus knew immediately he was obligated to tell him about Mary. He wanted to, anyway. He'd thought about it all the way back from Magdala and decided it was his place to inform Peter of the engagement. He also knew he needed to do this quickly before the news spread and Peter learned of it from someone else. Now here he was, right in front of him as confirmation that this must be done, and now.

"Peter!" said Jesus. "You look well, my friend!"

"Hello, Jesus. I feel well. I want to thank you and your family again for looking after me. Is James here?" he asked, trying to change the subject and move things along.

"He must be. Didn't you see him in the yard?"

"No, and I looked. There's no one in the yard."

"Huh, that's strange. I don't know where he could be. He didn't say anything about leaving. Is there anything I can do to help you?"

Peter sighed. Once again, he would have to deal with Jesus. He wasn't about to make an extra trip just to hand over his hard-earned money to the right bar Joseph. He reached into his pocket and removed the pouch. "Here are fifty-five of the ninety denarii I owe you for the boat. I should have the rest in two weeks."

"That's fine, Peter, thank you. I'll see that James credits your account."

Peter turned to leave.

"Peter, wait. I have something to discuss with you."

Peter sighed again. *What now? Is there no way to get around a conversation with this guy?* He turned and waited, but Jesus said nothing. Then, in frustration, he raised his hands in the air. "What?"

"Could you have a seat?" asked Jesus, gesturing toward an unfinished bench in the corner.

"Jesus, I have to get back to work."

"This will take just a minute."

"Fine." Peter went to the bench and sat.

Jesus pulled up a stool and sat in front of him. "I don't know exactly where to begin, Peter, except to say that I know you have feelings for Mary."

Peter's glance, which had been directed downward, suddenly went eye to eye with Jesus. *What business is it of yours how I feel about Mary? Where are you going with this?*

Jesus continued. "I also know you have feelings toward me that aren't the same as I have toward you. Despite this, I consider you a friend and would never do anything to hurt you intentionally."

Peter was halfway between aggravation and genuine puzzlement. "Are you trying to tell me something, Jesus?"

"Yes."

(Silence.)

"What? For God's sake!"

"I have feelings for Mary too. Strong ones. I love her, Peter."

"And what would you like me to do with that information, Jesus?"

"I want you to know that I have made a marriage contract with Mary's father, and she has accepted. I believe she loves me too."

The news was like a sword through Peter's heart. He knew he had no chance for a life with Mary. He had blown that. He knew it. But he still loved her, and he had managed to salvage their friendship. He hoped that that would somehow suffice. That it would be enough for him to be near her, to see her smile, hear her laugh, be her friend. He had already resigned himself to the fact that the day would come when he would hear this very news: Mary was getting married. He thought he could steel himself with good wishes for her happiness. And, maybe, he could have if the news had not come from Jesus. If the news had not *been* Jesus and Mary.

"Peter? Peter?" Eventually, the sound registered in Peter's brain.

"Screw you, Jesus. Of all the things you could have done to me, of all the things you could have taken from me, nothing could have hurt me more. And it's always been this way for you, hasn't it? Jesus is the most intelligent, Jesus is the most courageous, Jesus is the most handsome, Jesus is the best at everything, and everybody loves him."

"Actually it hasn't always been that way. There was a time when..."

"Shut up, Jesus! You think I have feelings for Mary? Yes, I do. Deep feelings. But there were no intentions toward marriage. We're only friends. So take her, Jesus! Take her as a consolation, because you know what? You aren't the best anymore. Your family is no longer affluent. Everybody knows that but your family. You're no longer better than me. I make twice, maybe three times, what you make in a year. The fact is *I'm* better than *you*! So good luck but know this: You didn't beat me. Maybe you thought this was a way to put yourself back on top. But it doesn't. You won a game I wasn't even playing! I hope you love her; for her sake, I do. But if you did this to beat me, you failed."

"Geez, Peter, no wonder you don't like me! I don't know where you got the idea that I feel, or have a need to feel, superior to you. I don't. And my engagement to Mary has nothing to do with you or our relationship. Obviously, you're pissed about a lot of things right now, but I don't feel insecure, and I don't need to be better than you. You can let those thoughts go because that's not the case. It never has been.

"I wanted to tell you about Mary and me, and I had hoped, maybe unrealistically, for your blessing. I had hoped we might remain friends."

"Listen to me, Jesus," Peter said angrily. "I'm not your friend. I never have been. I never will be. You want my blessing? Then God bless Mary, and God help her! But you are dead to me! We don't ever need to speak again. When I come here, I'd like to do business with James, and James alone. I hope you'll, at least, respect my wishes on this matter." With that, he stood up and walked out the door and back to the fishing dock.

Two weeks later, Jesus made another visit to Magdala, this time taking his mother with him to meet Mary's parents. They left just after daylight, with Jesus walking and leading a donkey. Part of the time Mary walked, and part of the time she rode on the animal's back. When they arrived, Jesus introduced his mother to Simon and his wife and reintroduced her to the young Mary. They embraced and kissed.

"Mary, we're so happy to have you as part of our family. It's nice to have a daughter with my namesake!" They laughed. Once they had sat down, Jesus' mother continued, "You have such a lovely place here."

"Well, it isn't our place," Mary's mother said. "We're simply the caretakers."

"Nevertheless, it's a beautiful place, and it's clear you're responsible for that. The gardens are lovely, and your cottage is wonderful, as is Magdala. I've never been here before."

"There are many homes like this in Magdala. It is a beautiful village. Why don't the three of us women go for a walk? We'll give you a full tour and that will give our men a chance to visit alone."

"I'd like that," the older Mary said.

Young Mary led the way. The two mothers followed arm in arm.

Jesus and Simon stayed inside at the table, as they discussed the marriage, the terms of their contract, and Jesus' plan to build a room onto his mother's house as a place for the couple to live. When they'd run out of things to talk about pertaining to the marriage, Simon told Jesus of the "welcome" news:

"There was a search party here several days ago. It seems the fat man never showed up at his home in Damascus. They expect the worst, possibly thieves attacked and murdered them all or, more likely, since they've found no evidence of an attack, the servants killed him and took off in another direction. I suspect the latter. Thieves wouldn't have covered their tracks so well. They would've killed, looted, and left. The search party would have found something: bodies, bones, the wagon, which they would have left behind. It's too easy to track if you're not going far. I think the servants and slaves hated the insolent bastard as much as I did, as much as anyone who worked for him. The fat man did something to cause one of them to snap, and the others piled on like a pack of dogs, or, at least, the others stood by and did nothing while the one did the deed. Either way, I can't say I'm sorry. The old fool got what was coming to him. And it saves me from having to deal with him when he comes back."

Jesus took a minute to process what Simon had told him. "Well, I can't say I'm not sorry. It's awful for a man to lose his life, and it's awful to take a man's life. It's a sad thing, too, for a man to die with so much to repent for. You always want to hope that bad people—people that do bad things—see the error of their ways and repent and make amends."

"I don't think it's awful. I think it's just!" said Simon. "But I hope the son of a bitch repented too. I hope he begged for forgiveness and had time to reflect on all the damage he had done to others. I hope he had time to feel sorry for all the evil that he had done. I hope he begged for his life and promised to be a better man. And I hope that God sees through all that bullshit and sends him straight to hell!"

"Simon, any man's heart can change. Any man can repent at any time. I'm not saying he did, or that he would have, but I won't celebrate a person's life being taken in retribution for sin. Only God can judge such things. It is good, at least, that neither Mary—nor you—will have to deal with him again."

"It is good," Simon said and then added, "He was an ass."

When the women returned, they all ate lunch together. Afterward, Jesus and young Mary went for a walk and discussed their wedding plans and all that had transpired in the two weeks since they'd last seen each other. Jesus told Mary about his encounter with Peter and his reaction to the news of their engagement. She listened as Jesus expressed his deep sorrow in learning how Peter had felt about him all these years. This upset Mary greatly.

"I'll talk to him," she said. "He had no right to say those things to you."

"He has a right to say what he feels, Mary, although I am sorry he feels the way he does, and I'm not at all sure *why* he feels the way he does about me. It's disturbing and disheartening."

"I don't understand it," she said in a stern tone. "The last time I saw him, he asked that we continue to be friends. That's what we are. That's all we are, or were."

"If you do talk to him, that's what you need to work on," said Jesus, "repairing and strengthening *your* friendship. His feelings toward me will have to be dealt with between the two of us."

When the two returned to Mary's house, Jesus and his mother thanked their hosts, bade them farewell, and began their journey back to Capernaum.

When the summer residents were not in Magdala, the market opened only one day a week. Mary was there waiting when the boats came in to sell their catch. She watched as Andrew maneuvered his small boat into the dock and began unloading several baskets of fish. "Hello, Andrew."

"Mary," he said, a bit cool.

"I was hoping Peter would be with you."

"I'm delivering for us and for my father. We don't bring as much of the catch over in the off season, so there isn't much use in both of us sending boats or even two fishermen. Peter's delivering to the ports on the other side."

"I need to talk to him, Andrew."

"Well, Peter doesn't want to talk to you. I don't think he's planning to come back to Magdala, ever. You broke his heart, you know."

"No, I don't know that, and I don't know why. I never gave him any indication that I was interested in him romantically."

"Yeah, you kind of did," Andrew said, as he unloaded the last of his baskets. You came to our house and lived there, Mary. You were with him every day."

"As a friend! I came there because I needed a friend. I still do. I still want Peter and me to be friends."

"Want my advice?"

She didn't. "What?"

"Find another friend." He looked down into a basket and started sorting fish.

Mary seethed for a moment and thought about pushing Andrew off the dock and into the water. She started to walk away, then turned and said, "Are you my friend, Andrew?"

He looked up, considered the question, and said, "I don't know. I suppose I am."

"Then, please tell Peter I want to see him. We have to sort this out. He can come here or I will come to him, but we have to talk."

"I'll tell him, but I doubt that he's going to come here."

"Fine, then just tell him I will come to Capernaum. I'll travel with the next group going that way. It shouldn't be more than a day or two."

"And will you be staying with us?"

"No, I have a place to stay."

"So we've heard," Andrew mumbled. "You know, that's part of the…"

"I don't want to hear it, Andrew!"

"Whatever. I'll tell him."

"Thank you," Mary said and walked away.

Mary explained the whole story to her parents and told them that she had to make the trip to try and correct the situation. "It's not just for the sake of my relationship with Peter, but for the relationship between Peter and Jesus, and Jesus and me, and all three of us! Jesus is really upset about this, and I need to try and make it right."

She asked her father to help her find someone or some group traveling the road to Capernaum and to gain her passage with them. He offered to take her himself but she resisted.

"There must be someone going that way, anyway," she said. "If I can get there, Jesus will bring me back, or I'll find another group coming this way."

"Jesus will bring you back," Simon insisted.

"I'm sure he will," she agreed.

"There are no caravans coming through here this time of year, but I will see if I can find someone traveling that way soon. If I trust them, you may go with them. If not, then I will take you, or you will wait."

The next day, Simon talked to some local merchants and learned that a small group of them were preparing to travel to Capernaum and beyond to sell wares and buy for their shops. They would be leaving in two days, and Mary could travel with them as far as Capernaum.

"They are trustworthy and neighbors," he said to Mary. "You can travel safely with them, but don't hinder them. Take enough food for yourself and carry your own load. You don't want to be a burden. And see that Jesus himself brings you home."

The night before she left, Mary packed a change of clothes and a lunch of bread and dates she could eat as she walked. (Her father had told her the group would be traveling fast and not stopping along the way.) She carried her own waterskin, so as not to infringe on the supplies of her hosts.

The day of the journey was quite pleasant and the trip uneventful. When they arrived at Capernaum, Mary thanked her fellow travelers and wished them good luck as they scurried off toward the marketplace. She thought about dropping in on Jesus but decided against it. She didn't want to explain what she was doing or why she was there before she talked to Peter. Neither did she want to risk the possibility of receiving advice or being coached on how to proceed with her task. So she made straight for the docks.

It was about two o'clock in the afternoon when she arrived. It was between fishing trips, so all the boats were in. A few men were napping in the shade, and a couple more were sitting on the dock, mending nets. She didn't see Peter. She figured he and most of the other fishermen had gone home to eat and rest before the afternoon haul. She started for Peter's house but then remembered her conversation with Andrew and his coolness toward her. She was afraid the rest of the family might have the same resentment for her, so she decided to wait for a time when she could catch Peter alone. She went back to the shore, found a tree, and rested under its shade, keeping a keen eye on the docks about thirty yards away.

A couple of hours later, she noticed the fishermen returning to their boats. Then she saw Peter walking with Andrew toward the big boat they worked together. There were already two others on the boat, whom she assumed to be their deckhands. She stood to approach him but then decided that this was not the right time for a surprise visit. At worst, there would be an unpleasant confrontation. At best, there wouldn't be enough time to have the long conversation necessary to work things out between them. She would wait until evening when he was finished for the day.

Mary was awakened by a sandaled foot lightly kicking at her ribs. She sat up, startled, and saw three men standing around her, all with devious grins on their dirty faces.

"Wake up, Missy," said the largest one. "We've come to pay you a call."

It was almost dark, but she could see that all the boats were in. She quickly searched the docks to see if there was anyone she could call to for help. No one. They had all gone home. How could she have slept through their coming and going? The man who had spoken to her squatted down beside her.

"I think I know every young woman in Capernaum, and you're not one of them. Where are you from, little lamb?"

"From Magdala," she said, in a trembling voice. She moved to get to her feet.

The man pushed her back to the ground. "Where you going, fig cake? You're not going to run out on our little party, are you?"

"Leave me alone!" she demanded. "I'll scream if you don't let me go!"

The man laughed, and his partners joined in with chuckles.

"Go ahead and scream, Missy. No one's going to hear you out here."

She screamed.

The man put his filthy hand over her mouth. She could taste the sourness of sweat and dirt and piss, and feel the crusty granules of who knew what on his palm. She bit down hard, and the man yelped, jumping to his feet. The other two men took a step back, startled by their leader's scream.

"You bit me, you little bitch!" He came down hard with his fist.

Mary's neck snapped back, trying to absorb the blow. She saw stars, and her face exploded with pain. Half conscious, she couldn't fight back as the man ripped at her tunic, exposing her breasts. He climbed on top of her. Regaining control of her senses, she began to scratch and claw at his face. At the leader's command, the other two men grabbed her arms, holding them tight to the ground. The gravel cut into her flesh as she struggled to free herself from their grip. He entered her. With every thrust, searing pain shot through her gut. She screamed again. Someone shoved something into her open mouth to muffle the sound. When the first man finished, a second took his place. She struggled again, briefly, then relented. Tears blurred her vision. The only sound she heard was a cadenced grunt from the pig on top of her. She closed her eyes and prayed to die. The third man took his turn. Her only movement now was the involuntary jerk of her body as the man violently thrust himself back and forth. She felt herself gradually slipping away.

When she awoke the men were gone. Her insides were burning— on fire—from the brutal violation. The muzzle was still in her mouth. She raised her arm to remove it but immediately let it drop again. Her whole body was racked with pain. Feeling nauseous, she willed herself to move. She took the cloth from her mouth, rolled onto her stomach and pushed herself up on her knees. She heaved and the sickness came immediately. She picked up the cloth (which was a piece of her own clothing) and wiped her chin and nose. She forced herself to her feet but staggered only a few feet before collapsing. Every fiber of her being ached, including her soul. She thought of Jesus. She thought of her parents. She thought of herself and the terrible thing that had been done to her.

As she lay there, looking up at the stars peeking through the trees, exhaustion and depression consumed her. Sleep mercifully took her away.

Mary awoke the second time to the shouts of the fishermen. The boats had cast off from the docks, and the men were calling out to one another as they raised the sails, which would carry them out to the deep water of the sea, and the fish. She sat up and wrapped her arms around her knees to steady herself. She still hurt, physically and emotionally. She tried to collect her thoughts. *What now?* There was nothing now. She couldn't undo what had been done. Her life was over. She imagined one last time her life with Jesus—their marriage, their family, their future—the happiness they would have shared. It was all gone. Jesus wouldn't have her now. She was damaged goods. She thought again about her parents. She wouldn't see them again, nor Jesus. She couldn't bear the thought of facing them, of telling them. It was suddenly clear to her what she had to do.

Mary struggled to her feet and tried to piece together her torn clothing. Then she remembered her bag and extra change of clothes. After a brief search she found the bag with its contents strewn around it. The men had apparently rifled through her belongings but, finding nothing of value, decided to leave it all behind. She went down to the lakeshore and cleaned herself up as best she could. There was dried blood on her arms and face, and cuts and scratches that stung when she touched the wet cloth to them. She cleaned the blood and dirt from the insides of her thighs. As she washed, she made her plans. She would go to the coast, probably to Caesarea. There were plenty of wealthy families there, and she could find work as a servant. She thought again of Jesus and her parents and the heartache she would cause them by disappearing without a word. But, she reasoned, it would be no worse than the heartache she would cause them if she stayed and told them of her attack.

As Mary made her way out of Capernaum, she stayed in the trees and off the road, avoiding human contact as much as possible. When she came to the edge of town, she started to second guess her plan. Hate for the men who ruined her life was beginning to fill her heart and mind. They should be brought to justice and pay for what they had done. But could she even identify them? It was dark, and when the men were on top of her, close enough for her to see them, her vision was blurred by tears or her eyes closed because she didn't want to see their horrible faces or witness their heinous act. And, even if the men could be found, what would happen to them? They could be stoned, but, more likely, if they were convicted at all, they would be required to pay reparations to her father for "property damage" and to abate *his* pain and suffering. It would change nothing. It wouldn't exact the revenge she desired in her heart. She decided to stay with her original plan.

The next concern for Mary was sustenance for her journey. She'd eaten the last piece of bread from her bag this morning. She had a few copper coins with her, enough to buy a meal tonight or tomorrow morning in Nazareth. But once she left Nazareth, she faced twenty-five miles of nothing but wilderness between there and Caesarea. Perhaps she should wait and talk to Peter, ask him for food or a small loan. She decided this wasn't an option. If he would talk to her at all, he would ask too many questions. She didn't want to face Peter, either. She would move on to Nazareth and decide her next step from there.

Not far out of Capernaum, Mary passed a farm and noticed, near the house, several fig trees. It was the season for fruit, and she could see that the trees were loaded with it. She left the road and headed for the trees, looking for anyone around the house and fields. She thought about going on to the house and asking permission to pick a few of the figs, but they were there for the taking, and what if she was told no? She quickly filled her bag and made her way back to the road, apparently unnoticed. She ate as she walked, thinking this might be a gift from God and a sign that her plan was the right one. However, she did not give thanks. She would have thanked God last night, if he had saved her from her cruel fate; if he had interceded on her behalf, but he didn't. And she would not give thanks. Not today. Not ever.

There was barely a soul on the road between Capernaum and Nazareth. It was well after dark when she reached the village, and most of its residents were asleep. She found a well, raised a bucket of cool water, and let it saturate her parched throat and stomach. When she could drink no more, she found a patch of grass just beyond the cobblestone square, laid her tired body down with her bag under her head, and went to sleep.

The next morning, Mary awoke, grateful that she wouldn't have to beg or steal for food. She went to the well and filled her waterskin. She drank it dry and filled it again. Then she took a single fig from her bag and resumed her journey. As she walked, she met women on their way to the well to fill their household jugs for the day. They didn't speak and neither did she. Within fifteen minutes, Nazareth was out of sight behind her, and the sun just beginning to rise. Ahead were the steep wilderness hills that would take her to Caesarea.

There was no real road between Nazareth and Caesarea. The highways were to the north, connecting the coastal town with Sepphoris, and to the south, between Caesarea and Nain. Mary followed a seldom used trail that allowed those traveling from Nazareth a straight shot to the port city. Few preferred the short cut to the safety of the more traveled roads. There were places where the trail was no more than a goat path and other places where it disappeared altogether. By the time she reached the highest point in the hills, she was completely lost. The twists and turns she had been forced to make as she traversed the mountain crevices made her question if she was even going in the right direction. At first, she could use the sun to navigate her way, but once it had begun its westward decline and the hilltops blocked her view, she had no bearing. She would have to stop until the sun was high in the sky again. It was her only compass.

Mary had seen no serpents or wild beasts, other than a single ibex, which had not welcomed her company and quickly pranced away. There had been a few scorpions that reluctantly gave her right of way. She knew, however, that the snakes and other creatures that could do her harm were nocturnal by nature. Once it was dark, they would begin their prowls for food, and encounters would be more likely. She had no way of building a fire. There was no particular place she could go to be safer, so she simply sat where she was and waited for the night. She ate until she was full; there was no shortage of figs in her bag. Then she lay down to rest with the bag beneath her head. She could smell the sweet figs inside. Suddenly, her brain registered that if she could smell the figs, they would certainly attract the olfactory senses of other creatures in search of food. She stood up and heaved the bag as far as she could down the mountain crevice, then sat back down, cupped her hands around her knees, and laid her head on her arms. She stayed awake as long as she could. Then sleep came.

It was late afternoon, and Simon was between worry and anger. He walked into the house and spoke to his wife. "Mary should've been home yesterday! I thought her business with Peter might have taken her all day and that she decided to spend the night, but the day is over and she isn't here. She should be here by now! I'm going after her."

"Simon," said his wife, "I'm worried about her too. She *should* be here, but it's too late to travel to Capernaum tonight. She and Jesus may be on their way now, almost here. Wait and see. If she doesn't come home, you can leave first thing in the morning."

"I'm not waiting," said Simon. "If they're on the road, I'll meet them. I'll get Mary and turn Jesus around in his tracks. It's irresponsible of both of them to worry us this way."

"Just wait, Simon, before you get too angry with either of them. There may be a perfectly reasonable explanation for why they're late. Calm down, and listen to what they have to say before you speak."

"She's done this before, you know. She was gone for two weeks without letting us know where she was. We shouldn't have to put up with this again!"

"Yes, she *was* gone before, and there *was* an explanation. You know that."

"I know why she left, yes. Don't remind me. But she could have talked to us before she left. And she shouldn't be doing this to us again. She should know we would worry!" He paced back and forth across the room. "I'm going," he said, and started for the door.

"Simon, *please* wait till morning."

He stopped. "I'll wait," he said, "but she'll never leave here again without one of us as an escort! Not until she's married."

They waited, until well past bedtime, the conversation between them sparse. Mary's mother knitted. Simon gritted his teeth and seethed.

"I'm going to bed," Simon said finally. "Have breakfast ready early." He closed the bedchamber door behind him.

The next morning, Simon ate in silence, with the exception of one word replies to his wife:

"Should I go with you?"

"No."

"When you get there, listen before you speak."

"No."

"Promise not to upset Jesus' mother."

"No."

When he had finished eating, he got up, grabbed his walking stick and head covering, and went out the door without a word. Ten seconds later, he came back in, hugged his wife, and kissed her cheek. "I promise to listen before I speak and not to upset Jesus' mother," he said and walked back out.

Simon arrived at Capernaum late morning. He asked directions to the carpenter shop and found Jesus there, working.

"Simon, greetings! What brings you to Capernaum?"

"I'm here for Mary," Simon said gruffly. "Where is she?"

Jesus looked puzzled. "Mary? What are you talking about, Simon?"

"She came here three days ago. She said she would have you bring her home the next day."

"Simon, I don't understand. I haven't seen Mary since I was at your place a week ago."

Simon felt sick. This was not good news.

"Why would Mary be in Capernaum, anyway?" asked Jesus.

"She came to see Pet—. I know where she is! Where she must be! Do you know where Peter lives?"

"Yes, of course," said Jesus. "But why would she come to see Peter?"

"Take me to his house," said Simon. "I'll explain on the way."

The two men walked quickly toward Peter's house, and Simon told

Jesus all about Mary's plan to set things right between her and Peter, and Peter and Jesus. "I think she intended to put Peter in his place regarding his behavior toward you, and to make things clear about their relationship, and about yours and hers."

"Brother!" said Jesus. "I told her to leave it alone. Peter has never liked me, and Mary intervening won't make things any better."

"He wouldn't hurt her, would he?" Simon asked.

"No. He may not like me, but he has deep feelings for Mary. He wouldn't hurt her."

It was just after noon, and Peter was home to eat and rest between the morning and afternoon fishing trips. He answered the door. "What are you doing here, Jesus? I thought I made it clear that I didn't want anything to do with you."

Simon stepped from behind Jesus, "Where's my daughter, Peter?"

"Simon? What are you doing here? What are you talking about?"

"Mary. She came here three days ago to see you. Where is she?"

"I don't know where she is. She came to see me?" Peter was excited but confused.

"Somebody in this town knows where my daughter is!" Simon shouted, now on the verge of real panic. "I want her found now!"

"We'll find her, Simon," said Jesus.

Peter's entire family was now standing behind him at the door.

"Peter, can we come in?" asked Jesus.

"Of course, you can come in," interjected Peter's father, as he pushed his son out of the way. "Come in, and we'll get to the bottom of this. We'll find Mary."

The men sat down together, as Peter's mother and sisters, also concerned about Mary, formed a perimeter around the room, listening. Simon explained everything, from the day she left with his merchant neighbors, to the reason for her trip, to her plans for coming home. "She's been gone for three days," he said, distraught. "She should have been home two days ago."

"Could she have traveled on with the merchants?" Peter's father asked.

"No," replied Simon. "Some of them have already returned. They said she arrived in Capernaum with them. She was safe and well when they said their goodbyes."

"Does she know anyone else here?"

"No. She'd never been out of Magdala before visiting your family and Jesus'. You men know about that better than I. Jesus? Peter? Andrew? Did she know anyone else in Capernaum? Any other fishermen from the market?"

"She knew everyone that sold at the Magdala docks," Peter said. "But from Capernaum? There were only Andrew and me and a couple of other fisherman from Capernaum who sold there. There are others from other towns, but if we know she was here, that rules them out. I can check with the others at the dock, but she never really seemed comfortable around anyone but us when she was here before." Peter waved his arm to include everyone in his family. "And now, I guess, Jesus and his family."

"Besides," said Jesus, "we know why she came here, so why didn't she talk to Peter? Why hasn't she come to see me? Why would she be in Capernaum and not be with one of us? Something's terribly wrong."

"I fear that is true, Jesus," said Peter's father, "and we shouldn't waste daylight making inquiries around town, not all of us, anyway. I'll send the girls around to the marketplace and door to door. We know she was here. Someone must have seen her, but, in any case, I don't think she's here now, and a cold trail will do us no good. If she isn't in town, I think our best bet is to assume that she may have tried to get back to Magdala on her own. We'll put together as many men and boys as we can in a hurry and make our way to Magdala. If she's out there, she may still be alive. Andrew, go to the docks and bring all of my hands back, and yours too. We won't fish this afternoon."

"Thank you," Jesus said, speaking for Simon, who had gone pale and silent. Simon and everyone else knew what Peter's father had just told them. He knew Simon had just come from Magdala and didn't see Mary along the way. That meant he believed she had been attacked on her way home by thieves or a wild beast and dragged off the road. She was somewhere in the trees and brush, dead or dying.

By the time they had gathered at the southern end of town and the road that led to Magdala, more than twenty men were with them. Peter's father, who had coordinated the formation of the search party, continued as leader of the group.

"I want half of you on this side of the road and half on the other." He pointed to direct the men into position. "Spread out thirty yards apart, and stay in a straight line. Those of you walking clear ground, slow down for those working through the brush. Stay together!" When everyone was lined up and in place, he said, "Alright, keep your eyes sharp. Let's go!"

Walking at a slow pace, and occasionally stopping as some of the men checked the caves and crevices in the rock formations that punctuated the landscape, it took them over seven hours to get to Magdala. They found no trace of Mary, so, now, they would turn and go back, this time placing their first man where the farthermost man had been on the way. They had covered three hundred yards on both sides of the road from Capernaum to Magdala; on their way back, they would extend their search to six hundred yards. If she had been attacked by man or beast, they would find her, or what was left of her. If they didn't find her, then she was still in Capernaum or had left by another road. But they couldn't continue their search today. It was almost dark. They would have to wait until morning.

Simon opened the large house for the men, and he and Jesus went to his cottage. He sat his wife down and explained the situation. Mary was missing. Neither Jesus nor Peter had seen her. They were searching the road to see if they could find her (or her body).

If they found nothing, he would continue the search in some other direction. Mary's mother took the news hard. Though she had hoped for the best, she feared the worst. She had tried to brace herself, as best she could, for a bad report, but she had failed. She collapsed into Simon's arms, and they cried together. After a time, he helped her to the bedchamber and into their bed, and left her alone to grieve.

The next morning, Peter's father lined the men up in proper position, and they began their extended search path on the way back to Capernaum.

The terrain was more rugged farther from the road. It took the entire day to get back to Capernaum. They found nothing, not even a shred of clothing. It was clear that Mary hadn't gone in the direction of Magdala.

When they reached Jesus' house, he asked Simon to stay with him while they devised a next step for finding Mary. Simon thanked Peter's father and all the others for their help. Peter's father told him that he and his household and all his workers were at Simon's service. They were very fond of Mary and anything they could do to help find her, they would do. He promised to continue the door-to-door search in Capernaum until every house and every resident had been questioned. Simon thanked him again, and the two men embraced. Farewells were said, and the rest of search party made their way toward their own homes.

By the end of the evening, the group decided that Jesus and Simon would leave the next morning for Cana. James and the two younger brothers would go in the other direction to nearby Bethsaida. In both towns, they would visit the marketplaces, wells, and any other public gathering places to ask about Mary, to see if anyone remembered seeing a beautiful young woman they hadn't seen before. They could describe her clothes and her unique appearance. (Mary still carried the dye marks of the indigo and henna that accentuated her eyes and lips.) If she had been there, someone would've seen her; someone would remember her. They were frightened but hopeful.

Just as they were saying good night, they heard a knock on the door. Everyone froze. Company at night was never good news. Jesus answered the door. It was Andrew and his father, who had a goatskin bag in his hand.

"We need to talk," the father said.

"Come in," said Jesus, worried. "Sit at the table. Simon, join us. The rest of you, go to bed."

"I'll stay," said Jesus' mother.

"Very well," said Jesus. "James, you can stay too. The rest of you, off to bed."

Once the others were gone, Peter's father began. "This was found late today, just before dark." He reached in the bag and pulled out

Mary's torn and dirty tunic. Everyone gasped. This was confirmation of tragedy, perhaps of foul play.

"Unfortunately," he continued, "it was not brought to me until after dinner, after dark. Some boys were playing near the shoreline today and found it half-buried. It appears someone tried to hide it. The boys dug it up but left it there, not thinking it important. At supper, the father of one of the boys mentioned a missing girl and the search. That's when the boy told him about the clothing they had found. The two of them went back with torches, found the clothes, and brought them to me. Are these Mary's clothes?"

He already knew the answer by the way Simon was caressing the cloth. When it was laid on the table, Simon had pulled it toward him and was gently running his fingers along the top of the cloth, back and forth, as if petting a newborn lamb. Tears were pouring down his cheeks.

"It's hers," Simon said, in a soft but firm voice.

"I'm sorry, Simon," Peter's father said sympathetically, but as a matter of fact. He had already examined the tunic. Clearly, it had been torn by human hands. There was blood at the neckline and, halfway down, more blood and other stains that indicated a rape.

No one else said a word. No one could look at another. One's gaze was up, another's down, another with her face in her hands. There were sniffles and sobs, with an eerie silence between that seemed to pall the room. But there were no words, not for a long time.

Finally, Peter's father said, "Peter couldn't come with us. He was too broken up and too angry. But all in our family extend our deepest condolences along with our broken hearts. We all cared deeply for Mary. May God bless her soul. And may God bring us justice!"

"You don't know she's dead," said Jesus. No one seconded his statement with affirmation or support. They all knew this was wishful but hopeless thinking. It was quiet again.

"We will go," said Peter's father.

There was no reply. No one got up to show them out. He and Andrew quietly exited the house, leaving the rest of them sitting at the table, lost in despair.

Mary didn't sleep well. It was cold in the hills, and every time she managed to doze off, she'd hear something (or think she heard something) and be wide awake again, waiting and watching for whatever was coming to get her. She watched as the stars began to disappear one by one and the sky fade from black to gray. She thought she would still have a while to wait before the sun was high enough to give her bearing, but suddenly she noticed a pinkish glow washing over the sky behind her. She knew it was the sun rising but where exactly? The sky in front of her was still dark, but behind her, the entire horizon was now lightening to a faint orange. It was impossible to determine precisely where the sun was and, therefore, what was east and what was north and south. She didn't want to wait another two hours for the sun to rise above the mountains, so she decided to move straight ahead toward the dark sky. She knew it could be leading north, south or west, but at least she knew she wasn't going back where she came from. West or north would take her to the sea and one port city or another, south into the desert mountains and likely death. She considered the odds and liked her chances. Besides, she thought, she was good with things either way.

Before beginning what she hoped would be the final day of her journey to Caesarea, she made a quick detour, sliding down a steep crevice to retrieve her bag and her food. It had taken a nice bounce when she pitched it down the hill the night before, but she could see it about fifty yards below her. It appeared intact. No animal had looted it. She eased herself down, trying to maintain control of her descent and not slide too far at once. She was starving, her mouth salivating just thinking of the figs. As she got closer, she noticed that the bag seemed to be moving, or not moving so much as changing, in color, in shape. What was it? The sun's heat reflecting off the ground, causing the bag to dance? No, it wasn't yet warm enough for that illusion. Was it her eyes (or her mind) playing tricks on her? She stopped about ten yards away to try to make it out. Suddenly, her eyes focused and she saw: ANTS! Ten thousand huge ants traveling in and out of the bag, covering every inch of it. She looked to her left and saw a trail of ten thousand more descending and ascending the crevice, not two feet from her hand. They would eat her alive if they managed to find her flesh.

She carefully climbed back up the trench, trying not to disturb the ants with too much falling debris. When she reached the top, she took a deep breath and drank from the waterskin. It was almost empty, and she knew she had at least as far to go as she had come the day before. Short of water and out of food, she considered her odds again. Not as good.

Once she had started down out of the mountains and the sun was high enough to see, she was relieved to know she was going in the right direction. Earlier, when she was at higher elevation, and before a haze had filled the air, she had seen the coastline, but, now, the only thing in view ahead was barren desert. She was hungry, dehydrated, and tired. There was one more drink in her waterskin, and she hoarded it as if it were the key to heaven.

Because the sun was directly in front of her, and the heat of the desert rising in waves and distorting her view, she didn't see the city until it was, perhaps, two miles away. She could hear the breaking waves of the ocean. It was blessed relief, and she almost gave thanks to God before catching herself. She stopped and drained her waterskin. Her throat felt as though it was cracking as the water trickled down, rehydrating at least the surfaces of her parched insides. She tried to walk faster but couldn't. In fact, she seemed to be moving much slower than before, dragging her body along with each anguished step.

When she finally reached the city gate, she collapsed in the shade of the wall, uncertain if she could take another step. A man watering his camel at a trough noticed her distress. He filled a cup and took it to her. She absorbed the liquid almost without swallowing. He took her waterskin, filled it, and brought it back to her. She drank thirstily until it was almost empty. With a cool, wet cloth, he wiped her sunburned face and then placed it on the back of her neck.

"Thank you. Thank you," she whispered over and over. She remembered the man handing her bread, and she remembered beginning to chew. Then her memory and consciousness faded into darkness.

When Mary opened her eyes, she saw the roof of a tent. She was lying on soft pillows. There was no one else inside. She began to recall the events of the evening before and deduced that she must be the guest of the camel herder. She felt rested, but her stomach was hurting with hunger. She started to rise but found that it was not an easy task. After several stretches to loosen her stiffened body, she managed to get to a sitting position. She looked around the tent and noticed a plate of food sitting on a milking stool beside her—bread, figs, and goat cheese—and next to the food, her own waterskin, presumably filled.

Mary grabbed the waterskin first. After a long, soaking, soothing drink, she replaced the cork and threaded the skin's strap around her neck and under her arm, letting it rest at her side. She ate hungrily, until the plate was clean, at long last feeling satiated. She could hear the hustle and bustle of traffic outside the tent and the closer sound of men's voices. When she bashfully opened the tent flap and stuck her head outside, she saw three men, including the one that had attended to her the previous night.

"Good morning," he said. "How are you feeling?"

"Much better, thank you," replied Mary. "I assume this is your tent?"

"It is. You weren't in very good shape when you came in from the desert last night. I thought it best to keep an eye on you until your health returned. You found the food?"

"I did. Thank you. I was starving!"

"May I ask your name?"

"Mary. My name is Mary. And yours?"

"Caleb, at your service." He stood and bowed.

The other two men had turned away and changed the subject of their own conversation. They were oblivious to the one going on behind them.

"And, if I may be so bold as to inquire, Mary, what brings you to Caesarea…through the desert…alone?"

Mary answered the question truthfully but selectively, "I came from Nazareth. I lost my employ as a servant and have come here to find work."

"Perhaps I can help you," the man said, "but first I must know why you were released. Did you steal from your master?"

"No," said Mary. "My employers moved from Mag...Nazareth to Damascus. My mistress wanted to take me with her, but the master had other plans. In the end, I was left behind."

"And you aren't a slave, run away?" the man asked.

"Of course not! I was born free, as my parents and grandparents were born free!"

Mary's legitimacy was not particularly what the man was fishing for. In fact, a thief or slave would have been much more useful to him in his line of work. "I beg your pardon. I didn't mean to offend, but you did come from the desert and not the road. For a woman alone, that is suspicious. I also ask because of your appearance. You have the marks of aristocracy. You appear either mistress or slave."

"My mistress treated me as her own child. She offered me paints and jewelry, and I accepted them freely, as a servant, not as a slave compelled to do so."

"Very well. Very well," said the man. "You understand I have to know about people before I can recommend them." He had no intentions of recommending Mary for servant work, because he had no connections with noble people, at least respectable ones. Perhaps Mary wasn't as desperate as he suspected but, then again, perhaps she was. It never hurt to ask. "How would you like to work for me?" he asked.

"You need a servant to tend your camels and tent?"

"This isn't my home, Mary. It's my place of business—one of them. I own three of the tents you see: this one, that one, and that one," he said, pointing. "The tents stay pitched here most of the time, but occasionally, we'll break camp and caravan to other cities. We buy and sell many things."

"I still don't understand. Do you want a servant girl for your home or your business? Whom exactly would I serve and how?"

"You would serve me, Mary, and you would serve many men. You are a beautiful woman and with face paint restored, you would be exotic! You would make a lot of money for me, Mary, and I would pay you a lot of money."

Mary was stunned for only a second. Then she quickly moved toward the street and the gate of the city. "Thank you for your hospitality," she called back to the man as she scurried away.

"Pity," he said to himself.

Mary thought her best bet for finding work was at the marketplace. There, both masters and servants would be shopping for food and other supplies as well as the baubles, bangles, and booty that kept the wealthy amused and occupied. At first, she tried to approach young women her own age. Perhaps they would tell her where they worked and if they thought the household had a place for another servant. Few would speak to her at all; some, she was sure, spoke a different language from hers; others seemed frightened to talk, as if they were being watched and would be punished by their masters if they deviated even slightly from their assigned tasks. When she tried to inquire of the shopkeepers, they would shoo her away, demanding that she buy or move along to make room for paying customers. Finally, she walked the city streets asking passersby about possible employment but got nowhere in the way of a positive response, or even a helpful lead. How could it be so hard to find servant work in a city of such wealth and gentry?

Mary's body had grown used to long periods without fuel, but after two full days of only water, her stomach began to growl. She considered stealing a piece of bread or fruit from one of the many food shops at the market, but every time she got close enough to make a grab at something, it seemed as though the vendor would train his eyes on her, as if he knew her thoughts.

Begging was officially illegal in Caesarea, but the guards didn't enforce the rule as long as the beggars restricted themselves to back alleys or outside the city walls. As hungry as she was, Mary couldn't force herself to compete for the little that was tossed to the blind and crippled outcasts of the city.

Sitting in the shade of a tree, and against a wall adjacent the main street, Mary watched as seemingly happy (and full) people passed by, some of them busily, others quite leisurely. They walked in pairs or groups, talking and laughing on the way, greeting their neighbors, and making friendly gestures toward one another. Mary vowed she wouldn't go to bed hungry tonight. And she knew the one place—the one person—who wouldn't turn her away.

She walked to the city gate and, once outside, turned right toward the sizeable encampment of sojourners. There were seventy or eighty tents pitched, she reckoned, but she knew which ones were Caleb's, so she made her way, ignoring a couple of cat calls and propositions as she dodged through the dusty maze of canvas cottages and smelly men. When she got there, Caleb was in negotiations with a man, who, after a word of protest, shoved some coins into Caleb's hand and disappeared through the flap of one of the tents. She moved closer, and Caleb looked up from counting his money.

"Mary," he said, surprised to see her.

"I've reconsidered your offer," Mary said without hesitation. She had done her thinking on the matter. She was a ruined woman already. Jesus would not have her, nor Peter, nor any decent man. Her virtue was gone, so what was the point of trying to protect it at the cost of going hungry? What was the use of anything anymore, except survival? And all she wanted to do today—all she needed to do—was to satisfy the beast that was gnawing away at the inside of her belly. "The first thing I need is food. Now, please."

Caleb almost broke his neck getting inside the tent where his food supplies were kept.

"Hey!" said the man who had just paid Caleb for the pleasure of one of his girls. He grabbed his tunic off the floor and covered his bare ass. "Get out!"

Caleb ignored him, grabbed a cake of cheese, a couple of pieces of flat bread, and some dried figs. He came out of the tent and shoved them at Mary. "I have a skin of goat milk cooling in the well. Would you like some?" he asked.

Mary nodded her head, as she stuffed her mouth with as much bread and cheese as it would hold.

Caleb was excited. He ran to the well. He'd never had a woman as beautiful as Mary. In fact, he thought he had never seen a woman as beautiful. She would make him lots of money! He would do everything he could to keep her happy, at least until she was clear that he owned her, body and soul. This usually didn't take long, perhaps a beating or two. But, for now, her wish was his command. He needed to keep her from second guessing her decision before she was in too deep. Eventually, she would accept her fate—the fact that she could never erase her whoredom. Then she would become complacent, lose her will, and simply do as she was told. That's how he came to own his girls. And they were his until he used them up and threw them away.

Suddenly, Caleb had an unhappy thought. What if she had taken his food and run? How stupid to leave her alone! He picked up his step and was relieved to see Mary still there, still stuffing her face. When he reached her, she grabbed the skin from him and drank several gulps, almost choking on the combination of the food and liquid together. When she had regained her composure, she stuffed another piece of bread in her mouth. Finally, she felt full, maybe too full.

"Now I want to lie down and take a nap, in private, please," Mary said.

Caleb was still excited but becoming a little perturbed. He wanted to keep her happy, but she seemed to know this game a little too well. "You're pretty demanding for someone in need."

"What I need is food and rest. You have been kind enough to give me food. Now I ask that you allow me to rest. We'll talk about terms afterward."

"Very well," said Caleb guardedly, "but you need to know my terms are set, and I don't negotiate. They are what they are. Take them or leave them." He said this knowing he could capitulate later, if necessary.

"We'll see," said Mary. She wouldn't be an easy mark because she didn't care. "Now, can I have a place to sleep, alone?"

It had been a week since Mary left Magdala, the last time she'd been seen alive. For all Jesus knew, she could have been dead the entire time, or she could have died as recently as the day her torn and bloody clothes were found, or anytime in between. Or she could still be alive, though the evidence strongly suggested this was not the case. No one held out any hope for that, including Simon, who had returned to his home the day after the discovery of Mary's tunic. He had taken it home, and this is what he and her mother buried in a private service with only the two of them present. They had put the clothing in a small stone box, along with some flowers from the garden, and buried it just outside her bedchamber window. This way, should they ever be asked to leave the estate, they could easily retrieve the box and take the remains of their only daughter with them.

There hadn't been a day that Jesus did not spend the *entire* day searching for Mary's body. Many of the others had helped, too, at first, but as the days passed, they all, one by one, returned to their homes and their livelihoods: Peter and Andrew back to their fishing boat, James to the carpenter shop, all of them given up hope of finding any trace of her. By now, the wild animals would have scattered anything that might have been left to find a few days before. The absence of vultures in the sky was proof that any flesh and bone had been carried to the dens and burrows of the land's carnivorous creatures.

On the seventh day, Jesus resigned himself to the fact that Mary was gone. He had wondered all the days before, if he could find her body intact, whether he could bring her back to life, like he had with the boys in Nazareth. Was it even possible for him to do again? And, if so, were there time limits for resuscitation? One day? Two? Three, when according to religious tradition, the spirit abandons the body? If her injuries were severe, her body mutilated, did he have the healing power to restore her, to put her back together, whole and new? None of those questions mattered anymore. His beloved Mary was gone, and there was nothing he could do.

So on that seventh day, when he finally crawled out of bed, he got on his knees and prayed, just as he had every day. Today, though, his prayer was different. It was for the repose of Mary's soul, for his own ability to cope with the grief of her loss, for God's justice toward the person responsible for her death, and for an understanding of why God would allow such a thing to happen. Last, he prayed for the capacity to forgive—the murderer, God, and himself for his unwillingness to do so.

After four hours of dead sleep, Mary collected herself, lifted the door flap, and emerged from the tent to find Caleb waiting impatiently. "Thank you for that," she said.

Caleb ignored the gratitude and immediately began his rehearsed speech. "You will keep yourself looking your best at all times. When there is available water, you will wash yourself every day. You will keep your face painted; you will wear clean and colorful clothing; you will wear jewelry: bracelets, necklaces, earrings. All of these things I will buy for you, and you will pay me back from your earnings. You will sleep with whomever I say. If there is any discernment in the selection of clients, I will be the one to do it. I will negotiate fees. Sometimes, it will be four denarii and sometimes one. If the fee is three or four, you will get half. If the fee is two or lower, you will get one-quarter of whatever I get. I will provide breakfast, lunch, and supper.

"Anything else you want, food or otherwise, you buy with your own money. You and the two other women will do the washing for all of us. I will do the cooking. I will decide what we eat and when we eat it. The busier you are with clients, the less menial duties you will be required to perform. I suspect you'll be busier than the others, so they will shoulder most of the chores while you entertain." He smiled. Mary didn't.

When she didn't counter, he added, "And I will require some attention from time to time. I'll use all of you, but I suspect you will be my preference for the present time." He smiled again. "Would you like that, Mary? A little extra attention? A little preferential treatment all the way around?"

Mary looked him hard in the eyes. It actually scared him a little. "I don't like any of this. I think you're an awful man who preys on misfortune for personal gain. I'm here because I have to be, not because I want to be. BUT you're the only person who's given any care to me or done anything for me since I arrived in this godforsaken town, regardless of your motivations. That is why I am here. Not because I like it but because it's all I have. You—sad to say—are all I have."

"Well...uh...okay then," Caleb said, not sure whether he should be hurt or flattered. "Go and wash. Do you have a change of clothes?"

"No."

"You are about the same size as Hannah," Caleb said. "You can borrow from her until we go shopping tomorrow. She has jewelry, powders, perfume, all those things, as well. Go and see her when you return. She's in the next tent, busy. Be sure she's not busy before you go in." He tossed her a wash cloth and another for drying. Mary made her way toward the well.

When Mary returned, Hannah, the younger woman was sitting outside the tents with Caleb. She was attractive but looked tired and despondent. Her eyes and lips were painted. She had several jeweled bracelets on her arms, and her ears and nose were pierced with metal rings. Caleb introduced the two women, who said nothing, and then sent them inside with instructions to Hannah to outfit Mary in appropriate attire. "Hurry," he said. "It's almost evening. Men will be coming soon."

When the women reappeared, Caleb was pleased. He knew Mary was beautiful, but washed, with fresh clothes and a painted face, he could hardly believe his eyes, or his good fortune. The older woman, Sarah, was sitting with Caleb. She looked to be in her mid-twenties, Mary thought, and appeared just as tired and defeated as Hannah. Sarah stopped eating long enough to hand Mary and Hannah a prepared plate of food.

"Eat quickly," Caleb said. "Two more caravans have just arrived for the night. It'll be busy." He dropped his plate on the ground and hurried off to solicit business from the camp's newest residents.

When Caleb returned, two men were with him. Mary was the first chosen, and, after a moment of haggling over price, the client counted three coins into Caleb's hand. He then grabbed Mary by the wrist and pulled her into the tent. She didn't resist. She knew this was her lot and complied without protest. The act was painful, but she gritted her teeth and didn't make a sound. When he was finished, he quickly dressed and left without speaking. Before Mary could get up, another man came in and climbed on top of her, and after him another, then another. Mary lay there, her body in shock, her mind a blank. By the time the night ended, she had been violated—five or six times? She couldn't remember, and she no longer cared. There were no tears. She would sleep tonight and eat tomorrow. For a woman like her, there was nothing else to hope for.

Mary spent her time away from camp, walking the streets of the city, visiting the marketplace, and strolling along the seashore. She had money to spend but nothing to buy. She thought of Jesus and her parents but quickly banished such thoughts from her mind. They were painful and pointless, and dwelling on the past or the future was a vain pursuit for a woman of her occupation. The day was her only concern. She did wonder, though, as she gazed at the horizon on the sea, what lay beyond, what people and lands? As she looked at the homes that lined the streets—the grand mansions with their courtyards, and the smaller dwellings that housed people of lesser means—she questioned what might be going on inside, what it might be like to live again in a pleasant family of respect and love, instead of with a pimp and two other whores?

Suddenly, Mary was brought back to reality by the cheers of people in the streets. She looked and saw soldiers marching with spears in their hands. Behind them were more guards on horseback and behind them a palanquin carried by servants, six in front and six in back. It was the king.

Herod Antipas was the grandson and a successor of Herod the Great. He had a palace in Caesarea, a favorite among his many outlying homes, and he vacationed there often to escape his Jerusalem responsibilities and the watchful eye of his overseers, the Roman authorities.

Mary quickly moved to the side of the street and stood with the others as the grand parade passed by. When the palanquin passed the place where Mary was standing, there was a command to halt.

One of the guards was called to the carrier and after a brief instruction from the king, his finger pointing in Mary's direction, the guard walked over to her.

"The king wishes you to join him at the palace," he said. Then he called for two of the foot soldiers, gave them instructions, and said to Mary, "Go with these men."

"Wait," said Mary, but he ignored her and returned to his troops. The procession started again, and the soldiers led her away.

When they reached the palace, one of the soldiers stood with Mary while the other disappeared through a door. A moment later, he returned with a distinguished and matronly looking woman, who said nothing before grabbing Mary's arm and pushing her toward the same door she'd come from. They went down a long, arched hallway then turned into a room that was larger than Mary's parents' entire house. There were several long tables, each filled with food: lamb, fish, beef, and poultry; vegetables and fruits and breads of every kind; honey, wine, pomegranate juice, and milk. "Eat," said the woman. And Mary did hungrily.

When Mary had finished her feast, the woman stood and said, "Follow me."

They continued down the hallway until they entered a room twice the size of the one they'd just left. There were four baths—pools, really—each filled with perfumed water that permeated the air with a sweet aroma. A servant girl hurried over with a basket of rose petals, which she emptied into one of the pools. The older woman ordered Mary to disrobe, which she did.

"In," the woman demanded and gave Mary a slight push in the back.

She stepped into the pool. It was wonderfully warm, and she stepped in deeper, and then sat, submerged in the perfumed water and flower petals. The servant girl scrubbed Mary's back and shampooed and rinsed her hair, all under the careful supervision of the matron's seemingly scornful stare.

"Out," the woman commanded. She held out a towel for Mary and wrapped it around her. "Follow me," she said, and they walked to the other end of the room, where another girl rubbed Mary with perfumed oil.

She was then taken to another room where the woman clapped her hands, producing more servant girls. They seated her in a chair and began painting the nails on her fingers and toes. They traced her eyes with indigo and salved her lips with a substance that turned them ruby red. Her face and body were powdered, and she was dressed in a silk gown that lay on her skin like baby's breath. She had never felt anything so soft. They brushed her hair and curled it with long, slender rods of heated marble. When they had finished, the girls stood back to admire their handiwork.

"You are beautiful," one of them said.

The matron clapped her hands again. The girls bowed toward Mary, then turned and ran away.

"You are ready," the woman said, without a smile. "Follow me."

Mary followed the woman up three flights of stairs and into a room, a bedchamber that composed the entire third floor of the palace. The walls, columns, and floors were polished pink marble. Silk draperies of every color hung from the ceiling and walls and gently swayed with the movement of the ocean breeze. In the center of the room's entrance hall was a large circular fresco showing a bearded man driving a chariot: Herod. It was surrounded by four smaller circles: Herod's seal, the Lion of Judah, an open book (the Torah), and a bull (representing the power and virility of the king). Beyond the entrance was a sitting area and beyond that, three steps up, a hallway lined with huge potted palms, leading to a canopied bed as big as a room.

As Mary was taking all this in, she heard the door close behind her. When she turned to look, the woman was gone. She was alone, but she surmised it wouldn't be for long. She now knew why she was here.

An hour later, the massive door swung open, and the king entered, along with four guards. One stood beside Herod while the three others hurried to inspect the room for any possible intruders. When they returned, they bowed before him, and all four made their exit, closing the door behind them.

The king stared at Mary, who suddenly remembered proper protocol and lowered her head in a respectful bow. He continued his stare, which made Mary uncomfortable. She kept her eyes pointed toward the floor.

"What is your name?" he said condescendingly.

"It is Mary, sire."

"And what is your station? Do you have family?"

"Not here, sir. I am from…" *Screw it,* she thought. "I am from Magdala."

"Mary of Magdala." He let the phrase roll off his tongue, thinking himself brilliantly poetic. "What brings you to Caesarea?"

"My parents are dead. I have no other close family. I came here seeking work as a servant girl."

He nodded. "And have you found employment?"

"I have not."

"Well, perhaps I can find work for you here. We shall see." He offered his hand and she took it. "So, what do you think of the palace?" he asked boastfully. He made a wide sweep with his hand, inviting a panoramic view of the apartment before she gave her opinion.

"It's lovely," Mary replied.

"It is spectacular!" he corrected. He led her through the sitting room and up the steps.

The king was fat and effeminate. His voice carried a tone of arrogance, and his eyes projected the venomous cruelty that lived in his heart. He reminded her of the master, and she immediately despised him. When they were ten feet from the bed, he wrapped his arm around her and began to force her toward it. She resisted, more out of surprise than protest. After all, she'd known her fate from the second she entered the king's apartment. This didn't particularly bother her. It was something she did every day and would be doing now at the tent if she wasn't here. Besides, he was the king. Resisting his affections could mean death, but she didn't like the sudden violent change for no reason. She pushed back, which he seemed to enjoy. Then he threw her on the bed and began tearing at her clothing. Once he had exposed her body, he climbed on top of her. He didn't undress himself but simply raised his gown above his waist. For no reason, he slapped her across the face, causing her jaw to sting. Then he had his way with her. When he had finished, he collapsed on the bed beside her, breathless. In fact, she wasn't sure he would survive his full minute of physical activity. As soon as he recovered, he got up without a word. He stood above the bed and looked at her. She moved to cover herself.

"No!" he demanded. "I want to look at you." He stared at her for a long time. Then he said, "You will do. I will keep you. Now get dressed." He walked to a table and poured himself a cup of wine. "Guards!" he shouted.

Mary tried to piece her clothing back together, but it was torn too badly to repair. She had to hold the front of her gown with both hands to keep from exposing her breasts. The guards entered, along with the woman who had brought Mary to the apartment. Apparently, they'd been stationed just outside the door, awaiting the king's command. The woman took Mary's elbow and led her away, followed by the guards.

Mary was taken to a bedchamber where she was bathed and dressed in a nightgown by the servant girls, then left alone. She thought about her lot. This was certainly better than the tents and her situation at the camp. But she was still a whore, and she hated Herod more than Caleb. In any case, her life was not in her control. It was now the king who controlled her. He would decide her fate. She couldn't care less. She went to bed and slept well.

The next morning, breakfast was brought to her on a tray. She was dressed and attended to in every possible way. Unsure of what to do, she stayed in her room until noon, and then strolled about the palace for the rest of the day. She didn't see Herod or the matron that day or the next. If she wanted for anything, she simply asked, and it was brought or done for her.

In the days and weeks that passed, she was occasionally summoned to Herod's bedroom. She did her duty, and enthusiastically so, to gain and keep his favor. It was easy work, compared to what she had been doing for Caleb. Instead of several men each night, she had to entertain only the despicable Herod occasionally. Her lifestyle had certainly improved. This was the better way, she thought. Still, she didn't trust the king. Mentally, he was unstable. She feared his violent nature and his need to express his power over her.

When it was time for Herod to return to Jerusalem, he decided to leave Mary at the palace at Caesarea. There had been pillow talk about Mary accompanying him to the capital city, but, in the end, Herod decided that this wouldn't sit well with his queen. Herod had become affectionate toward Mary, and he knew his feelings would show. That, coupled with Mary's incredible beauty, would cause him headaches he didn't need. There were enough political tensions awaiting him in Jerusalem. He didn't need marital ones, as well. He would just have to make his trips to Caesarea more frequently than before.

Fearing his decision would be devastating to Mary, he decided to send the matron to break the news. Mary pursed her lips trying to restrain a smile as the woman explained that Herod would be going without her. The additional good news was that only a skeleton crew would be left behind to maintain the palace while Herod was away: a few servant girls to maintain the house and attend to Mary, four guards, and the two year-round gardeners—both local men who lived offsite with their families. Mary would have the run of the house and, by decree of the king, would be in charge of all the staff, including the guards, while he and the matron were away. It seemed Herod trusted her implicitly. *Big mistake.*

Mary watched from a window as the procession headed out of the city, complete with all the fanfare it had received upon its arrival weeks before. She waited an hour to make sure the caravan was well on the road—that nothing had been forgotten or that the king hadn't had a change of heart about leaving her, causing an unexpected return. Then she began to case the palace, room by room.

Mary took only money and jewelry, and only as much as she would be able to carry without slowing her down. She would have to travel fast. At first, she considered taking some of the palace's gold and silver items—plates, chalices, candlesticks—to the camp outside the city and fencing them to the caravan merchants. But most of the items carried the king's seal. Dishonest as most of them were, they probably wouldn't want to risk dealing or being caught with Herod's stolen property. Same with Caleb. Greedy as he was, he wouldn't want to be complicit in looting the king's palace. She didn't want to see Caleb again, anyway, ever.

Over the next week, Mary planned her departure. On Monday, she went to the dock and booked passage on a ship carrying supplies from Caesarea to Joppa. She paid the captain half in advance and was instructed to be aboard and ready to sail on Thursday. She spent all of Wednesday sewing pockets inside the tunic she would wear and more in the others she would take with her. Before going to bed, she filled the bottom of her bag with money and jewelry, and then packed her clothes, also lined with money and jewels, on top. On top of that, she packed more clothes, unencumbered with loot, just in case a guard, for some reason, decided to inspect her bag. She didn't really expect this. After all, she was in charge of the house, but better safe than sorry. If one of the guards did happen to see her leaving, and did have the audacity and gall to search her bag, he wouldn't rifle farther than the top layers of clothing to be convinced of its contents, and for fear of being too forward toward the king's new mistress.

When morning came, Mary dressed in the heavily weighted tunic, put the bag over her shoulder, and quietly slipped out of her room. She went down the hallway and out the back entrance facing the beach.

Her heart was racing. If she were caught stealing, she would surely be executed. She suddenly realized that, for the first time in a long time, she did care. She cared for herself, her safety, her future. If she could pull this off, she'd have a chance to start again. She would have her life back. And she would've stolen it back from at least one of the pigs that had stolen it from her.

Mary arrived at the ship just before daylight. She paid the captain the other half of her fare and went to the front of the boat where she could see the palace. No one would expect her to be up this early, nor would they even question her absence until the noon meal. Then one of the girls would come to her room to check on her. Curious, but not alarmed, they would search for her for an hour or so before alerting the guards. By the time they had searched the palace and the market and the rest of town, it would be evening. Then panic would set in. The next day, they would search and discover the missing treasures. Then they would panic some more and argue over who would be the emissary to go to Jerusalem and tell Herod. He would be violently furious. Heads would roll, perhaps their own. By that time, Mary would be safe in Joppa, preparing her next move, charting the course for the rest of her life.

The captain's voice called out to the ship hands to release the lines and cast off from the dock. The sails were raised, and, as the first winds caught hold, Mary's head jerked, and the boat veered right and pushed out into the sea. She kept an eye on the palace as long as she could and then the southern edge of the city until it, too, disappeared. She turned forward to face the wind and a new life and, at that moment, determined she would never look back again.

Chapter 4
Jesus' Journey

The peace of God that passes understanding fell upon Jesus like rain in the desert land. He welcomed it in gratitude and received the life-giving spirit that revived his withered heart. His love for Mary had not died with her. The pain of losing her had almost killed him too. In a blessed instant, though, his faith was renewed. He felt, and somehow knew, that her spirit was alive and well and at rest with God. He wept for the first time in weeks, as the hardened shell encasing his heart cracked and fell away. This time, his tears were born not of sadness but of joy, knowing that Mary was in the loving arms of a loving God. He knew he would see her again. He was at peace.

He also knew, suddenly and completely, that he could not remain in Capernaum. God was calling him into the world, and he yearned to see all of his Father's creation, to learn all the things God wanted him to know. Those places and things held the clues to his destiny. They were a part of his destiny. His time at home was at an end. It was time for his journey to begin.

Jesus' mother listened quietly as he told her of his plans. She didn't protest or interrupt as he talked. When he finished, she surprised him by saying that, in her heart, she knew this day would come. She had hoped and prayed that God might allow Jesus to stay near her, and she thought God had answered her prayers when he and Mary became engaged. "I just hope you're leaving for the right reasons, my son. That you are walking toward God's call and not away from a broken heart and the pain of what has passed."

"It is God's call, Mother. I am sure of it."

"Then I'm sure of it too," Mary said. "Go with God, and he will show you the way."

The next morning, all of Jesus' family gathered to bid him farewell. His brothers and sisters weren't as sure as his mother about his decision to leave. They were concerned about his mental state, considering the tragedy he'd just suffered, and the fact that he had no real destination other than where God would lead him. They worried, too, that perhaps Jesus relied on and talked to God a little too much.

"Can you at least tell us where you're going first?" asked Marion.

"I really don't know," said Jesus. "Probably to Jerusalem and then east from there."

"Please, let me give you some more money," James said. Despite pleas from both James and Mary, Jesus refused to take more than fifty denarii from the money he'd saved. The rest he'd placed in the shop account.

"I'll work as I go," Jesus said. "I prefer it that way. I don't want to get robbed of family funds on the road." He smiled, trying to lighten the air.

"But you're a partner in the shop," James pleaded. "You should take your share. At least put it in the bank."

"I have no need of it, James, really! Do what you want with it. Now, enough conversation. I have to get going." He hugged and kissed them all.

Then he and Mary walked down the street together. When they reached the edge of town, they embraced again. Jesus kissed her on the forehead and said, "I will see you again, Mama."

Mary nodded her head affirmatively. She wanted to speak but couldn't. Wiping tears from her eyes, she watched Jesus until he was out of sight. She believed she would see Jesus again, but her heart was heavy and her thoughts troubled as she considered the days to come.

On the second day of his journey, Jesus came to the village of Nain. Instead of continuing south to Jerusalem, he decided, instead, to go west to Caesarea. He wanted to visit the rich Greek and his son, with whom he had traveled the Mediterranean years before. Perhaps the man had never made his trip along the trade routes to the Far East, or, perhaps, he was planning another trip. In any case, it was only a small detour to Caesarea, and he wanted to see the man and his son again.

When he came upon the city, it was much bigger than he remembered, perhaps twice the size. But he knew that finding the house would not be a problem. It was right on the seashore and just north of the harbor tower. As he got closer, he wondered if the Greek would be there. It was the season for him to be in Caesarea, but what if he was on a caravan heading east or another sea cruise of the Mediterranean? He did love to travel. Or what if, for some reason, he had decided to spend the summer in Greece instead of Caesarea? He would find out soon enough.

Jesus made his way through the town and down the street that ran parallel with the harbor. When he passed the tower, he began looking for some familiar feature to help him distinguish the Greek's house as one among the many that lined the street. It suddenly occurred to him that he'd never seen the house finished. It was still under construction when he was last here, and there wasn't another house near it. Now, there were dozens of homes, stacked one after the other, with not twenty feet between them. He didn't have to wonder long. About five houses down from the harbor wall was a house unique to all the other Roman-style structures. Jesus recognized the Greek architecture immediately. Its roofline and columns reminded him of the Greek temples and government buildings he had seen in Athens. There was no doubt that this was the house he was looking for. A stone wall ran the length of the property, which Jesus followed halfway down to a gate with a wooden door. The gate wasn't locked, and there appeared to be no guards on the grounds. He walked through the gate to the front entrance of the house and pounded on the door, using an attached huge bronze doorknocker. An elderly man opened the door.

"Hello, Homer," said Jesus.

The man cocked his head slightly, trying to identify the stranger in front of him. There was some familiarity in the face and voice. "May I help you, sir?" he said finally, unable to make the connection.

"It's Jesus, Homer."

Homer's face brightened immediately, his recognition of Jesus suddenly clear. "Master Jesus, my dear friend. How good it is to see you again!" He started to bow, but Jesus grabbed his shoulders, raised him up, and kissed him on both cheeks.

"What brings us the honor of your presence, Master Jesus?" Homer asked.

"I'm here to pay respects to your masters, Sarba and Temarus."

Homer's smile faded. "Alas, Jesus, Master Temarus is here, but you will have to pay respects to Sarba in the grave. He died almost two years ago."

"I'm very sorry to hear this news, Homer. Your master was a good man."

"He was good to me," said Homer. "That is all I know."

There was a respectful silence. Then Jesus spoke. "So, Temarus. He is here in Caesarea?"

"He is. Please come in. I will get him." Homer disappeared and a minute later returned with an excited Temarus, barely maintaining protocol by letting his manservant lead him to his old friend. Just before he reached the door, he could stand it no more and shot around Homer, embracing Jesus with a hug that lifted his feet off the floor. "Jesus, I cannot believe you are here. It has been so long!"

"Ten years," Jesus said.

The two men spent the rest of the afternoon catching up on each other's lives. Jesus told Temarus about Joseph's death (which he had already heard about), his inherited trade and partnership in the carpenter shop (and subsequent boatyard), and his intention to see the world, traveling along the trade routes to the east. When Temarus asked Jesus if there was a woman in his life, Jesus answered, no. Temarus told

Jesus about his father's death, about the trip he and his father did take along the trade roads east (they didn't ask Jesus along because of the tragedy of Joseph's death), and about all the things inherited money can buy a young man. Temarus told Jesus there was not a woman in his life, either, but many women.

After dinner, Jesus asked Temarus about the possibility of another trip east and his tagging along.

"Like I said, already been there," Temarus replied. "It is a long trip and a long way between cities. The conditions are harsh and the bandits many. I still do a lot of importing and exporting with the East, but I rely on others to haul the merchandise.

"However," Temarus continued, "what I will do is finance a trip for you. I will furnish as many men and camels as you want. It is the least I can do for the kindness you showed me as a young boy and for your friendship to me and my father."

"I thank you, Temarus," said Jesus, "but I cannot accept your offer. If you were going anyway, yes, but if not, I'm just as happy to be on my own. I can go in whatever direction I want, stay as long as I want, or not return at all if I want. And traveling alone, I can earn my room and board along the way. That isn't as easily done in a crowd."

"At least let me furnish you a camel," said Temarus. "There is a breeding farm just outside the city."

"Thank you, Temarus. I may accept *that* offer, but animals can be a burden as well as an aid on the road. Especially for one in no hurry. The transportation is nice, but it's one more mouth to feed. Let me sleep on this and give you an answer in the morning."

"As you wish," replied Temarus. He clapped his hands, and two beautiful women appeared. "I am off to bed with one of these women. Take your pick, Jesus."

"Nothing for me, thanks."

"Seriously?"

"Seriously."

"Suit yourself," sighed Temarus. "Then I will take them both. Good night." He motioned to the girls, and they followed him from the room.

In a matter of seconds, Homer entered the room. "Follow me, Master Jesus. I will show you to your sleeping quarters." Jesus followed, and then slept.

The next morning, Jesus and Temarus were having breakfast on a terrace overlooking the sea. "I've decided I would like to take you up on your offer of a camel," said Jesus. "If it's still available."

"Of course. But why not spend a week with me before you leave? It is so good to see you again."

"It's been good to see you, too, and I appreciate the invitation, but I really should be on my way. I have many miles to travel."

"Indeed, you do," said Temarus. "If you take the main trade route from here to Chang' an, you will be covering a distance of more than seven thousand miles. One way! Any detours will add to that."

"And there will be detours, for sure," said Jesus. "Long ones. I'd like to go as far south as Nepal and, maybe deeper, to the Indian coast."

"Then you will be gone a long time, Jesus. Years."

Jesus nodded his head. He knew the journey would be long, and that was fine with him. He was in no hurry. As far as he was concerned, he had a lifetime to discover whatever it was God was calling him to. That was his life's goal. He looked at Temarus, who was looking at him. "So…"

"Let's go get you that camel," Temarus said.

Camels are remarkable animals. They have adapted physically and physiologically over a myriad of time to become the desert's best suited and most efficient form of transportation. Camels can go for a week without water, due to their uncanny ability to store and efficiently release and use this precious and rare desert commodity. A camel can lose up to a third of its body weight to dehydration without ill effects. And when it does have the opportunity to replenish its supply, it can "refill" itself by drinking in up to three gallons per minute!

They are able to eat almost anything due to tough mouths and strong stomachs, which is important in the desert where grass and grain can be scarce and where the sparse plants that do grow are generally scrubby and brier-covered.

Camel humps are made of fat and can supply the animal with energy when food can't be found. Their feet or paws are huge and uniquely adapted for walking over the desert sands without sinking. Their nostrils can close and their eyes are surrounded by shaggy eyebrows and long lashes to protect them from sand and dust storms. The camel's manure is dry enough to be used almost immediately as fuel for campfires.

They can haul up to seven hundred and fifty pounds in passenger or cargo. Because of an ability to tolerate body temperature changes of 10 degrees Fahrenheit, they can withstand the desert extremes of boiling hot days and freezing cold nights. In addition to their desert readiness, camels can provide meat and milk for food and fur (camel hair) for clothing.

The breeding farm was about ten minutes northwest of the city. There were forty or fifty camels, at least that many donkeys, half a dozen horses, twenty head of cattle, and hundreds of sheep and goats. Temarus greeted the breeder, introduced Jesus, and explained the purpose of their visit. The breeder instructed his drivers to gather a dozen camels into a corral near the barn.

"Take your pick," the man said. "They're all adults, trained and fit for the journey."

Most of the animals were the one-humped Arabian type, but there were a few of the Asian Bactrian (two-humped) variety. Jesus hadn't seen a two-humped camel before and, therefore, was attracted to the rarity of them.

"They're actually the more prevalent animal where you're going," said the breeder, "and better suited for the colder weather you'll experience as you move eastward."

Jesus knew nothing about camels, but he liked what he saw in the furrier Asian beasts. He examined their almost comical faces: huge glamorous eyes with long lashes, a flat ridiculous nose, and a mouth with a grin that seemed to extend from ear to ear. And while they all looked the same, generally, there was a personality or demeanor or *something* that distinguished each one from the other and reminded Jesus of people he knew. He amused himself by matching each camel with a person. One reminded him of Mary's father, Simon; another of Sarba the Greek; and one, Jesus thought, carried a peculiar and comical resemblance to Peter. Interestingly, this one seemed taken with Jesus too. Unlike the others, when Jesus took the camel's face in his hands, the animal didn't turn away. Instead, the two exchanged gazes for a full minute. Jesus' face broke into a smile, and the animal's face seemed to brighten as well. Then, with only a second of warning, the animal spit at Jesus, who managed to jerk his head out of the way just in time to avoid the thick projectile saliva aimed at him. It was Peter, alright. "I'll take this one," he said.

> *When Jesus and Peter were children in synagogue school, Peter had a nickname among the other children. They called him, "Rocky." This is the name Jesus gave to his camel. Rocky.*

Temarus paid the breeder for the camel, a saddle and reins, and various other supplies he insisted Jesus would need. After a brief riding lesson, Jesus and Temarus said their farewells, and Jesus rode away, south toward Jerusalem.

Just east of the city of Jerusalem was a place called the Mount of Olives: a beautiful and peaceful place where groves of olive trees dotted the landscape. Jesus' approach to the city from this direction was intentional. He'd come this way on his first trip to Jerusalem with his parents many years ago. He remembered, as a boy, seeing the city from this vantage point and how breathtaking it was. The top of Mount of

Olives was actually higher than the hill on which the city was built. From there, he could look over the wall into the great Judean capital, the City of God, built to its grandeur first by King Solomon and then again, after its near destruction, by Herod the Great.

At the southeast corner of the Temple Mount was the pinnacle of the Temple. It had been built on Jerusalem's highest point, and it rose high above all other structures. This was his destination. He would go to the Temple and pray for God's guidance and direction before continuing his journey far eastward. But first, he would pray here, among the olive trees, in this lovely and refreshing place that would always hold specialness for him. There was something about it that strengthened his heart and his spirit.

After an hour in prayer, Jesus started down the mountain toward the city. At the bottom, he took the less traveled path toward the northern wall. Near the northeast corner of the wall was a gate, seldom open for major traffic into the city. However, built into the gate was a smaller door just large enough for a man to pass through but not wagons and not camels. The door was known as "the eye of the needle." Jesus found a boy and gave him a coin with instruction to feed, water, and watch after Rocky until he returned. He then slipped through the small door and made his way up the street toward the Temple.

Jerusalem was a bustling and exciting city. It seemed that half the people he passed were either Roman soldiers or the religious elite: scribes, lawyers, priests or some other sort, each one wearing the robes of his particular sect. Some had phalanxes strapped to their foreheads. Some were carrying scrolls under their arms or reading aloud from parchment, constantly bowing as they walked. There were women, their faces covered with veils, dragging their children along with them, going who knows where? And beggars—so many of them—blind and crippled, sat along the sides of the streets, calling out for food and money. Shop owners were barking from their booths, trying to lure people toward them to examine "the finest merchandise in all of Jerusalem." Visitors—merchants and businessmen—from all parts of the world were walking in pairs or groups conversing in different languages, some of which Jesus understood and some which he did not.

When he finally reached the Temple, Jesus did the ritual bathing required before entering but bypassed the moneychangers selling doves for sacrificial offering. (He didn't believe God required or appreciated the blood sacrifice of animals for atonement and worship.) When he had finished his prayers, he walked back through the city, feeling at peace. God had still not given clear direction for his journey, but Jesus trusted that the Lord had brought him this far and would be with him to direct him the rest of the way.

Jesus exited the city through the eye of the needle and found the boy and Rocky waiting. "Thank you for your help," he said to the boy, and handed him another coin.

"Did you know your animal does tricks?" the boy asked.

"No," said Jesus. "I haven't owned him long."

The boy knew enough about animal training to teach them a few simple tricks and, as one who often "animal sat" for people with business in the city, this talent sometimes gained him another coin from amused owners. Rocky was sitting with his legs folded beneath him, making his shoulder height about the same as the boy's. "Watch," he said. "Rocky, are you glad to see your owner?" He discreetly placed his hand on the nape of Rocky's neck and pinched. Rocky nodded his head up and down.

Jesus smiled. "Excellent!" he said, and clapped his hands together.

"Now get up, Rocky," said the boy, lightly kicking the camel's ribs. Rocky reluctantly struggled to his feet. "Now, I want you to count to five." The boy placed his hand behind the highpoint of Rocky's right leg and pinched. The camel raised and stamped his paw on the ground five times.

"Very good!" exclaimed Jesus, aware of the boy's secret and not so slight-of-hand movement.

"Now," said the boy, standing in front of the camel, "I want you to give us a big smile!" He reached forward and flipped his finger against Rocky's upper lip. It did look as though Rocky was about to smile but, instead, a long stream of camel spit sprayed from his mouth and hit the boy's face with a syrupy splash. The youngster stood there for a second, slightly bent forward to let the goo drip from his face, and then used both hands to scrape the remaining mess from his mouth, nose, and eyes.

"Oops!" said Jesus.

"It happens sometimes," the boy lied, still in surprised disbelief and more than a little embarrassed.

Jesus genuinely felt sorry for the boy and tried desperately to suppress laughter, as he studied the boy's combined expression of shock and disgust. He took another coin from his pouch and carefully dropped it into the boy's slimy hand. "Well, thanks again," Jesus said, holding down a chuckle and quickly wiping tears from the corners of his eyes. "I guess we'll be going." He took Rocky's reins and led him away.

The boy said nothing, his head still tilted toward the ground, as the last drops of camel spit rolled off his face and joined the puddle at his feet.

Jesus traveled east from Jerusalem to the Jordan River and followed it north to Sartaba, then Pella and Gadara. From there, he veered northeast to Dium and then to Navah, where he rested and replenished supplies for the trip through the desert to Damascus. At Damascus, he took the main trade route east, known as the Silk Road. Silk was one of the chief items exported from the eastern lands, but there was as much business traffic going east as coming from it. Gold, silver, jewels, fabrics, furs, glass, ivory, spices, coffee, tea, tobacco, and opium were transported from land to land as each had abundance and in exchange for merchandise more rare and in demand.

The Silk Road was not a single highway but a series of routes that traveled east to west and north to south. And while the road created many towns and villages to service its travelers along the way, there were hundreds of miles of uninhabited wasteland, hot and cold, dry deserts and treacherous mountain terrain. There were also the beautiful cities, nestled in valleys surrounded and protected by mountains, where the earth was green and fertile. Though isolated, these great self-sufficient and cultural metropolises were populated by educated and prosperous people, who wanted for nothing except the business the caravans brought their way.

Braharam was one of these cities and the first place Jesus planned an extended stay. Bordered by the great rivers, the Tigris and the Euphrates, Braharam was known as the *Garden City*. Its abundance of water allowed for fruit orchards and farms growing virtually every kind of crop. Every home had green lawns and multi-colored flowering trees and shrubs. Braharam was also an intellectual center, with great libraries and schools of every kind, attracting both permanent and visiting scientists, philosophers, and scholars from all over the world.

Jesus had planned to study at Braharam for some time. In fact, he would stay until he was compelled to move on by God's call. Never again would he have the opportunity to read, study, and contemplate so many collected volumes of work from some of the world's greatest minds, or to sit with great teachers to listen and learn and debate the philosophies and religions of men.

After asking directions, Jesus found a caravanserai, where he rented a room for himself and corral space for Rocky. He ate and slept, and the next morning, he oriented himself to the city's opportunities for scholarly pursuit. The largest of the libraries was connected to a kind of walled cloister or monastery housing dozens of men. There were laboratories where the scientists conducted their experiments and theaters where philosophers posited their views to colleagues and students alike. The scholarly spent their days in booths along the sides of the library, reading and writing and sending their assigned assistants scurrying to retrieve books as references for their work.

Jesus spent the next several days pouring himself into his studies. He applied every waking hour to reading, attending lectures, and joining in the discussions of the many small groups of men that would gather each day at the cloister. In the evenings, he would visit Rocky and either walk or ride him to keep him exercised and their relationship familiar for the next leg of the journey.

As the days and weeks passed, Jesus became well known among the cloister community as one with promise. "He argues well," said one of the philosophers. "He is too religious, too focused, maybe even obsessed with his god, but he raises good points, in many areas of study, that are hard to counter."

"And you are not religious enough, my friend," said another. "Perhaps you could learn something of God from him if you listened."

"The gods are poppycock," said the first one. "They are an excuse for ignorance and a barrier to true wisdom. We will come to a full understanding of the place of men only when we lose the notion that there are gods above us who control our lives."

"Or," said the other, "we will come to an understanding of God only when we acknowledge the supremacy of One greater than ourselves and our place as his subjects."

"One? You believe there is only one god? Then, which one is it? There are many people who believe in many gods. And there are many kings who believe that *they* are gods. Maybe each person has his very own god. So who is right? Which is really God?"

"I cannot say which, but I believe there is a God who is God above all gods, the Lord of lords, the King of kings. That One, who is God of all, is the One God and, thus, the only God. Perhaps we do not yet know of this God, that we have no knowledge of him because we cannot yet conceive of him. This is why we must continue to seek him until we find him, to study and debate, to meditate and pray, until he reveals himself to us."

"Poppycock! Knowledge is the only god I seek, the only god I desire and will submit to. When your argument convinces me there is a god, then I will submit to you, O wise one. You can be my god." When he said this, he made a low sarcastic bow.

"You make light of a serious thing, my friend. It does not become you. But this is a debate for another time. Today we are deciding whether to accept Jesus into our cloister."

"You are right," said the first man. "Discussions about religion do not bring out the best in me, in speaking or listening with an open mind. As I said, Jesus argues well in many areas of study. He is a worthy opponent in disagreements and has good ideas concerning the issues of the day. I would accept him as a brother of the cloister."

"As would I," said the other man, "and as my student unless one of you others wish to claim him." No one spoke. "Then I will take it to council. Thank you, brothers." The small group dispersed to pursue other activities.

After the evening meal, the man approached the council room where the cloister leaders were conducting their daily business meeting. He took a seat in the chamber and waited his turn as other petitioners brought their concerns before the council. When his name was called, he walked to the front of the room where a group of fifteen men sat behind a large table.

"My brothers and teachers," he began, "a young man named Jesus has been studying at the cloister for several weeks. I bring a request from myself and seven other brothers to allow Jesus to become a resident of the cloister. His main interests are religion and philosophy, but he is well versed in other areas of study, including languages, and seems to have a real thirst for learning all the things we can offer him. I believe he has much to offer us as well."

"Is he a local man?" asked one of the council members.

"No, brother. He comes from Israel: Galilee, to be precise."

"And who will take him as a student?" asked another leader.

"I will. Our interests are much the same. I believe such a relationship would be of mutual benefit."

"Israel is a backward and violent place," said another council member. "It is occupied by the Romans and its king, Herod, is a frightful and horrid man. Does your Jesus carry any of the qualities we would expect from a resident of such a place?"

"He does not. As I have said, he is quite well educated. His demeanor is peaceful. There is no guile in him."

There was silence.

"Are there any other questions for Latamar?"

Silence again.

"Then I suggest we accept Jesus into the cloister with the customary one-year probationary status. If, after one year, he has proven himself worthy to be among us and made positive contributions to the community, he will be accepted permanently. Agreed, raise your hand."

All fifteen of the council members raised their hands.

"You may extend the invitation. Next petition, please."

The next day, Latamar found Jesus and extended the invitation. "You will live here with us. Your meals and clothing and any other needs will be supplied."

"That's wonderful," said Jesus, beaming at the news. He thought of Rocky. "I have a camel. May I bring him here?"

"We have camels, and asses, too, of the human and animal variety," Latamar quipped. "Many of our brothers travel from time to time, so we need them for transportation. You can bring your camel here, but everything is community property. Once here, he belongs to the cloister."

Jesus swallowed hard. He knew he would not remain at the cloister forever, and, when he left, he would want to take Rocky with him. "Perhaps I should just continue to board my camel elsewhere."

Latamar began to get the picture. "Look, Jesus, not everyone stays in the cloister for a lifetime, but that should be your intention going in. Your monetary needs will be supplied while you are here, but that does not include money for maintaining your own private property. Unless you have a great amount of wealth, and if you do, it should be given over to the cloister, you are not going to be able to board your camel elsewhere. If keeping your camel means more to you than living fully immersed in this community, then perhaps you should decline the invitation."

"I should think about this," said Jesus. "I really do want the experience of living in community, but I wouldn't be truthful if I told you my intention was a lifelong commitment. I can't commit to that because I've already made a commitment to God. I know that, eventually, when my time here is fulfilled, God will call me to continue the journey, and I must follow where he leads me. This is one stop along the way."

Latamar took in a deep breath and slowly exhaled. "Then there is nothing to think about. I know you are right, Jesus. I believe you have a true calling from God, and you must follow it if you are to be faithful to the One who sent you. You can continue to do here as you have done. Come to the library every day and continue your studies. Join in the discussions and debates with the brothers. Learn from us and allow us to learn from you. When the time comes for you to go, go in peace and follow God's direction. Perhaps, some day, when your journey is done, you will return to us and tell us what God has revealed to you, so that we, too, may know him and live according to his truths."

Jesus smiled at Latamar and laid a hand on his shoulder. "You already know much more than you think you know, Latamar. And, in time, God will reveal these things to you."

Latamar was suddenly overcome with emotion. As he looked at Jesus, he felt a great love for the man but also a sense of grief. He couldn't tell if it was because of the loss of a true friend (he knew Jesus would very soon be moving on) or because of a premonition that Jesus' journey would be a difficult one, filled with suffering and pain. "Well, if you will excuse me," he said, "I have a rather embarrassing report to make to the council." Sadness consumed him as he walked away from Jesus.

It didn't take long for the call Jesus was expecting to come. He was awakened from sleep one night by a voice that told him it was time to move on. Jesus immediately got up and dressed, made sure all his belongings were in his bag, made his bed, and quietly slipped out the door and into the stable yard. He lit a lamp and saddled Rocky, who seemed as eager to go as Jesus. *Maybe the camel had heard a voice as well.* As was establishment policy, the room and stable rates had been paid a day in advance, so there was no settling up to do. Jesus quietly led Rocky out of the corral, past the house, and into the street. It was dark and quiet; not even a dog was barking. The whole town was asleep. When they reached the edge of the city, Jesus had Rocky kneel. He climbed into the saddle, tapped the camel's neck as instruction to rise and then gently dug his heels into the animal's ribs. Rocky responded by moving forward in a motion that was slower than a trot but faster than a walk. It was still hours till daylight, but the moon was full and lighted their way.

By the time of the next full moon, thirty days into their journey from Braharam, Jesus was beginning to realize just how isolated and harsh sections of the trade route could be. In almost all that time, except for a couple of small caravans traveling in the opposite direction, they hadn't seen another living soul. For the last ten days, they had not even seen a wild animal, not even an insect! The land they were traveling was barren and dry, void of any grass or shrub or tree. During the day the temperature exceeded 100 degrees Fahrenheit; at night, often less than 20.

Jesus didn't mind the isolation from other people. In fact, he felt certain that he was meant to travel these "between times" of his journey alone. It was the nothingness of the desert Jesus found disconcerting, the eerie emptiness and lifelessness that surrounded him, as far as the eye could see.

It had been ten days since they passed any hold of water and almost a week since Rocky had drunk. Five days ago, Jesus had given Rocky a full waterskin but even that was little more than a drop to a dehydrated camel. Jesus was down to the last third of his last waterskin. He knew sharing this would do nothing for Rocky, and almost certainly mean death for him. They had to find water soon but where? The snow-capped mountains that surrounded the desert floor and provided occasional streams and oases had, apparently, taken a sharp turn without Jesus noticing. By the time he did, they were so far away, he could barely see them, and so were their chances of catching any runoff from the melting snow. If it was even still heading in their direction, it would likely pool or evaporate before reaching them. It was too late to turn north toward the mountains and pointless to continue east in the hope of finding water. Yet, this was the main route. Countless people had traveled it before, and they must have found water. He wished he had traveled with a caravan over this worst part of the wilderness. He wished he was with some experienced traveler with knowledge of the route, someone who knew the exact location of the next water source. Surely, there is something—a pool, a stream, a well—and surely it is soon, and surely it is here on the main road east! He made his decision. He would stay the course.

Then he abruptly turned north!

An hour later, Jesus was certain he'd made a mistake. The rocky terrain rose over hills and then down into deep gullies. As he maneuvered back and forth to find a passable route, he lost all sense of direction and regretted not following his initial instincts, staying on the road and the course east. But he had wasted too much time. An hour off the road, it would be suicide to turn back now, even if he could find his way.

Rocky was clearly in distress. His breathing was labored, and his nostrils flared as he inhaled and exhaled the dry air. His head was hung low, searching for the slightest hint of moisture in the arid ground. They traveled for another hour, and nothing in the landscape changed. They could be going in circles for all Jesus knew. He had long ago loosened his grip on the reins, allowing Rocky to determine their path through the desert maze.

The hot sun, the monotonous scenery, and the sway of Rocky's gait was causing Jesus fatigue. He was just beginning to nod when Rocky suddenly stopped in his tracks. He lifted his head high, and his parched nose twitched as if detecting some new and unfamiliar scent in the air. He let out a loud, pitiful, almost panicked cry and then took off in a dead run up the hill in front of them. Jesus feared his friend might be dying and, this, the beginning of his death throes. He pulled back on the reins to try and slow Rocky's gait but it had no effect. The camel continued to struggle up the embankment as fast as he could go. When he reached the top, he hesitated for a second to survey the gully below and then began bounding down the hill at breakneck speed. Jesus held on for dear life as Rocky stumbled down the steep decline. Jesus knew, if the animal lost its footing completely and fell, it would probably kill them both, so he did the only thing he could to save himself and possibly his friend. He threw his right leg over the saddle and leaped off his steed, hoping the lighter load would help Rocky keep his balance and reach the bottom of the ravine safely. Jesus landed on his feet, but the steep bank and rocky ground caused him to lose his equilibrium, and he slid face first several feet down the hill. When he finally stopped, he sat up and wiped the dirt and tears from his eyes. His face and chest stung from a hundred tiny cuts and scrapes inflicted by the sharp rocks, some of which were still attached to his body. When his eyes cleared, he saw that Rocky had made it to the bottom safely, and then he saw what had caused the animal's sudden bolt. Water! A tiny stream, maybe a few inches wide and just as deep trickled along a crease at the gully's base.

Rocky fell to his knees and sucked at the life-giving liquid. He bit up chunks of the mud trying to absorb its moisture into his parched mouth and throat. Jesus ran down the hill and frantically began digging with his hands to make a pool from which Rocky could drink. The trickle of water was not enough to keep up with the animal's intake, and as blood cells and muscles battled over the small amount of moisture trying to hydrate his system, Rocky cried out in pain. Too little water was worse than none at all. The shock was killing him. Jesus grabbed the last of his water from the saddlebag and emptied it into the pool. It was less than a quart and was sucked up in a single swallow. Rocky was now stretched out on his side and in agony as the severe dehydration caused his muscles to contract and cramp.

Suddenly, the wind began to blow. Jesus smelled moisture in the air. Billowing clouds rolled in above them. *Please, God, let it rain.* As he looked up at the sky, a single rain drop fell on his face, then another and another. Within a minute, it was pouring down. Within five minutes, the tiny stream had widened to two feet, and five minutes after that, it had become a rushing torrent that caused them to have to retreat several feet back up the hill. Rocky drank gallon after gallon until his body was saturated and his thirst quenched.

The rain lasted little more than an hour, and the stream receded as quickly as it had risen. It was almost dark, so after filling his waterskins,

Jesus took a blanket from his saddlebag and settled in for the night.

The next morning, knowing that water flowed south, he led Rocky along the path of the stream, following it back to the trade road. Once on the road, they didn't travel far before coming upon a small oasis and caravanserai. There they rested for two days, allowing Rocky to recover fully.

For the next three months, Jesus and Rocky traveled without incident. The closer they came to their next destination, the city of Samara, the more populated the area. There seldom was a time when they were more than two days between villages or caravanserais. The traffic had increased along the road, and they often passed two or three caravans in a single day. At night, if they were between villages, they could usually camp with a caravan for safety.

The only thing troubling Jesus now was a lack of funds. He hadn't intended to spend so much on food and lodging, but after their near brush with death in the wilderness, he found it difficult to pass up shelter and meals when they were available. He wanted them to be in their best condition in case such hardship confronted them again.

At the next village, Jesus paid room and board for himself and Rocky with one of his last two coins. There was no work to be had and, thus, no way for him to earn money in the small villages, and they were still a couple of hundred miles and ten days from Samara. Once there, he could find a job and replenish his funds. Until then, he and Rocky would either go hungry and cold, or he would have to find another way to restore his money pouch.

He emptied the saddlebags that Temarus had prepared for him to see if there was something he could sell. The only things of worth were a silver chalice and the three thick camel furs he used to make his bed on the cold nights when he slept outside. The chalice he could do without. He hardly used it anyway, usually choosing the convenience of drinking directly from his waterskin. In Samara, the cup would bring the equivalent of five, maybe six, denarii, but here he would be lucky to get one. The furs, on the other hand, would be more valuable in this outpost town than in Samara where such things were plentiful. He could get three, maybe four, denarii for each of the furs. If he sold them all, that would be enough to get him the rest of the way. However, if he sold all his furs and found himself stranded between villages and out in the elements for a night along the way, he would surely freeze to death. He determined he could survive with two furs: one to lie on and protect him from the ground and another for covering himself. He also had a couple of cloth blankets to wrap himself in as added protection. He would still be cold but he wouldn't freeze. He would sell one fur now and, if he needed to, make a decision on his other belongings down the road.

He rifled through the rest of his bag to see if there was anything else he might have missed—a couple of tunics, a couple of books, a flask of wine, a few pieces of stale bread and some dried meat. Then he saw something else in the bottom corner of the bag. It was a small dark lump of cloth he hadn't noticed before. Inside the cloth, he found a leather pouch tied at the top with a string. He opened it and inside were twenty shekels (equivalent to fifty denarii)! Temarus must have put them in the bottom of the bag, knowing Jesus wouldn't have accepted them if they had been offered, and also knowing that Jesus wouldn't find them until he was well on the road, unable to refuse the gift. Jesus smiled, thinking of his friend who, apparently, knew his travel needs better than he did. It was a long journey, he had told Jesus—"seven thousand miles, one way." Jesus never imagined how far seven thousand miles could be.

For the next eight days, Jesus and Rocky ate, slept, and traveled well. There was no shortage of food, bed, company or means to supply their needs. By design, they traveled alone during the day as Jesus continued to contemplate the meaning of his journey. The mountains had turned back inward toward the road, and, as they climbed in elevation, the weather turned colder. All day, they had been on a steady incline and Rocky was clearly fatigued. Jesus dismounted, so as to ease the animal's load, and walked alongside the grateful beast until his own legs began to ache.

When they reached the top of a mountain pass, it afforded Jesus a view of what lay ahead: another wilderness—miles and miles more of mountainous terrain. He could see the serpentine road as it wound its way up and down and around through the uninhabited land. There would be no warm place to stay tonight (or for the next few), so he began to look for a cave or an outcropping of rocks to give them shelter from the wind.

He found a wide crease between two huge boulders, and they were able to slip in deep enough until the rocks formed a ledge over their heads. They were protected from the weather on three sides, but it was still cold. Jesus had Rocky lie down, and he got out his furs to make a bed, one beneath him and two on top. Then he pressed his back against Rocky's side for extra warmth. He was thankful again to Temarus for the furs, and for the money that prevented him from having to sell them. He was thankful to God for the shelter and the friend beside him. He finished his prayers, closed his eyes, and went to sleep. And then it started to snow.

The next morning, Jesus awoke to find several inches of snow on the ground and a tall drift at the opening of the shelter. After building a small fire from camel dung, he emptied a saddlebag of grain on the ground for Rocky, and then shoveled snow from the drift into the bag. He held it over the fire until the snow melted, then repeated the process again, and again, until the bag was full of water. When Rocky had finished eating, Jesus lifted the bag to the camel's mouth and held it there until the animal drained it dry. After Jesus fed himself with bread and water, he led Rocky out of the shelter and began the trek across the mountains.

By the end of the day, Jesus reckoned they had traveled at least ten miles. They were at a lower elevation, so he couldn't see far beyond him. From what he could see, though, there were only more mountains and wilderness ahead. It had been cold all day. He was freezing; the mountain wind chilled him to the bone. It was almost dark, and he'd not been able to find any sort of enclosed shelter like the night before. The best he could do was to find a large boulder to shield them from the north wind. It was barren land, and there was nothing with which he could build a fire suitable for providing substantial warmth. (A little camel dung was fuel enough to melt snow, but it wouldn't even begin to thaw his cold bones.) Jesus had Rocky lie down, feet and legs beneath him, and straddled himself across the animal's back. He then covered them both with the blankets and furs to keep them as warm as possible. Between the fur and Rocky's body warmth, Jesus felt almost cozy, at least warmer than he'd been all day. He hoped, for Rocky's sake, the pile of flesh and fur was symbiotic.

Jesus awoke warm and rested. He would remember this sleeping arrangement for future cold nights. He took out a piece of bread for himself. There were only two more saddlebags of grain for Rocky, so he wouldn't feed him until evening. He wasn't sure how many more days of wilderness they had left. By Jesus' reckoning, they should've reached Samara by now—a day ago, in fact. They were still on what appeared to be a well-traveled road, but the suddenly diminished traffic and the extra day of travel made Jesus wonder if they had somehow strayed from the trade route and missed Samara altogether.

Almost immediately after starting out, the road began to rise again. The steep incline made Jesus' legs ache, and the higher elevation and labored walking made his breathing short and more difficult. He wanted to ride but knew that would add stress and weight to the camel, so he continued to walk, stopping frequently to rest.

When the better part of the day was done, Jesus noticed that they seemed to be coming to a mountain peak. From there, he would be able to get a clear view of what lay ahead. As soon as his vision cleared the top of the mountain, he couldn't believe his eyes. A bucolic valley lay below them. Vineyards and tea fields, orchards and cultivated gardens stretched up the mountainsides to form a giant green bowl. At the bottom, in the center of the valley, was majestic Samara, the *Gem City of the East*. Not five hundred yards below them was thick emerald-colored grass and below that wheat and barley fields.

Rocky let out a bellow of relief and excitement and began pulling Jesus down the mountain. He reluctantly allowed the animal to bite off stalks of the grain as they walked, hoping not to raise the ire of some observant and protective farmer. The closer they got to the city, farmhouses began to dot the landscape, then larger estates with opulent palaces. The stone-built city was a bustling metropolis and magnificent as well, with businesses and trading markets, monasteries and temples, schools and observatories. Every street was paved, and an elaborate aqueduct system provided running water to individual homes. A city of great wealth and trade, Samara was also a center for religion, philosophy, and astronomy, and some of the world's greatest minds were resident here. It seemed to Jesus that every culture, race, and people were represented among its citizenry.

As tired as Jesus was, he was fascinated by Samara's beauty and busyness, and he walked the entire length of the city's main street before settling in at a caravanserai at the other end of town. By the time he got Rocky stabled and had had a brief rest in his room, it was evening and suppertime. He washed and then joined the other guests at a table where his host had set the evening meal. Jesus ate ravenously from a spread of rice, meat, fruits, tea, and wine. The conversation at the table was lively, and he learned much about all the things Samara could offer him during his stay there. He listened with particular interest when the subject turned to astronomy and the great observatories of the city.

The next morning, Jesus rose and joined the others for breakfast. After checking on Rocky and seeing to the animal's food and water, he got directions to the largest of the observatories, *Observatorie Asmara*, and made his way back toward the center of town.

The *Observatorie Asmara* was a formidable stone structure that stood four stories tall and was capped with an oval-shaped dome in the center of the roof. The building was surrounded by a twelve-foot-tall wall with a double-door gated entrance allowing access from the street. There were no guards and no apparent admission procedure, so Jesus went through the gate and entered the building. The entire first floor was a single room lined with large stone columns. In the center of the room were several glass-topped tables with parchments beneath the glass, showing hemispheres of stars and constellations, and with lines drawn between the stars. Some of the lines were straight from star to star, with numbers written alongside the lines; others had connecting lines forming animals or men. On the walls of the giant hall were stone tablets, some with writing, others with objects resembling the sun and moon and other heavenly bodies carved into them. There were also other parchments hanging from the walls, each one framed under clear glass. Only a few other people were in the great hall, meandering around the room and observing the various exhibits. In the back corner was a spiral staircase that led to the upper floors. After a few minutes of minimal curiosity and courteous study of the first floor displays, Jesus decided to take the stairs to the second floor.

The make-up and activity on the second floor was quite different. There were doors to rooms on each side of a wide hallway that traveled the entire length of the floor. In the center of the hallway were rows and rows of filled bookshelves and cabinets with all kinds of tools and instruments used for drawing and measuring. People were scurrying in and out of the rooms to replace a book or instrument, and then they would retrieve another and disappear into a room again.

Jesus walked over to one of the open doors and peeked inside. At the far end of the room was a little round man sitting on a stool and working at a table. He was using a compass to draw circles on a large piece of paper and a ruler to measure the distance between the circles. Jesus lightly tapped on the side of the door. The little man held up a hand to silence the interruption. He made one last mark and scribbled something—numbers or words—beside it, then spun around to acknowledge his guest. He stared at Jesus for a few seconds, then his eyes widened as a slight smile appeared on his face.

"Your Majesty," he said. He stood and made a sweeping bow.

Jesus simultaneously turned and stepped aside to make room for the royal visitor. There was no one behind him. He turned back to the man at the table. "Pardon?" he asked.

"King Jesus! We've been expecting you. The stars said you would come."

"How do you know my name?" Jesus asked, puzzled. "And why do you call me king?"

"Because that is what you are," said the little man. "King of what, we do not know. We had suspected you to be the king and deliverer of Israel, but since the Romans still rule the land, and Antipas, Herod's grandson, sits as their puppet king, perhaps you have not yet come into your kingdom. Perhaps you have come *here* to conquer and rule. Do you have your army with you?"

"I have a camel," said Jesus. "I haven't come to conquer anything, but to study and learn."

"Ah, then you are in preparation for your kingship. This is wise."

Jesus was growing more uncomfortable with the conversation. "How do you know me?" he repeated.

"We visited you, when you were born. Or, at least, when you were still a babe. A star directed us to you. We traveled months from this place to Bethlehem, and then to Jerusalem and Nazareth. The heavens said a new king would be born, a great king, so we followed a star that led us to you. We brought you gifts—gold, frankincense, and myrrh— as homage and to celebrate your birth. You are a king, Jesus, or you will be. The stars have predicted it, and the stars are never wrong. One must only learn to read them correctly."

"Then, perhaps, you misread them. I am no king. I am Jesus, son of Joseph the carpenter, son of Mary, the daughter of Joachim."

"You know as well as I do, Joseph is not your *real* father. You are from a royal bloodline, conceived in your mother's womb before Joseph knew her as his wife. The stars told us this, and so did your mother."

Jesus' head was reeling now. How did this man know these things? Neither Joseph nor Mary had told Jesus this story, but somehow he had always known this to be true. Even as a child, he knew Joseph was not his birth father. He had always loved Joseph as a parent, but he had never seen anyone as his father except God. "Do you know who my father is?"

"We do not. We have asked this question of the stars, but they have not revealed the answer. Your mother told us the spirit of god came upon her and impregnated her; which god, she did not say. We did not question her hard on this matter. We are not much for belief in gods. We have seen no evidence of them in the stars."

"Then who directs the stars and who speaks through them?" Jesus could not resist the opportunity for a little theological banter.

The little man grinned broadly, revealing the very few yellow teeth left in his mouth. "This is a wise question, King Jesus, one that we have pondered, but the answer remains elusive. Perhaps we can argue this with you when we are all together, but now I have important work to do, so if you will excuse me. We are excited you have come. Come back tomorrow, and we will set aside some time to talk."

"You keep saying '*we*,'" Jesus questioned. "Who are '*we*?'"

"My name is Gaspar. My friends, Melchyor and Balthazar, traveled with me to find you. We have all looked forward to your predicted visit to Samara. Unfortunately, Melchyor died last year. Balthazar is at a foundry, just outside of town, overseeing the making of some instruments we need for our work. He will be back tomorrow. You come back tomorrow."

Jesus left, feeling a bit queasy in his stomach and troubled in his mind by his conversation with Gaspar and all that the man knew about him. Still, he was eager to meet with him and Balthazar tomorrow. He spent the rest of the day touring the city and thinking on the things Gaspar had told him.

The next morning, Jesus was up and on the street early. He was anxious to meet and talk with the two men, but he didn't want to arrive before Balthazar, so he continued his sightseeing around the city. At noon, he had lunch at an outside teahouse, then slowly made his way back toward the observatory. He climbed the steps to the second floor and went to the laboratory where Gaspar had been working the day before. No one was inside, so he went to the next room, which was also empty, then to the next, where a man was bent over a table measuring and writing on some sort of celestial chart.

"I'm looking for Gaspar," said Jesus.

"Next floor," the man said without looking up.

Jesus took the stairs to the third floor. It was similar to the one below: a large open hallway with bookshelves and cabinets in the center and surrounded by small individual workrooms. He walked down the corridor, peering into each open doorway until, finally, he saw Gaspar and another man carefully examining several strange looking objects, no doubt the newly manufactured devices Balthazar had brought from the foundry.

"Gaspar?" Jesus said softly.

"Ah, King Jesus!" Gaspar said, as he turned in Jesus' direction.

"Please don't call me that," said Jesus.

"Have you changed your name?" Gaspar questioned.

"King, I mean. Don't call me king."

"As you wish, sire." said Gaspar. "Balthazar. This is him. King Jesus."

Jesus winced and bowed his head toward the man. He looked younger than Gaspar, though there were streaks of gray in his long hair and beard, and where Gaspar was short and round, Balthazar was tall and lean.

"Gaspar told me you had come," said Balthazar. "We have long awaited your visit. I am sorry Melchyor is not here to meet you and witness this day. Gaspar tells me you have come to learn the ways of astronomy and astrology. It is wise for a king to know of these things or, at least, to know people who do."

Jesus ignored the mention of his royal title again. "I am on a journey to learn, and I am open to learning many things. But mostly, I seek to learn God's will for my life—my purpose and destiny as a servant in God's kingdom."

"A servant in another's kingdom? That is not the talk of a king."

"I am not a king!" Jesus protested, a little louder than he intended. The two men studied him in silence.

Jesus sighed. "I must admit, a study of the stars hadn't crossed my mind. Still, if you're willing to teach me, I'm willing to learn. There may be something in it that will aid my personal quest. First, I'd like to know more about your visit to Nazareth and what my parents told you. Gaspar said my mother confided in you that Joseph was not my father, but that God's spirit came upon her and conceived in her womb."

"We have heard such stories before," said Balthazar. "Surely, you have as well. Mythological stories abound of gods seducing human women and producing offspring that become demigods themselves, or the favorites of gods who grant them special blessings and powers. We did not question your mother's indiscretions then, and we do not now. They were likely forced upon her, anyway, by some passing prince or king. You do have a royal bloodline, however; the stars have told us this. That is why we traveled to pay homage to a new king. That is your destiny, King Jesus: to find *your* kingship, to come into *your* kingdom."

"I have felt this, without knowing it," Jesus said. "What my mother told you. No one has told me of these things before, but I've always known that God was my true Father."

"And which god would this be?" Balthazar asked.

"There is only one God," said Jesus emphatically. "The God of Israel."

"I'm sure the other nations of the world would be surprised to learn this," Gaspar said, with a near toothless grin.

"Then you don't believe in God, even a God of the stars?"

"We believe in *no* gods; we *can* believe in *all* gods," said Gaspar.

"We just need someone to show us a god, to prove the gods' existence, scientifically. And that is the argument you and I promised each other yesterday. Come, let us teach you about the stars, and you can teach us about your God."

The two men then began to show Jesus all their different tools for plotting charts and measuring distances of millions of miles, the formulas for figuring complicated mathematical equations and the meanings of the movements and changes in the sun, moon and stars.

When it was evening and their stomachs were growling with hunger, the men decided to call it a day. They all agreed to meet the next morning to continue Jesus' tutelage.

"King Jesus, have you ever seen a sextant?" Balthazar asked.

"I don't even know what a sextant is," said Jesus.

Balthazar raised his eyebrows and smiled. "Tomorrow morning, fourth floor."

"I'll be there. Well, good night."

The two men bowed in unison and said, "Good night, Your Majesty."

"Oy vey!" Jesus muttered to himself, as he turned and left the room.

The following day, Jesus entered the observatory and climbed the stairs to the top floor. It was different from the others in that it consisted of only one large room. It was bare except for a huge machine of some sort that sat in the center of the floor and extended up through a hole in the roof. Balthazar and Gaspar were there, waiting. Upon seeing Jesus, they bowed together and greeted him, "Your Majesty."

Jesus tried again. "Please do not bow to me, and please call me Jesus." He thought about commanding them to do this but decided that would defeat the purpose. "And what is this?" he said, amazed and staring at the contraption before him.

"This is a sextant, an astrolabe," said Balthazar, "the largest and most complex in the world. Smaller ones are used to navigate the sea. With this one, we can measure distances between the earth and the stars or that between the stars.

"For instance," said Gaspar proudly, "with this instrument, we can tell you that the sun is ten, maybe eleven, million miles from the earth! And some of the stars as much as four times that far away!"

"Wow!" said Jesus, as he walked around the machine. Its frame and gears were made of metal, most intersecting with another so that they turned together. There were giant wooden spokes, like those on a ship's wheel, protruding from the machine and about waist high. These were for manually rotating the machine, the base of which sat on a round platform that rolled inside a metal track. There were wooden parts, such as the heavy braces that held the instrument together and steady, and various hanging ropes to pull high levers back and forth and open and close lids on the tops and bottoms of long tubes. In the center of the sextant was a long cylindrical tube, like a giant column, that rose up and through a hole in the roof about three times the size of the tube. They walked Jesus through the workings of each part of the machine.

"And what does that do?" Jesus asked, pointing to the cylinder.

"That, King Jesus, is the only one of its kind in the world! It is a stargazer," said Gaspar excitedly. It has a special magnifying glass at each end that brings the heavenly bodies closer. We can observe the moon closely enough to see what appear to be mountains and valleys in what we suspect to be some sort of sponge-like material."

"The moon is made of sponge?"

"Sponge-like," interjected Balthazar. "We can't be certain of its composition."

"If you'll come back tonight, we'll let you have a look through the stargazer," said Gaspar. "In fact, Balthazar and I have talked, and if you could humble yourself enough, dear king, to live here at the observatory with us, we could work together day and night and teach you all that we know of the stars."

"And I could teach you about God?"

"Uh, sure," said Gaspar, less excited about the idea of being a student than a teacher.

"Great!" said Jesus. "I accept! I'll go and get my things now, and I have to make some arrangements with the caravanserai for my camel. I should be back here by noon. Then we can get started."

"Good. We'll be working in Balthazar's lab on the third floor," Gaspar called out to Jesus, who was already bounding down the stairs.

Jesus settled his bill with the caravanserai and paid a month in advance for Rocky's boarding. The caravanserai had a lush green pasture where the camel could graze and roam, and once each week he would receive a sweet-feed treat of barley and oats. Jesus packed his things and hurried back to the observatory to begin his new education.

For the next several weeks, Jesus worked closely with the two astrologers, absorbing as much as he could of their knowledge and skills. He read from assigned books, learned the names and uses of their many instruments and the new mathematics of geometry and calculus. He listened to lectures, posed questions, and argued well the various astronomic theories of the day. His teachers and the other resident scientists were most pleased with his rapid progress and abilities in the field. He spent hour after hour at night, looking through the stargazer, fascinated by all that he saw. Though he did not mention it, as he observed the moon, he doubted his teachers' theory that the moon was made of sponge. He did not see it. To him, it looked more like the desert wilderness he had crossed between Braharam and Samara.

Gaspar and Balthazar taught Jesus about the stars, and he taught them about the God of Israel, who ruled over the heavens and the earth. He told them the stories of Abraham and Moses and Joshua and Elijah: of how God had caused fire to rain down from the sky to destroy the cities of Sodom and Gomorrah and, again, to defeat the priests of Baal at Mount Carmel; and of how God caused the sun and moon to stand still during the battle of Jericho. He told them of how God created the sun and the moon and the stars and set them in their places. He told them that the God of Israel was, in fact, the God of all creation—of all people and things—and they believed Jesus, and they believed in God.

Jesus spent a portion of every day, speaking and teaching about God. Many of the observatory's scientists listened to him, and they, too, became believers. Each day, Jesus grew stronger in spirit and felt closer to God. He was renewed in the purpose of his journey—that he had been sent by God to learn and prepare for the task God would set before him. God's plan for Jesus' destiny.

Jesus and Balthazar and Gaspar spent many more days together teaching and learning from each other. Until, one night in a dream, Jesus heard a whispering voice that told him it was time to go. The next morning, as Gaspar and Balthazar and the observatory slept, Jesus rose and packed his things. He did not wake his friends. He went to the caravanserai where Rocky was waiting at the gate of the corral. Once again, it was as if the camel had heard the voice as well. Jesus retrieved his saddle and gear from the barn and left money with a sleepy stable boy to cover any remaining debt. He saddled and loaded Rocky, then mounted himself on the animal's back, and the two ventured into the darkness toward Turfan.

The first three hundred miles from Samara to Khular was uneventful and pleasant. The weather was fair, and there was plenty of grass and water and farms along the way. Jesus camped comfortably at night, in agreeable temperatures, and made good progress over the relatively flat land during the day. They made it to Khular in eleven days. Jesus had planned to spend a couple of days there, but since neither he nor Rocky was fatigued from their journey, and with expected good travel ahead, they stopped only long enough for supplies before going on.

Traffic along the Silk Road from Khular was fairly constant, and the good weather and terrain continued for twelve more days until they were at the base of Tianshan Mountains. Though it was only midday, the view of the mountains was formidable enough to cause Jesus to stop at a nearby caravanserai. While eating supper with the other guests, he learned that the Tianshan mountain range stretched for some eight hundred miles. However, once one had traversed the initial climb into the higher elevations, the road leveled off and wound its way between the higher mountains that provided a shield from the cold winds at night and shade from the scorching heat of the day.

There were caravanserais about every three days along the way, so supplies would be available, at least until the last leg of their journey—a one-hundred-and-fifty-mile trek through the harsh desert land of the Flaming Mountains. There were also small packs of bandits that lived in the Tianshans, but they usually limited their attacks to individuals and small groups that were less able to defend themselves and ward off the robbers' assaults. Since all of the other guests were traveling west, it was suggested that Jesus wait for a large eastbound caravan and travel with them through the range. He waited.

Two days later, a caravan of forty camels, a dozen donkeys, and fifty men arrived at the caravanserai. Jesus bought passage with their leader for a trade of the silver chalice he never used and an agreement to lighten the load of their pack animals by carrying two hundred pounds of their merchandise on his own camel. To offset the extra weight on Rocky, he would walk the entire distance of the mountain range.

The first day up the mountain was rough on everyone. It was a one-thousand-foot climb up a steep, narrow trail that wound through rocks and around deep gullies. But true to the report, once they reached the top, the trail leveled off and widened to resemble the trade road they had left at the bottom of the mountain. They set up camp for the night to allow themselves and the animals a chance to rest and regain stamina for the next day's travel.

There were rises and falls in the elevation, and some days were harder than others, but, for the most part, Jesus found the journey through the mountains to be as advertised. There were never more than three days journey between caravanserais, the evenings were brisk but not unbearable, the days were warm but not torrid. Occasionally, they would see a single man standing on a ridge above the trail (obviously, a thief standing lookout for suitable prey), but they were never attacked or even threatened by bandits.

A month after they had entered the mountain range, they began a steady descent into the lower elevations of the Flaming Mountains. Jesus could see how they got their name. The bare and eroded cliffs shimmered as the sun's heat reflected off their jagged surfaces, causing them to appear on fire with dancing flames. At the base of the mountains was a flat desert floor, cracked and dry. The mountains that had given the caravan shade all those days were behind them now, and the sun beat down on them furiously. They had replenished their supplies at their last stop a day ago, but they would be seven or eight days in the desert before they reached Turfan. They would make it, their leader had said, as long as they rationed wisely.

They traveled the rest of the day and through the night and the next day until about noon. Then they pitched their tents for shade and rested until the sun went down again. The rest of the way, they traveled only at night and early morning, and rested uncomfortably during the day.

Seven days later, the desert ended as abruptly as it had begun. A line of cedar trees stood against the dry ground like a sentinel of green guards holding the desert at bay. Behind the cedars were fields of grass and cultivated land with fruit trees and grapevines and even rice fields. Along both sides of the road, a stream of water flowed and fed irrigation ditches that ran along the rows of planted land. Their animals lined up along the stream to drink, and the men soaked their head cloths and squeezed the water onto their faces and into their mouths. They had reached Turfan, well known as the *Oasis City in the Desert.*

In the midst of some of the harshest land on the earth, Turfan was an island of green, but it was a man-made oasis. The five-mile-by-five-mile city was watered by a series of wells and irrigation caves that ran hundreds of miles to the base of the Tianshan's snow-covered mountains. The mountains, as well as the valley floor at their base, consisted of porous rock that soaked up water from rains and melting snow. Over centuries, and because the rock was porous and soft, the citizens of Turfan were able to punch holes in the rock at the mountain base to release the trapped water. They then dug tunnels, as underground canals, to carry the water from the mountains through the desert and to the city. The underground shafts not only prevented evaporation but allowed the water to move along a slight down hill slope, ensuring a constant flow. All along the way, additional holes were drilled into the rock above the canal to release even more trapped water. Once the canal

reached the city, pools were dug to collect the water for use. The
same process was repeated for irrigating the outlying areas of fields,
orchards and vineyards. The result was plentiful water in an arid
land: the Oasis City in the Desert.

Jesus stayed in Turfan only a few days. After some rest and relaxation
to recover from their time in the desert, he and Rocky resumed their
journey toward Chang' an, the easternmost point of the Silk Road.

The next hundred miles east was as hot and dry as the desert
leading to Turfan, but Rocky was loaded with water and food, and
Jesus was confident they could make the journey safely. He followed
the caravan leader's wisdom by traveling at night and resting in the
shade during the hottest parts of the day. At sunrise on the fifth day,
Jesus spotted the first hills and spots of grass that marked the border
of the desert. As he rode further, he began to see trees and more green
ground, which meant water. By the end of the day, they began to pass
by houses and farms and, finally, a caravanserai, where they spent the
night and restored their supplies. When Jesus paid his bill the next
morning, he realized his funds were running low. He would have to
find work soon to replenish his money pouch.

For the next two weeks, Jesus and Rocky traveled with ease. There
were artesian wells and springs releasing streams of water that ran
beside the road, feeding rice and melon fields. Jesus ate from his own
supplies and gleaned from the fields. Rocky grazed on green grass that
sprang from the fertile soil. The weather was mild, and Jesus reflected
that this was the best leg of their trip so far. They camped along the
road at night, feeling safe in the rural but fairly populated land. They
took a slight detour south to the city of Loulan, where they spent the
night, and then caught the main route again at the banks of the Yellow
River. The river was deep and swift, and the only way across was a toll
bridge. Jesus paid the fee from his meager funds and crossed over into
the heart of China. They were six hundred miles from Chang' an.

The next two hundred miles were as smooth and comfortable as the
land on the other side of the river. Water and food were plentiful, the
population sparse but constant, and the road traffic steady all the way to

Danhuang. This would be the last city before Chang' an. Jesus checked with other travelers about the conditions between the two cities and was told to expect another hundred miles or so of good travel before entering the Ordos Desert, a two-hundred-mile stretch of wilderness also known as the Badlands. Rather than spending money on a room for the night, Jesus spent the last of his funds on food supplies. He filled his bags with as much as they could hold, packed them onto Rocky, and left Danhuang at the first light of day.

Jesus continued to glean the fields along the road, and Rocky continued to graze from the ample grasslands as long as it lasted. They would save their own supplies for the desert. When they entered the hill country four days later, the grass began to disappear, and the rocky, red soil turned sandy and brown. By the next day, all vegetation had vanished. As they topped a hill—the last one—Jesus looked out on the desert floor below, stretching as far as the eye could see. On the north and south horizons, there were mountains that looked as bare and dry as the desert. Rocky let out a long, bemoaning bellow, as if to say, *please, not again!* But when Jesus gently kicked his heels into Rocky's sides, the animal began descending down the hill without protest or resistance. It was almost evening. They would travel throughout the night.

Ten hours later, when the sun rose in front of them, Jesus reckoned they had covered at least twenty-five miles of desert. They could go another four hours—maybe twelve or fourteen miles—before the heat would force them to stop. If they could average thirty-five miles a day, Jesus figured they could be through the desert in six days. There was enough food for both of them for eight days. Water was the issue. Rocky was fairly hydrated and could easily go three more days without a drink, but then would need their whole supply to make the rest of the trip. Jesus, on the other hand, would have to drink at least a gallon of water each day to stay hydrated enough to survive the desert.

They stopped when the sun was at about eleven o'clock in the sky. Jesus pitched a canopy large enough to shade both of them and draped two sides to shield them from the remaining morning sun. In the afternoon, as the sun moved, he switched the drapes to the other side to maintain their shade. They napped fitfully in the stifling heat. When the sun set behind them, Jesus dismantled the tent and loaded it back onto the camel. After mounting the kneeling Rocky, and being careful not to let the animal see him, Jesus uncorked a waterskin and took a long, thirsty drink. He would not drink again until the next morning. On Jesus' command, Rocky rose to his feet and began to walk slowly toward the wilderness that lay ahead.

As the next day passed, and the next, the mountains to the north crawled nearer. By the morning of the fourth day, they were at the base of a long jagged wall that stretched eastward out of sight. The desert floor was rocky here, and Jesus knew this would make night travel treacherous. But the mountains provided morning shade, so they traveled on until midday in relative comfort.

When they finally stopped to make camp, Jesus unloaded all the gear off Rocky and began pitching the tent. He then removed the top from one of the four barrels of water he had brought for Rocky. The camel bellowed as he saw and smelled the sweet liquid before him, then sank his long snout beneath the surface and began sucking it down. While Rocky was occupied, Jesus quickly opened another barrel and submerged a waterskin, allowing it to fill, then he did the same with another. He now had two gallons of water for himself. It would have to do. Rocky would get the rest. The camel finished off his ration of water in minutes and bellowed for more. But Jesus knew the cry was more out of gluttony than anguish.

"Quiet," he said. "You'll be fine. Just let that settle into your system. It's more than enough to get you the rest of the way."

Rocky bellowed again in dissatisfaction, then turned to work on the grain Jesus had poured out for him.

Suddenly, Rocky let out a yelp and jumped away from his food. Jesus, startled, turned just in time to see a rock fall from the animal's side. As he was trying to figure out what had happened, another rock landed on the ground between himself and Rocky, causing the camel to flinch again. Jesus quickly looked up, fearing a landslide, and saw a man standing on a ledge far up the mountain. He was waving his hands frantically and yelling at them, but Jesus couldn't make out what he was saying. Jesus raised his hand and made a broad waving motion. But the man picked up another rock and chunked it toward them.

"Hey!" Jesus shouted. "Cut it out!"

The man responded with another rock, causing Jesus to have to jump out of the way. He grabbed the rope around Rocky's neck to move them both out of the man's throwing range. Jesus looked at the man who was still screaming at them and making obscene gestures with his hands. After an hour of this, the man finally turned and walked away from the ledge, disappearing from their sight.

It was almost dark, and Jesus wasn't about to be ambushed in the night, so he tied Rocky's rope to a huge stone and carefully climbed up the mountainside to the ledge where the man had been. About ten feet back from the ledge's edge there was a cave, and just outside the cave's entrance, a small campfire. Above the fire, there was a bird cooking on a skewer.

"Hello?" Jesus called.

The man appeared in an instant with a large stick in his hand. "Get out!" he screamed. "This is my mountain and my desert, and you are trespassing! You are off the road. Go back immediately!"

"Take it easy!" said Jesus. "I left the road only to travel in the shade of the mountains, and I came up here only to make peace. We'll sleep tonight and be gone tomorrow."

"Why don't you travel at night like a sane man? The sun will broil you by day."

"We were traveling at night until we left the road. It's too dangerous to travel on this rocky ground at night, especially with no moon."

"Then go back to the road! The moon will return to you tomorrow."

"And tomorrow night, we will resume night travel, but tomorrow morning, we will stay close to the mountains."

The man responded with a primal scream. "Arghhh! Get off my mountain! Sleep tonight, but then move on. Go! I do not wish to talk to you anymore!"

"Thank you," Jesus said sheepishly, and he started to climb back down the mountain. It was dark now, and he couldn't see where he was placing his feet. He started to sweat. Falling would mean certain death, but he suspected interrupting the caveman again would have the same result, so he continued to inch his way down. Then he heard a voice from above.

"Wait, traveler! Why are you leaving so soon?"

"Uh, because you told me to."

"Nonsense! Don't be rude," the man said. "Join me for supper and conversation."

"Gladly," Jesus mumbled, confused and scared. His knees were shaking so badly, he didn't know if he could move. He finally inched his way back up to the ledge, where the man took his hand and hoisted him up.

"Welcome, welcome! It's good to have company visit me."

"O...kay," Jesus said, wondering if the old man were more dangerous than the cliff.

"I have a bird here we can share, and some tea I make from berries that grow in the rock crevices." The man talked and talked, as if he and Jesus were old friends catching up. Some of what he said made sense and some of it didn't. Finally, he asked Jesus to speak about himself and listened respectfully as Jesus shared the details of his journey.

"It is a long way to travel," the man said to Jesus. "And what is your business when you arrive at your destination?"

"I seek God,' said Jesus. "I seek to know God's will for my life, my purpose in God's plan, and my place in God's coming kingdom."

"It is the same with me," the man said. "That is why I came here twenty years ago. Sometimes I find God, and sometimes I lose him."

"You've been in this cave for twenty years? How did you survive?"

"I don't know if I have been here for twenty years! Who told you that?"

"You just did!"

"Well, then, perhaps it is true. I'm a hermit, you know. I have been living in this cave for twenty years, and I haven't spoken a word in all that time."

"But you're talking now."

"No, I'm not. You are. Besides, why wouldn't I talk? It would be rude not to talk with a guest. It's not like I am a hermit who has taken a vow of silence."

"But..." Jesus decided to let it go.

"Well, I wish I could talk to you more, but I can't. Vow of silence, you know. So, I'll say good night. See you in the morning." And with that, the man got up and disappeared into the darkness of the cave.

Jesus laid down on the hard rock, wondering if he would be able to sleep. That was the last thought he had before daylight awakened him.

Jesus had just sat up and was clearing his eyes from sleep when the man appeared from the mouth of the cave. He jumped back when he saw Jesus. "Who the hell are you, and what are you doing on my mountain?" he exclaimed, reaching for a rock. "Go away!"

"Wait!" yelled Jesus, jumping to his feet. "I was here last night. Don't you remember? We talked! We ate together!"

The man considered this, studying Jesus' face. "Well, then, let's have some breakfast!" He went into the cave and quickly returned with two birds on a skewer. He placed it on the fire, which Jesus noticed was still burning from the night before, though, to his knowledge, no sticks or fuel had been added. In fact, he didn't remember the man adding anything to the fire the night before.

"How is it that your fire continues to burn without wood?" Jesus asked, looking all around the ledge for sticks or some other possible fuel. He saw nothing.

The man ignored his question. "Tea?" he asked.

"No, thanks," said Jesus, remembering how horrid last night's tea had been. "Do you have water?"

The man gave Jesus a disgusted look. "You can't have tea without water."

"Where do you get it?"

"There's a pool in the cave. I'll show you after we eat," said the man, ripping one of the birds from the skewer and handing it to Jesus. "I'll show you how I catch these birds too."

When they finished their meal, he took Jesus into the cave. Just inside, there were several nets stretched out and hanging from jagged points of rock along the cave's roof and walls. "Pigeons fly into the cave all the time, bats too, though I prefer the birds. They fly into the nets; the nets collapse and trap them. More than I can eat, really." He pointed to a small pile of dead birds. "I can't let them go. They would tell the other birds."

"And the water?" asked Jesus.

"It's a little deeper into the cave. We'll have to let our eyes adjust." After a minute, he said, "Follow me." They went about twenty feet deeper in, where the cave widened and the light from the cave's opening ceased to exist.

Jesus could see nothing, but he could hear dripping sounds, some closer and some farther away. "What is it?"

"Water drips from the roof of the cave and falls into this pool." He took Jesus' hand and placed it into a pool of water about six inches deep. "It has never dried up and, really, never overflowed. There's a trickle of runoff that goes deeper into the cave, but it seems to produce just about the amount I can drink in a day. That's why I can't invite you to stay."

"It's okay," said Jesus. "I have to be going anyway, and I should be leaving now, while the morning is still cool."

The two men walked back out of the cave into the bright light. They squinted as their pupils adjusted.

"Thank you for your hospitality," Jesus said.

"Why don't you stay?" pleaded the cave man.

"But you just said…"

"We could eat your camel."

"I have to go," said Jesus. He looked over the naked, dirty man—his skin turned to leather from the sun. "Would you like some clothes? I have an extra tunic in my things."

"I cannot leave this ledge," the man said. "Why don't you give me the clothes you have on." Jesus thought about this and decided it was a better idea than going down and having to climb up again with what he had below. He undressed and gave his clothes to the old man.

"Excellent!" the man said, admiring the tunic and head cloth in his hands.

"Thank you, again, for your hospitality," Jesus said. "God bless you." As he started to climb down, just before his eyes lost sight of the top of the ledge, he saw the man toss the clothes onto the fire.

"Excellent!" the man said, rubbing his hands together, his eyes excited by the rising flames.

When Jesus reached the bottom of the mountain, he dressed himself, saddled and packed Rocky, and rode away following the shade of the mountains. At about noon, they stopped and camped until evening. Then they veered south, connecting with the main road again, and traveled throughout the night and until mid-morning the next day.

The first signs Jesus noticed of the desert's end were sparse clumps of bush and the changing composition of the ground beneath them. The sand was turning to harder, darker soil. Then there was grass, and then hills and trees on the horizon. Cultivated fields began to appear, and farmhouses. By the time they had reached the shade of the trees, the road was full of people going in both directions.

There were booths along the roadside, selling vegetables and fruit, jade and ivory and silk. He thought he had finally reached the edge of Chang' an, but the village was small, and, in minutes, he was riding into rural territory again. The farms continued and, eventually, they came to a river, where several people and camels waited to cross on a ferry. People were speaking in languages he couldn't understand, so he approached a camel driver from a small caravan to ask directions. Fortunately, the man was a westerner who spoke Aramaic. He told Jesus that he, too, was on his way to Chang' an, which was across the river and eighty miles further. He invited Jesus to ride with them the rest of the way.

Rocky drank from the river until he was full. Jesus refilled his waterskins but not the water barrels. The skins would be plenty for Jesus. Rocky would be fine the rest of the way and would appreciate the lighter load. When they all had ferried across to the other side, the caravan regrouped, with Jesus and Rocky as new additions, and they began their final approach to Chang' an.

Chang' an (meaning "eternal peace") was the capital city of China and the seat of the country's king. With over a million citizens, it was the most populated city in the world and, perhaps, the richest. Its silk farms were massive, with hundreds of thousands of mulberry trees filled with silkworms that fed on the tree's leaves. Each farm had house after house where the silk was spun and woven into the sought after fabric. Outside the city, there were mines that produced more precious stones and metals than the rest of the world combined. It was an international city, where people of all races, cultures, and languages lived and worked in harmony. As the political, religious and cultural hub of the East, it was, indeed, "the City of Peace."

As Jesus rode through the city gate, he was amazed. The wall surrounding the city stood thirty feet high and stretched as far as he could see in either direction. People were everywhere, and the sounds of the marketplaces were deafening. Musicians played on every street corner, and the smell of food and sweet incense filled the air. Pagodas and temples stood eight, ten, and twelve stories high. Jesus dismounted Rocky, who was distressed by the traffic, and led him along the streets toward the center of town and the tallest of all the buildings. It was the king's palace. In reality, it was not as tall as some of the other buildings, perhaps only three or four stories in all. But it stood on the city's only hill, and this caused the palace to rise up high above all other structures. Jesus reckoned this vantage point allowed the king to overlook Chang' an from end to end. The palace itself was surrounded by its own wall, though only about half the height of the city wall.

After an hour of sightseeing, Jesus decided his first order of business was to find a job. He was completely broke. He would need a place for Rocky, so he thought his best bet was to go back to the farms outside the city and seek a job tree-dressing or harvesting produce from the fields. Hopefully, the farmers would allow him to board Rocky in the pastures with their own animals. Just as he was turning to leave, a guard on the palace wall called out to him.

"You there, with the camel: Hold where you are!"

Jesus turned back and saw the man pointing to him. He waited until another guard rode out on a horse. "The king wishes to see you."

"Me?" Jesus asked, puzzled.

"Get on your camel and follow me."

Jesus did as he was told and followed the guard up a winding, paved road to the top of the hill and the palace. They stopped at the bottom of some stairs that led up to a set of gold-gilded doors. Two boys ran out to take the reins of the horse and camel. The guard dismounted and started toward the stairs. "Come with me," he said, without looking back.

Jesus had Rocky kneel. He dismounted and followed the guard up the stairs and through the doors. "I don't understand," he said. "I don't know the king."

The soldier didn't answer and didn't look back. When they came to another set of carved gilded doors, the guard turned and said, "Wait here." He went through the doors, closing them behind him.

In a few minutes, the guard returned. "The king will see you now. This way."

Jesus walked into one of the most magnificent rooms he had ever seen. Gold and copper and silver paneled every wall. The furniture was made of jade and some black, gleaming wood that Jesus didn't recognize. Giant jade planters held miniature trees, and painted pottery vases, filled with flowers, were everywhere. Multi-colored silk fabric was draped from the ceiling and swayed in the breeze.

"Move forward," the guard said, now following behind him and occasionally giving him a slight shove in the back to move him along.

At the other end of the room, the king sat in a jade chair with red cushions on its arms and seat. He was a boy, maybe sixteen, Jesus thought.

"Leave us," the king said to the guard.

He bowed and left the room.

Jesus, taking the cue from the guard, remembered royal protocol and bowed deeply.

"Who are you?" the king asked.

"My name is Jesus."

"Aha!" said the king. "I knew it! They told me you would come."

"Who?"

"Balthazar and Gaspar."

"You know them?"

"Who doesn't? They are some of the wisest sages and scientists in all the world. They were here for my father's funeral a year ago. They told me to expect you, and I have been looking for you ever since. I saw you today from my window. You were staring back at me."

"I did not see you, Your Majesty. I was just looking up at the beautiful palace."

"It doesn't matter. I saw you, and now you are here. You are a king, too, they say."

"I am not a king. I do not wish to be a king."

"Me either!" said the king. "I want to be a monk. Perhaps you will tell me how you managed to abdicate your throne without raising the ire of your people."

"I am not a king!" Jesus repeated loudly.

"They told me you would say that."

Jesus raised the heel of his hand to his forehead and pressed, trying to ward off a headache. "Really, these wise men are mistaken. I am not a king and have never been a king."

"They are never mistaken, King Jesus. Perhaps, you are not *yet* a king, but if they say you are, then you are, or will be. But I will not belabor the issue. You are here, as predicted, and you will be my guest for as long as you wish to stay. I believe that you can be wise counsel in this matter and, perhaps, I to you."

"What matter is that, Your Majesty?"

"The matter of kingship. Me losing mine and you finding yours."

Jesus decided to give up the argument. "I would be honored to be your guest."

In the weeks that followed, Jesus and the king became true friends. Chang' an and China were home to many religions: Daoism, Confucianism, and Buddhism, to name a few. The king was remarkably adept in the faiths, especially these three, and he instructed Jesus in them.

Jesus, in return, taught the king about Judaism and the one true God of all. He helped the young king with his administrative duties and tasks and taught him that a good king is really a faithful servant to his people, working always in their best interest and well-being.

"Give and share from the blessings of your kingdom," he told the king. "If your people are faithful and loyal, then you must be faithful and loyal to them.... Do to others as you would have them do to you.... You cannot own two coats until everyone has one.... Love your enemies and do good to them.... Ask and it will be given; seek and you will find; knock and the door will be opened.... If you learn these things and do them, then you can rule as a great king and be a good monk too."

After three months in Chang' an, Jesus heard the voice again in his dreams. "Go," it said. The next morning, Jesus said goodbye to the king.

"I think you are a king, Jesus," the king said, "The servant king you speak of. If you will search your soul, you will find this to be true. And you will find your kingdom."

"I will continue to search for God's kingdom and my role in it," said Jesus.

"Then may God go with you, and lead you there," said the king. The two embraced and Jesus took his leave.

An hour later, Jesus passed through and out the gates of Chang' an. For the first time in more than two years, he was headed west. He veered slightly south to avoid the desert and the same route he had come, and found the way delightful. He loved the rural country of China. There were melon, rice, and cotton fields, and streams of water everywhere. The people were friendly and gracious. They dressed in modest but colorful clothing, and many of them had covered their bodies with equally colorful tattoos. When Jesus stopped to camp, they would offer him food and, sometimes, even a bed in their homes.

When he arrived at the Yellow River, he followed it south until he found a place to ford, then continued along the south side of the Attun Shan mountain range. Day travel was easy in the shade of the mountains. The weather was cool but not cold. The villages and farms became less and less frequent as he followed the path of the mountains. Eventually, the road came to an end but Jesus continued on. There were people in the area, Chinese nomads—Bedouin-type tribes—that chose to live in isolation outside of society. Though disengaged from civilization, they were quite welcoming to strangers, and Jesus spent many days in their company and encampments as he traveled along the way.

Jesus continued to follow the Attun Shan range west until it intersected with the Himalayas running north and south. Caught between the two ranges, Jesus had no choice but to take to the mountains. Having been a guest at many tables over the weeks prior, he still had most of his supplies, but there was no way to know what lay ahead of him or how long it would take to cross over the mountains. Jesus had noticed that the height of the Himalaya's mountain peaks seemed to be dropping as he continued to travel west and north, while the peaks of the Attun Shan were rising. By the time he came to a canyon that boxed him in between the two ranges, the Himalayan range was at its lowest elevation and the choice was easy. He headed up the gradual but steady slope into the Himalaya Mountains.

For the next ten days, Jesus and Rocky traveled upward, and every day it became a little colder. It snowed at night, and the wind blew ferociously during the day. Jesus wore a heavy wool tunic—a gift from the king—and draped a fur over him to try and ward off the wintry blast assaulting his body. He used part of his head covering to wrap his face so that only his eyes were exposed.

When his feet were too cold to walk, he would mount Rocky and bundle them in blankets to try and restore some warmth. They slept little and tried to keep moving most of the time, knowing that any sustained inactivity could cause them to freeze. Their best chance of survival was to spend as little time in the mountains as possible.

On the fourteenth day, they reached the peak and began their descent. At various passes, as they made their way down, they could see the forests and fields beyond the mountain base. Five days later, they were out of the snow, and the wind was less brutal, but it was still cold, and they continued to move without sleep. They had eaten more than usual to re-energize their bodies, so their supplies were dangerously low.

When they reached the base of the mountain, they made camp and ate their last morsels of food. The ground was warm, but the air still cool, so they slept without a tent to let their bodies thaw in the sun. It was late afternoon when they laid down to sleep. They did not awake until the next morning, and they were starving.

Jesus watered Rocky and himself, and then they set off on a path west through the forest until they came to a road. He knew they were in the northern portions of India, a land he had intended to see on the trip home, so he took the road south until he came to the town of Talaxia.

Talaxia was a good-sized village of about four hundred people. It was mostly a farming community, but there were shops with paintings and jewelry and fabrics, a few restaurants, and a single boarding house. Jesus didn't lack for money. His friend, the king, had insisted on filling a saddlebag full of it for Jesus' journey home. He checked into the boarding house, secured a stable and food for Rocky, then he washed, ate, and set out for one of the nearby farms to see about buying supplies for the road. A young boy was working in one of the melon fields beside the road, and Jesus asked him about the possibility of making some purchases.

"My name is Sanjai," said the boy. "I work for the man who owns this farm. He is a good man and will sell you what you need."

"Wonderful," said Jesus. "Can you take me to him?" He followed the boy to a barn, where the farm owner was working on an ox yoke. The boy introduced the two men, and Jesus stated his business.

"We can take care of you," said the farmer, "but right now, I'm burdened with this damned thing. It won't sit right on my oxen and keeps making sores on their backs."

"You know," said Jesus, "I'm a carpenter and pretty good with this sort of thing. Why don't you let me have a look?"

"Be my guest," said the farmer. "I'd appreciate the help."

Jesus studied the yoke. "Have you got a wood plane?"

The farmer disappeared and a minute later returned with a plane, handing it to Jesus. "It's a new yoke, so be careful," he said. "I can always return it, though I would have to travel a long way to do so."

"No need," said Jesus. "It's just a little uneven." He made a few strokes with the plane on one side of the yoke, then measured both sides with his fingers and repeated the process on the other side.

After a few times going back and forth, taking careful measurements in between, he stooped to make his eyes level with the yoke. "There, that should do it," he said. "But you'll have to let your oxen's backs heal completely before you put them back to work. The yoke's sides were slightly off, and that was causing it to rub hard against the animals' hides. It will pull evenly now and won't injure them anymore."

"Thank you," the man said. "Now, let's get you fixed up with supplies."

As Jesus called out his list of wanted items, the man sent Sanjai running in one direction or another. Finally, they had accumulated everything Jesus requested, and a few other recommended items, and placed them on the floor of the barn.

"I'll pick them up on my way out of town tomorrow," Jesus said.

"They will be here waiting," said the farmer, "and Sanjai will be here to help you load them."

Jesus thanked the farmer, paid him, and then went back to the boarding house for supper and a good night's sleep. He still had some catching up to do.

The following morning, Jesus got up, ate breakfast, checked himself and Rocky out of the boarding house, and started down the road toward the farm. When he arrived, Sanjai was waiting to help him load the supplies.

"I'd like to go with you," Sanjai said.

"I don't even know where I'm going, now," said Jesus, "but, eventually, I'll be traveling all the way back to my home in Israel. I won't be coming back this way to drop you off, and, surely, you don't wish to be so far away from your family."

"I have no family," replied Sanjai. "I am an orphan, since I was six. The farmer took me in and gives me room and board in exchange for work. I would like to travel and learn the ways of the world. Or I would, at least, like to be educated in a school. There is no school in Talaxia."

"And your farmer?" asked Jesus. "What would he think about your leaving?"

"Perhaps he'd be glad not to have to feed me anymore."

"Nonsense. I've seen what a good worker you are. Besides, I'm sure he cares about you. He would miss you."

"Then let's ask him. If he says I can go, will you take me?"

"I'm not sure about all of this. I…"

Sanjai didn't wait for Jesus to finish but ran toward the farmhouse to retrieve his guardian. In a moment, the two of them returned.

"Good morning, Jesus," the man said, as he entered the barn behind Sanjai. "Do you have everything you need?"

"Yes, thank you."

"Sanjai said you wanted to ask me something."

Jesus shot a disturbed glance at Sanjai. "I think *Sanjai* has something to ask you," he said, concerned that he might be opening himself up to a proposition to which he had not yet agreed.

"What is it, Sanjai?" the farmer asked, starting to feel a bit irritated by the mystery.

"Jesus has asked me to go with him."

"I did not!" said Jesus, more than a little flustered.

The farmer looked at Jesus, then at Sanjai. "Would someone like to tell me what's going on?"

Sanjai quickly dropped his head and stared at the ground, obviously, deferring to Jesus.

Jesus sighed. "Sanjai asked me—and I have not agreed to this, nor do I think it is a good idea—if he could leave with me. He says he wants to see the world and learn of other places. Or he, at least, wants to go someplace where there's a school so he can be educated."

"And where are you going?" the farmer questioned Jesus.

"I don't know! I told him that!"

The farmer looked down at Sanjai. He took the boy's chin in his hand and lifted his head so he could look in his eyes. "Do you want to leave me, Sanjai?"

"No. Yes. I don't know, sir. I want to learn. I want to learn to read and write and see things I've never seen."

The farmer stared at Sanjai lovingly and then looked at Jesus. "He is a smart boy and a good one. He's a good worker and a fast learner, but there is nothing for him here in Talaxia, except farm work. That's all there will ever be. He deserves an education."

Jesus swallowed hard. He could certainly teach the lad, but he wasn't ready to take on a student or companion, much less the care of a young boy. He didn't know where he was going, but he knew where he had been. This child would've never survived the deserts or mountains he had crossed. He didn't doubt that there would be equal hardships ahead.

"I cannot take you," he said to Sanjai. "You would need your own camel. You would need your own supplies. You would need to be able to fend for yourself. You aren't old enough for the journey I am taking."

"I agree," said the farmer. "He isn't ready for the journey you are on, but he has relatives in Patella by the sea. It's a large city, and there are schools there and universities. If you'll take him there, I will pay you."

"How far is it?" Jesus said, all but conceding.

"Two months' travel, give or take a week. But ten days west of here is a main trade road. Once you're there, the travel will be safe and agreeable."

Jesus sighed again. He was uncomfortable with the idea, but the sea and farther south to Gandari were places he intended to go. "Get your things," he said.

Sanjai ran to a haystack, reached beneath the straw, and pulled out a small sack he'd hidden away. "Ready!" he said, with an excited smile.

All three of them finished packing the supplies and loading them onto Rocky. Sanjai and the farmer embraced, the man holding on to the boy for a long time. They said goodbye, and the man watched as they walked away. Jesus noticed that Sanjai occasionally looked back and waved. He assumed the man was still watching and waving back. He handed Sanjai Rocky's reins and said, "Lead the way." The boy gladly did so, stepping out in front of the camel. When Jesus turned to see if the man was still watching them, he saw the farmer on his knees with his face in his hands, no doubt weeping for his loss.

Jesus, Rocky, and the boy made good time through pleasant lands as they traveled south and west. They passed no villages but the farms continued, so they were able to stock their food supplies every few days, which was necessary, since the boy ate like twelve-year-old boys do. Jesus knew the time would come when they would find themselves in barren and uninhabited lands. He decided it would be wise to stop at the next town they passed and buy extra saddlebags and two more barrels to stock additional food and water. Ten days into their journey, just as the farmer had said, they met the main road and headed south.

Conditions changed. They stayed in caravanserais when they found them and camped when they didn't, which was most of the time. Though the road was a main trade route, the traffic was light and the villages few. There were no farms and, seemingly, no people in this part of India. There were animals, though. At night, they heard the roars of tigers and the screams of leopards. In the daytime, they saw herds of elephants and all kinds of deer and antelope grazing far off the road. When they camped, and could find wood, they made fires in hopes of warding off the nocturnal flesh-eaters that roamed the hills and forests.

Six weeks later, they arrived in Patella, no worse for wear, and though Jesus had become quite fond of the boy, he was glad to be delivering him to his family, and relieved of the responsibility of his safety and care. Patella was, by far, the largest city he had seen in India. Fifty thousand people, Jesus reckoned, maybe more. It was a port city, and merchandise was being unloaded from and on-loaded to the many ships docked there. The markets started at the docks and spilled into the town, an unending line of booths selling gold and silver, fabrics and furs, spices and animals, and women.

Jesus held tightly to Rocky's reins in one hand and the boy's hand in his other as people shoved and pushed by. He wondered how he would ever find Sanjai's family in this sea of humanity. He had a name and that was all.

They found a hotel with a livery stable to board Rocky. Jesus paid in advance for a week's stay, hoping that would be more than enough time. He could pay for additional days, if necessary, but he didn't want to be here any longer than he had to be. The sudden burst of civilization and so many people packed together made him anxious and uneasy. He and Sanjai went to their room and washed, then went back to the main room and asked the manager about the boy's family.

"Their name is Ujjayi," Jesus inquired.

"I know many Ujjayis," the manager said. "My sister is married to one, and there are a thousand others with that name."

Jesus closed his eyes and took in a deep breath, imagining how long this could take. "Can I start with your sister's family?" he asked.

"She lives in Amarivati, a thousand miles from here. I would not start with her."

"Okay," said Jesus, rubbing his temples with his fingers. "Let's start with an Ujjayi that lives here in Patella."

"Which one?"

"I don't know!" barked an exasperated Jesus, trying to keep his composure. "How about a family you know, and the one that lives closest to your hotel?"

"That would be Abu. He lives about a mile from here. He is married to my sister."

"I thought you said your sister lived in Amarivati?"

"That is my other sister."

Jesus counted to five slowly. "Can you give me directions?"

"Yes, of course." The man gave him directions.

"Thank you," Jesus said. He took Sanjai's hand and started to leave.

"He won't be home now," said the manager. "He is at work."

Jesus turned, "Do you know when he will be home?"

"He gets off at six. Maybe you can just talk to him now. Abu!" the manager called out. "This gentleman would like to speak to you."

Abu was twenty feet away, setting a table in the dining room. He walked over. "May I help you?"

Jesus looked at Abu, then the manager. "He works here," said Jesus, incredulously.

"Of course," said the manager.

"Of course," said Jesus.

Jesus introduced himself to Abu and relayed the whole story to him: where the boy came from, how he came to be an orphan, his six years in the guardianship of the farmer.

"I'm afraid I cannot help you," said Abu, "but I can check around. All the Ujjayis are related in some way. We do not all know each other, but there is a network in the family. If he belongs to a family here, I think the chances are good that we will find them."

"Thank you," said Jesus.

"How long will you be in Patella?"

"For as long as it takes," Jesus said, hopeful that it wouldn't be for long.

"I will be in touch," Abu said.

Jesus slept well that night, encouraged by Abu's help and optimistic about finding Sanjai's family.

Jesus and Sanjai were having breakfast when Abu appeared at their table. "My cousin, Fatali, will come to you this morning. She is the cousin of Sanjai's mother. She knows the story of Sanjai's family, and she will come here to take him as her own."

"That's good news, isn't it Sanjai?" Jesus looked at the boy, who nodded his head.

"I knew of this story, too, when you told me yesterday. But I had to speak to Fatali first, to be sure she was willing to claim the boy."

"I understand," said Jesus. "When will she be here?"

"Soon. She has boys of her own. She has to get them off to school."

Sanjai's eyes lit up "Will I go to school?"

"Of course," said Abu. "You are of school age. You must go to school."

Sanjai smiled, and so did Jesus. He put his hand on the boy's head and ruffled his hair.

"I must go to work now. Stay in the hotel. I will come for you when she arrives." Abu left them.

An hour later, there was a knock at their door. Jesus pulled the curtain and a beautiful woman, about Jesus' age, was standing with Abu. "This is Fatali, cousin of Sanjai and of his mother."

"It's good to meet you," Jesus said.

Fatali clasped her hands together in a praying position and bowed slightly, but she was already looking around Jesus and at the boy behind him. She quickly maneuvered past him and took the boy in her arms, pressing his head against her chest. She was crying.

Jesus felt at ease, knowing the boy would be cared for and loved.

They talked for a brief time—but there wasn't much to say, in words. Finally, Jesus said goodbye to Sanjai, kissing him on the top of his head. The boy embraced Jesus in a tight hug. Then Sanjai, Fatali, and Abu left, and Jesus was alone. He sat on the bed and said a prayer of thanksgiving to God. He asked God to watch over Sanjai and his new family.

He spent the rest of the day buying supplies for the next leg of his journey. Then he slept. In the morning, he would ride south toward Gandari.

Jesus was up early and out of town before sunrise. There was a small caravan just in front of him, and he fell behind a good hundred yards to allow the dust they were kicking up to settle. He camped with the caravan that night and learned that Gandari was another eight-day journey. The road turned inland the next day, and the caravan followed its path toward Japar. Jesus continued along the coastline on his own. He passed no villages or people the rest of the way.

When Jesus arrived at Gandari, he was surprised by the smallness of the city. It was no bigger than Nazareth and seemed to be made up mostly of shrines and temples, holy men and gurus. There was a small market and the few women and children he saw were working its booths. There was no pier and no ships, and only a few small fishing boats anchored several feet off shore. About a half a mile out into the sea, there was a small island and, taking up almost every inch of the island's surface, a monastery within a surrounding wall. This was Tankah, the island and monastery that claimed to hold the Ark of the Covenant. Jesus didn't know if he believed the story, but the Ark was somewhere, and if it was here, he wished to see it. As a boy, Jesus had dreamed of traveling here to rescue the Ark from its apostate keepers and returning it, as King David had, to its rightful place in Jerusalem.

Jesus found a fisherman and offered to pay him for passage to the island.

"I will take you," the fisherman said, "but it will do you no good. Outsiders are not allowed entrance to the monastery."

"We'll see," Jesus said, handing the fisherman a coin.

When they landed on the island shore, Jesus instructed the fisherman to wait.

"I will wait," said the fisherman. "You will not be long."

Jesus climbed up the rocky shoreline to a path that led to a huge wooden door. He pounded on the door with his fist, but the massive thing was so thick and solid it barely made a sound. "Hey!" he called out. "Hel-lo!" he yelled again.

Finally, a man peeked over the wall. His head was shaved, except for a long braided ponytail in the back. He had red and white paint markings on his chest, arms, and face. "What do you want?"

"I want to visit your temple."

"Sorry," said the man. "Only the residents of the monastery are allowed to worship in our temple."

"I do not wish to worship there. I would just like to see it. I am a traveler visiting many places and seeing many things. I've come a long way to see this very place."

"Wait," the man said and disappeared.

In a moment, Jesus heard the door unbolt from the inside and it slowly opened. The man he had been talking to and another older man stepped into the opening of the door.

"Greetings," said the older man. "Have you come to visit us, or is your hope to stay, as a member of our community?"

"Just a visit,' said Jesus. "I would like to see your temple."

"Come in," the man said. He gave Jesus a guided tour of the place, ending at the temple. "We pray to many gods here. Is there a particular one you seek?"

"Yes," said Jesus. "The God of Israel."

The man looked at Jesus with a curious interest. "Ah, the god of the golden box. The stone writer."

So it is here! Jesus thought to himself. "Yes," he said.

"Then you may pray to him, but then you must leave."

"Do you have a shrine for the box?" Jesus asked. "I would like to see it and to pray there."

"You can pray here. He will hear you."

"I would like to pray at the shrine," Jesus insisted.

"You cannot see the box!" the old man said, with an irritated voice. "It is too powerful. It will kill you if you look upon it."

"Have you seen it?" asked Jesus.

"Of course, I have."

"Then why didn't it kill you?"

The man's face was turning red with anger. "I am a priest. I serve in the room where the box is kept. I haven't *exactly* seen it. It is kept behind a curtain to shield our eyes from its power and wrath."

"How did it get here? Where did it come from? How did the people who brought it here escape death? If no one has actually seen it, how do you know it exists?"

The old priest reeled from the rapid succession of questions. "It was brought here centuries ago. I don't know how they escaped death. Maybe it was covered when they found it. We know it exists, because it's here!"

"I don't believe you," said Jesus.

"Get out!" screamed the priest.

"Look," Jesus said, "show me the room. I'll look behind the curtain. If it kills me, you can bury me here and write FOOL on my tombstone. At least you'll know."

"Get out!" the priest screamed, again.

Jesus turned and started for the door, thinking. *If I can just get out of his sight and find a place to hide, I'll find the room tonight while the monks are sleeping.* He started down the temple steps and was looking for some suitable place of concealment when he heard the priest call out from behind him.

"Wait!" The priest caught up to him. "You know, the truth is, I've always had doubts myself. A hundred times I've wanted to peek behind that curtain, but I was afraid."

"I'm not afraid," said Jesus. "Even if it's there, I don't think looking at it will kill me. Israel possessed the Ark for millennia and in all the stories told, I've never heard of anyone dying from simply looking at it!"

"Come with me," the priest said.

They went to the front of the temple and down some stairs below ground. The priest took a torch from a barrel and lit it. They went down a short corridor and through a door into an anteroom. The priest lit some lamps on the wall and then slid back a curtain that led into another longer room. He lit more lamps. At the back of the room was another curtain.

"It's behind there," the old man said, his voice trembling.

Jesus hesitated for a moment, himself, not out of fear but anticipation. He walked to the curtain, took a deep breath, and slipped in behind it. It was dark and he could see nothing. "Torch!" he called to the priest, who crept forward and put it into the hand reaching out from behind the curtain. When Jesus brought the torch in, what he saw at first gave him a shock. There, in the flickering light, was a golden box! But, in an instant, he knew it wasn't the Ark of the Covenant. It was too small and carried none of the designs or markings he had read about in the scriptures: no rings on its side for carrying the Ark, and no carved cherubim atop the box with their wings spread out above it. He raised the lid of the box. There were bones inside.

"Do you want to see this?" he called out to the priest.

The priest eased through the curtain and looked in the open box. "What is it?"

"It appears to be someone's ossuary, but it certainly is *not* the Ark of the Covenant."

"Crap!" said the priest. "Are none of the gods real?"

"None of them," said Jesus, "except the one God. He is the God of all people and places and things."

The two men walked up the stairs and out of the temple.

"I'd appreciate it if you didn't mention this to any of the others," the priest said to Jesus.

"I'm leaving," Jesus said. "What you tell them is up to you."

The priest walked Jesus to the gate and closed the door behind him without saying goodbye.

Jesus walked down to the shore and found the fisherman in the boat asleep. "Let's go," he said.

"What took you so long?" the fisherman asked.

"Just go."

Jesus spent the next two weeks traveling north along the coastline of India. He thought of stopping in Patella to check in on Sanjai but decided against it, feeling a sudden great compulsion to return home. At Patella, he joined a main trade route northeast, then another northwest. Two thousand miles and a hundred days later, he crossed the border from India into Persia.

Jesus was ten days into the Persian wilderness when he stopped to make camp for the night. He unloaded Rocky, gathered some sticks for a fire, and pitched his tent before sitting down to eat supper. Suddenly, he heard a sound behind him and turned to see three men coming down the hill toward him. He didn't have a good feeling about them.

"Hello," said the man in front.

"Hello," responded Jesus.

"Got any food for some weary travelers?" They were carrying only walking sticks, no packs and no waterskins. They didn't look like travelers.

"There is food, and water too. Help yourself." Jesus pointed to the water barrels and rose to get bread from a saddlebag.

"How about money?" asked another man, grinning.

"I have no money," Jesus lied. He noticed the three men positioning themselves in a circle around him. "Here is your bread. Now, take a waterskin and go."

"We'll see what you've got," said the man closest to Rocky and the gear lying on the ground. He began to look through the bags.

"Get out of there!" Jesus said, starting toward the man.

Suddenly, one of the other men brought up his stick and hit Jesus across the face. He covered himself with his arms for protection as another of the bandits joined in the beating. Rocky bellowed, and the man nearest him turned. The camel sent a stream of slimy spit into his eyes. The man screamed. One of the other men turned his attention from Jesus toward his screaming friend. Rocky whirled around and kicked a hind leg into the robber's face. Blood and pieces of flesh splattered on the ground, and the man fell dead. Jesus quickly grabbed the dead man's stick and turned to meet the last aggressor. The man looked at Jesus, then at the dead man, then at his spit-covered friend, then at Rocky, who bellowed again angrily. He turned and ran, deserting his fellow bandits, feeling less brave as a single assailant. Jesus turned toward the temporarily blind man and swung the stick into the man's side. The man screamed again. Jesus grabbed him by the back of his tunic and pushed him in the same direction the other man had run. "That way!" he shouted, and the man stumbled off, holding his side and trying to find his way through blurred vision.

Jesus quickly saddled and packed Rocky, then climbed on his back, and the two galloped away. After a few miles, they slowed to a walk, but they didn't stop until the next evening.

Jesus met the Silk Road at Bokara, thirty days west of Braharam. From there, it was another thirty days to Damascus and through the edge of the Syrian Desert to Galilee. Those sixty days passed too quickly for Jesus. The nearer he came to home, the more anxious he was about his return. Where would he go from there? What was he to do? And what was the purpose of his long journey? He felt no closer to discovering God's will for his life, his destiny in God's great plan for Israel.

At Damascus, Jesus stayed in an inn. During the night, the voice came to him in a dream: "Do not go home to Capernaum. Go to Jerusalem, to the Mount of Olives. Pray to me there, and I will answer you."

The next morning, Jesus left Damascus and traveled south through the desert toward Jerusalem. It was the same route he had taken on the beginning of his journey. He traveled two days to Dium and two more days to Pella. At the end of the fifth day, he crossed over and made camp at the Jabbok River. He was sleeping when he heard a lion's roar and then Rocky's scream. He sat up and saw three lions: one with claws attached to Rocky's hind-quarter and two others crouched in front, ready to pounce on the panic-stricken animal. Jesus jumped to his feet and rushed the lions, shouting and waving his arms. The two cats in front of Rocky quickly turned and roared at Jesus, then, seeing him as no threat, turned back toward their desired prey. Rocky took off, running past Jesus with the lion still clinging to his side. The other two cats bypassed Jesus, too, following the bellowing camel into the night. Jesus turned but didn't follow. He couldn't. The animals were too fast, and the night too dark. He hoped Rocky would get away, that he might be able to cripple the cats with his kicks or, at least, hurt them enough to cause them to run away. But he knew in his heart it would not end this way. His friend was outnumbered, and the lions too strong. From far away, he heard Rocky cry out in his final death throes. He heard the growls of the lions. They had him on the ground. Then it was over. Silence. Jesus wept.

When it was daylight, Jesus filled three waterskins from the barrels and packed a single bag with food. He fit these over his shoulders and walked away, leaving the rest behind. In the distance, he could see the dark bump on the desert floor. Vultures were piled on top of it, picking away at the remaining flesh. He took a wide berth around the scene he didn't wish to see. He followed the Jabbok until it merged with the Jordan, then followed the Jordan for the rest of the day. He spent the night beside the river, and the next day traveled west to Jericho.

Jesus stood on the Mount of Olives, looking down on the Kidron Valley and across to the City of David. Crowds of people were moving in and out of the east gate. It was the Festival of Weeks, and Jerusalem was bursting with pilgrims from all over Israel. He went to his favorite place to pray. It was a rock at the top of the mountain and hidden away from the rest of the garden by a row of cedar trees. The rock jutted out of the surrounding ground, about two feet high, and its flattened surface gave the appearance of a short table or altar. He knelt there beside the rock, placed his elbows on its surface, and folded his hands in a praying position. He could see the Temple, its white stone walls gleaming in the sun. Whatever his destiny was to be, he knew it would come to pass in Jerusalem. He prayed there in earnest for an hour, always listening for the voice to speak, to give him direction as promised.

Finally, Jesus broke his concentrated prayer. He suddenly realized that his knees were on fire from pressing into the rocky ground below, his elbows bloodied by the stone table's jagged points and pits. He raised himself and rubbed the sore parts of his body, disappointed that the voice had not come. Then God spoke to him. "You have done well by me, Jesus. Like Abraham before you, you followed my call to go, not knowing where you were being led. You have been faithful and obedient, and you have learned much of what you need to know. But your quest is not done. Now, go to the wilderness of Judea, to the place I will show you. Your cousin, John, is baptizing at the Jordan and preparing your way. Go to him and be baptized. I will lead you from there."

Jesus left that same day and made his way back to the Judean Wilderness and the Jordan River.

John the Baptizer was the cousin of Jesus, the son of Elizabeth and Zechariah. He grew up strong in the Lord and believed in the coming of God's kingdom and the messiah, who would bring this about. John was an ascetic. He lived in the wilderness and wore clothes made of camel hair, and his food was locusts and wild honey. John preached repentance for the forgiveness of sins and baptized those who accepted his message as a sign of being cleansed from sin and made ready for the kingdom of God. John knew his destiny: to prepare the way for the one who was to come.

People from all of Judea and Jerusalem heard about John and his message of repentance, and they came to him to be baptized. "Repent, for the kingdom of heaven is near," he would say to them. "Hear my voice, the one crying out in the wilderness: Prepare for the coming of the Lord! Make your crooked ways straight. Fill the valleys in your hearts and flatten the mountains that block the way of your souls. Make your rough places smooth. And you will see the salvation of God!"

There were people of high status and political power, Pharisees and Sadducees, coming to receive the baptism of John, but they were not sincere in their hearts.

John said to them, "You brood of snakes! Who told you to run from the wrath of God? For you follow God with your lips, in prayer, and through keeping the ritual acts and ceremonies of the law, but your hearts are far away! Go and bear the fruits of repentance, then come and be baptized!"

They went away angry and, from that day, conspired against John, to discredit him and destroy his ministry.

To the others who came to him, John said, "I baptize you with water for repentance, but there is one near; he will baptize you with the Holy Spirit."

One day, when John was baptizing, he saw Jesus approaching. Though he was still far away, John knew this was the one for whom he was preparing the way. "Behold!" he shouted, pointing at Jesus, "The Lamb of God, the messiah, has come!" John came out of the water and walked to meet Jesus. When they met, he knelt before Jesus, who took John's hand and lifted him up.

"I have come to you for baptism," Jesus said.

"It is I who need to be baptized by you," John replied.

"Let it be as I have said," Jesus answered. "For God has sent me to you, and it must be fulfilled in this way."

So John relented and baptized him.

When Jesus came up out of the water, a white dove descended from the sky and hovered above his head. Then a voice from heaven said, "This is my Son, the Beloved One, in whom I am well pleased." The voice was heard by everyone, including Jesus, and he was filled with the Holy Spirit.

Jesus and John talked for a long time together. John told Jesus that he should take over the ministry he had begun. "I've been preparing the way for your arrival. Now it's time for me to step aside and follow you."

"It is not the time," Jesus said. "God will tell me when my time has come. You must continue to baptize and preach. Witness to all who will listen; make them ready for the kingdom that is surely coming."

"I will do as you have asked, Lord, but do not be long. Already, the sickle is at the root of the crop and the harvest is at hand."

Jesus placed his hand on John's shoulder. "I'll return when the time is right. Now, go. You have work to do."

"At least, let me send some of my disciples with you," John said.

"I have no need of disciples, John. For I cannot teach what I do not know. God has yet to reveal his plan to me. When he does, I will gather my own disciples. What I do now, I must do on my own." Then, compelled by the Spirit, Jesus turned and made his way deep into the Judean wilderness.

John returned to the river and was baptizing when one of his disciples waded out to him. "That guy is trouble," the disciple said.

"Did you see how they all looked at him? How they wanted to follow him?"

"And they will follow him. Soon we'll all follow him," John said. "I must decrease and he must increase."

"Please, don't talk that way, master! I won't follow anyone but you!"

John grabbed the disciple by the nape of his tunic and shoved his head under the water. He held him there for a while, the man's arms and legs flailing. Finally, he released him, and the man shot up straight, coughing water from his mouth and nose.

"Didn't you hear the voice from heaven?" John shouted angrily. "Don't you know who this man is? He is the messiah! The one we've awaited!"

The disciple stared at John from his wide open eyes, wiping water from them and quickly backing away. The people were staring too.

"Next!" John yelled. It took a moment for the next person to step forward.

Jesus had been in the wilderness for four days. He hadn't eaten in all that time, and his waterskin had run dry two days ago. His throat was parched and his lips cracked. The skin on his face was burned and raw. There were snakes and scorpions about, and an occasional curious ibex, precariously perched on the rocky cliffs above him, staring down. There were a few birds in the air, mostly vultures searching the desert floor for something dead. Of late, they seemed to be keeping a watchful eye on Jesus. At night, the air grew cold, and the extreme shift in temperature caused his body to shiver. The wind whipped down the mountain creases and around boulders, making haunted sounds like tortured demons condemned to fly blind in the wasteland's darkness. He drifted off to sleep.

At dawn, Jesus opened his eyes and saw a man standing in front of him. He was dressed in a dark tunic, and a hood was pulled over his head, so Jesus couldn't see his face.

"Jesus," he said. "Why do you suffer so? You heard the voice, didn't you?" If you are, indeed, the Son of God, then command these stones to become loaves of bread, and eat."

"It is written that one does not live by bread alone," Jesus replied, "but by every word that comes from the mouth of God."

Suddenly, Jesus was whisked away from the wilderness. He could see that he was moving but at a speed so great the ground below him was flashing before his eyes and he couldn't focus. When his feet touched the ground again, he looked and saw the city of Jerusalem below him. He wasn't standing on ground at all, but on the pinnacle of the Temple. He didn't see the man but heard his voice:

"If you are the Son of God, throw yourself down from here. God will command angels to save you. Is it not written in the psalms, 'God will command his angels concerning you, to guard you in all your ways. On their hands they will bear you up, so that you will not dash your foot against a stone.'"

Jesus said, "It is also written, 'Do not put the Lord your God to the test.'"

In an instant, he was taken away, again, to a high mountain. The man stood beside him and before them were all the kingdoms of the world. "You know who I am, Jesus. I have the power to give all these to you. Just bow down and worship me, and they are yours."

"You have no power unless God gives it to you. And you have no power over me. So, away with you, Satan! For it is written, 'Worship the Lord your God and serve only him.'"

Immediately, Jesus found himself back in the wilderness, and the devil left him to await a more opportune time to test him. And the angels came and waited on Jesus, giving him drink and healing his wounds, but he didn't eat. He fasted for forty days in the Judean wilderness and then returned home to Galilee.

Chapter 5

Jesus' Ministry

I t had been four years since Jesus left Capernaum. When he topped the brown-grass hills overlooking the Sea of Galilee from the west, his spirit was full. He knew God's plan for him now, his life's purpose and destiny. He would spend a few days in Capernaum with his mother and family, and then begin the ministry to which he was called.

It was the Sabbath, so the streets were empty as Jesus made his way toward home. He passed the boatyard and carpenter shop and was surprised to see no boat under construction. There was only a small amount of lumber in the shed, and the furnace sat on its side, a rusty hulk. The boatyard sign he had made was gone.

Jesus went to the familiar house, which was no worse for wear, and knocked on the door. He didn't wait for it to be answered. When he entered, Mary stood before him. She clasped her hands to her mouth and tears filled her eyes. Then she ran to Jesus and threw her arms around his neck. She kissed him again and again on his cheeks, while he picked her up and spun her around in circles until they were both dizzy. He embraced his brothers Jacob and Simon, and Mary gave the young men instructions to go and get their siblings.

"Not tonight," Jesus said, stopping his brothers in their tracks. "It's late. Let's just sit and visit, the four of us. I'll see the rest of them tomorrow."

They stayed up late into the night, talking. Jesus learned that Marion, Anna, and Salome were all married and had families of their own. James was not married but had added a room to the carpenter shop and was living there. Jesus had walked right past the place and missed the added space. Finally, after much conversation, Jesus was the first to say good night. He was tired and he slept well, and late.

When Jesus got up the next morning, most of his family was there. They hugged and kissed, and Jesus greeted his new brothers-in-law, men he already knew. Marion had married Silas, the fisherman. Anna's husband, Caleb, was the son of a local merchant, now in business with his father. Salome, the youngest of the girls, wasn't there. She lived in the Judean town of Lydda and was the wife of a local vinedresser. Jesus counted four young nieces and nephews, not yet sure who belonged to whom.

After breakfast, Jesus asked James about the business. "I didn't see any boats in the yard."

"Nah, I gave it up." James said.

"How come?"

"There just wasn't enough business. It took a year to sell each of my last two boats. I couldn't tie up that much capital for so long a time and so little profit. I've built a few smaller boats, but that really doesn't hold much interest for me. I might as well be building furniture. Besides, since you left, the work at the shop was backing up. People were starting to place their orders elsewhere. I couldn't build boats and furniture too."

"I'm sorry," Jesus said.

"It's okay. I've taken both Jacob and Simon on as apprentices. They're both pretty good carpenters, though I don't think Simon will stay. He has his mind set on sailing the seas. He wants to travel, like his brother."

"Uh-oh," Jesus said.

"Yeah," said James. "But it's okay. The shop can't support three households, and, eventually, that's what we'd have. I hope you're not looking for work."

Jesus laughed. "Don't worry. I'm just here for a short time. The Spirit of the Lord is upon me, James. God has called me to preach and teach that the kingdom is near."

"I hope that is so," James said. "The Roman dogs are worse since you left. Taxes are twice what they were, and the soldiers are everywhere, abusing women and extorting money from merchant and farmer alike. Herod is in league with them and does nothing to protect the people."

"Herod is no king but a greedy puppet. He cares only for himself."

"When will you go?" James asked.

"Soon. Why don't you come with me? There is much to do to prepare the people for the Lord's Day. I could use your help."

"I'll give it some thought," James said.

The next day, Jesus was walking by the sea. When he came to the main fishing dock, he saw Peter there with his brother, Andrew. They were cleaning their nets on the shore.

"Peter. Andrew," Jesus called out.

The two men looked up.

"Jesus of Nazareth," Peter said, condescendingly. It was an attempt at a slight, using Jesus' birthplace as a title and reminding him that the people of Capernaum did not hold Nazoreans in high esteem. Peter had always enjoyed harrassing Jesus in this way.

"Well, look what the cat dragged in," Andrew said, following Peter's lead.

"You're a sight for sore eyes, gentlemen," Jesus responded. He noticed their large boat was nowhere in sight. "Where's your boat?"

"Sunk. Last year," Peter said, in painful remembrance. "Just as well. There aren't as many fish as there used to be. These small boats do just fine."

What Peter said was true. The fishing had been so poor that many believed the lake was dying. Many of the fishermen had left Capernaum and the surrounding villages for the coast. Peter's father's once large fleet now consisted of only himself and his four sons.

"Get in your boat and row out seventy yards. If you cast to the west, you'll find fish."

Peter chuckled. "The great Jesus has returned. And now the carpenter is teaching the fishermen how to fish."

"Just do it, Peter. I promise you, you'll find fish. What have you got to lose?"

"A good deal of energy from two tired men," Peter replied. "There are no fish, Jesus. We've been out there in the hot sun all day and caught nothing. Now, at the end of the day, you want us to go back out?"

He threw his net in the boat and walked toward Jesus. When the two were face to face, Peter said, "Look, I'm glad to see you. I'm glad you're back. There's something I've wanted to say to you for a long time. I know you think I hate you, Jesus, but I've never hated you. I resented you, maybe. You always seemed to have such a charmed life, and I wanted that. I wanted to be you, since we were kids. You were always the perfect student with the perfect family. You had money, at least until your father died. You were funnier. Smarter. The girls liked you better. You never had to work as a child. You were always free to do whatever you wanted after school, while I had to come to these damned docks every day and help my father. When we grew up, you were more successful. You had your own business while I continued to work as my father's slave. Then, when you took Mary, the love of my life, I took it personally. I know, now, that you loved her, too, and she loved you. But, at the time, it just seemed as if you were trying to best me, again. Anyway, as I said, I know better now, and I'm sorry. I don't hate you. I just wanted you to know that."

Jesus smiled and reached out to embrace Peter, who shielded himself and backed away.

"Uh, I don't really need a hug," Peter said. He reached out his hand and Jesus accepted it happily.

"Thank you, Peter," Jesus said. "But the fish are out there, you know, if you'll just…"

Peter interrupted him with laughter. "You haven't changed. That's for sure. Maybe tomorrow. Tonight, I'm going home."

The next afternoon, Jesus was walking along the shore again. He saw Peter and Andrew casting their nets and drawing them in empty. "Peter!" Jesus shouted. "Come this way!"

"Son of a bitch. He doesn't give up, does he? Is he trying to tell us where to fish again?"

"Let's just go in," Andrew said. "It's pointless. There are no fish and I'm tired."

"Pull in the nets, and we'll go." Peter replied.

They stored the nets and lifted the sail. It barely caught wind, so they manned the oars to help the boat along. As they headed toward the dock, Jesus was running along the shore, yelling.

"No! No! Toward me!" He was motioning with his hands.

Peter and Andrew were staring at him. "He's crazy," Andrew said. "He must have lost his mind during his travels."

Jesus became almost frantic, jumping up and down and waving his arms above his head.

"This is ridiculous," Peter said, finally. "Row over to him."

When they were about thirty yards from shore, Jesus yelled at them to stop. They did. "Now cast your nets south and behind you."

"Jesus!" Peter shouted. "You know nothing about fishing! The day is hot and the water here is shallow. If there were fish, they would be deeper."

"You've already fished the deep water," Jesus shouted back. "Trust me."

"Crap," Peter said. "Let's get this over with." He and Andrew threw their nets in the direction Jesus had said. "Now, pull them in and we'll go home."

There was a quick jerk and pull, like fish bumping against the net, then a steady, slight resistance.

"I'll be damned," Andrew said. "It feels like we have fish."

Suddenly, the boat was being pulled in the other direction, toward deeper water. Then it stopped and began to tilt to the side where the net was sinking to the bottom.

"Pull!" shouted Peter. "If the net hits bottom, it'll open and the fish will swim away!"

"Don't pull!" Andrew replied nervously. "If we try to pull it to the surface, it'll capsize the boat. Just keep the line taut and the top of the net will stay closed."

"Yeah? So how do we get the fish in the boat?"

"I don't know!"

"Help! Help!" They both called out to another fishing boat on shore. The three men standing beside their boat couldn't believe what they were seeing. They stood there, motionless.

"Go help them!" Jesus shouted, running toward the men on the shore.

The three men suddenly came to their senses and pushed their boat into the water before climbing aboard. They rowed out and positioned their boat beside Peter and Andrew. Then all five men hoisted the net up between the two boats and tied off the lines. Using baskets and their bare hands, they began shoveling fish into both boats. Finally, when the net was light enough, they pulled it in the boat. They had so many fish, both boats were practically sinking as they rowed them to shore. The adrenaline rush caused the men to whoop and laugh and clap their hands in excitement. Except for Peter, who sat, leaning against his boat with his arms folded and his eyes fixed on the ground. He knew he had witnessed a miracle, and that it was Jesus who had performed it.

When Jesus walked over to him, Peter looked up into his eyes. "Who are you?" he asked.

"You know who I am," said Jesus.

Peter fell on his knees before Jesus, and said, "Go away from me, Lord, for I am a sinful man."

Jesus looked at him. "Come with me, Peter, and I will make you a fisher of people ."

"I will go where you go," Peter said in surrender.

"So will I," said another voice. Jesus turned to see Andrew standing behind him.

Jesus walked over to the other boat, where the three men were separating the flopping fish by kind and size.

"I am Zebedee," said the older man, "and these are my sons, James and John."

"I have need of you," Jesus said to the two younger men. "Will you go with me to proclaim the good news of God?"

"I'll go," John said, without hesitation.

"As will I," James replied.

"I will not go!" said Zebedee.

"You weren't invited," Jesus said. "Your place is here. Your sons' places are with me."

Zebedee started to protest but said no more.

"We'll travel light," Jesus said to the men. "No coat, no staff, no purse. Now go make yourselves ready. Say your goodbyes. We leave in the morning."

Jesus and James said goodbye to their mother and met Peter, Andrew, James, and John on the road. Only Peter was leaving a wife. He'd married a woman, ten years older, on the rebound from Mary. It was a marriage of convenience. She was a childless widow with a house and some money, and Peter's business was in dire financial straits. On the other hand, husbands were hard to find for barren forty-year-old women. After three years together, neither was devastated by Peter's departure.

From Capernaum, the men traveled to Bethsaida. Peter and Andrew had a cousin there whose name was Philip. He devoted himself to the study of scripture and was looking for the coming of the messiah. When they told Jesus about him, he agreed that they should find Philip and invite him to come with them. Philip believed in Jesus and followed him.

From there, they journeyed to Gergesa, where Philip had a friend named Nathaniel, a man also awaiting the kingdom of God and the restoration of Israel. Jesus sent Philip to search for him, and he found Nathaniel in the fields, dressing fig trees. "Nathaniel, we've found the messiah. Come and see." Nathaniel left the fields and followed him.

When Jesus saw him coming, he said to the others, "This man is faithful and true."

Nathaniel heard what Jesus said and asked, "How do you know me?"

"I saw you under the fig tree before Philip found you," Jesus said.

Nathaniel fell on his knees before Jesus. "You are the messiah, the king of Israel!"

Jesus took Nathaniel's hand and lifted him up. "Do you believe in me because I said I saw you under the fig tree? You will see much greater things if you will follow me."

"I will follow you," Nathaniel said.

The eight men traveled throughout all of Galilee, and Jesus taught in the synagogues, proclaiming the good news of God's kingdom. People were amazed at his wisdom, and word spread about him. He healed the sick and those afflicted with various diseases and pains, and great crowds began to follow him. From these, he chose four more disciples: Thomas, Simon, Bartholomew, and Judas.

When Jesus and the disciples came to Lydda, they stayed at Jesus' sister's home. Once word spread that he was there, people began coming from nearby villages and towns to see him. One day, the house was full, and people were standing outside, surrounding the house, listening as he taught. Some men from another village brought their friend, who was paralyzed, to see if Jesus would heal him. But when they got to the house, they saw the great crowds and were unable to push through them to the door. They carried the man on his stretcher to the back of the house, where stairs led to the roof terrace. They took their friend to the rooftop and then, using their hands, began to tear away at the clay roof and ceiling. The people below, especially Jesus' sister, were yelling at the men to stop, as they waved away the dust and dodged the clumps of dirt and straw falling on their heads. Jesus held up a hand to quiet them. The men continued to dig until they had made a large enough hole; then with ropes on each corner of the stretcher, they lowered the man down to Jesus.

Amazed at the faith of the men above him and their great love for their friend, Jesus looked at the crippled man and said, "Friend, your sins are forgiven."

Some Pharisees who had come to hear Jesus teach were in the house, and they said to him, "How do you speak such blasphemies? Only God can forgive sins."

"Why do you question God's forgiveness?" asked Jesus. "Are your hearts too hard to conceive of this? Isn't it easier to offer forgiveness than to say to a crippled man, 'Stand and walk'? But so that you may know I have the authority to forgive sins, I say to this man, 'Stand up and take your bed, and go to your home.'"

Immediately, the man stood, and, praising God, he took his bed and made his way through the crowd to the door. The people began to cheer and celebrate with the man and his friends, but the Pharisees were indignant and left in a huff to report Jesus' actions to the high priest.

After he had finished teaching, Jesus sent the people away. To calm his sister, he and the disciples spent the rest of the day repairing the roof. They left the following morning for Emmaus.

Matthew had not always lived in Emmaus. He had grown up in Bethany, in an upper middle class family, and then was sent to live with relatives in Jerusalem to attend secondary school there. After finishing his education, he took a job as an agent of the Roman government, collecting taxes from his own Judean people. He wasn't paid for this work but, like all tax collectors, was allowed to set a surcharge on the taxes he gathered as a means of support. And, like all tax collectors, Matthew paid himself very well. Tax collectors were despised by the Jewish people and looked upon as traitors, in collusion with the Roman oppressors.

Matthew spent many sleepless nights wrestling with his chosen occupation. But what choice did he have? He was, in fact, conscripted into service by the Romans. Education was his basic skill. He knew accounting and math and reading and was well schooled in the Roman tax laws and codes. He didn't know farming or fishing or carpentry or shop-keeping or any other trade that would provide him with half the living he was making in his current position. In the end, he justified his work with a "somebody's-got-to do-it" resolve and the feeling that he really had no choice at all. Still, he hated what he did and, most days, hated himself for doing it. His family had all but disowned him.

He had no friends, except other tax collectors. He wasn't welcome at the Temple or synagogue or many of the shops or neighbors' homes. He was a tax collector: lonely, well-off, ungodly, scum. That's how Matthew thought of himself. That was his fate. Or his choice?

When Jesus entered Emmaus, the crowds were waiting. Some who had been with him in Lydda, once they knew where Jesus was going next, ran ahead and told the people of Emmaus he was coming. They also reported to the people there about the healing of the paralyzed man. When they saw Jesus coming, they met him with cheers and shouts of "Hosanna." They lined the streets, and the sick were brought to him as he walked, so he could touch them.

Matthew, sitting in his tax booth, heard the commotion and saw everyone running toward the city gate.

"Jesus is coming!" shouted one, as he passed by.

"It is Jesus, the messiah!" shouted another.

"Jesus!"

"Jesus!"

The name sounded again and again.

It wasn't the first time Matthew had heard it. Some called him "rabbi," others "the messiah." Some referred to him as a miracle worker or healer or a great preacher. Some believed he was Elijah returned. And some, particularly among the religious leaders, believed him to be a charlatan and false prophet, drawing people away from God. Matthew had longed to meet him and see for himself who and what the man was. But he would have to wait. He couldn't leave his station and his money. He would have to hope Jesus would pass by.

The entire street was deserted. Matthew didn't see even a dog or a bird. It was as if the whole world had gone to Jesus. At least, all of Emmaus had. Matthew wanted to see too. He thought of grabbing up his books and money and risking himself to being fleeced by robbers in the midst of the crowd. Here, in his booth, within shouting distance, there was always a Roman soldier that he could call on should a robber or an irate taxpayer decide to accost him. And there were grave penalties to pay for such an offense. (It was, after all, Caesar's money.)

Surrounded in a crowd, however, there would be little a soldier could do to protect him and the money, or even identify the thief or thieves. He would stay where he was, even though he suddenly realized there wasn't a soldier in sight. *Had they, too, gone to Jesus?*

After a time, Matthew saw the crowd coming around the corner. They were definitely coming his way. He readied himself, hoping to catch a glimpse of the man he'd heard so much about. As they came closer, the shouts grew louder. Some in the crowd were dancing and singing. He could hear music—a drum, flutes, tambourines. There were townspeople in front, leading the way, but when they passed, there was an open space of about ten feet separating the crowd from Jesus and several men following close behind him. Matthew could clearly see him, and his heart raced as he watched him pass by. Then Jesus saw *him*! He stopped and looked at Matthew, and then walked right toward him. Matthew braced himself for the worst—yet another public condemnation of his work and place in society—when Jesus smiled at him and called him by name. *How did he know my name?*

"Matthew," Jesus said, "come and follow me." Matthew, to his own surprise, immediately got up, leaving the books and money on the table, and fell in behind Jesus, who was already moving again.

A Roman soldier, who had suddenly reappeared, yelled at Matthew, "Hey! You can't leave this booth unattended! Get back here!" He ran over to the booth and began to swat away the hands that were reaching in at the unprotected funds.

"Where is your house?" Jesus asked Matthew, as they walked.

"Not far from here," Matthew replied. "I'll show you." He walked beside Jesus, speaking directions as they went. When they arrived, Jesus had the disciples lift him up to the top of the wall surrounding Matthew's house, and from there he taught the people.

That night, Matthew gave a dinner party in honor of Jesus. There were no others Matthew knew of to invite, or who would even enter his house, so the guest list was made up mostly of other tax collectors.

A few of the local dignitaries were there too. They had invited themselves, because they couldn't resist the opportunity to rub elbows with Jesus, but they came reluctantly because of Matthew and the other less desirable persons present. They were offended that Jesus was showing deference toward such riffraff and practically ignoring *them*! "Why does he eat and drink with tax collectors and sinners?" they complained to the disciples.

Jesus heard them whining and, excusing himself from his conversation, went to them. "Why are you complaining?" he asked.

"Because you treat these sinners as if they are righteous, and us as if we are sinners," one of the Pharisees said. "Why do you spend all your time with them and none with us? You insult us!"

"You call yourselves righteous and them, sinners. If this is so, what need do you have of me? If you are well, what need of healing? Only the sick need a doctor. I have not come to save the righteous but the sinner. And I tell you this: Because you believe you are righteous before God and not in need of his forgiveness and healing, you will not receive it. You cannot receive it because, though it is offered, your hearts are not open to accept it. As for these sinners, they know their faults well and their need for God's mercy. They confess that they fall short of God's will for them, and they open themselves to receive God's forgiveness and grace. Therefore, I tell you, they will receive it and will enter into heaven before you."

"Outrageous!" said one.

"How dare you!" said another. "Sinners cannot enter the kingdom of heaven!"

"Unrepentant sinners, no; that is what I am telling you," Jesus said.

"Certainly not!" said a self-righteous priest, smugly. "You… Wait! … He's talking about us! You're talking about us!"

Jesus had already turned to walk away and leave them to think on what he had said. The Pharisees and other dignitaries had had enough. Those still seated stood to leave with the others.

"We should never have come here! We have defiled ourselves by being in the company of sinners," a Pharisee said.

"Ah, but we have also uncovered evidence that this Jesus is a false teacher, perverting the faith and leading the people astray," the priest said. "Our time here has been valuable. Let us take our report to the chief priest and the Sanhedrin. This man is dangerous and must be dealt with."

"We should deal with him ourselves," another man said. "We should stone him now!"

"Do not be foolish," said the priest. "The people adore him. They would kill us if we laid a hand on him. Let us continue to gather evidence against him. We will keep our eye on him wherever he goes. When the time is right, we will expose him, and the people will be with us. For now, just let him keep talking, and he will hang himself."

"Yes," said a Pharisee, "we will keep making our reports to Jerusalem. That is where we will get him. Sooner or later, he will go to Jerusalem. We can have him arrested there and tried. If we have our stories straight and our evidence against him, he will be convicted and that will be the end of him."

Just then, there was laughter from the other side of the room. The priest looked and saw Jesus enjoying himself with the others. He gritted his teeth.

"That is fine," he muttered loud enough for those around him to hear. "If he likes to be with thieves and sinners, we will soon give him all the company he can handle—in prison."

One Sabbath, while Jesus and the disciples and a crowd following them were walking on the road, they came to some wheat fields. His disciples were plucking some heads of grain and rubbing them between their hands to remove the husks, then eating them. There were some Pharisees in the crowd, spying on him, and they complained to Jesus. "Look at your disciples! It is the Sabbath. Why are you allowing them to do this? Do you not know that it is unlawful to do any kind of work on the Lord's day?"

"Is it wrong to hunger on the Sabbath, or to eat?" asked Jesus.

"It is wrong to work, and this is what your disciples are doing. It is the work of their hands that exposes the grain."

"Have you read the scriptures?" asked Jesus. "When David and his soldiers were hungry, did they not enter the house of God and eat the bread of the Presence, which is unlawful for anyone to eat but the priests? Those who work deserve to eat, and these followers of mine are doing the work of God."

On the same day, Jesus passed by a woman standing with the crowd along the road. She was crippled and her back was bent, so she was unable to stand up straight. She would've said nothing to Jesus, having been this way for many years, but Jesus felt her longing for him and stopped. "Woman," he said, "come out of the crowd and come to me here."

No one knew who he was talking to, so his disciple, Philip, asked, "Lord, who do you want?"

"The one who wants me," Jesus said.

The woman knew Jesus was calling her, but she was embarrassed and ashamed and shrank farther back into the crowd.

Jesus walked toward her. "Woman, I know you. Your back has been bent, and you've suffered in pain for eighteen years. If you'll come to me and tell me what you want, I'll do what you ask. God will make you well today."

Another, who knew the woman, was standing beside her. She said to her, "He's calling you. Go to him."

Still the woman hesitated, so the other woman took her by the hand and led her to Jesus. When they were in front of him, the woman fell to her knees and wouldn't look at him. Jesus placed his hand under her chin and lifted her face so that her eyes met his.

"I called you, but another led you to me. You must have faith in God and believe."

"Lord, I do believe," she said. "Help my unbelief."

"Then tell me what you want."

"I wish to be healed."

"And do you believe God can do this?"

"Yes. And I believe you are the Son of God, sent to do these things."

"Then stand and be well. Your faith has healed you."

Immediately, the woman stood up straight and began praising God, and the people joined her.

"Stop! Stop!" A Pharisee stepped forward from the crowd and stood in front of the woman and Jesus. "Do not celebrate this blasphemy! Again, this man proves he is not from God, for he breaks God's commandment by working on the Sabbath. And you, woman!" the Pharisee said, pointing his finger in the woman's face. "Do you not know that God crippled you in the first place as punishment for your sins? It is not God who healed you, but it is the devil himself." He turned his finger toward Jesus.

The woman was no longer shy but addressed the Pharisee boldly, "I may not know the scriptures as well as you, but you do not teach what you know. Why would the devil heal to alleviate the suffering of humans? The devil wishes only evil upon God's people. How can the devil heal? Only God can heal. This man has healed me, and I believe he is from God. But day after day, when I came to the Temple, the Pharisees said, 'Go away from us for your sins are upon you.' If God does good and the devil evil, then who is from God and who is from the devil?"

"How dare you, woman! Do you address a leader of Israel this way? Your sins *are* upon you, and they show in your speech!" He looked at the crowd and raised his arms in the air, questioning them. "I study the laws of God as my daily food and this uneducated woman dares to challenge me?"

By this time, the other Pharisees were coming out of the crowd to stand beside their spokesman. Some of them held rocks in their hands.

Jesus had enjoyed the banter and let it continue because he thought the woman spoke well and was holding her own with her opponent. But he could see she was becoming intimidated and scared. (She had seen the rocks in the men's hands.) He stepped in front of the woman. "Does it not say in Isaiah, 'The wisdom of the wise shall perish, and the discernment of the discerning will be hidden'? Woe to you, Pharisees. For you have eyes but do not see, and ears but you do not listen."

He then looked toward heaven and said, "Father, I thank you that you have hidden your truths from the wise and revealed them to your children." He looked at the Pharisees and asked, "Are you going to throw stones at the healing work of God?"

As he said these words, the men dropped the rocks from their hands but not on purpose. Each one involuntarily lost his grip, and the stones fell to the ground. They looked at each other, puzzled and afraid.

"Go in peace," Jesus said to the woman and gently nudged her back into the crowd.

As he started to walk away, one of the Pharisees, still massaging his numbed hand, shouted, "Just a minute, Jesus! We are not finished here. There is still the matter of your breaking the Sabbath law. And you sinful people! You come out on the Sabbath for healing, when you should be home at rest! You have six days when work is allowed and ought to be done; come on those days to be cured but not on the Sabbath day."

Jesus had had enough. "And you, teachers of Israel, what brings you out to me on the Sabbath day? Shouldn't you be at home and at rest? Or, have you come for healing too? You are hypocrites! For which one of you, if his ox falls in a ditch or if his donkey needs water would leave it for another day? If there is necessary work to do, even on the Sabbath, then do the work that is necessary. The Sabbath is made for man, not man for the Sabbath."

Though there were grumblings among them, none of the Pharisees wanted to argue further with Jesus, at least not today. Instead, they would regroup. They decided to continue following Jesus and wait for their next opportunity.

On the next Sabbath, they were in Jericho. Jesus entered the synagogue and taught the people there. When he was leaving, he saw a man whose hand was withered, so he went to him. The Pharisees were watching to see if Jesus would again heal on the Sabbath, so that they could bring another charge against him. Jesus knew what they were thinking, and he told the man to stand beside him. Then he said to the crowd, "I ask you, is it lawful to do harm or to do good on the Sabbath, to save life or destroy it?"

He waited. When no one answered him, he said to the crippled man, "Stretch out your hand." Before their very eyes, the man's arm straightened and was fully restored. The people praised God and rejoiced with the man made well. But the Pharisees were furious at this, and they discussed with one another what they might do about Jesus.

Jesus was anxious to get away from the people, and especially the Pharisees, so he set out for the Samarian wilderness. Samaria was a land mostly off limits to Jews, and certainly upstanding ones. He knew the Pharisees wouldn't follow him there. While it was acceptable, if necessary, to travel through Samaria, Jews were to travel through the land as quickly as possible and were not to speak to any of its residents along the way. Samaria and Samaritans were once a part of the Jewish nation and its northern tribes. They worshiped God, as the Jews did, but they had intermarried with those from other nations and, thus, were considered by the Jews to be permanently impure and unclean. By their sin, they had separated themselves from Israel and given up their birthright to be counted among God's people.

Just as Jesus predicted, when they came to the Samarian border, the people stopped and began to grumble. "Why does he go into the wilderness, and why does he go into Samaria?"

The Pharisees seized the opportunity. "So this is the man you wish to follow? Look where he goes, to a cursed land, no doubt to cavort with a heathen people. Do not be fooled by this charlatan. He has shown his true colors today!"

But some in the crowd defended Jesus. "You teach the law, but he fulfills it. You tell us the ways of God, but he shows us."

"He has a demon!" one of the Pharisees shot back. "He shows you the tricks of Satan and teaches the ways of the devil. We are men of God and the teachers of Israel. We will show you the true way! Now, follow us away from this godforsaken land, where, even now, Jesus and his disciples are going!"

Some in the crowd agreed and began to shout insults at Jesus, who, by now, was some distance away. Others said nothing, as they turned and walked toward home. The Pharisees felt good about the developments of the day and couldn't wait to share the news with their friends.

Jesus and the disciples came to a Samaritan city called Sychar. There was a well at the edge of the city, and Jesus stayed there while his disciples went to buy food. While he was waiting, a woman came to the well to draw water. She didn't speak to Jesus or look at him (because it wasn't proper for a woman to acknowledge or initiate conversation with an unfamiliar man). She tied her bucket to the end of the well's rope, dropped it down to the water, and then quickly raised it.

As she was untying the rope, Jesus spoke to her. "Give me a drink."

The woman caught Jesus' Galilean accent. "Sir, how is it that you, a Jew, would ask a woman of Samaria for a drink?"

"If you knew who you were talking to, you would be asking me for a drink," Jesus said.

She looked at Jesus and around his feet. "You don't even have a bucket. How are you going to give me a drink?"

"It isn't water from the well that I would give you, but the living water of God."

The woman was intrigued. "And where do you get this living water?"

"It is a gift I give to those who believe in me," Jesus answered.

"I see. And are you greater than our ancestor Jacob, who gave us this well?"

"Everyone who drinks from this well will be thirsty again, but those who drink the water I give them will never be thirsty."

"I would like to try this water," the woman said. "It's a long way to come to this well every day."

"Go and call your husband then, and you can drink together."

"Um...I don't have a husband, *really*."

"Really, you don't. That is true. But you have had a husband. In fact, you've had five husbands, and the man you're living with now is not your husband at all. So, you're right when you say you have no husband, *really*."

She looked at Jesus, now more intrigued. "Okay. So…are you some kind of prophet? I mean, you see me and you see my life. How do you know these things?"

Jesus didn't answer.

"Then let me ask you this: Our ancestors worshiped at the Temple on Mount Gerizen, but the Jews say people must worship in Jerusalem at the Temple there. Who is right?"

"Neither is right. We can worship God at any place and at any time. And God is present in all places and at all times. There isn't a place where God is not, and there isn't a place where God is, only. It isn't the *place* that makes our worship acceptable and worthy before God; it is the worshiper's heart. And I tell you this: The day is coming when all God's people will worship in spirit and in truth."

The woman was moved by Jesus' words. "I know the messiah is coming, and when he comes, he will reveal all these things to us. Are you the messiah?"

"I am," Jesus said.

Just then, the disciples returned from the city. The woman bowed and kissed Jesus' hands and then hurried away.

"Teacher," said Thomas, "why were you speaking to a Samaritan woman? What did she want?"

"What did you bring to eat?" Jesus asked.

The woman returned to the city and told everyone about Jesus. "He is the messiah," she said to them. "He knew everything about me and spoke great truths about God."

Many from the city went out to him, and Jesus taught them about the good news of God. They invited him to stay in the city, and he was there with them for many days. When he was leaving, they said to him, "At first, we believed because of what the woman told us, but now, we have heard for ourselves, and we know that you are the savior of the world."

From Sychar and Samaria, Jesus continued north to Galilee and the city of Nain.

Just as they were approaching the gate of the city, he saw a large funeral procession carrying the bier of a dead man above their heads. He asked one of those in the procession about the man and learned that he was the only son of a widow—and her sole support. When he saw the widow and how she grieved, his heart went out to her. "Woman, do not weep, for God is with you."

"God may be," she said through her tears, "but my only son is gone."

"Have faith," Jesus said.

He went to the bier and told the bearers to stop and lower it. They stopped but didn't lower the bier from above their heads.

"You're a stranger," one of them said. "Are you curious about this man at his poor mother's expense? Now stand aside and let us proceed."

"Do as he says," the mother of the dead man replied. "I trust him to be a compassionate man and a servant of God."

The bearers lowered the bier to the ground.

The man was covered with a shroud, and Jesus couldn't see his face. "Come and stand with me," he said to the widow. When she was beside him, he placed his hand under the shroud and coupled it with the hand of the dead man. "Son," Jesus said, "I say to you, rise up and live."

The man immediately sat up and threw the shroud from his face. He looked around at the stunned crowd, then down at himself and his bier, then at his mother. "What the hell, Mama!"

She slapped him for his language, then fell to her knees and wrapped her arms around her son's neck. "My son! You were dead but now live again!"

Some in the crowd thought he was a ghost and were so frightened, they began to run away. Others were praising God and saying, "A great prophet has come among us! God has looked with favor on our city!"

And the word spread throughout all of Galilee and Judea that Jesus had raised the dead.

Nazareth was the boyhood home of Jesus. When the people there heard that he was returning, they were excited because of all the wonderful things he had done. The whole town went out to greet him, and they claimed him as their own. "He is one of us!" they said. "He is Jesus of Nazareth!"

Many of the older citizens recalled memories of Jesus as a child (somewhat differently than before). "Didn't we see his greatness when he was just a boy? The signs he did, even then? We knew there was something special about him!"

On the Sabbath day, Jesus went to the synagogue to worship and pray. The synagogue leaders had invited Jesus to read the scriptures and preach, and the whole town came out to hear him. When he stepped to the podium, he was handed a scroll. He unrolled it and began to search for a passage from Isaiah. When he found it, he read aloud:

> *The Spirit of the Lord is upon me,*
> *because he has anointed me*
> *to preach good news to the poor.*
> *He has sent me to proclaim release to the captives*
> *and recovery of sight to the blind,*
> *to let the oppressed go free,*
> *to pronounce God's favor upon all his people.*

He then rolled up the scroll and handed it to the attendant. He said to the people, "Today, this scripture has been fulfilled in your hearing."

There were murmurs among the congregation, and people began to squirm in their seats.

"Did he just say *he* was the fulfillment of the scriptures?" someone finally said aloud.

"His powers and gifts have gone to his head. He thinks he's the messiah!" said another.

Everyone stood up and began to shout out at the same time.

The synagogue leaders tried to restore order, but they were angry at Jesus too. When they finally got the people relatively quiet and seated again. One of them spoke directly to Jesus. "You've come to our city, and we've welcomed you home, but you have done no great works here. We've heard many things about you, but we have seen nothing. You are purported to be a great healer and teacher, a worker of miracles, but there have been no healings here, and the teachings we've heard seem to us as blasphemy. You tell us you are messiah, the Son of God, but we know you, Jesus. You are the son of Joseph and Mary. We knew you when you were just a snot-nosed little boy, up to mischief and not greatness. Your family was run out of town because of you and your unruly ways. And you want us to believe that you are the messiah, the fulfillment of the scriptures concerning God's anointed one?"

"He's anointed by the devil!" shouted an old man. "I told you when he was a boy, he had a demon. Now evil has consumed him. We should've killed him then. We ought to kill him now!"

The people erupted again, in agreement with the old man.

It was clear to the synagogue leader that he had a lynch mob on his hands. He raised his hands to quiet the crowd. "Jesus can show us if he is good or evil, of God or the devil. For the devil can do no good works among men. Come forward, Jesus, and show us some sign, some miracle, to convince us that you are from God."

Jesus stood up and faced the crowd. "I say this to you: No prophet is ever accepted in his hometown. You ask for a sign, and here I stand before you, but you do not see. Therefore, no other sign will be given to you, except the sign of Jonah. For when he preached to the people of Nineveh, they repented and believed. You have heard this day the proclamation of God, and yet you do not believe."

When the people heard this, they became enraged. "Kill him!" they shouted. "Stone him! And his disciples too!"

"There will be no killing in the house of God!" said the synagogue leader. But the people were already pressing in toward Jesus.

"Quickly," Jesus said to his frightened disciples, "go out the side door. Get out of town. Run, don't walk. Go on to Capernaum, and I'll meet you there."

"But what about you, Jesus?" Peter asked, as the others quickly made their exit.

"I'll be fine. Just go."

"I'll stay and fight with you, and die with you," Peter said defiantly but pessimistically.

"I'm not fighting or dying, today, Peter. Now go and catch up with the others. I'll see you in Capernaum." He forced Peter out the side door, following him, but, once they were outside, Jesus turned and went the other way.

By now, Peter had lost his nerve and was running as fast as he could. When he realized no one was chasing him, he turned to look for Jesus. He saw him climbing a hill with what seemed like the entire town in pursuit behind him. He wanted to go back, but when Jesus disappeared behind some trees, he turned and began running again to catch up with the others.

When Jesus reached the top of the hill, there was nowhere else for him to go (and nowhere else for his pursuers to go). Jesus had remembered the hill and the cliff from his childhood. He stood at the edge, and the people came toward him to push him over the side. Just when the first men were about to lay hands on him, Jesus vanished from their sight. When the rest of the people reached the top of the hill, the eyewitnesses tried to explain to the others what they couldn't believe themselves.

"He was there, and then he wasn't there!" said one of the men.

"Are you sure he didn't just fall over the side?"

"That's what we thought must have happened," said another witness, "but we checked. He's not there. Look for yourself."

"I'll tell you what happened," said a third witness. "He just disappeared, right before our eyes. I saw it! He was there, then he faded into this transparent mist. You could see right through him! Then he was gone!"

The old man (the same demon-obsessed, lifelong Jesus hater) struggled to the top of the hill, caught his breath, and spoke. "He has a demon, if he isn't the devil himself! I told you this when he was a boy. We should have killed him then."

Eventually, the people left the hilltop and went to their homes—confounded but glad to be rid of Jesus, again.

The disciples avoided all the towns and villages between Nazareth and Capernaum. When it was evening, they made camp along the road. They had no food and were famished.

"We shouldn't have left him," Peter said.

"We did what he told us to do," Andrew replied. "He said he would meet us at Capernaum. We have to trust this is true."

"What if it isn't true?" asked Philip. "What becomes of us? We've left everything to follow him."

"Shut up!" James snapped. "Are you worried about yourself? Worry for all of Israel if something's happened to him. Do you doubt he is the messiah, the hope of our people? You're right, Peter. We shouldn't have left him. Woe to us, if harm has come to him."

"If he is the messiah, then God will protect him," Thomas said. "Let's not speak more about things we do not know. We'll go to Capernaum and wait, as he told us."

"Ho!" a voice called out from the darkness. "Have you any food for a fellow traveler."

"We have nothing, friend," Peter said to the disembodied voice. "But you're welcome to come into our camp and share our fire."

A figure stepped out of the darkness and into the light of the fire. It was Jesus. "Then, perhaps, I can share my food with you."

"Master!" Peter exclaimed. He rose and embraced Jesus. The others stood, too, and happily greeted him.

"Now, sit and eat." Jesus sat with them and unrolled a cloth sack filled with bread and dried fish. He also had a waterskin.

"But where did you get this?" asked Nathaniel.

"Didn't the Lord provide food and water for Moses and those who followed him? God will provide for you and me as well."

They asked him no more questions but listened as he told them parables about the kingdom of God.

The next evening, they came to Capernaum. Peter and Andrew took their cousin Philip and his friend Nathaniel to their father's house. James and John took Thomas and Simon to stay with them. Jesus and James took Bartholomew, Judas, and Matthew home with them. "Let's take a few days and rest up before we begin our journeys again," Jesus said before they parted. "I'll let you know when it's time to go."

Mary was pleased to see her two oldest sons. They had supper, and Jesus and James told Mary all about their experiences on the road (though they didn't mention Nazareth). Mary caught them up on the happenings of the rest of the family.

"There's a wedding in Cana next week," Mary said. "It's your cousin Esther's. You should plan to go."

"A wedding feast would be fun," Jesus said, "and a nice diversion for the men for a few days. What do you think, James?"

"I agree. I would like to see Esther and the woman she's become. I haven't seen her since she was a young girl."

"Do you think it would be okay to bring the others along?" Jesus asked Mary.

"Of course. The entire village will be there, and family and friends from all over. A few more won't make a difference."

"It's settled, then. When do we leave?"

"In five days."

"We'll let the others know tomorrow," said Jesus.

The next day, Jesus was on his way to the carpenter shop to visit his brothers, Jacob and Simon, when the local elders came to him. They told Jesus about a Roman centurion, who'd been living in Capernaum for the past year.

"He's a believer in the Lord God, and he keeps our ways," one of the elders said. "Further, he knows of you and the things you have done. When he heard you were here, he called for us and asked us to speak to you on his behalf."

"What does he want?" Jesus asked.

"He has a servant, whom he loves, and who is deathly ill. He asked us to ask you to come and heal her. The centurion is a good man, Jesus. He isn't like other Romans and is worthy to have you do this for him, for he loves our people. It is he who is funding the construction of our new synagogue."

"Very well," said Jesus. "Take me to him."

As they were on their way, a neighbor of the centurion met them. He genuflected before Jesus, then rose with his head still bowed, and spoke. "I have a message from the centurion, Flavius."

"Then speak it," replied Jesus.

The neighbor unrolled a small scroll and read:

"Lord, please do not trouble yourself for my sake, for I am not worthy to have you come under my roof. For this same unworthiness, I do not come to you. But for the sake of my good servant, have mercy, Lord. Only speak the word from where you are, and I know my servant will be healed. For I am a man of authority with soldiers under me. When I say, 'Go,' they go. And when I say 'Come,' they come. I know it is the same with you, Lord, and with your authority, which surely comes from God."

When Jesus heard this, he was amazed. He turned to the elders and said, "I tell you, not among all the children of Israel have I found one with such faith!"

"Go back," he said to the neighbor, "and tell your friend that his faith and God's power have made his servant well."

When the neighbor returned to the centurion's home, the servant was up and about, completely healed. And the neighbor told the centurion everything Jesus had said.

Four days later, Jesus and his disciples and all his family arrived at Cana for the wedding feast. Hundreds of people had gathered for the event—most of Cana, as well as relatives and friends from all over Galilee.

The father of the bride was Mary's brother, Jacob. After welcoming his sister and the rest of the Capernaum party, including the uninvited friends of Jesus, he hurried off to look after the details of the just beginning five-day feast. It was the responsibility of both families of the couple to provide for the feast. Jacob had secured and paid for the wedding venue; he had also made arrangements for all the food and drink for the feast, the cost of which would be shared by the two families equally. Guests, other than those invited to stay in the homes of family, were to provide for their own lodging. Most of the guests camped in tents just outside of town, creating their own new village, virtually half the population of Cana itself.

As it turned out, Jesus' disciples weren't the only uninvited guests. Many more people showed up than were expected, so, by the third day of the feast, supplies were running dangerously low. Jacob shared his concern with Mary. "We're out of almost everything," he said. "The food we can ration to a degree, and I can get more from the merchants and farmers, if needed, but there isn't enough wine in all of Cana to last through the day. It was my responsibility to supply the feast, but how could I have known so many people would come? If we run out, I'll be disgraced and so will my new in-laws, and so will Esther and her husband. I don't know what to do, Mary!"

"I think I do," Mary said. "Let me speak to Jesus."

Mary found Jesus with his disciples and some of his cousins enjoying themselves in the courtyard of the city's common hall. (This was the center location of the feast, where the food and wine were served.) She had brought one of the stewards with her. "Jesus," Mary said, "I need to talk to you alone."

Jesus excused himself from the others and followed his mother to a corner of the courtyard. "What is it?" he asked.

"They are almost out of wine, and there are two days left for the feast."

"That's not good," Jesus said.

"No, it isn't," said Mary. They looked at each other, each waiting for the other to speak.

"So...maybe they should get more?" Jesus queried.

"There is no more. Not in all of Cana or the surrounding area."

"Okay. And you're telling me this because...?"

"Because this could become an embarrassing situation for my brother and niece, and *your* uncle and cousin."

Jesus looked perturbed. "Am I the father of the bride or groom? What does any of this have to do with me?"

"This is my family," Mary said. "It is *your* family. You need to do something about this."

Jesus looked puzzled, and then began to see where the conversation was going. "Oh no, Mother! I'm not getting into this! This has nothing to do with me or my ministry. I came here to enjoy myself and celebrate Esther's wedding. That's all I intend to do. I'm here as a guest. That's all I intend to be."

"Yes, you are a guest. You and your uninvited friends!"

"*You* invited them!"

"It doesn't matter, Jesus. The point is there are a hundred unexpected people at this feast. It isn't as if Jacob planned badly or skimped on supplies. He just didn't prepare for this onslaught of people. This isn't his fault, and you need to help him fix it. Do you want your Uncle Jacob to be humiliated in front of his new in-laws and the whole town? Do you want your cousin Esther and her husband to be embarrassed in front of all their wedding guests?"

"Of course not, but I still don't see what this has to do with me. Why is it my responsibility? What you want me to do?"

"You know what to do. Now, do it." Mary turned to the steward and said, "Do whatever he tells you." She turned back toward Jesus and shot one last stern look at him before walking away.

Jesus shook his head in disbelief as he watched his mother disappear into the common hall. Mary hadn't made a request but a demand, and he was actually a little frightened about failing to comply. He looked at the steward. "What?" he asked, irritated.

The steward shrugged his shoulders as if to say, *Hey, she's your mother. I'm just doing what I'm told too.*

"Take those six jars and fill them with water," Jesus said. "Then bring them back to me."

The steward called for two more servers, and they took the jars, each with a capacity of about ten gallons, and filled them with water. They returned with the full jars and set them in front of Jesus.

"Taste it," he said.

The steward dipped a cup into one of the jars and tasted it. "It's wine!" he said, surprised and now a little frightened himself.

"Take the rest of your cup to the chief steward and have him taste it."

He did so.

When the chief steward tasted the new wine, he found Jacob.

"Where did you get the new wine?" the steward asked.

"What new wine?" Jacob asked.

Mary was sitting beside him. Smiling, she leaned over to Jacob and whispered something in his ear.

"It doesn't matter," the steward said. "There is plenty to avert the crisis. I don't mind telling you I was a little worried. In fact," he said with a grin, "I did tell you, many times, didn't I? This is a great relief, Jacob. We wouldn't have lasted another hour without this new supply."

"Uh, yes, we were fortunate to find it," Jacob said, also relieved.

"And it's some of the best I've ever tasted," the steward said. "You know, it's funny—ironic, even. At most weddings the best wine is served first and the cheaper stuff brought out at the end. Yet, here we are, after worrying about having no wine at all, serving the best last. People will be impressed by the quality of this feast, Jacob, from beginning to end."

Jacob leaned over and kissed his sister on the cheek. "Thank you," he said.

"You're welcome," Mary said. "When the time is right, we'll thank Jesus together."

"You know, I doubted him, Mary. Despite all the stories our father told me about him, all that you've told me, all the wonderful things I've heard about him, I doubted. I mean, I've always said to myself, he's family. How can he be this great miracle worker and man of God? Now I no longer doubt. I believe."

"I believe too," Mary said. "But he's more than a miracle worker, Jacob. He is the messiah."

When the wedding feast ended, Mary and the rest of the family from Capernaum returned home, while Jesus and his disciples went south to Judea.

When the Pharisees heard that Jesus had left Samaria and was in Galilee, they sent a contingent to spy on him. They had heard the reports of his raising the dead in Nain, and of the near riot in Nazareth, and of his healing the centurion's servant in Capernaum, but they could find him nowhere. Finally, in Cana, they learned that Jesus had left there for Judea, so they returned to Jerusalem, hoping to find him there, and to tell the high priest and council all that had been told to them.

Now it was time for the festival of Passover, and Jesus and his disciples went to Jerusalem. Beside the Sheep Gate was a place where many of the city's invalids—the blind, the lame, and the paralyzed—gathered by a pool called Bethzatha. It was said that the waters of the pool had healing powers but only when a breeze from the wind would cause the waters to ripple and move. Those desiring to be healed waited there patiently, day by day.

Sometimes the wind would not come at all, and, sometimes, when it did come, the stirring of the water was only momentary—perhaps only a second or two. Another unfortunate element to these healing waters was that they seemed to heal only one person at a time. That is, once the waters began to move, the first one in the pool would be healed. For all others, even the moving waters were ineffective.

When Jesus passed by the pool, he saw a middle-aged man there, paralyzed from the waist down. "Why are you here?" Jesus asked.

"I'm crippled. Have you come because you are blind?" the man replied sarcastically.

"I was just asking," Jesus said.

"I've been brought here every day for thirty years, waiting to get to the waters. I watch continuously for the waters to stir, but every time it happens, someone gets there before me."

"Perhaps you should move closer," Jesus said.

The man gave Jesus a venomous look. "You *are* blind," he growled. "Can't you see I'm as close as I can be on this ledge? I can't move as fast as others because I must drag my legs with me."

"Do you believe these waters can heal you?"

"I know they can. I've seen it happen."

"It isn't the waters that heal. It is the mercy of God."

"This I have not seen or experienced."

"Do you wish to be made well?"

"Uh, yeah. Duh! That's why I'm here."

"Then you will experience God's mercy today. Stand up. Take up your mat and walk."

Suddenly, after feeling nothing but the dead weight of his lower body for as long as he could remember, there was a tingling in his legs, then a searing pain, and then tightness, as palsied muscles began to twitch and straighten. He lifted himself, first with his arms and then with a new strength in his ankles and knees. He stood there, amazed, as his joints convulsed and then loosened. He took a step on shaky but able legs, then another, then another. He looked at Jesus. "You've healed me! God bless you!"

"Don't give praise to me," Jesus said. "Praise God. It is he that has healed you. Now take your mat and go, and tell others what God has done for you."

The man picked up his bed and went through the streets to his home, telling everyone along the way about the man he had met at the pool, and of the great thing God had done.

The Pharisees and the Sadducees were the two main religious schools in Judaism. Their leaders held high positions of honor in the Temple, and in the faith. The two groups differed, politically and theologically, on many points of view, but in one thing, they did agree. They hated and feared Jesus. Too many people were believing in him and the teachings he espoused: that the poor and needy were as special to God as they were; that the sinner was as loved by God as the righteous; that it was God's mercy and grace that effected salvation, and not the complex and precise keeping of the purity laws and the hundreds of commandments written by the religious leaders to separate themselves from the lesser classes of society. He had called them hypocrites for following the letter of the law but missing the spirit of what was behind the law and the reason for it—to strengthen relationships among God's people, not to strain them. He had accused them of supplanting God's commandments with their own, of making up rules for purity and righteousness too difficult for common people to follow, and for making additions to the ritual and ceremonial requirements that only they themselves could attain. He had even told the people that they could disregard all these laws so long as they followed two: Love the Lord with all your heart, soul and mind; and love your neighbor as yourself. If they followed these two laws, he had told them, they would be following all the commandments of God. Jesus was trouble. The people were believing in him. The Pharisees and Sadducees were losing control and losing respect. Something had to be done.

When the Temple leaders heard about the paralyzed man's healing, they sent some men to question him.

"Tell us what happened," they demanded.

"I was at the pool of Bethzatha, where I've been going every day for thirty years. I was waiting there when a man came up to me and asked me what I was doing. I told him I was waiting for the waters to move, so I could try to be the first in the pool and be healed. He told me that I didn't need the pool but a belief in God's mercy, and that if I believed in God, I would be healed. Then he told me to stand and walk, and I did."

"And who was this man?" they questioned.

"He didn't say."

"Have you seen him before?"

"No."

"Then he does not heal at the pool every day?"

"I haven't seen him before, and, as I said, I've been going there every day for thirty years."

"We heard what you said, but how do we know you were even crippled in the first place? Perhaps you are working with this man to make the people believe he is a healer."

"I wouldn't spend my time at the pool if I didn't need healing," the man replied. "As for how you can know if I was paralyzed, you can ask others there. You can ask my parents or others in my family, or my neighbors who have known me my whole life."

"Still, for all we know, you could have been faking."

The man chuckled. "This is some conspiracy I'm in with this man you are after. For thirty years, we have plotted together, and I've spent my life as a crippled man, waiting for this day to come so that, together, we could fool the world."

"Do not speak to us like we are idiots!" warned the man's questioners. "We are respected men and leaders of the Temple!"

"Then don't behave like idiots," the man said, still smiling at the preposterous accusation. "You've asked me to tell you what happened to me today, and I've told you. Whether you believe me is up to you. I don't care. All I know is this morning I was paralyzed, and now I'm healed. I praise God for this."

"Do not be too quick to praise God for what may be a work of the devil," one of his questioners said. "Tell me: Was this man's name Jesus?"

"I told you already. I don't know the man or his name. I've never seen him before. I don't know if he is from God or the devil, but if I see him tomorrow, I will thank him all the same. He told me to praise God for the healing, though. I doubt this would be something the devil would propose."

"You are a blasphemer!" shouted another of the questioners. "Do you not know we have the power to punish you for this sin? If you were crippled, it was God who crippled you because of sin. Can you tell us what great thing you have done to gain the Lord's forgiveness and favor and be healed?"

"I cannot," said the man. "I know I'm not a good man in the Lord's eyes but a sinner undeserving of God's favor. Still, in God's mercy, today he chose to make me well. For that, I am grateful, and I will praise God today, tomorrow, and for the rest of my life."

"*If* you stay healed," one of them said.

"Regardless of whether I stay healed," said the man, "I will praise him always for this one day."

"You know nothing of God. Why should we even listen to you?"

"I didn't invite you here. You came to question me."

The men got up to leave. "Watch yourself, charlatan. And watch the company you keep. These are dangerous times and accomplices will fall with their masters."

When they were out the door, the same questioner turned to him again. "Beyond what you have already said, say nothing more—to anyone."

"Sorry," said the man. "I'll be in the streets tomorrow, telling all of Jerusalem what God has done for me."

"You suck!" the questioner said.

"Bite me!" the man replied.

Jesus and his disciples were staying outside the city at the Mount of Olives. On the Sabbath, they went to the Temple, where they worshipped and made an offering, but none of the Temple leaders recognized them. Afterward, Jesus went out to the portico and sat down. Then he began to teach and many came to hear him.

Finally, one of the leaders noticed him and went inside to tell the others. "It is Jesus! He is outside the Temple and teaching the people!"

Some of the priests and scribes started out to confront him.

"Wait!" the high priest said. "We must be careful with this one. The people love him. If we try to arrest him, they will turn on us. It will be better to question him about some of his teachings. If we can find fault with him in front of the crowd and trick him into making some of the outrageous and blasphemous statements we have heard of, we will win the people to our side. Then we can have the Temple police arrest him."

"Or better," said another priest, "we can incite the people to stone him."

"Let us counsel together quickly. We will decide on some questions to ask him and then send our best to argue with him."

When they had finished their discussion and determined how they would test Jesus, they sent a lawyer, a Pharisee, and a Sadducee to infiltrate the crowd and pose their questions.

The lawyer went first. "Teacher, we know you are guileless and show deference to none, for you do not regard people with partiality but teach the way of God in accordance with the truth. Please tell us, what must we do to inherit eternal life?"

Jesus looked into the man's soul and knew him. "You are the lawyer. What does the Law command?"

The lawyer was taken aback because Jesus had recognized who he was. He was careful to answer with the words he had expected from Jesus, thereby keeping his follow-up question intact. "You shall love God with all your heart and soul and strength and mind; and you shall love your neighbor as yourself."

"You have spoken rightly," said Jesus. "Do this and you will live in the kingdom of God."

The lawyer had hoped Jesus would respond in this way, since he had taught this to the people before. He smiled. "But, teacher, surely you know that we have another law regarding this to help us determine who our neighbor *really is*. Do you reject this law or accept it?"

> *The law the lawyer was referring to was a law of technicality that determined who was a person's neighbor, based on class and a geographical radius surrounding one's residence. If a person was not of a similar socio-economic station or was one who lived outside the radius of the other's "neighborhood," then that person was not considered a true neighbor, and, thus, the obligation to love was removed.*

Jesus answered, "This is not God's law, but man's law, written to justify your hardness of heart."

"So," the lawyer said, "you argue, then, that everyone is my neighbor, entitled to the same love I have for myself and my family? Even sinners? Even Samaritans? Even Romans?"

Gotcha! If Jesus said 'no' to the idea of loving the enemies of the Jews, then he would have to contradict himself and conclude that there is need for all the commandments, laws, and codes—not just the two, as he had preposterously espoused before. If he said 'yes,' to loving even the hated Roman oppressors of Israel, then surely the people would turn on him and come to their leaders' side.

"Consider this story," Jesus replied. "A man was traveling from Jerusalem to Jericho. While on the road, he was attacked by robbers, who stripped him of his clothing, beat him, and left him bleeding and half dead. Later that day, a priest was going down the same road. He saw the man lying there but crossed to the far side of the road to avoid him. The same thing happened when a lawyer and a Pharisee traveling together came upon the man. To avoid any involvement or responsibility for the man, they passed him by.

"But a Samaritan traveling down the same road saw the bleeding man and came near him, and, having pity for him, he bandaged his wounds and gave him water to drink. Then he lifted the man onto his own donkey and took him to an inn. He gave the innkeeper money and said, 'Take care of him until he is well. When I come back this way, I will pay you any extra money that is owed.' Now, which of the four men, do you think, was a neighbor to the wounded man?"

"I am sure I do not know," the lawyer said smugly.

"You are a lawyer, and you do not know? You have no answer?"

The people's gaze was fixed on the lawyer, who stood mute, knowing Jesus had turned the tables on him.

"Answer him!" whispered the Pharisee beside him, elbowing him in the ribs.

"Hazard a guess, lawyer!" shouted someone from the crowd.

"I...I suppose the one who showed him mercy." (The lawyer couldn't even bring himself to say "the Samaritan"—the "S" word!)

"Then I say to you, go and do likewise."

Jesus then addressed the crowd. "If you love those who love you, what great thing is that? Even the heathen does this. If you do good only to those who return good, is that a virtuous thing? The Law says, 'Love your neighbor.' I say to you: Love your enemies, do good to those who hate you, bless those who curse you, pray for those who abuse you. Then you will be doing a great thing and truly following the way of God, for God loves the sinner and the righteous alike. Be merciful, just as your heavenly Father is merciful."

It was the Sadducee's turn. "Teacher," he said to Jesus, "Moses wrote a law for us that said if a man's brother dies, leaving a wife but no children to care for her, it is the man's responsibility to take the widow as his own wife and care for her. But I am confused about how these things work in the resurrection. (He said this because the Sadducees did not believe in the resurrection, and he hoped to trick Jesus.) Consider this parable, then, and give us your answer. There were seven brothers; the first died and left his wife childless. The second brother married the widow, but then he also died childless. Then a third brother married her but died without children too. And so it was the same for the next, and the next, until all seven brothers died. Finally, the woman died as well. Tell us: Whose wife will the woman be in the resurrection?"

"You are, indeed, confused," said Jesus. "Marriage is an intimate union and partnership between two people for this age but not for the age to come. In this age, marriage is given and blessed by God as a way for two to become one together. But in the age to come, there is no need for marriage for we are all intimately bound together as one in God."

Now, the Pharisee stepped forward to question Jesus. "Rabbi, is it right for the Jewish people to pay taxes to the emperor?"

"Do you pay the tax?" Jesus asked.

"I pay the tax because it is Roman law—because I must. I am asking you if it is right. Should we pay taxes to the emperor or not?"

Good! The Temple leaders thought, as they listened to the exchange. The Pharisee had held his ground and forced the question. Jesus would have to answer one way or the other.

> *The Temple leaders had formed this question as their failsafe. The Jews hated the Roman tax. It supported the very enemy that occupied their country and oppressed their people. If Jesus said the people should pay the tax, this surely would cause the people to turn against him. On the other hand, if he spoke against the tax, the leaders could take this to the Roman authorities and accuse Jesus of inciting the people against the emperor. He would be arrested and either imprisoned or executed. It didn't matter which. They would be rid of him, and the people would soon forget about him—except for the example this heretic would set for any who dared to challenge their authority, and the law, and the status quo of their religion.*

"Do you have a coin?" Jesus asked the Pharisee.

"I have a denarius."

"And whose image and title is on it."

"The emperor's."

"Then give to the emperor the things that are his, and give to God the things that are God's. You claim to hate Caesar, and yet, you follow him to retain your places of honor. You claim to love God, and yet you do not follow him faithfully. Woe to you Pharisees and Sadducees! You keep ceremony and rituals, but you neglect justice and fail to practice the love of God. Woe to you! You love the seats of honor in the Temple and to be greeted with respect in the marketplace, but there is deceit in your heart for others and for God."

The lawyer spoke. "Teacher, why do you say such harsh things to us? It is disrespectful! We are followers of the Law!"

"Woe to you lawmakers and scribes, as well!" Jesus said. "Your complex laws load people down with burdens too heavy to bear, while you yourselves do not follow the simple laws of love God has set for you."

After Jesus had finished speaking, the Temple leaders said no more to him but tried to convince the people to turn away from him. "He has a demon and is out of his mind!" they said. "Why do you even listen to him?"

Some in the crowd agreed, but others said, "How can a demon speak such words of love and truth? And how can a demon do the healing works this man has done? Truly, he has the spirit of God."

When Jesus heard the crowds arguing, he gathered his disciples and left the city for the Mount of Olives, fearing that the Temple leaders might try to arrest him.

That night, a man named Nicodemus came to him. Nicodemus was a Pharisee and a member of the Sanhedrin, the Temple council, but he believed in Jesus and thought he might be the messiah. He came in the dark, and in secret, so the other Temple leaders wouldn't know.

"Rabbi, I know that you are from God, for no one can do the signs you are doing apart from the presence of God, and no one can teach as you teach without the wisdom of God."

"What do you want from me?" asked Jesus.

"I wish to know when the kingdom of God will come," Nicodemus said.

"I will tell you the truth," Jesus said. "No one will see or know the kingdom of God without being born again."

"I do not understand," said Nicodemus. "I am old and was born long ago. How is it that I can be born a second time? Can I reenter my mother's womb and come out again?"

"That is a birth of the flesh. To enter the kingdom of God, one must be born of the Spirit. Do not be astonished that I say to you, 'You must be born again.' For just as the wind blows and you hear it but do not know where it comes from or where it goes, so it is with the Spirit. It will come upon you as a mystery and gift from God. If you open yourself to receive this gift, it will come to you."

"This is a mystery," Nicodemus said. "How can I receive what I cannot see?"

"You are a teacher of Israel and you do not understand these things?" asked Jesus. "We speak of what we know and testify to what we have seen, yet you have seen me and do not know me. You have heard my words, and yet you come to me at night, in secret. If you believe in me and the works that I do and still do not testify to what you have seen, then how can you testify to what you have not seen? How can you expect to know of heavenly things? Truly, I tell you that God's light has come into the world, but its people love darkness more than light. However, those who come to the light will see clearly and will know the truth of God. It is these who will see what others cannot see and will know the kingdom of God."

Nicodemus went away, pondering all the things Jesus had said to him.

The next day, Jesus and the disciples left the Mount of Olives and went to Jericho. He was teaching the people there when a man came to him.

"Teacher, my father has died, and my older brother has claimed all of the property for himself. Tell him to be fair and divide his inheritance with me."

"Am I a judge," Jesus asked, "that I should decide this matter for you? But I say to all who will listen, take care! Be on your guard against all kinds of greed, for your life isn't about the abundance of possessions. Do not store up for yourselves earthly treasures but seek the treasures of God for where your treasure is, there your heart will also be. And I tell you, don't worry about your life or all the things you think you need. God knows your needs and will supply them. And don't be like the one who sits idly by and cries out for God to save him. Work out your own salvation. Be dressed for action and have your lamps lit; be honest with others and labor for your needs if you are able. Give to those who are not able, as God gives to you, and you will be blessed, for the measure you give is the measure you will receive. Strive for the kingdom of God and for righteousness, and be faithful, and all that you need will be given to you. Do not be afraid, little children, for it is your Father's good pleasure to give you the kingdom."

Zacchaeus was a tax collector and a rich man. He had heard of Jesus and very much wanted to meet him. When he arrived at the place where Jesus was teaching, he tried to push through the crowds but could not get close enough to see him. Zacchaeus was a short man, barely five feet tall, so even standing on the short walls that bordered the square where Jesus was speaking would not afford him a view. When Jesus had finished teaching, he left the place, but the people continued to surround him. Zacchaeus looked ahead of him and saw several persimmon trees lining the street, so he ran to one and climbed it to be above the crowd.

When Jesus came beside him, he looked up at the little man. "Zacchaeus, come down," he said. "I wish to stay at your house."

Zacchaeus sat frozen, wondering how Jesus could possibly know his name.

"Today, Zacchaeus."

Zacchaeus slid off the limb and shimmied down the tree.

The people parted, making a path for Zacchaeus to get to Jesus, but they began to grumble, saying, "Of all the people in Jericho, why would Jesus stay at the home of this sinner?"

Jesus heard their murmurings and said, "Zacchaeus is chosen because he will do a great thing for the Lord today, not the least of which is welcoming me and my friends into his home. For foxes have holes and birds have nests, but too often I have no comfortable place to lay my head. You were with me all day, but not one of you invited me into your home. You offered me no water, nor even a morsel of bread."

"But you didn't ask this of us," they said.

"Should I ask for hospitality?" Jesus asked. "Doesn't the Lord require this of you when a stranger is in your midst? Zacchaeus climbed a tree to greet me! Indeed, he has prepared a meal for me! We will go to his house today."

> *This was true. Zacchaeus, upon hearing that Jesus was coming to Jericho, had that morning instructed his housekeeper to prepare a large feast for supper, on the outside chance he could meet the great teacher and convince him to be a guest at his table.*

Zacchaeus welcomed Jesus and the disciples into his home. At supper, he announced to Jesus that he had seen the error of his ways and wished to repent. "Half of my possessions, Lord, I will give to the poor. I will check my books and to all I have overcharged, or if I have defrauded anyone, I will give them back four times as much. All I ask, in my unworthiness, is your blessing and God's forgiveness."

Jesus smiled. "Today salvation has come to you and your house! For you have welcomed me, and, in doing so, you have welcomed the One who sent me. You have my blessing and God's forgiveness."

"May I follow you, Lord?" Zacchaeus asked.

"Stay here and do what you have said you will do. Be a witness of God's love to these people. In this way, you will be my follower."

The next morning as they were leaving, Peter came to Jesus. "Lord, it is good to see these things and witness one like Zacchaeus coming to you, but what of us? We've left everything to follow you. Is there blessing for us?"

"Peter, how can you ask such a thing?" Jesus said, disappointed. "Truly, I tell you there isn't one of you who has left your home and family for my sake, and for the sake of the good news, that won't receive blessings a hundredfold. But remember, in the kingdom of God, many who are first will be last, and many who are last will be first."

The following day, they traveled from Jericho to Galilee and remained there for a long time, teaching and healing and doing great works in God's name. Jesus didn't wish to go to Judea because the Temple leaders were looking for him there and plotting against him to have him arrested or killed.

It had been weeks since Jesus and his disciples had had any time alone. By now, all of Israel had heard about Jesus, and they were coming to Galilee to hear him speak, and bringing their sick to be healed. Everywhere they went, large crowds followed them, and when they arrived at a place, many others were waiting. One day, when Jesus was teaching by the Sea of Galilee, the people were pressing in on him, so he got into a boat, had the disciples row him out a little way from shore, and taught them from there.

"Do not judge, and you will not be judged; do not condemn and you will not be condemned. Forgive and you will be forgiven; give and it will be given to you.

"Why do you see a speck in your neighbor's eye but fail to see the plank in your own eye? And how can you say to your neighbor, 'Friend, let me take that speck out of your eye,' before you remove the plank from your own? First, take the plank out of your own eye, and then you can see clearly to remove the speck from your neighbor's eye.

"A good tree will bear good fruit, but a bad tree bears bad fruit. Is it not true that we know the tree by the fruit it bears? Figs are not gathered from thorns, and grapes are not picked from caper vines. A good person produces good from a rich and fertile heart, but a bad person produces evil from a hard and withered heart. For it is out of the abundant heart that the good harvest comes.

"Why do you call me Lord, but do not do what I say? If you hear my words and do them, you are like one who builds a house on a foundation of rock. When the rains come, the house will stand strong and will not be washed away, but the one who hears my words and does not do them is like one who builds a house on sand, with no foundation. It will stand for a while, but when the rains come, the sands will wash away and the house will fall. In this way, not everyone who calls me Lord will enter the kingdom of heaven, but only those who hear my words and act on them."

After he had said these things, Jesus told the disciples to row the boat to the other side of the lake, leaving the crowd behind. Many saw where he was going, so they ran on foot to meet him and joined the crowd that was already waiting. When Jesus saw how many there were, he had compassion on them. He healed their sick and spoke to them about the kingdom of God.

At the end of the day, Jesus called Philip to him. "These people have been here all day and have nothing left to eat."

"Exactly!" said Philip. "That's why you need to send them away, so they can buy food for themselves, and so we can have some peace. Just demand that they leave. Otherwise, they'll stay here all night!"

"Ah, but some of them have no home here and no place else to stay." Jesus said. "There's no use sending them away to buy bread. It's late. The markets are closed. Why don't we feed them?"

"Us?" Philip asked, shocked. "Where would we get food, even if we could afford it? Which we can't, by the way. There must be five thousand people here!"

"Get the others and bring them to me," Jesus said. "And see if you can find anyone nearby with any food at all."

Philip started to say more but, instead, shook his head and walked away. Several minutes later, he returned with the other disciples and a young boy carrying a basket.

"This lad has two fish and five biscuits." Andrew said.

Jesus smiled at the boy. "Come," he said.

The boy stepped up to where Jesus was standing and offered his basket.

Jesus accepted it and placed his hand on the boy's head, gently tousling his hair. "Thank you," Jesus said. Then he looked at the disciples. "Have the people sit down."

When they had done this, Jesus took the food from the basket and lifted it in the air. He blessed it, then broke it into pieces and placed it back in the basket. "Collect twelve more baskets, one for each of you," he said to the disciples.

They did as instructed.

Jesus took the pieces of fish and bread and placed some in each of the baskets. He then told the disciples to distribute the food to the people.

Reluctantly, they started through the crowd. Every time they reached into their baskets, there seemed to be as much as before. When they had finished feeding everyone, they returned to Jesus, amazed.

Jesus collected the baskets and served each of the disciples. Then he emptied the remains of all the baskets into the boy's. "Shall we eat now?" Jesus asked the lad. He reached in the basket and took out a whole fish and two biscuits, handing them to the boy, and then took the same for himself. Curiously, the boy looked into the basket. There was one biscuit left.

Once the people had eaten and realized the miracle that Jesus had done before their eyes, they began to talk among themselves. "Surely, this is the messiah," they said. "He is the one who will lead us to victory over the Romans and liberate Israel from its oppression! He is David's son! The one spoken of by the prophets! Today is the day of our salvation!"

Jesus heard the shouts from the crowd as they grew louder and louder. He saw the people rising and beginning to come closer to him. When he sensed that they were about to take him by force and make him king, he told his disciples to go ahead of him and make a boat ready to cross the lake. As they were doing this, Jesus, standing at the top of a hill, began to speak to the people. When he had finished, he slipped away behind the hill. The people stood and followed, but when they came to the top of the hill Jesus was not there. He had vanished!

Just as suddenly, Jesus appeared at the boat and got in. "Quickly, push off, and let's go to the other side."

The disciples followed his orders.

It was the end of the day when they left for the other side of the lake, and, by the time it was dark, a storm had arisen. The rain was pouring down, and the wind and waves were tossing the boat about violently. Water was coming in over the sides of the boat, and they were sinking. Jesus was asleep in the boat's cabin, so Peter came to him. "Master! Wake up! Can't you hear the storm? Save us!"

Jesus sat up and wiped the sleep from his eyes. He looked at Peter. "Seriously, Peter? You and James have known me longer than any of the others and, still, neither of you know who I am." He pushed past Peter and went onto the deck. He raised his arms above his head and shouted over the sound of the storm, "Be still!" Immediately, the wind and rain stopped and the waves calmed. He looked at the frightened and tired disciples. "Do none of you have faith in me? Do none of you trust me?" He went back below to the cabin.

The disciples looked at each other, unbelieving of what they had just witnessed.

In a moment, Jesus emerged from the hold and said to them, "Man the oars and make your way to Gergesa. I'll meet you there." He climbed over the side of the boat and began walking toward the far shore.

The disciples—dumbfounded—watched him going away.

Finally, Peter called to him, "Lord!"

Jesus turned to face him.

"I have faith, Lord. Let me come to you."

"If you have faith, then come." Jesus reached out his hand.

Peter carefully placed a leg over the side of the boat and pressed down. *Solid.* He put his other leg over and felt the water lapping at his ankles, but he didn't sink. He cautiously pushed himself away from the boat and stood there for a second, trying to fit his brain around what was happening. He was standing on water! He took a step, then another, balancing himself on the moving surface below him. He was twenty feet from the boat and halfway to Jesus when he looked back and began to doubt. He stopped, afraid, and started sinking, slowly, as in quicksand. "Jesus, save me! I'm sinking!"

Jesus walked over and took his hand, lifting his feet back to the surface. He walked Peter back to the boat, and they both climbed inside.

"None of you is ready for the things that lie ahead of us," he said to the disciples. "Why have you come with me if you don't believe? You see all that I do and, still, you doubt. You must believe, for there are hard days ahead of us. You must have faith or you will falter. I'm going below to pray." He started for the cabin.

"Lord," Peter said, still trembling, "teach us to pray."

Jesus turned and faced them. "Very well. Whenever you pray, pray in this way:

> *Our Father in heaven, holy is your name.*
> *May your kingdom come,*
> *and may your will be done on earth, as in heaven.*
> *Give us today and provide for our daily needs.*
> *Forgive our sins as we forgive those who sin against us.*
> *Strengthen us for the trials of this world, and save us*
> *from its evils.*
> *For you are the God of all things,*
> *and all glory is yours. Amen.*

After Jesus had said this, he went below to the cabin, leaving the disciples alone. They discussed the events of the day and all they had seen and heard. They said, "Who is this, that he can feed thousands with only a little food? And who is this, that even the wind and sea obey him?"

When they reached the shore at Gergesa, a madman came out to meet them. He was vile and vicious, and cursed continuously. He didn't live in the village but in the cemetery, in a tomb. He wore no clothes, and the people were afraid of him because he was a violent man. When he saw Jesus, he fell down on his knees, frightened. "Why have you come here?" he cried out. "What are you going to do to me, Jesus, Son of God?"

"I've come to release you from your suffering," Jesus said.

"You have come to torture and kill me," the man growled.

"Tell me your name," demanded Jesus.

The man's speech suddenly changed from a single voice to a chorus. "We are legion," they snarled. "For we are many demons living in this man."

"I know who you are. And I command you, in the name of God, to leave this man's soul."

"We beg you not to send us back into the abyss," screamed the voices.

There was a herd of pigs, rooting on a nearby hillside.

"Spare us and send us, instead, into those pigs."

"Very well," Jesus said. "Go."

The man fell to the ground and shook violently. A strong wind began to blow, and the evil spirits transferred themselves to the swine. Immediately, the pigs stampeded toward a cliff overlooking the sea and hurled themselves over the side and onto the rocky shoreline below. When the swine herders saw that the pigs were dead, they ran back to the village and brought all the people with them.

"Look what you've done!" they shouted at Jesus.

"Yes, look at this man," Jesus said. "He has suffered among you for a long time, and now he is well. The demons that tormented him and lived among you are no more."

"Do you think we would trade the health of one man for all the pigs in our village? Go away before we stone you, and don't come here again!"

Jesus and the disciples got back in their boat and went home to Capernaum. They stayed there for several days, resting in the homes of their families, but Jesus also taught the people and healed their sick.

When it was, again, nearing Passover, Jesus gathered his disciples and they left Capernaum for Jerusalem. Along the way, some disciples of John the Baptizer came to him. They told Jesus that John had been arrested and imprisoned by Herod. John had confronted Herod about his marriage to Herodias, Herod's brother's former wife, and he was criticizing the king before the people, calling him a perverse leader and a great sinner.

"John has sent us to you," they said. "He doesn't understand why you hesitate to initiate the kingdom of God and the deliverance of Israel. Evil grows in the land. Herod is corrupt and Caesar's oppression worsens. John is doubting if you are the messiah, the true king, who will lead us to a new day. He sent us to ask of you: 'Are you the one or shall we wait for another?'"

Jesus answered, "Go and tell John what you see and hear: The blind see, the lame walk, the deaf hear; the diseased are cleansed and the dead are raised, the poor have good news brought to them, and the captives are set free. Perhaps I am not what Israel expected—a warrior to destroy and overthrow—but I am the messiah of God. I come to bring peace and to build up in God's name. And I will give myself in love to redeem a lost and hateful world. Blessed are those who believe these things and believe in me. Go and give this message to John."

Jesus was greatly troubled by the news of John's arrest and wondered if it was wise to continue on to Jerusalem. He went away from the disciples to pray on the matter. When he returned, they continued on their way.

When they were near Jerusalem, some people came to Jesus from Bethany and told him that his friend Lazarus was deathly ill. "His sisters are calling for you to come and heal him," they said.

"Go back and tell them I'm on my way," Jesus replied. When the people had gone, he said to the disciples, "We won't go to Bethany just yet. Make camp here for the night." They did this.

The next day passed, and the next. Finally, Peter questioned Jesus. "Lord, it's been more than two days since those people came to us. Shouldn't we go before Lazarus dies?"

"He is already dead," Jesus said, "But we'll wait here another day, so that the glory of God may be revealed."

> *It was the belief of the Jews that, whenever a person died, or apparently died, the soul left the body but continued to hover over it for three days—just in case—hoping to reenter the body if, in fact, there was some miraculous recovery. Once three days had passed, however, and it was clear the body was indeed dead, the soul would depart, permanently separating the spiritual life force from its physical container, thus ending any possibility of reunion and reanimation.*

By the time they arrived in Bethany, Lazarus had already been dead for four days. When Jesus was still a distance away, Lazarus's sisters, Martha and Mary, were told that he was coming, and they went out to meet him.

"Jesus," said Martha, "why did you delay in coming? If you had been here, my brother would not have died." She wrapped her arms around Jesus and wept.

Mary didn't approach Jesus but stood away. She, too, was weeping.

"Mary, come to me," Jesus said.

Mary shook her head and raised the palm of her hand toward him, rebuffing the invitation. Her other hand covered her mouth, as she tried to hold back her cries. She started to walk away.

Jesus called to her again, "Mary."

"Don't!" she said angrily, between tears. "Lazarus loved you. We all loved you. How could you be so cruel to us and let him die? And why are you here now? Did you come to grieve with us this death that you could have prevented? You open the eyes of the blind and heal those who don't even know you, but you can't lift a finger to help your friends? You could have saved him, Jesus, but you let him die. Now, please go, and leave us to our pain and grief." She started to walk away again but collapsed to the ground and began to sob.

Martha released Jesus and ran to her sister's side. Jesus was moved with compassion when he saw how distraught the two sisters were, and he began to weep too—for them.

The people standing nearby saw Jesus crying. "See how much he loved Lazarus," they said. "But Mary is right. If he really loved him, why didn't he come and heal him?"

Jesus heard what they were saying. "I could have come earlier, but I stayed away for your sake, so that you may see and know the greatness of God, and believe that it is he who sent me." He went to Mary and Martha. "Your brother will rise again. Do you believe this?"

Martha looked up at him. "I believe that, even now, God will give you whatever you ask of him."

"Do you believe, Mary?"

Mary spoke but did not look up at Jesus. "I know that he will rise again, in the resurrection on the last day."

"Mary, I am resurrection, and I am life. Those who believe in me, even though they die, will rise again. Lazarus will live again. Take me to where you have laid him."

He helped the women to their feet and, together, they went to the tomb where they had buried Lazarus. A large crowd followed behind them.

When they got to the place where Lazarus had been laid, Jesus saw that it was a cave in the side of a hill. A boulder had been used to seal the entrance. "Roll away the stone," Jesus said.

"Lord," said Mary, "he's been dead for four days. His body is decomposing by now. There will be an odor."

"Did I not tell you that if you believed, you would see God's glory revealed today?"

There was a Pharisee in the crowd. "This man is dead, Jesus. He is not sleeping or catatonic or comatose like the others you *supposedly* raised. He is dead! Spare this grieving family your delusions and leave them in peace."

"Take the stone away," Jesus repeated. Several men stepped up to the boulder and began pushing against it. Finally, when the stone had been moved enough to allow for an opening, Jesus cried out, "Lazarus! Get up and walk."

Nothing happened.

After a tense moment, people began to mumble against Jesus.

The Pharisee spoke again. "Why don't we put this fool in the tomb and roll the boulder back in place?"

There were quiet chuckles from the crowd, and the mumbling increased.

"Lazarus, come out!" Jesus shouted into the opening of the tomb.

Suddenly, a figure appeared out of the darkness. Lazarus came forward, wrapped head to feet in white linen cloth, shuffling his feet and trying to maintain his balance. No one moved to help him. In fact, everyone was backing away from the mummy coming slowly toward them.

"Unbind him and let him go," Jesus ordered.

Mary and Martha ran to their brother and began untying the bands of cloth. At the same time, they were showering him with kisses on his face and chest.

There was a roar from the crowd, and then everyone moved forward to surround them and share in the joy of the reunited family. Except for the Pharisee, who quietly slipped away and hurried back to Jerusalem to report what he had seen.

After spending two days in Bethany, Jesus and the disciples arrived in Jerusalem just in time for the Passover feast. The city was packed with people, and Jesus spent most of his time in the Temple courtyard, teaching them about the good news of God's kingdom.

The Temple leaders noticed the large crowds he was attracting, but they didn't dare confront him for fear that the people would turn against them. "Look," they said, "the whole world is going to him." They conspired together for a way to separate him from the people, so they could arrest him in secret.

One day, as Jesus was sitting in the portico of Solomon and watching the people bring their offerings to the Temple, he noticed how the rich made a spectacle of their offering.

The receptacle, into which people placed their offerings, was horn-shaped at the top and made of metal. When the offerings were placed in the opening, the money dropped down the stem of the receptacle and into a collection box below. Those wanting to be showy in their offerings didn't drop but, instead, threw their money into the treasury receptacles a few coins at a time. As the coins hit against the metal sides of the receptacle, they would make a loud noise, signaling the contribution and attracting the attention of all in the courtyard. In this way, the rich could be assured that everyone nearby would take notice and see them offering up their generous gifts.

Jesus said to those with him, "Beware of those who practice their piety before others. They love to wear colorful robes, and pray in public, and to be greeted with respect in the marketplace, and have the best seats in the synagogue and places of honor at banquets. But, I tell you, those who do their good works before others and gain praise in this world have received their reward."

Then he saw a widow come to make her offering. She had two copper coins and quietly placed them in the receptacle. "Behold, a true giver!" he said to the people. "For this poor widow has given more than all the others before her. The rich give much but little according to their abundance, but this woman with little has given much more. Indeed, she has given all that she has. Blessed are those who seek no praise and who do their good works in secret. They will receive their reward from their Father in heaven."

Just then, a child came up to Jesus, and he took her in his arms. "Unless you become like a child, and have the trust and faith and love of a child, you cannot enter the kingdom of heaven. And woe to anyone who causes one of these little ones to stumble or turn away from me; it would be better for them if they had not been born."

Some of those with him were talking about the Temple and its majesty—how it was adorned and furnished with beautiful things, dedicated to God.

"The days are coming," Jesus said, "when this Temple will fall and not one stone will be standing on another."

"When will this be, and how will it happen?" they asked him.

"When you hear of wars and insurrections, do not be terrified, for these are things that must take place. Nation will rise against nation, and kingdoms against kingdoms. And do not be led astray by those who will come and say, 'I am the One.' Be faithful to God. You will be betrayed by parents and siblings and relatives and friends. You will be persecuted and hated because of my name. But I tell you, you will not perish. By your faithfulness, you will gain your souls. Do not fear those who can kill your body. Be faithful to the One who can save your soul. When you see Jerusalem surrounded by armies, know that the last days of the Temple are near. Many will be killed by the sword, and many others will be taken away as captives. Jerusalem, because of her unfaithfulness, will fall and be trampled by its enemies. But when God's people are ready to return to the Lord, then Jerusalem will be restored." Then he told them a parable. "Look at the trees. As soon as they sprout leaves, you know that summer is near. So, too, when you see these things taking place, you will know that the kingdom of God is near."

Every day, he taught at the Temple, but at night, he would go out of the city to the Mount of Olives because he knew the Temple leaders were seeking to arrest him when the people were not around.

As Jesus continued to teach and to heal the sick, the people were saying, "Isn't this the man our leaders want to kill? Yet, here he is, speaking openly, and they do nothing. Could it be that the authorities really know he is the messiah?"

Jesus did many signs in the presence of the people. And they were astonished, and many believed in him.

The Temple leaders had heard reports of what Jesus had said about the Temple being destroyed. Because they themselves were afraid of confronting him among the people, they hired some men to infiltrate the crowd and question him.

They approached Jesus. "By whose authority are you teaching these things?" they asked.

"My teaching is not my own but of God, who sent me. Those who speak on their own seek their own glory. I seek only the glory of God and to speak his truths. Now let me ask you a question. Why are you looking for an opportunity to kill me?"

"You have a demon!" one of them sneered. "Who is trying to kill you?"

"Those who sent you," Jesus said. "I heal the sick, and they say I am the devil. I do God's work on the Sabbath, and they say I am a sinner. I preach good news to the poor, and they say I am a blasphemer. They know who I am, and they know from whom I come. Yet, because they refuse to recognize me, they deny the One who sent me.

"Enough!" one of the men said. "If you are the messiah, tell us plainly."

"I have told you, but you will not believe. The works that I do in my Father's name testify to me. Yet because you do not believe, you cannot see and will not hear. My sheep know me; they hear my voice and follow me."

The men picked up stones, as they had been instructed to do, to see if the others in the crowd would follow suit.

"I have shown you many good works that come from God," Jesus said. "For which of these are you going to stone me?"

"We're not going to stone you for good works. We're going to stone you for your blasphemy. You're only a human being, but you try to make yourself a god."

"I have said I am God's Son because God has sent me into the world to speak his words and do his works. If I am not doing the works of the Father, then do not believe me, but if I do them, even if you do not believe in me, believe in the works themselves, so you can know and understand that the Father is in me, and I am in the Father."

"You've heard him with your own ears!" one of Jesus' opponents said. "He is a blasphemer! Pick up your stones!"

Then one in the crowd answered, "Could the messiah do any greater works than this man has done? How can he have such learning and power if he isn't from God?"

Others said, "This is the messiah!" and they began to jeer at Jesus' accusers, who dropped their stones and quickly went away.

It was the last day of Passover, so the next morning, people who had come from all over Israel were leaving Jerusalem and beginning their journeys back home. Jesus and the disciples, who had spent the night at the Mount of Olives, left from there and returned to the region of Galilee.

Using Capernaum as a home base, Jesus spent the next several months, traveling around all the cities and villages of Galilee, but he didn't go to Nazareth because the people there didn't believe in him. One day, as he was passing through the city of Nain, the place where he had raised the widow's son from the dead, crowds formed along the road to greet him. He hadn't planned to stop there, but the people kept pressing in on him, so he sat down in the road and began to teach them.

"You are the salt of the earth. Salt is good, but if it loses its taste, it has no purpose. Why should it be kept in the house?

"You are the light of the world, but no one after lighting a lamp puts it under a basket. Instead, it is placed on a lamp stand to give light to the whole house. Just so, let your light shine for all the world to see.

"When you stand before the Lord to be judged, he will separate the sheep from the goats. Then he will say to the sheep, 'Come, you blessed ones, and inherit the kingdom prepared for you; for I was hungry and you gave me food, I was thirsty and you gave me drink. I was a stranger and you welcomed me, I was naked and you clothed me, I was sick and you cared for me, I was in prison and you visited me.' Then the righteous will say, 'When was it that we saw you hungry or thirsty and served you? And when was it that we saw you as a stranger or naked and took care of you, or sick or in prison and visited you?' Then the Lord will say, 'Whenever you did this for any of my children, you did it to me.' But to the goats, the Lord will say, 'Depart from me, you unrighteous ones; for I was hungry and you gave me nothing to eat, I was thirsty and you gave me no drink. I was a stranger and you did not welcome me, naked and you did not clothe me, sick and in prison and you did not visit me.' Then the unrighteous will say, 'Lord, when did we see you hungry and give you no food or thirsty and give you nothing to drink? And when was it that we saw you as a stranger or naked and did not care for you, or sick or in prison and did not visit you?' And the Lord will say, 'Whenever you failed do this for any one of my children, you failed to do it for me.' When you serve another, you are serving the Lord. When you care for another, you are caring of your Father in heaven. When you love each other, you show your love for God. So, be kind to others as you would have them do kindness to you, and you will be blessed by God."

When Jesus had finished speaking, he got up and started on his way.

There was a woman in the crowd who had been sick for many years. She believed Jesus could heal her, but, because of her weakness and the size of the crowd surrounding Jesus, she could neither push through nor call out to him. "I must get to him," she said to herself. "If I can just touch the hem of his garment, I know I will be healed." She dropped on her hands and knees and began to crawl around and through the legs of the people in front of her. Some of them kicked at her as she moved underneath and between them, but most, eventually, moved out of the way, if only to maintain their balance and stay on their feet as she passed through. Finally, bruised and covered in dust, she broke through the front of the line just as Jesus was passing by. She lunged for him, barely touching the bottom of his tunic, before being swallowed up by the crowd following him.

Jesus stopped. "Who touched me?"

Peter and the other disciples were circled around Jesus trying to keep the crowd from crushing him. "Teacher, don't you see this crowd pressing in around you? People are touching you constantly, including us."

"No, someone touched me for healing. I felt power go out of me."

"Master," Judas said, "it's all we can do to hold this mob at bay. Surely, you don't expect us to identify a certain one who touched you. Now, keep moving, please!"

Jesus raised his hand above his head, and the crowd quieted. "Who was it that touched me? Who has been healed just now?"

The woman struggled to her feet. "It was I, Lord. I'm sorry. I've been sick for a long time, and I just thought if I could touch even your clothing I would be healed."

"And, are you healed?" Jesus asked.

The woman had to consider this for a moment. She'd been so busy trying to keep from being trampled to death, she hadn't had a chance to think of her condition. She did a quick, internal self-examination and realized her pain was gone! She felt around her body and moved her limbs about to be sure. "I am healed!" she said gratefully.

"Daughter, it is your faith that has healed you. Now, go in peace."

"Yes, and may we go in peace as well!" Judas said. "Before this mob kills us all! Please, Jesus! Move!"

The crowd continued to follow them to the edge of town and beyond, but eventually, they turned back, while Jesus and the disciples went on their way toward Sepphoris.

From Sepphoris, they went to Cana, and from Cana to Heptapegon, and from Heptapegon to Capernaum, and Jesus taught and healed all along the way. When they arrived back at Capernaum, they rested for seven days.

Then Jesus called the twelve together and blessed them with his own power and authority, and sent them out two by two to cast out demons and heal the sick. "Go and proclaim the kingdom of God," he told them. "Whatever you ask in my name will be done for you."

When they were gone, Jesus went out of the city to a lonely place where he spent many days in deep prayer. It was nearing Passover again, and Jesus knew he would be going to Jerusalem for the last time. He asked God for the strength and courage to see his journey through and complete his mission. This was the special purpose God had for him, the purpose for which he was born and had sought all his life, his part in bringing about the kingdom of God. Now he was filled with anxiety but no less determined.

A month later, the disciples returned from their journeys and told Jesus all that happened to them and all they had done. "Lord, in your name, we were able to speak as you speak, and heal as you heal. Even the demons submitted to us!" they said excitedly.

Jesus was pleased with their reports and thought his companions were, at last, beginning to get it—to understand the power and grace of God. "See, I have given you authority to do all these things! I watched the devil fall before you for you've been given power over the enemy. Nothing can defeat you so long as you believe. Nevertheless, do not rejoice in this, but rejoice that you are children of God." Jesus then had the disciples kneel, and he laid hands on each of them, blessing them, as he prayed:

Father, I thank you for hiding these things from
the wise and mighty and revealing them, instead,
to your meek and faithful children. For this is your
will, Father: that you have handed all things over to
me, and that no one can know you unless I choose to
reveal you to them.

Jesus then said to the disciples, "Blessed are the eyes that have seen what you have seen! For I tell you that many kings and righteous people have desired to see what you have seen but did not see it, and to hear what you have heard but did not hear it. To you, it has been given to know the truths of the kingdom, but to them, it has not been given."

"But, why is this so?" Judas asked. "Why don't you reveal all things to everyone?"

"Indeed, I will reveal all things," Jesus said, "but not everyone will choose to receive it. With them, the prophecy of Isaiah is fulfilled, when he says, 'You will listen but never understand, and you will look but never perceive. For people's hearts have grown dull, and their ears are hard of hearing, and they have shut their eyes, so that they may not look with their eyes, or listen with their ears, or understand with their hearts and turn—and I would heal them.'

"And so, I say to you, blessed are you who see and hear and understand; yours is the kingdom of heaven. For to those who have, more will be given, and they will have it in abundance; but to those who have little, even what they have will be taken away."

After he had finished teaching them, Jesus sent the disciples away to rest, instructing them to return in three days, so they could resume their journeys. Jesus spent time at home, too, with his mother, but most of his hours were spent in prayer.

When the disciples returned to Jesus on the third day, he told them of his plan to go to Jerusalem for Passover.

"Teacher, it isn't good for us to go to Judea," Peter said. "The authorities are looking for you there, to kill you. Why can't we celebrate Passover here with our families?"

"I tell you, whoever is not willing to give up father and mother and sisters and brothers to follow me cannot be my disciple."

"Master, how can you say this to us?" Philip asked. "Haven't we done all this for you? We don't have to be with our families. We can stay here with you, but we don't have to go to Jerusalem, either."

"I agree," James said. "Why should we put ourselves in such danger?"

"Then stay here, you faithless ones!" Jesus said angrily. "I am following the will of my Father, and I won't be dissuaded or hindered by your selfish fears. If you believe in me, follow me. If you don't, then go your own way." He turned and began walking away.

The disciples stood still, looking at each other.

"We might as well go with him," Thomas said. "He can't do this without us."

"Perhaps we can talk some sense into him along the way, talk him out of Jerusalem, at least," Philip said.

"Yes, let's go with him," James sighed. "This is madness! Surely, it isn't God's will that he die, and us along with him!"

They all walked quickly to catch up to Jesus and fell in behind him, but they didn't say anything to him or to each other for a long time.

Despite his recent respite in Capernaum, Jesus felt weary. He was disappointed in his disciples and distressed by what he knew awaited him in Jerusalem, so they avoided all the cities and towns along the way. When they came to Mount Tabor, Jesus sent the disciples to a nearby village to buy food while he went up the mountain to pray. When he came down, the disciples weren't there, so he went to look for them. As he entered the village, he saw a crowd gathered around the disciples, shouting at them.

Philip saw him first and raised his hand to wave to him over. "Here is Jesus!" he called out to the crowd. "He will fix this!"

Everyone turned to look at Jesus, and a man ran to meet him. "Jesus, I beg you, look at my son. He's the only child I have, and he's been seized by a strange sickness. Sometimes he's fine and as normal as ever, but other times, without warning, he falls to the ground convulsing and foaming at the mouth, and I fear he'll die. Now, it happens more and more, and it's happening to him now! Come and see!"

Jesus walked over to where the boy was lying on the ground, stiff and shaking. Two men were trying to hold him still.

"I asked your disciples to heal him, but they couldn't," the boy's father said, desperate. "Please, have mercy on him, Jesus!"

"Let him go," Jesus said to the men holding him.

Immediately, the boy calmed and sat up.

"The sickness has left him," Jesus said to his father. "It won't come again."

The man kissed Jesus' hands. "Thank you!" he said and then ran to his son and hugged him.

"Let's go," Jesus said to the disciples, who were still looking like scared rabbits.

As they were walking, Philip asked, "Teacher, why couldn't we heal the boy? Why couldn't we do what we had done before, when you sent us out alone?"

"Because you sought the healing for your own glory, and not for the boy's sake and the glory of God. The things you did before, you did in my name. Tell me, did you pray to the Father, and ask in my name, before you attempted to heal the boy?"

No one answered him.

"You are faithless ones," Jesus sighed. "How long must I be with you? What will it take for you to understand? I know what it will take, so let this sink into your heads: I will be betrayed and beaten and killed, and on the third day I will rise again. Then you will truly know who I am."

This was the first time Jesus spoke to them plainly about what was to happen to him in Jerusalem.

From Nain, they traveled east and south to the Jordan River. When it was evening, the next day, they made camp, and Philip, on behalf of the others, came to Jesus.

"Please don't be angry with us, Jesus. Of course, we believe in you, and our faith is strong, but we don't understand why you must go to Judea. You aren't welcomed there, nor are your teachings and works accepted. Isn't there enough to do in Galilee, where you are loved and respected by the people? Can't you initiate your kingdom from there, where the people follow you?"

"It is for this reason that I go to Judea," Jesus said. "The people of Judea are like sheep without a shepherd, and their leaders are like wolves preying on the flock. I am the good shepherd, and I will lay down my life for my sheep. There are sheep that do not yet belong to the fold. I must bring them also, so there will be one flock and one shepherd. The people of Judea will hear my voice, and those who belong to me will come to me."

"I'm sorry," Philip said, "I don't understand."

"Get the others and bring them here," said Jesus.

When they all came to him, Jesus began again. "You say you have faith, but, I tell you, if you had faith the size of a mustard seed, you could say to one of these trees, 'Be uprooted and planted in the Jordan,' and it would obey you. You could say to a mountain, 'Move from here to there,' and it would move, and nothing would be impossible for you. Believe in God, and believe in me!

"We are going to Judea because the people of Judea have a right to hear the good news. We are going to Judea because Judea is Israel, too, and my message is for all God's People. Judea, like Galilee, needs to see and know that things, which had grown old, are being made new, and things, which were cast down, are being raised up, and that all things will be brought to perfection in the coming kingdom of God. We are going to Judea because what is about to take place must take place at Jerusalem. Therefore, I'm telling you now that I am setting my face toward Jerusalem, and I will not turn back, for all these things must be fulfilled so that the kingdom of God can come. Do you understand this?"

The disciples nodded their heads and said they did, but they didn't. And Jesus knew this was the case.

People were coming out to the Jordan to see Jesus and hear him teach. One day, a man came to him and said, "Lord, I will follow you wherever you go."

"Then come and follow me," Jesus replied. "We're leaving now."

"I need only go home and say goodbye to my father and mother. Then, I'll pack my things and meet you on the road."

"Your invitation is for this moment only," Jesus told him. "If you cannot come now, you cannot come at all."

"I can't leave without saying goodbye," the man countered.

"Then you should stay," Jesus said. He then addressed the crowd: "If you are plowing a field, you know you cannot look backward, or your furrow will not be straight. It is the same with discipleship: Anyone who would follow me cannot look back. If you hold anything more important than the kingdom of God, you are not fit to be my disciple."

Another man heard this and said, "Lord, my father has just died and my mother, years before him. I can follow you faithfully, because there is nothing for me here and nothing to look back to."

"Good," Jesus said. "We're just leaving. Follow me now."

"But the funeral is tomorrow. Let me bury my father, and then I will be free to follow you."

"Let those who are not following me bury your father. Are there not enough in your village to do this for you?"

"Yes, but it would be dishonorable to leave now and not attend his burial."

"Then stay and be honored here, for you do no honor to me if you do not put God's kingdom first." Jesus felt compassion for the man, and for the crowd, because they didn't understand. "I do not speak these words to be harsh or to offend, but I speak the truth. If you follow me, you must put God first, above all things. If you love God, then you must love God most, and set all other things below him."

The next day, Jesus and the disciples were in the wilderness near the Dead Sea. They came to a mountain, and Jesus, leaving the others, took James, John, and Peter up the mountain to pray. When the four men reached the top, Jesus could see that the others were exhausted, so he told them to rest while he went a short distance away to pray.

The disciples were sleeping when a thunderclap awoke them, and they saw that the entire mountaintop was covered in a cloud. They looked at where Jesus had been and saw a bright light in the haze of the cloud, so they went to investigate. When they were close enough to see Jesus, they noticed two other men standing with him. At first, they assumed two of the other disciples had climbed the mountain behind them and were speaking with Jesus, but as their vision adjusted to the light and the cloud began to dissipate, they could see that the two other men were older than any of the disciples. Their hair and beards were gray, and their tunics were long and white. Then they realized that the light they were seeing was emanating from the three men.

"Master?" Peter called out, "Is everything all right?"

Jesus looked in the disciples' direction, and Peter saw that his face was glowing like the sun. He walked toward the three dumbfounded disciples, and, as he did, the other two figures with him began to fade away, along with the light and the cloud.

"Who were those men?" Peter asked.

"I thought you were asleep," Jesus said. "I don't think you were supposed to see that. But since God has revealed this to you, I will tell you. It was Moses and Elijah."

"But they are dead—centuries dead!" Peter said.

"Really," Jesus said, with a slight smile. "They looked pretty good to me."

"But..."

"Don't say any more, Peter. Just know that all I have said to you about the kingdom of heaven is real. If you didn't believe me before, you have no excuse now. You've seen it with your own eyes."

"No, I believe it!" Peter exclaimed. "The question is what do we do about it? This is fantastic! We have to let people know! They'll want to come here and worship! We should build a monument, and we should keep someone here at all times to explain to everyone who comes what just happened!"

Jesus closed his eyes and considered the idea of leaving *Peter* here—forever. It was a fleeting thought. "Let's go, Peter." Jesus looked at James and John who hadn't moved or said a word. They were both still staring at the place where Jesus and Elijah and Moses had been, their mouths hanging open. "You two okay?"

"But...what...who...why were they here?" John asked.

"The Father sent them here to comfort me. I've been under some stress lately, in case you haven't noticed."

"But...," James finally managed to say.

"Come on, guys," Jesus said, as he started down the mountain.

"Jesus, wait!" said Peter. "Seriously, let's, at least, build a shrine before we go. You know, just set some rocks on top of each other or something to mark the spot. This is a big deal! One of those kinds of things you read about in the scriptures!"

Jesus turned. He walked over to James and John and shook them both to reanimate them. "Listen to me, all of you. James? John? Look at me. Are you listening?"

They both nodded their heads.

"You cannot tell anyone about this—nothing that you have seen until my departure. Do you understand?

"Where are you going?" James asked, still befuddled.

Jesus dropped his head and heaved out a breath. "WE are going to Jerusalem. THERE, I will be arrested and killed and, on the third day, I will rise again to be with my Father. My departure? Remember?"

"You were serious about that?" James asked.

Jesus looked at James, then John, then Peter. They all looked equally clueless. "Forgive me, Father." Jesus said, confessing his murderous thoughts. He was already on his way down the mountain when he yelled back, "Down! Now!"

Jesus had promised the disciples that before going to Jerusalem, they would, first, go to Bethany to stay a few days at the home of Lazarus and his sisters, Martha and Mary. The disciples were pleased with the news. They had experienced the hospitality of the Bethany family before and were excited about the idea of being off the road for a while.

While they were traveling toward Bethany, Jesus noticed that several of the disciples, including John and James and Peter, were not keeping pace with the rest of the group. They had dropped back and seemed to be arguing about something. Jesus stopped and called for the lagging disciples to catch up.

"What were you talking about back there?" he asked Peter.

"Nothing. Just a bit of a misunderstanding."

"Yeah, a misunderstanding by you," John said.

"Shut up, John!" Peter shot back.

"You shut up!" James, John's brother said, as he bumped his chest against Peter's.

"Enough!" Jesus said, as he separated the two. "What's going on?"

"We were arguing," Philip said, looking embarrassed. "These three, and Andrew, and your brother James and I. We were all arguing over who is the most important to you, and which one of us will be the greatest in your kingdom."

"Unbelievable," Jesus said, almost to himself. Then he got considerably louder. "Have none of you heard a word I've said?"

"But surely, Jesus, you can name a favorite among us and settle this once and for all. If you had to choose," said Philip, "who would it be? Would it be James your brother? Or James or John, the sons of Zebedee? Or Peter? Or me, Lord?"

"Or me?" said Judas.

"Or me, Lord?" said Nathaniel.

"Or me?"

"Or me?"

A couple of others chimed in, not wanting to be left out of the contest.

"Look," James said, interrupting the sudden stream of applicants for the coveted position, "it's obvious that John and Peter and I have a bit of an inside track here. I mean, Jesus chose *us* to go with him up the mountain and reveal to *us* things that you others don't know about—can't know about. Am I right, Jesus?"

"James..." Jesus warned.

"We may be able to reveal these things to you in time," James continued, "but, for now, Jesus has sworn us to secrecy. My point is we were chosen already. But the question is which one of us will sit at Jesus' right hand when he sits on his throne, and for that matter, who will sit at his left? They are both seats of honor. Jesus, I would ask that my brother be allowed to sit with us, he on your left."

"You asshole!" Peter shouted, charging James and reaching for his throat.

Jesus quickly stepped between them.

The other disciples were pushing and shoving and arguing as well.

"Everybody! Calm down!" Jesus said. "I can't believe you're doing this! I can't believe I'm hearing this! If the choice were mine, right now? I would choose none of you! However, God, in his infinite wisdom, gave you to me—for some reason! And I will not lose one of you or one thing the Father has given me. But I will hurt you! So stop it!

"As for this nonsense, it is not for me to decide who will sit at my right hand or my left. That is the Father's decision. But your ideas of the kingdom are wrong! You dream of worldly kingdoms, but my kingdom is not of this world. And I tell you this: The One who sits on the throne in the kingdom of God is servant of all, and whoever sits next to the throne is servant of all. If you would be the greatest in my kingdom, you must be least, for the first are last and the last are first. You should know this! I worry about you! There isn't much time left for you to learn these things, and you are still so immature in your faith.

"Now, I want you to think about what I've just said to you. It will take us the rest of the day to get to Bethany. We will walk single file and *in silence* the rest of the way. I think we all need some alone time. I know I do. Now…let's go…*single file.*"

Jesus was hoping some of what he had said would sink into thick heads over the next eight hours of quiet journey, but he was sure he would have to tell them this again. He was disappointed by the whole, sad episode, and his disappointment made him tired. He would be glad to get to Bethany.

Like his father before him, Lazarus was a wealthy man. As an only son, he had inherited the sprawling estate where he and his two unmarried sisters lived together. The house was large and spacious and able to accommodate the thirteen weary travelers easily. Jesus and the disciples were in Bethany for three full days, and they cherished their time there, safe and among good friends and enjoying the luxurious surroundings and hospitality of their hosts. They ate from plates: beef and mutton, cheeses and honey, figs and sweet plums. They drank good wine and fresh chilled cow's milk. They bathed each day and wore clean clothes provided for them, and they slept in actual beds that had been set up for them. Every day was a feast, and every evening was spent in conversation and laughter. It was the most enjoyable time any of them could remember.

At the end of the third day, Jesus announced they would be leaving the next morning for Jerusalem. The disciples were disappointed with the news. They knew they couldn't stay in Bethany forever, but they tried to talk Jesus into one more day. That evening, when Jesus was alone on the porch, Peter went out to him.

"We are just rested," Peter said, "and you know how it will be when we get to Jerusalem. The people will smother us all day long—those for us and those against us—and at night, we'll be in hiding from the authorities, camping again, and living on bread and water."

"I've enjoyed our time here too," Jesus said, "but we've lived with little for three years. Have you grown soft in three days? Besides, Passover begins at dusk tomorrow. I want to be in Jerusalem by then."

"Why can't we do Passover here?" Peter asked, in a stern and demanding tone. "Or anywhere but Jerusalem? They want to kill you there. You know that. Do you have a death wish?"

Peter's questioning frustrated and angered Jesus. "Get behind me, devil! You know exactly why I am going to Jerusalem! The evil one has put it in your heart to try and stop me from what I have to accomplish there. Stay here if you want. All of you can stay here if you're afraid. I am going to do the work my Father has given me to do."

"Jesus, you hurt us when you say these things. You know that we love you and will go where you go."

"Then tell the others to be ready in the morning. We're leaving for Jerusalem at first light."

"I will tell them. We will be ready." Peter turned to go back inside.

"Peter?"

Peter turned back to face him.

"Those who follow me must deny themselves for my sake. For those who seek to save their life will lose it, but those who would give their life for my sake will be saved. Do you understand this?"

"Yes," Peter said. He didn't.

At the same time Jesus was in Bethany, the Sanhedrin—the Temple council—was meeting to discuss what they would do about him.

"Report," said Caiaphas, the high priest.

One of the Pharisees who had been sent to spy on Jesus stood to speak. "He is in Bethany now, at the house of Lazarus. We believe they are meeting there to plot a coup against us and Rome."

"Does he have an army?" Caiaphas asked.

"He may be gathering one as we speak. Most of the Galileans are followers. There are many already in Jerusalem expecting him, and others from all over Israel will be coming to meet him here. When he arrives, he will make his entrance as the messiah and incite the people, and the insurrection will begin. Too many people believe in him, and once he enters the city, it will be too late. We must arrest or kill him before he gets here. We can do nothing once Passover begins."

Caiaphas considered this. "No, let him come. It is better to have him here than outside the city. It may be that the people are with him, and it is true that we cannot kill him during Passover. Once he is here, though, we will trap him with his own words and let the Romans deal with him. They are nervous about Passover and the crowds, anyway. Reports of an insurrection will put them on their guard against him."

"But what of the people?" a council member asked.

"Once he is in prison, the people will lose faith and forget him, just as they did with the Baptizer."

When the council had adjourned, some of the Pharisees gathered together to discuss the decision.

"This is a bad plan," one of them said. "He is too powerful among the people. If he enters Jerusalem, there will be a revolution, and the Romans will come down hard on all of us. Much blood will be shed. Pilate could destroy us all."

"We should send emissaries to Bethany now," said another. "Perhaps we can ward him off with the threat of death if he comes to Jerusalem."

"He already knows the danger of coming here," responded another. "You won't turn him around. We must send assassins to deal with him."

"And do you know any assassins?"

The question went unanswered.

"Are there any murderers among us?"

Again, no response.

"Then two of you will go and try to dissuade him. Tell him Herod is waiting for him and plans to do to him what he did to the Baptizer."

They decided which two should go and set them off on the road for Bethany.

Jesus and the disciples were five miles from Jerusalem when the Pharisees met them.

"Teacher, we have come to warn you," they said. "Herod seeks your life. His soldiers are lying in wait for you, and he has vowed, if you come to Jerusalem, he will kill you, just as he killed John the Baptizer."

"John is dead?" Jesus asked, shocked and distressed.

"Have you not heard? Herod's stepdaughter asked for John's head as a birthday present, and the king had him beheaded to satisfy the heartless whim of a young girl. He is ruthless, and he will do the same to you if you show your face in Jerusalem. You must turn back and save yourself while there is still time."

Jesus, forlorn by the news of John's death, sat down in the road and folded his arms around his knees. His heart sank and his stomach churned; he bowed his head and closed his eyes, trying to fight back sickness. The reality that his time had come, and that his own death was near, was clearer than ever before. After a moment, he collected himself and stood. "Thank you for the report, but the work my Father has sent me to accomplish is in Jerusalem. We will continue on."

"Teacher, did you not hear what we said? We come to you as friends, to warn you."

"You? My friends? You? To warn me? Haven't you sought to destroy me from the first? You care only about yourselves and your place and status as the leaders of Israel. Publicly, you hope for the messiah and pray for the kingdom of God to come, but, secretly, in your hearts, you don't want these things, for you know when the messiah comes, when the kingdom of God is established, your seats of power and prestige will be taken from you. You say you come to warn me, but John tried to warn *you* to repent and that the kingdom was near. Now, I warn you that it is here. Go back and tell your real friends that I am on my way."

"Herod will be waiting for you," one of the Pharisees said.

"Tell that fox for me that I am coming to bring good news to the people of Israel. Tell him his corrupt house that kills the prophets sent to it will fall and that his day of reckoning is at hand."

When the Pharisees had gone, Jesus led the disciples off the road to a small grove of trees. "We'll go no further today. Make camp here. I must go and pray and grieve for John." He left them there and went a distance away to be alone.

The disciples began to discuss the situation among themselves. "We have to make him listen to reason," Andrew said. "He heard what we just heard. They're waiting there to kill him. We have to change his mind about going to Jerusalem."

"We should go back to Bethany," Nathaniel said, "at least until after Passover. Things will cool down after that."

"I agree," said Simon. "In fact, we should insist on it. We should go back, even if he refuses. He won't go to Jerusalem without us. If we all go back, he'll have no choice but to follow."

"Are you insane?" retorted Peter. "Is he our follower? He doesn't follow us. We follow him. We will go where he goes. Nevertheless, I'll talk to him. He'll listen to me."

"Yeah, like he's listened to you before," James mocked. "You better let John and me talk to him. He likes us better, and respects us more."

Peter stood up to go after James, but Andrew and Matthew grabbed him.

"Don't you guys start this favorite son thing again," Matthew said. "All three of you are going to get sent home if you don't stop this ridiculous argument."

"I'm not sure I'm not ready to go home," Philip said. "This is getting pretty sticky. Maybe we all need to go home for a while, including Jesus."

"Again, Philip?" Thomas interjected. "Didn't you hear Peter? We follow Jesus. He doesn't follow us. I don't like this any better than the rest of you, but he is going to Jerusalem. And he is going to die there. Haven't you heard him say this countless times? That this is his mission, his purpose, his fate? That he would go to Jerusalem, where he would be arrested and beaten and killed and, on the third day, rise from the dead?"

"He was serious about that?" James asked.

"How is he going to raise himself from the dead? He'll *be* dead!" Philip protested.

"I don't know," Thomas said. "I don't know what any of this means. All I know is he's determined to follow this plan through, and we will go with him. We will follow Jesus to Jerusalem so that we, too, can die with him."

Judas had been sitting against a tree, listening to everyone else but not speaking. "Jesus is right. You guys never listen and never learn. Or you hear with your ears but don't comprehend with your minds. This whole death thing is metaphorical. He is going into Jerusalem as Jesus, the son of Joseph and Mary, but, once there, he will rise up as the messiah and establish his kingdom as the Son of God. The old dies away; the new comes to be. And where else would he do that but Jerusalem, and when else but at the Passover festival with all the people there to witness it? They will rise up in revolution with him and fight with him to overthrow the Romans. And when he's sitting on his throne, we'll be right there with him, to rule as his chief officers. I can't believe you guys haven't figured this out. Do you think this has all been for nothing? Jesus knows what he's doing. It's just been a matter of timing, and the time has come."

"But he said he would be arrested. What about that?" Philip asked.

"Of course, they will *try* to arrest him. Maybe they will, but, again, it's timing. The people won't stand for it. They'll rise up and fight for him, and that will begin the revolution. Look, go home if you want, but you'll be giving up three years of earning your place in the new kingdom, and you'll miss the great battle for independence from Rome. Besides, who knows what Jesus will do to you when he's king if you desert him now? He may very well see it as an act of treason."

"And why are you suddenly so much smarter than the rest of us? How do you know this is right?" James asked, somewhat jealous that he—a favorite—had not figured this out himself.

"How else could it be?" Judas said smugly, leaning back against the tree with his hands behind his head. "This has been Jesus' plan all along. How else could it work out? It's just a matter of timing." He closed his eyes, and added, "Do what you want, but I'd think twice about leaving Jesus now or, for that matter, getting in his way."

At dawn, Jesus returned from prayer and roused the disciples from sleep. They ate breakfast in silence. When they had cleaned up and packed everything away, Jesus, without a word, started walking toward Jerusalem, and the disciples followed him. Jesus seemed troubled, and this troubled the disciples—all except Judas.

The Pharisees who had spoken with Jesus on the road returned to report their conversation to the others. "He is coming, and our fears were correct. He plans an insurrection to overthrow Herod and the Romans."

"He said this?"

"He told us to tell Herod that his house would fall."

"This is bad news," said another Pharisee. "His army may be strong enough to take Herod's palace, but they cannot defeat the Romans. The Zealots have tried this before and failed. If Jesus starts a war, we will all pay the price, and it will be a heavy one. Pilate is no friend to Herod, but he will not stand for any resistance that threatens the status quo. Who serves as tetrarch is Caesar's decision, and Caesar has appointed Herod. Any attempt to remove him will be met with Roman force. Pilate will squash Jesus, but he may squash us, too, in the process. With Passover and the city full of people, it could be a massacre. We must stop this."

"But how?" asked one of those who had met with Jesus.

"We have to report what Jesus has said to Caiaphas but without letting him know we went to Jesus to try and warn him to stay away. Remember Caiaphas told us to let him come. If he finds out we went against his decision and things go awry, he will blame us for our insubordination. Caiaphas has the ear of both Herod and Pilate. He will report what Jesus has said, and they will listen to him. Perhaps this can still be stopped before it starts."

One of the Pharisees went to the Temple and found Caiaphas. "Rabbi, Jesus is on his way to Jerusalem, and we have evidence that he plans to attack Herod's palace and take the throne."

"What evidence?"

"One of our spies heard him say this."

"Good," Caiaphas said, revealing an evil grin. "He has done our work for us and condemned himself. I will go and speak to Herod at once."

Caiaphas was ushered into the palace's throne room and left alone for an hour, waiting for the king to appear. When Herod entered the room, Caiaphas reluctantly bowed to the arrogant and self-indulgent fool he secretly despised. Behind the king hurried two naked girls, perhaps ten years old. When he took a seat on his throne, one of the girls climbed in his lap and began kissing his chest and neck. The other sat at his feet and immediately placed her hand underneath his robes, massaging him as she had, no doubt, been trained to do. This was all done, Caiaphas knew, for his benefit—the king knowing his high priest would find it disgusting and repugnant.

"What is it, Caiaphas? I am a busy man."

"Your Eminence, you know of this Galilean named Jesus, who has the people believing he is the messiah."

"I have heard of him," the king said, feigning disinterest. "I hear he does good magic tricks."

"You should take him more seriously, my king. He has many people fooled, and he means to do you harm."

"What harm can he do to me?" Herod said, waving his hand to dismiss the remark.

"He is coming to Jerusalem today, and he has vowed to take your palace and replace you as king." Caiaphas smiled inside, as he watched the smirk melt from Herod's face and fear fill his eyes. Then rage.

In a single motion, Herod stood, picked up the girl on his lap and threw her hard over the side of his chair. She landed with a thud, and her head cracked like an egg, as blood and gray matter splattered across the marble floor. He grabbed the girl at his feet by her hair and, raising her above his head with both arms, hurled her ten feet across the room. Caiaphas heard the girl's spine pop as her small body wrapped around a column and, slowly, slid to the floor. Her eyes were wide open, but she did not move or appear to breathe. Caiaphas hoped, for her sake, she was dead.

"Get them out of here!" Herod shouted to the guards at the door. "And don't let them bleed on my floor!"

The guards quickly removed their cloaks, wiping up the blood and brains as best they could, then used them to wrap the girls' bodies before carrying them away.

The king paced back and forth a few steps, then fell back into his chair and covered his mouth and chin with his hand. "How dare this common preacher threaten me and my throne!"

"Do not take him too lightly, my king. As I said, the people hold him in high esteem and follow him, especially the Galileans."

"The Galileans," Herod said, repulsed. "They are ignorant north-country hicks. No better than Samaritans. How do I deal with this man? Why do I have to continue to deal with these riff-raff preachers who try to set my people against me? These preachers for the kingdom of God! Am I not the anointed king of God? Is this not the kingdom of God? Is Jerusalem not the city of God?"

There was a little bit of vomit coming up Caiaphas's throat. He swallowed it back down. *You are Caesar's anointed lapdog,* he thought. "You must take action against Jesus before he takes action against you," Caiaphas said. "If he riles the people and rallies them, he could do you great harm. If he riles the Romans…well, I don't need to tell you how that would end, or who would be held accountable."

Herod ignored the remark. "You know, John thought he could turn the people against me. You see what happened to him."

"Yes, and so it must be for Jesus. I tell you, sire, he is a much bigger threat than the Baptizer."

"I have not slept well since executing John," Herod said, looking across the room at nothing. "He believed in Jesus, you know. He predicted that Jesus would come for my throne."

"It does not have to be so, my king, not if you act first. Go to Pilate and tell him of Jesus' plans to lead a revolt. He will listen to you."

"Pilate has no respect for me," Herod lamented. "He thinks I am a powerless worm. Just another inferior Jew, coddled and tolerated by order of the emperor."

"Then, perhaps, I should go to him."

"No! Do you think he holds higher regard for you than me, you arrogant ass? You are just tolerated, too—you and all your Temple cohorts—simply to keep the peace of Rome. Besides, Pilate would either ignore you and do nothing or overreact, cancel Passover, and kill half the men in Jerusalem."

"What then?" Caiaphas asked, irritated.

Herod put his troubled face in his hands and rubbed his weary eyes. Then he looked up at Caiaphas. "Take your Temple guards and arrest him as soon as he comes into the city. Then bring him to me."

Jesus arrived at the Mount of Olives in the early afternoon, but he was weary and wanted time to pray before entering the city. "We'll camp here tonight," he told the disciples. "Tomorrow, we will go to Jerusalem."

They rested that afternoon, and in the evening Jesus went to his special place to pray. When he had finished, he sat down and took in the view of the valley below and the holy city on the hill on the other side. He was filled with anxiety, and his heart pounded in his chest, as he thought about what tomorrow and the next few days would bring. He remembered his first view of Jerusalem from here when he was just a boy, and how many times he had been here since, and how the city called out to him, even when he was far away. He wanted to cry out, but, instead, his voice whispered, "Oh, Jerusalem, Jerusalem, the city that kills prophets and stones those who are sent to it! How often I have wanted to gather you as a mother hen gathers her children under her wing, but you were unwilling. Now, you will greet me saying, 'Blessed is the one who comes in the name of the Lord' but, still, you will turn from me. Woe to you, Jerusalem, for your house will fall. And you will not see me again until you are ready to truly receive me, until you are ready to say, 'Blessed are you who is sent by God for the salvation of the world.'"

The disciples were asleep when he returned to them, so he lay down beside them and looked up at the stars until he, too, was asleep.

Now, some of the Pharisees were frightened by the report their friends had brought to them: that Jesus was coming to overthrow Rome and Herod and establish his own kingship in the new and liberated Israel. They questioned whether Jesus might really be the messiah, in which case the coup would have God's power and protection behind it. The new Israel would be the inauguration of the kingdom of God, and Jesus would be the Lord predicted by the scriptures. They decided to hedge their bets. They would hold the establishment line in the presence of the authorities, including the other Pharisees, but, at the same time, secretly, they would try and cozy up to Jesus—*just in case*. Plans were made as to how they might meet and befriend him once he was in Jerusalem. They decided a dinner invitation would be a good place to start.

The next day, when Jesus and the disciples were to enter Jerusalem, he took Philip and Andrew aside. "I want you to go ahead of us. When you come to the city gate, you'll see a donkey tied to a post. Take it and bring it to me."

"You want us to steal someone's donkey?" Philip asked.

"We're only borrowing it. If anyone says something to you, tell them the Lord has need of it. They won't object."

"How do you know these things, teacher?" Andrew asked. "How do you know there is a donkey tied at the city gate, and how do you know there will be no objection to our taking it?"

"My Father has placed the animal there for me, and he will put it in the heart of the owner to accept your explanation for taking it. These things are a foreshadowing of what is to come, and for your benefit, so that you may have faith and believe."

The two said no more (in front of Jesus) and went on their way to do as they were told. When they arrived at the east gate, there was the donkey tied to a post, just as Jesus had said it would be. They untied it and started to lead it away.

"Hey, you two!" a man called out, in an unfriendly tone. "That's my animal, there! Where are you taking it?"

"The Lord has need of it," Philip said, following Jesus' instruction. The man looked at them warily, but then, incredibly, he nodded, giving them permission to proceed. The two disciples were amazed, and hurried on their way.

Halfway back, they met Jesus and the others with a large, excited crowd following them. They were singing and dancing, and shouting, "The Son of David has come to deliver us!" and "The messiah is here!"

Jesus mounted the donkey, and Philip led it back toward the east gate.

Some of the others in the crowd had run ahead of them and announced to the city that Jesus was coming. When they entered through the gate, throngs of people lined the streets, and they waved palm branches as a sign of honor to Jesus. They were shouting, "Hosanna, Lord! Save Israel!" Others were crying out, "The revolution is here. Prepare to fight! The Lord has come!"

Jesus rode on to the Temple, and it seemed that half the city was following him. When he arrived at the Temple courtyard, he dismounted the colt and taught the people there. They brought their sick and wounded to him, and he healed them.

The Temple priests and scribes watched all this from a distance, but they didn't dare confront or try to arrest Jesus, fearing the crowd would riot and kill them.

At the end of the day, Jesus dismissed the crowds, promising to be with them again tomorrow, and went into the Temple to pray. Traders crowded the place, hawking worshipers as they went to and from their prayers. The money changers were there, too, with booths set up to convert—at a high profit rate—the profane Roman currency to Jewish money acceptable for Temple offerings. The traders had had a bad day of business, thanks to Jesus and the people's obsession with him, and they cursed at him when he walked by.

Suddenly, an irrepressible rage welled up in Jesus, and he grabbed a walking stick that was sitting next to one of trading tables. He began swinging it wildly across the tables, sending the merchandise flying and smashing the breakable wares. He pushed over the money-changing booths as the merchants hurried out of the way to protect themselves.

"God's house is to be a house of prayer," Jesus shouted, angrily. "But you have made it a den of robbers! Get out! All of you!"

The shocked and appalled businessmen looked around them, assessing the damage. They looked at Jesus, still holding the walking stick above his head, ready to strike. His eyes were piercing and full of fire. No one said a word but began picking up what they could salvage of their merchandise. Finally, one of them ran into the Temple's inner court and, in a moment, returned with three priests and a dozen Temple guards.

"How dare you!" said one of the priests, walking briskly toward Jesus. When Jesus tightened his grip on the stick and raised it slightly, the priest stopped his movement forward. "You have no authority in this place! You do not determine what does and does not happen here! These men are here by the permission of the Sanhedrin. They pay a fee to the Temple to do business here. They, therefore, have the protection of the Temple guard."

"Arrest him, then!" shouted one of the now more brave merchants.

"Yes, arrest me, then," Jesus said. There was the slightest smile on his lips, as the stick above his head began to twirl in small circles.

The guards gripped their spears tight, waiting for a command.

"No, no. There's no need for that," the priest said, trying to calm the situation. He was well aware that arresting Jesus now, before they had enough evidence to turn the people against him, could have disastrous consequences for himself and the other Temple hierarchy.

It might spark the insurrection they feared. "Go your way, Jesus, and pay heed to this warning. You do not direct the ways of this Temple."

"Pay heed to my warning, priest," Jesus said. "Repent of your evil ways. You corrupt my Father's house and teach lies to his children. You are in collusion with these robbers for your own gain and steal from your own people. Woe to you, unless you repent, for judgment is coming soon!" Jesus lowered the stick and threw it to the ground in front of the priest's feet. Everyone stood in silence as Jesus walked out through the portico and into the courtyard.

"Clean this up and leave," the priest commanded angrily. "You can come again tomorrow." He motioned for the guards to follow him and the other priests as they went back into the Temple proper.

A meeting of the Sanhedrin was called to discuss the confrontation with Jesus.

"I am sick of this false prophet and his antics," said Nehemiah, a member of the council. "You should have had the guards arrest him."

"On what charge exactly?" asked Ezekiel, the priest who had confronted Jesus.

"Destruction of property. Desecration of the Temple. Assault. Take your pick! Would we allow anyone else to come in and wreak havoc the way this man did? He has become violent now. How far are we going to let him go before we take action against him?"

"He challenged me to arrest him," Ezekiel said. "That is what he wants. If we arrest him now, it will spark the insurrection we fear, and Pilate will destroy us all."

"Ezekiel is right," said Caiaphas, the high priest. "If we arrest him now, the people will fight for him and against us. The Romans are already nervous about the Passover festival. They won't tolerate any unrest or divisions among the people. We must wait until we can bring charges against Jesus that sway both the people and the Romans to our side."

"So, what is our strategy?" asked Nehemiah.

"Let him alone," Caiaphas said. "Let him continue to roam freely among the people, for we can do nothing else now. But let us keep an eye open for everything he does and a listening ear for everything he says. We will keep spies close to him to report to us. Sooner or later he will stumble, and we will have the evidence we need to condemn him before the people. I already have Herod's orders to arrest him, but we need something substantial enough to convince Herod, or Pilate, to put him to death."

Nicodemus stood to address the council. "Caiaphas, I must speak for those of us who disagree with this course of action against Jesus. Some of us find no fault with the man. I do not know if he is the messiah, but, surely, he is anointed by God. He speaks good news to the people, heals the sick, and does great works in God's name. Why is it the work of this council to condemn such a man and such a message? Are we not all looking for God's promised deliverance of Israel? Do we not all hope for the coming of the kingdom that he proclaims?"

"Have you become his disciple too?" Caiaphas asked in a condescending tone. "Have you not read the scriptures? Is there any mention of a prophet from Galilee? The prophet Micah has said that the messiah will come from Judah, not Galilee; from Bethlehem, not Capernaum; from David's royal line, not from a carpenter's offspring!"

"I did not say he was the messiah. I said I believe him to be a man of God," Nicodemus replied. "Obviously, I am not the only one who believes this, not even in this room."

"Enough of this nonsense!" Caiaphas shouted. "His talk of a new kingdom is a threat to this Temple and our authority. He is a threat to Herod and Caesar and the sovereignty and peace of Rome, and that makes him a threat to Israel! He is a blasphemer against God and treasonous against Caesar. These are both capital offenses. We need only clear evidence of this to arrest and convict him. Then we will be done with this devil. So send men out to follow him and get this evidence for us." Caiaphas stood to adjourn the meeting. He looked around the table, his eyes settling on Nicodemus. "Be careful, Nicodemus, and all you who would align yourself with Jesus, lest you find yourselves beside him at the executioner's hand."

Jesus didn't return to the Mount of Olives that evening, as was his custom, but instead he and the disciples left the city through the north gate and went to a place with a garden called Gethsemane.

"We'll make camp here," Jesus said, "and this is where we will stay each evening until my work is accomplished. If we are separated during the day, return to this place, and I will meet you here."

He sent Nathaniel along with Judas, who kept the group's purse, back to the city to buy food for supper and breakfast. While they were gone, Jesus took Peter and Thomas aside from the others.

"You and the others have been with me for a long time, but I fear in my hour of need you will run away from me."

"I cannot speak for the others, Lord, but, as for me, I will never desert you," Peter said.

"Nor will I," Thomas said. "I will die with you before I will leave you."

"I would like to believe this is true," Jesus said. "My heart would not be as troubled if I knew I would not be left alone."

"Lord, we are with you," Thomas assured him. "We will not leave you. *I* will not leave you."

"We shall see," Jesus said. "The time is coming soon when your faith and loyalty will be tested. Do not fail this trial."

"You can count on us, Jesus. You can count on *me*," Peter said.

"And me," Thomas agreed.

Then, looking at his friend, Jesus asked, "Peter, do you love me?"

"Lord, you know that I love you."

"Then feed my sheep." He asked again, "Peter, do you love me?"

"Lord, you *know* that I love you!"

"Then care for my children." He asked a third time, "Peter, do you love me?"

"Lord," Peter said, painfully, "I have told you that I love you! I love you more than life!"

"Then, be faithful, Peter. Be faithful and believe."

When they went back to the others, Peter lagged behind, hurt and confused by the questioning. He knew what Jesus was implying: that he might not love enough to remain faithful when their lives were on the line, or, if Jesus were taken from them, that he might not love enough to continue the work Jesus had begun—to heal and teach and proclaim the coming of the kingdom of God. But wasn't Jesus the hope and promise of the kingdom? If Jesus was taken from them, what would be the point of it all, anyway? He didn't understand any of it. Why an hour of need for Jesus? Why a time of testing for the disciples? Why did Jesus keep talking about dying? Had they come this far, invested all this time, to fail? Was there to be no kingdom with Jesus in power and them at his side? Or, was Judas right about Jesus? All the cryptic messages—the metaphors and parables about death and rising to life—were just Jesus' way of clueing in "the chosen ones" about his plans to usher out the old and usher in the new. *Let those with ears listen, right?* Perhaps Peter's test was the doubt he allowed to enter his mind. Jesus was just biding his time, waiting for the precise hour, testing his disciples to measure their true grit for the moment of truth. *Yes, that was it! That had to be it!* This was the test. It was Peter's test—doubt or belief—and he would not fail!

When Judas and Nathaniel returned with food, they all ate supper together. Then Jesus questioned the disciples. "Who do the people say that I am?"

"Some say you are Elijah returned, but others, John the Baptizer; and still others, that you are Isaiah or one of the other ancient prophets arisen."

"And what of you?" asked Jesus. "Who do you say that I am?"

"You are no other but the messiah of God, the anointed one," Peter said.

Jesus smiled at Peter, and Peter smiled back, proud that he had pleased Jesus.

"Blessed are you, Peter, for God has revealed this to you! But I say to you all, tell this to no one until my work is complete and the scriptures have been fulfilled. I must undergo great suffering and be condemned by the elders and priests and scribes, and be killed, and on the third day rise again. All this must take place, so that others will believe and know that I am the Son of God."

And, just like that, Jesus had managed to spoil the mood again. Peter's heart sank. He had gone from being recognized by Jesus as the favorite among them, due to his God-given insight and acclamation of Jesus as the messiah, to just one of twelve confused disciples with no understanding at all of what Jesus was telling them. A moment ago, he had been so sure. Now, doubt was creeping in again, and Peter's stomach ached.

The next morning, after breakfast, they went back to the city. Just inside the gate, Jesus saw a blind man, begging for money.

"What do you want?" Jesus asked.

"Just a copper coin or two will do, sir," the blind man replied.

"What is your name?"

"Bartimaeus."

"What is it that you really want, Bartimaeus?" Jesus asked.

The man studied the blackness between himself and the voice addressing him. "Do I know you, sir?"

"I am Jesus, and you will know me today, Bartimaeus, if you will ask. What do you want from me?"

Bartimaeus threw the blanket from his lap and rose to a kneeling position before Jesus. "You are Jesus of Galilee, the one sent by God?"

"I am. Do you believe I can heal you, Bartimaeus?"

"I have been blind from birth. I've never seen the light of day, or my mother's face, or a building, or a stone or a blade of grass. Yet, I know of these things and desire to see them. I believe that you have the power to heal me, if you choose."

"I do choose," Jesus said. He placed his hands over the man's eyes, then removed them. "What do you see?"

Bartimaeus stood on his feet. He squinted, as his eyes adjusted to the sudden appearance of light. Amazement and joy filled his face. "I can see!" Bartimaeus shouted. "I can see trees, but they're walking like people!"

"Those *are* people," Jesus sighed. "Wait a minute." He spat on the ground and made mud from the dirt, then placed it on Bartimaeus's eyes. When he removed the mud, he said, "Now, what do you see?"

"I can see people! I can see buildings and the sky. I can see you!" He fell to his knees and wrapped his arms around Jesus. "Thank you, Lord! Thank you for giving me sight!"

Jesus lifted him to his feet. "Do not thank me. God has given you sight so that his works may be revealed. Now, go and testify to these things."

Bartimaeus went to his home and told his family and all his neighbors about what Jesus had done. But some of them doubted. "This can't be Bartimaeus," they said. "It's someone who looks like him."

"Are you blind now?" Bartimaeus asked. "You all know me. You've known me my whole life. I have no twin, and there is no one in Jerusalem like me. It is I, who once was blind, but now I see."

"But how can a man born blind be made well?" asked a neighbor. "Didn't God create you? Why would he heal you now?"

"I'm not wise enough to know the mind of God," Bartimaeus said. "But I testify to the truth. The man Jesus opened my eyes and told me it was God who gave me sight."

"Perhaps it isn't God who has done this but the devil," said another.

"Why would the devil do a good work such as this? And why would the devil do any good work and give the credit to God?" Bartimaeus asked.

"Then you must go to the Temple and testify this to the priests," they said. "Let them decide if this is a good work, and if Jesus' works are the works of God."

"I will go anywhere and tell anyone what has happened to me, and who it is that has done this for me."

The news of Bartimaeus's healing swept through the neighborhood, and a large crowd gathered at his home. While he was speaking to them, several Pharisees came and heard his testimony, and they compelled several of the men to seize him and take him to the Temple. The Pharisees ran ahead of them and told Caiaphas of all they had heard.

"Quickly," Caiaphas said. "Go and tell the other priests to come immediately. We will convene a hearing for this man. He may tell us just what we need to know to bring charges against Jesus."

"Shall we send for the members of the council?" the Pharisees asked.

"No. Some of them are too quick to make excuses for Jesus and even defend him. We will deal with this matter and report to the council once we have our facts."

Bartimaeus stood alone in the center of the council room. In front of him, seated, were seven priests. One of them, Caiaphas, the high priest, was sitting in the center in a larger throne-like chair flanked by side tables. On the tables were several items, including a bell, a wooden hammer, a small leather whip, and some other things Bartimaeus didn't recognize. To his left were two temple guards standing on either side of a railed platform—the witness box. To his right was a long table, and behind it sat four scribes, with quills in hand, waiting to transcribe the proceedings.

Bartimaeus was nervous but not so much from fear. He was still reveling in his newly found vision and slightly stunned by all that his sight sense was trying to absorb, including the grandiosity of the great Temple. He was a bit anxious, and confused, by the negative attention his miracle had caused and about being dragged before the Temple priests for questioning. He didn't understand why his healing was being seen as a source of consternation and worry and fear rather than one of joy and blessing. No matter. He knew what God had done for him through Jesus, and he would testify to this, just as Jesus had told him to do.

Caiaphas picked up the hammer beside him and rapped it on the table. "Let the proceeding begin," he said.

The scribes readied their quills on the open scrolls in front of them.

"Bartimaeus, you stand before us as one who has been healed of blindness. Is this true?"

"It is."

"And who is it that healed you?"

"It was God," Bartimaeus said sincerely.

"Do not be coy, Bartimaeus. It will not serve you well here. Our report is that you were blind from birth. Is this true?"

"It is."

"Then it was God's will for you to be blind. Do you question God's will?"

"I have never questioned God's will. And I do not question it now. Do you?"

Caiaphas gritted his teeth. "I warn you, again, Bartimaeus. Do not mock this court."

Bartimaeus was silent.

"Now I ask you to tell us exactly how this healing took place."

"I went to my usual place this morning, at the north gate. I sit there every day, all day, and beg for money to live on. A man came to me and asked me what I wanted. At first, I asked him for money, but when he asked me again what I really wanted, I told him I wanted to see. He touched my eyes, and I could see light and people moving about, but my vision was blurred, so he made mud and put it on my eyes. When he took the mud away, I could see clearly."

"And who was this man who healed you?"

"His name is Jesus, of Galilee. Have you heard of him?"

"We know of him. He is a blasphemer and a false prophet, and he deceives the people."

"No, I think he is a true prophet. He speaks the truth and does great acts in the name of God."

"My point, exactly," Caiaphas said, contemptuously. "See, he has deceived you."

"I am not wise enough to know the things you know," Bartimaeus replied. "All I know is that I was blind, and now I see. The man who healed me said this was God's doing and told me to testify to this. That's what I'm doing. Jesus healed me in God's name. That's all I know. How can a false prophet do such things in the name of God? And why would one who isn't from God give credit to God for the works he does?"

"You are right when you say you are not wise," Caiaphas said. "If you were, you would see what we see in this Jesus. He does not follow our laws and rituals. He does not keep the rules of Sabbath. He associates with sinners while shunning the righteous. And he incites the people with teachings we do not know or understand and that threaten the faith: Love your enemies, blessed are the poor, the last shall be first. These are not the words or acts of a godly man."

"Have you brought me here to confirm that I am not wise or that Jesus is an ungodly man? To the first, I will confess: I have been blind since birth, I have no education, I beg for a living. I am not wise; but I do believe the works Jesus does are by the power of God, for what he asks in God's name is done for him. It would be a foolish man, indeed, who witnesses these things and still does not believe."

"We know this man is a sinner!" Caiaphas snapped. "We do not need another sinner to confirm this for us! We have witnesses who tell us that you were never blind at all, that this whole episode is a ruse, and that you are in league with Jesus to lead the people astray!"

"I don't know these witnesses you speak of, and, if their testimony is that I wasn't blind, they don't know me. Untrue testimony usually comes by way of threat or reward, and you know better than I which method has been employed."

Caiaphas picked up the wooden hammer beside him and threw it at Bartimaeus, who dodged out of the way (once again, thankful for his eyesight). "How dare you accuse us of such deceit! How dare you speak to your elders in this way!" He lifted the cat-of-nine-tails from the table next to his chair. "Your back is very close to the ends of this whip, Bartimaeus. Watch your tongue."

Bartimaeus dropped his head in deference to Caiaphas (or, more correctly, to Caiaphas's whip).

"Now," Caiaphas said, regaining his composure and taking his seat, "you will tell us again *exactly* what happened. What did Jesus do to you? How did he open your eyes?"

Suddenly, Bartimaeus's courage and resolve returned to him. They were offering him an opportunity to recant his story and give them incriminating evidence against Jesus. He would do no such thing. "I've already told you *exactly* what happened. Were you not listening or do you need Jesus to heal your deafness?"

Caiaphas was seething. "If you are healed, it is God's doing, not Jesus'. Give glory to God and confess this man as the sinner we know him to be."

"Again, I don't know if he is a sinner. All I know is I was blind and now I see. It was Jesus who touched and healed me and told me it was the work of God. If God does his works through him, then he must be from God."

All the priests began to shout insults at Bartimaeus.

"Why should we listen to this fellow?" Caiaphas asked. "He has become one of Jesus' disciples. Bartimaeus's testimony is that he was blind from birth. If this is true, it was God's will that he be blind. If, then, Jesus healed him, he has usurped the will of God. It is, therefore, an evil act and the work of a demon. Our other witnesses say that Bartimaeus was never blind. If this is true, then Jesus, along with Bartimaeus, is a charlatan and deceiver of the people. I suggest we retain the testimony of these other witnesses and dismiss Bartimaeus's tale as false. This will give us one more charge against Jesus. All agreed, say, Amen."

"Amen," the other priests said in unison.

"Very well," Caiaphas said, as he eyed Bartimaeus with evil intent. "You are dismissed, Bartimaeus, not only from this hearing but from the Temple and all synagogues as well. You and your whole family. Now you can go and follow your Jesus, and die with him if you wish. If you decide you are ready to deny him, you can send word to me that you wish to repent, and we will consider your penance and reentry into the faith." He clapped his hands, and the guards manhandled Bartimaeus out of the Temple.

Caiaphas was pleased. He knew Herod was waiting for Jesus to be brought before him, and he had his paid false witnesses ready to testify against the Galilean. His popularity with the people was still a problem, but Caiaphas had plans for one more confrontation, and a trap that would show Jesus to be a true blasphemer. This would turn many away from him and cause many others to question. Then a careful arrest by night, and Jesus would be out of sight and out of mind, at least until after Passover. Once the crowds had dispersed—the pilgrims to their villages, and the locals to their homes and work—they could deal with Jesus properly, and without fear of a riot. They would try him and convict him, and if they could make insurrection charges stick, Herod or Pilate would have him executed. Then things could get back to normal. All this talk of Jesus as the messiah would end. The Temple leaders' authority and respect would be restored among the people. One more troublemaker's actions and memory erased from Israel's history.

Later, some of the Pharisees (those who were hedging their bets and hoping to associate themselves with Jesus—*just in case*) sent an envoy to request that Jesus join them for supper. "Rabbi, there are many of us who believe in you," the messenger said. "We have rented a room and would have you come and eat with us, and teach us."

Jesus knew what they were up to, and that they had chosen the evening meal and darkness, and an undisclosed location, to keep the meeting secret from their anti-Jesus colleagues. "I would be happy to accept your invitation. Our camping fare is little more than bread and cheese and is growing monotonous. It will be nice for all of us to sit at a table. We're staying at Gethsemane, in the garden there. When you're ready, send someone for us."

"Uh, actually, we were thinking it would be only you joining us. There may not be enough room for all of you."

"I'm afraid, when it comes to dinner invitations, we're a package deal. I would never feast and leave my disciples to scraps by the campfire. We come together or we don't come at all."

"Very well," said the Pharisee reluctantly. "We will send someone for you at dusk—*all of you*. He will bring you to the place where we are meeting."

"We'll be ready," Jesus said. "Thank you for the invitation. It should be an interesting meeting."

The Pharisee walked away with the uneasy feeling that he had just been played, and that he and his friends were in for a teaching they wouldn't like.

It was just getting dark when a servant of one of the Pharisees came to the garden to collect Jesus and the disciples. He was carrying a torch, which helped them find their way back along the narrow path that wound through the garden. Once they reached the city gate, the servant extinguished the torch and reached for a lamp he'd apparently stowed in a small alcove in the wall. "Please follow me," he said. The men complied, following the lamp's dim glow through the dark streets. When they had gone a few blocks, the servant stopped beside a door. "Through here and up the stairs," he instructed, then led the way.

As Jesus stepped through the door at the street, he noticed more doors on either side of a short hallway. Just beyond these was a set of steep stairs leading to another single second-story door. They followed the servant to the top of the steps. He opened the door and then stepped aside, bowing and gesturing with his hand for the others to enter. Inside was a large room with tables set in a rectangular shape. The head tables at the other end of the room were being set with pitchers of wine and plates of food. Several male servants scurried back and forth from the tables to another room that was, apparently, a kitchen. There were six columns, three on either side of the room, and each set supported the weight of a huge wooden roof beam. From these, several lamps hung from braided ropes over the tables. Lamp sconces on the walls provided additional light. Most of the guests were gathered in small groups of three or four and, though everyone noticed the large contingent that had just entered the room, no one made a move to greet them.

Finally, the Pharisee that had extended the invitation entered the room from the kitchen and noticed Jesus and his entourage. He barked out a few final instructions to the servants, then hurried over and bowed in front of Jesus before embracing him and kissing him on both cheeks. "Thank you for coming. Please let me introduce you to some of the others." He led Jesus away, as the disciples held their places just inside the door.

After Jesus had accompanied the Pharisee to every one of the small groups, the disciples noticed the man gesturing for Jesus to take a seat at the center of the head table (no doubt next to himself). They saw Jesus point toward them and say something to his host, who shook his head and shrugged his shoulders as he replied. As the two separated, the man clapped his hands loudly and gave direction for everyone to take their seats. Most scrambled toward seats closer to the head table.

When Jesus rejoined the disciples, he instructed them to sit on the benches closest to them and farthest from the head table. Then he taught them, saying, "Do you see how everyone seeks the closest seats and the places of honor near the host? But whenever you are invited to a feast or banquet, do not seek the most prominent places, for if someone more distinguished than you should arrive, you may be asked to move to a lower seat. Instead, take the least important place at the table, so that when your host comes, he can say to you, 'Friend, move up to a higher place,' and you will be honored. For so it is in the kingdom of God: Those who exalt themselves will be humbled and those who humble themselves will be exalted."

After supper was over, the servants moved the tables to one side of the room and dozens of blankets and reclining pillows were brought in. The guests all gathered in the center of the room and made themselves comfortable on the pillows.

The host Pharisee asked Jesus to speak to them, and he taught them many things about the kingdom. Finally, he said, "I notice with the exception of myself and my friends that this is a rather elite gathering."

There was a proud chuckle from the room.

"But I would say to you, whenever you give a dinner like this, don't just invite your neighbors and friends and those equal to or better off than you. For in doing so, you are inviting only those who can repay you by returning the favor. Instead, when you give a feast, include those lower than you. Remember the lame and blind and poor, for these can never repay you. You have simply done to them an act of kindness without thought of reciprocation. Nevertheless, when you include those who cannot repay your favor, God will bless you, and you will be repaid through the riches of his grace."

One of the Pharisees, troubled by Jesus' words, spoke. "But is not such behavior wrong before God? Eating with sinners and the unclean renders *us* unclean and defiles our own righteousness. This is what we do not understand about your behavior. You call us to truth and obedience to God, yet you ignore the very laws that keep us pure."

Jesus looked at him and said, "Woe to you, Pharisees, and to the Sadducees and priests and scribes, who pervert God's simple laws of love with complicated laws that separate and exclude. You rewrite God's laws—or expand them—to serve your own purposes and to fabricate your own righteousness. God gave you ten laws, which you do not follow. Instead, you have written hundreds more to suit your ways. But I will tell you again, as the prophets before have told you, this is what God requires of his people—his true children: Love mercy, do justice and walk humbly with your God; Love the Lord your God with every fiber of your being and love every person with the same love you have for yourself; Do to others as you would have them do to you. If you do these things, you are following the commandments of God. It is not hard. It does not require the rituals and ceremonies and sacrifices and the many rules that you demand. Love God and love one another. That is enough. And yet, you fail to do this simple thing."

There was a tense silence.

Finally, one of them said, "We do not need to be lectured by the likes of you." He pointed his finger at Jesus. "We invited you here because we want to help you bring about your kingdom."

"No," Jesus said, "you invited me here, not because you are for me, but because you fear I am speaking the truth. You seek both my favor and the favor of my enemies, so that you may claim allegiance to the dark and the light, to God and to man, to earthly power and the power of heaven. You are hypocrites."

"How dare you speak to us this way!" said another angrily. "We know the law better than you. And we know that we are on the side of God. It is not us who associates and eats with sinners. Do you not know righteousness from sin, and that God loves one and hates the other?"

"If you were righteous, then you would know that God loves the sinner as well as the righteous."

"Then why is it that the righteous are blessed and the sinner is condemned by God? Why is it that the righteous are saved and the sinner obliterated?"

"These are not God's ways but yours. It is my Father's will that all should come to him. This is why I have been sent: to preach this good news and to seek out the lost and bring them home." Jesus knew they didn't understand, so he continued, "Which one of you, if you had a hundred sheep and one of them strayed, would not leave the ninety-nine and go in search of the one that was lost? And when you have found it and brought it home, would you not rejoice with all your household that the lost sheep was found? Such is the way with God and the kingdom of heaven. For there is more joy in heaven over one sinner who repents than over ninety-nine righteous persons who need no repentance."

There was grumbling throughout the room as the Pharisees considered what Jesus had said.

Finally, the host posed a question to Jesus. "Rabbi, we do not understand how it is God's will that everyone should be saved. Are there not those who are enemies of God? Will God not destroy even them?"

"It is God's will that all should come to him and love him, but, sadly, some will not. Nevertheless, we must love as God loves, extending mercy to all and withholding judgment, for God alone knows our hearts, and God alone is our judge. The truly righteous will know this."

Just then, the door opened, and a woman entered the room, carrying a jar of perfumed oil. She went straight to Jesus and poured a few drops on his head, then used the rest to wash his feet as a sign of her servitude and his Lordship.

"This is an outrage!" shouted one of the Pharisees. "No women are allowed in this room!"

Some of the others stood to remove her.

"Leave her alone," Jesus said. "This woman is preparing my body for burial." (Jesus was announcing to the Pharisees that he would soon die, if not at their hands then at their urging, but none of them understood what he was saying.)

The woman continued to bathe Jesus' feet with the oil and wipe them dry with her long hair.

The men in the room watched, appalled. Many of them knew her very well; she was a prostitute, and they were her clients. One of them whispered to another, "This cannot be the messiah. If he were, he would know who it is that is washing his feet."

Jesus sensed what they were saying and responded. "This woman washes my feet because she loves me and wishes to honor and serve me. Yet you have sought her out for an act without love or honor. Therefore, the sin for which you condemn her is yours."

"We are not whores," one of them said. "Yet you place her sin on us?"

"She does what she does out of necessity, because you make no provision for her or others in need. You take advantage of her poverty and abuse her by giving little from your abundance and demanding something in return from one who has nothing. Her fault is forgiven, but for the acts you have committed with her, yours is the double sin."

"We do not know what you are talking about!" shouted one of the woman's frequent visitors. "You are the one who associates with sinners, not us. If she is a whore, she has chosen her lot. If she is poor, then God has made her poor. It is not our responsibility, or even our right, to change God's judgment on another."

"You *are* hypocrites," Jesus said. "For you have been given much, and you hoard your blessings. But I tell you, in the kingdom to come, what you have will be taken away. Learn from this woman; for the little she has, she has spent on this oil and given it to me. Therefore, I tell you, in the kingdom to come, she will be blessed and given much more."

"Enough of this!" said the host. "Jesus, we offered you our friendship, and you have refused it! It will not be offered to you again. Take this woman with you and leave this place. Leave this city and do not return, or, I warn you, the consequences will be dire."

Jesus stood to leave. "You know where we are staying. Tell Caiaphas we will be back in the city tomorrow. What will be will be, for it is my Father's will that these things must take place."

When Jesus, the woman, and the disciples had gone, the host Pharisee said to the others, "You have heard him. He intends a revolt and plans to make himself king. This is all the evidence we need to charge him with insurrection and treason against Herod and Rome. Let us go to Caiaphas and stand as witnesses to his words."

"If you say this is what we have heard, then this is what we have heard and will testify to it," said another, confirming the lie. "But what will we say of this meeting with him? Will we not be implicating ourselves with this stupid act—your stupid idea—of enlisting with him?"

"We will say nothing, except that we called him here to interrogate him. And since we have the evidence Caiaphas wants to arrest him, that will be enough."

When Jesus returned with his disciples to their camp in the garden, a crowd was gathered there. Many of them had swords and clubs, and they cheered as Jesus came among them. Jesus' mother and his brothers and sisters were also there, and they greeted him.

"Why have you come, Mother? What are all these people doing here?" Jesus asked with concern.

"We've come with others from all over Galilee and Judea," said Jesus' brother, Jacob. "Your disciples sent word that you're ready to overthrow Rome and claim your kingship as the messiah of Israel."

Jesus looked at his disciples. "Why have you done this? How could you have done this behind my back? Can I not trust even you, my closest friends? Do you follow me or the devil?"

"But, Lord, what evil have we done?" Philip asked. "We can't fight without an army. And there are many more who will follow you. They only await your command."

"Oh, Philip," Jesus said, with great disappointment. "Have I been with you this long and, still, you don't know me? Have I taught you all this time and, still, you don't understand? The time of my kingdom has not yet come, and when it does come, it will not be the kingdom you are expecting. My kingdom isn't an earthly kingdom of armies and power and might but a heavenly kingdom of peace with good will and forgiveness for all."

"But we must fight!" exclaimed Judas. "Do you expect the Romans to simply stand aside in peace and let your rule and kingdom usurp theirs? Without an army, they will crush us, and the hope of Israel's freedom will be destroyed forever."

"Send these people away!" Jesus demanded. "And if you don't believe in me and that I know the Father and am doing the will of the Father, you go with them! Look, this is a heavy burden I bear. I need you with me, but if I must do this work alone, then so be it, for this is my purpose and the reason I was sent—to accomplish the will of God and to bring his people to him through me."

"If we send them away, they won't come back to us," Judas said. "They'll look to another to save them. They'll turn to Barabbas and the Zealots."

"Send them away," said Jesus, and he left them and went into the darkness to pray.

The disciples stood silent for a moment, confused and disappointed.

"I will say nothing to these people," Judas said. "If Jesus wants to send them away, then he can tell them himself." He walked away.

Finally, Peter spoke to the crowd. "Jesus says we will not fight. Put away your weapons. If you've come from other towns or villages, stay for Passover or return to your homes, but you cannot stay here with us. Now, please go."

There was murmuring in the crowd.

"We were told to come here for war!" someone shouted. "Have we come all this way and risked our lives gathering for nothing?"

"Jesus is not the messiah," said another. "If he were, he would lead us into battle!"

"Jesus is a deceiver!" shouted someone else. "The Temple priests are right! Let us find him and kill him!"

Others in the crowd began to roar their disapproval.

The disciples took Jesus' family and slipped away for fear the people might turn on them.

Eventually, most of the crowd dispersed, but some gathered in groups to plan new strategies.

Jesus didn't return to the camp until the next morning. The disciples, except for Judas, were waiting for him there. Jesus' family was with them.

"You have decided to stay with me?" he asked.

"Where, and to whom, would we go, Lord?" Peter said. "We will follow you even to death."

"You would give your life for me, Peter?" Jesus asked. "I tell you, before the cock crows at the next dawn, you will deny me three times."

"I will never deny you, Lord," said Peter, hurt.

"Today will be the day that your faith is tested," Jesus said to them all. Then he looked at them with love and compassion and said, "Do not let your hearts be troubled. Believe in God and believe in me. In my Father's kingdom, there are many houses. If this were not so, I would tell you. I am going away from you for a while to prepare a place for you. And I will come again to take you to the place where I am going, so that where I am, you may be also."

"Teacher, we have followed you all this time," Thomas said. "Tell us what you would have us do, and we will do it. Show the way you would have us go, and we will follow."

"Dear Thomas," Jesus said, smiling, "*I* am the way, and the truth, and the life."

Judas had left the night before to find the camp of the Zealots. Before becoming a follower of Jesus, Judas was a member of the Zealot

organization, an underground band of revolutionaries set on the overthrow of the Roman oppression of Israel and responsible for the murders of many Roman soldiers and government officials. When he made contact with one of his former colleagues, he learned that their leader, Barabbas, had been captured and arrested and several dozen of his soldiers put to death. Barabbas himself had been kept alive for interrogation but since had been tried and convicted of insurrection and was in Pilate's prison, awaiting crucifixion. To appease the Jews' sensibilities about such things, the death sentence was not to be carried out until the Passover feast had ended. Because the Romans had become quite relentless and brutal in their efforts to quell the Zealot uprising, Judas's friend told him they had decided to lay low for a time. The Zealots had paid close attention to the Jesus movement, however, and many of their soldiers believed that he could be the messiah. Barabbas was not one of them, believing Jesus to be weak and indecisive. Judas's friend was disappointed to hear the report that Barabbas was apparently right, and that the "Jesus Revolution" had fizzled.

As Judas made his way back to the city, he decided there was only one course of action. He would force Jesus' hand before it was too late. If Jesus was arrested, perhaps he would see the gravity of the situation and call on the people to revolt. And even if he didn't, the disciples could rally the troops and, in Jesus' name, the revolution would begin. But he had to act fast. It had to happen during Passover, when there were enough people present in Jerusalem to actually make the overthrow possible. Right now, the Romans were greatly outnumbered, and an all-out attack might make success possible. But once the people had returned to their own villages throughout Galilee and Judea, they could never muster the enthusiasm that was with them now, especially without Jesus. His plan was the better plan. It had to be this way.

Judas didn't relish the idea of going against Jesus and having to explain himself to his master later, but that was a risk he would have to take—for Jesus' sake and for the sake of Israel! Once Jesus realized why he did what he did, perhaps he would understand and forgive him. But left to his own devices, Jesus would stall and avoid confrontation as long as possible. By that time, he would have alienated the people with his false or delayed promises, and they wouldn't come to his rescue. They would turn against him, and Jesus' ministry would have been for nothing. Yes, his was the better plan, and he would do what had to be done.

The next morning, some of the Pharisees who had secretly met with Jesus came to Caiaphas and reported all he had said.

"We questioned him," one of them lied. "He told us he would establish a new kingdom where the laws of God would no longer stand and where sinners would rule over the righteous."

"He was intimate with a whore in our very presence and praised her as a favored one of God," said another.

Caiaphas tore at his clothes in theatrical grief, but his heart rejoiced at the news. "This fool has blasphemed for the last time!" he said, in thrilled anger. "Take the Temple guards and arrest him. If you will testify to these things, we have what we need to convict him before Herod."

"We will testify," one of them said, "but the people still follow him. There could be a riot if we arrest him."

"Then bide your time. Wait until he is alone, if you must. But if he continues to spew his blasphemies, you can turn the people away from him by his very words. Seize the opportunity whenever it presents itself and bring him to me—today!"

They left with the guards to find Jesus.

When the Pharisees came upon Jesus, he was teaching a large crowd.

"We do not dare arrest him in front of all these people," one of them said. "We must wait."

"Or," said another, "we can find a way to turn the people to our side. Wait here. I have an idea." He ordered two of the guards to follow him and left.

A short time later, they returned, the guards pulling and dragging a woman along with them. "He likes whores so much," the Pharisee said to his friends, "we'll see what he has to say to the people about this one. Disperse yourselves among the crowd and be ready to incite them."

"Wait!" said another. "What are you doing? What is your plan?"

"Just follow my lead!" the first one replied. "This woman is a known whore. If Jesus defends her acts, the people will be ready to stone both him and her. If he condemns her, then encourage the crowd to kill her."

"But we cannot do this during Passover. We will be guilty of a great sin."

"It will not be our sin, will it? Take up your stone, but do not throw it. If the crowd kills them both, then we will be witnesses to their sin. If Jesus should condemn the woman, and the people stone her, then he bears the guilt and sin of her death. Now, make yourselves ready. Guards! Bring her!" he commanded and began parting the crowd to make his way to Jesus.

The guards threw the woman to the ground at Jesus' feet. She rose to her knees but kept her face bowed low toward the ground.

"Rabbi," said the Pharisee, "we have found this woman to be guilty of prostitution and adultery, for she has slept with many married men, causing them to sin against their wives. The Law of Moses commands us to put such women to death. What do you say about her?"

Jesus knelt beside the woman and wrote with his finger in the dirt in front of her. *M-A-R-Y.*

She read her name and looked up at Jesus.

He whispered to her, "Don't speak and don't move." Then he stood and said, "Let the one among you who is without sin be the first to throw a stone."

"Stone her!" the Pharisees began to shout, but no one in the crowd reacted.

"Do you follow the laws of God or this man's laws?" said the Pharisee standing beside Jesus. "Stone her!"

Jesus walked over and picked up a rock from the ground. He handed it to the Pharisee. "You are a leader of the people, aren't you? You are a keeper of the law. Do what you will."

The Pharisee was still for a second. Then he raised his arm above his head, as if ready to strike a deadly blow. His hand began to shake, and he threw the stone to the ground beside the woman. Without another word, he angrily pushed his way through the crowd and left. The other Pharisees let their rocks drop from their hands and followed.

Jesus helped the woman to her feet. "Your accusers do not condemn you," he said, loud enough for everyone to hear. "Neither do I." He called Peter to him. "Peter, take Mary back to the garden and take the others with you. I will meet you there this evening."

Peter suddenly recognized the woman. "Mary! We thought you were dead!"

"Go now," Jesus said. "We will all talk later." Peter put his arm around the weak-kneed Mary and led her away.

"Master, some of us should stay with you," Philip said.

"I'll be fine," Jesus said. "My enemies are men of darkness. They cannot do their work while it is light, but only in the dark of night. I must continue while it is light, for darkness will surely come."

The Pharisees arrived back at the Temple to report to Caiaphas.

"How long must I put up with you?" Caiaphas said. "I have orders from Herod to bring Jesus to him. He is probably wondering now why I have not done this. You have evidence against him. Why did you not arrest him?"

"The crowd around him was too large, and they were with him. We tried to turn them to our favor, but they hang on his every word. If we had tried to arrest him, they would have surely stoned us!"

"And, yet, you say he forgave this woman's sins. Is this not blasphemy? Do you not have tongues in your mouths to rebuke him before the people and to convince them that he is a sinner?"

"We have argued this, but they will not listen. They believe he is the messiah."

"Then they are fools!" Caiaphas shouted. "We can wait no longer for the people to come to our side. Once we have dealt with him, they will realize the truth about this man, and their folly in following him. They will thank us for saving them from their false hope, and all of Israel from a cruel fate at the hands of the Romans.

"Tomorrow is the day of Passover. He will make his move sometime between now and then, while the city is still full of people who will follow him. We must act first to prevent the insurrection he is planning. If a revolt begins, we will pay the highest price. Go back and take the guards with you. Find him and do whatever you have to do, but arrest him and bring him to me."

The Pharisees didn't have to go far. They found Jesus just outside in the Temple courtyard, teaching a large crowd of people.

"Truly, I tell you, I can do nothing on my own but only as God directs me, for I see what God does, and I do likewise through the power of God. The heavenly Father is in me and I am in him. As God loves, I love; as God heals, I heal; as God raises the dead to life, so I give life to whomever I wish to give it. And, I tell you, you will see greater works than these, and very soon.

"God judges no one but has given all judgment to me so that all may honor me just as they honor God. Anyone who does not honor me does not honor God, for God and I are one."

"Holy crap!" one of the Pharisees said excitedly. "We have him!" He ran forward through the crowd and stood in front of Jesus. He turned to face the people. "We have warned you about this man. Now you have heard it with your own ears. He is equating himself with God!" He turned to Jesus. "You say you and God are one. Not even the messiah would make a claim to be God! You pronounce the forgiveness of sins, but only God has the power to forgive sins. You are not God, and you are not from God but from the devil!"

Some in the crowd were astonished at what Jesus had said and began to jeer at him and side with the Pharisees.

Jesus spoke, "Very truly, I tell you, those who hear my words and believe them will know that it is God who sent me, for my words are true, and God is truth. The devil is the father of lies and his sons are liars. You have seen the good works that I do. How can I do these things apart from God?"

He looked at the Pharisee. "You say that only God can forgive, but I say to you, only God can condemn. Woe to you who so easily condemn your neighbor but find it impossible to forgive. This is the will of the devil and his children. But *this* is the will of God: Do not judge, and you will not come under judgment but have everlasting life. Do not condemn and you will not be condemned. Forgive and you will be forgiven. The hour is coming, and is here now, when the living and the dead will hear the voice of God, and those who hear will live. Let anyone who is thirsty come to me, and let the one who believes in me drink of the water of life. As the scripture says, 'Out of the believer's heart shall flow rivers of living water.'"

When the crowd heard these words from Jesus, some of them said, "This really is the messiah who speaks the words of God." But others said, "How can he be equal to God? This is blasphemy! How can he even be the messiah, for he comes from Galilee? Do the scriptures not tell us that the messiah will come from Bethlehem?" So there was a division among the people.

The Pharisee who had confronted Jesus went to the Temple guards. "Now is our chance. The crowd is divided among itself. Make the arrest."

None of the guards moved.

"I am giving you an order!" he screamed. "Arrest Jesus!"

The guards looked at each other. "We do not take our orders from you," one of them said, "but only from Caiaphas."

"Your orders *are* from Caiaphas!" the Pharisee continued screaming. "He sent you with us to arrest Jesus! Arrest him now!" He pointed in the direction where Jesus was standing.

"Where is he?" one of the guards asked.

The Pharisee turned to look at where Jesus had been. He was gone. "Quickly, spread out, search among the crowd!" he said in a panicked voice. "He must not get away! We must find him!"

The guards and the other Pharisees did as they were told, but there was no sign of Jesus.

A half an hour later, after the crowd had dispersed, the search party regrouped in the middle of the courtyard. The Pharisee ordered them all back to the Temple and Caiaphas's meeting chamber. Caiaphas listened as the Pharisee recounted the story of his confrontation with

Jesus and the insubordination of the guards in their reluctance to arrest him.

"Tell me why you did this?" Caiaphas asked angrily. "Why did you not arrest him when you had the opportunity?"

One of the guards sheepishly stepped forward to answer for the group. "It was the things he said, sir. Never have we heard anyone speak this way."

Caiaphas sighed, "So now you, too, have been deceived by him? You, too, have become his disciples? Do you realize you may have cost us our last opportunity to get this man before he starts a war? Get out of my sight before I have *you* arrested!"

When the guards had left, Caiaphas looked at the several Pharisees standing in front of him. "What now? Does anyone have any ideas about how we might find Jesus and arrest him before morning? Before it's too late?"

One of them spoke. "We know he is staying outside the city, but we do not know where. Perhaps we could offer a reward and send the guards into the streets and to the city gates to see if anyone can lead us to him."

"Do you trust the guards?" Caiaphas growled, with disdain. "You are the leaders of the community. Call all the Pharisees and the Sadducees and send them out to question the people. Offer forty pieces of silver to anyone who will lead us to him."

Just then, a scribe entered the room. "Excuse me, sir, but there are two people who wish to see you."

"Who is it?" Caiaphas roared, irritated.

"One is a soldier from Herod's palace. He says Herod has sent for you."

Caiaphas coved his face with his hands. Herod would want to know why Jesus hadn't been brought to him. He would not be pleased with what Caiaphas had to say. "And who is the other?"

"His name is Judas. He says he is a disciple of Jesus and has some important information for you."

Caiaphas's face brightened. "Send in Judas first," he said.

Judas spent several minutes lying to Caiaphas about the reasons for his falling out with Jesus and the motives behind his betrayal. "He deceived us," Judas said. "Now I know he is a false messiah, just like all the others before him. I want him stopped before he turns the hearts of others away from the true faith of Israel."

"You are wise in coming here, my friend," Caiaphas said. "For we, too, want only what is best for our nation. Jesus is a dangerous man with a dangerous message. If he is not stopped, he will lead many astray and put all of Israel at risk of destruction."

"He is not an evil man," protested Judas, already feeling remorse and doubting his resolve. "He is...just...disturbed. Perhaps, delusions of grandeur."

"Of course." Caiaphas said, faking sympathy. "He is a son of Israel, like you and I. We wish him no harm but rather to compel him to repent and save his soul. You are doing the right thing for him and for us. Now, where can we find him?"

"I can take you to him, but I want one thing in return."

"What?" Caiaphas said, suspicious and impatient.

"Complete immunity for me and the other disciples." (He said this not only out of fear of arrest for their complicity with Jesus, but, also, hoping that after Jesus' arrest, he and the others could rally support for their master's cause.)

"Done," Caiaphas said. "Now, please have something to eat and rest in my quarters. You can take us to him tonight."

One of the Pharisees escorted Judas out of the room and to the high priest's resting quarters.

"Now send in Herod's soldier," Caiaphas said confidently.

The soldier entered and saluted Caiaphas by placing his right arm across his breastplate. This was followed by a low bow.

Caiaphas nodded his head as a return gesture. "I know why you are here. Go back and tell Herod I am occupied, seeing to the arrest of Jesus this very hour. The prisoner will appear before him tonight."

"I will give him your message," said the soldier. He repeated the salute and bow, then turned and left the room.

"Call a meeting of the Sanhedrin," Caiaphas said to another priest. "Seven o'clock tonight at my house."

The priest nodded and followed behind Herod's soldier.

Caiaphas felt as if a huge burden had been lifted from his shoulders, and not a moment too soon. "Gentlemen," he said to the Pharisees and priests still in the room, "I think a celebration and a bit of wine would be appropriate." He clapped his hands, and a servant standing beside him scurried off to see to the high priest's order.

It was near dusk when Jesus arrived back at the garden. The disciples were waiting for him, along with Mary, his mother, and Mary Magdalene.

"Mary, come with me," he said to Mary Magdalene, taking her elbow in his hand and leading her away from the others. When they were a distance away and out of sight, he embraced her and held her close. "Mary, you're alive! This is wonderful! But, how? We found your bloodied clothes. What happened? Where have you been?"

Mary was transfixed. For a few seconds, she ignored his questions. Instead, she gazed deeply into his face, studying every line and crease, his beautiful eyes. He was older, weathered, but so familiar. For eight long years, she had tried to forget about him—about *them*—but, in an instant, it all came rushing back. She loved him. And, as he looked back at her, she could see his love for her. She wrapped her arms around his waist and held him close, her head against his chest. She felt him reciprocate, his strong hands pressing against her back.

"Mary?"

She pushed herself back and raised her head to look at him again. This time she saw anguish in his eyes, no doubt, from the weight and questioning of her sudden reappearance from the dead. (She didn't know the true reason for his anguish was his impending fate.) She quickly dropped her gaze to the ground. She couldn't bear to look at him as she recounted her story. "I've already explained to Peter what happened. I came to Capernaum to try and make things right between Peter and me, and between Peter and you—about us. Before I found Peter, I was attacked and raped by three men. After that, I simply left town, knowing our life could never be as we had planned, that it was the best thing for all concerned."

"But your clothes? We found them."

"I had brought a change of clothes with me. I had planned to stay in Capernaum a day or two. I buried the clothes you found. Obviously, not well enough. They were torn and bloody and carried the stench of those animals that raped me."

"You should have come to me, Mary."

"No, I shouldn't have. Even if you still would have wanted me, you didn't deserve me or my shame."

Now Jesus was looking at the ground, too, forlorn and as broken-hearted as when he had first believed Mary to be dead. "But, your parents, surely they know."

Mary shook her head. "No, they didn't need the burden of my shame either. It would have killed my father. Knowing the truth would have been harder on them than thinking I was dead."

"This is all so hard for me to take in. I mourned for you so long and, now, you're here, alive." He reached for her. Mary wanted to back away, feeling unworthy of him, but she couldn't resist and met his embrace.

"Nothing has changed since that day, Jesus, except I am more defiled. I am a prostitute, and I have chosen this life on my own. I am an unrepentant sinner, not worthy even to tie your sandals, much less to receive your mercy and love."

Jesus looked at her. "You have my mercy and my love, Mary. And I tell you this: You didn't choose your life. If you had, you would have chosen differently. Others bear the guilt of your fate."

"Ah, but, in the end, our fate is what we own, and it owns us. Isn't this true?"

"God, alone, owns us, Mary, and we are his. This is the truth. God determines our final fate. If we follow his will for us, we will be saved."

"I would have his forgiveness, if he will have me."

"I promise you, this day, this moment, you have it. You are forgiven."

Mary looked at Jesus, frightened but overjoyed. "You *are* the messiah, the Son of God."

"I am."

She bowed at his feet. "From this day, I will follow the Lord, and I will follow you."

Jesus raised Mary to her feet, and they went back to join the others.

At dark, Caiaphas reentered the Temple meeting room, took his chair, and instructed the Pharisees and guards who were to accompany Judas. "Go with him to the place where Jesus is staying. When you find him, arrest him and bring him to my house. I will be there with the council to interrogate him." He pointed his finger at the guards. "Do not fail to arrest him this time, or you will be dealt with harshly."

Judas led them away.

When it was time for supper, Jesus had the disciples gather around him, and he taught them, saying, "You have stood by me in my trials; therefore, I confer on you, just as the Father has conferred on me, a kingdom, so that you may eat and drink at my table when my kingdom comes. First, you must undergo your own trials. Pray God will send his Holy Spirit to be with you and guide you. This is the Spirit of truth who will abide in you forever.

"I no longer call you servants but friends, and no one has greater love than to lay down one's life for one's friends. You did not choose me. I chose you. I appoint you to go and bear good fruit so that the Father will give you whatever you ask in my name."

Then Jesus looked up into heaven and prayed. "Father, I pray to you not only for these who believe but for those who will come to believe in me through their witness. May they be one, even as you and I are one. As you are in me and I am in you, may they also be in us, so that the whole world may believe that you sent me."

When he had finished praying, he called his mother and Mary Magdalene to join them, and they sat down for supper. "Tomorrow, others will celebrate the Passover meal, but I will not be with you tomorrow. Let us eat our Passover meal tonight."

"But, Lord," Philip said, "we don't have a lamb or the other things we need to celebrate properly. Let us go into the city and buy what is required."

"I am the Lamb of God," Jesus said. "I am the Alpha and the Omega, the beginning and the end. Is that not enough? My body and my blood will be your Passover sacrifice, now and forever."

He took a loaf of bread, and after blessing it, he broke it into pieces and distributed it among them. "This bread is my body. It is broken for you. From now on, whenever you celebrate this feast and eat the bread of Passover, remember me, for I am the sacrificial lamb, given for the world."

He then took a cup and filled it with wine. "This is my blood, which is poured out for you and for many others for the forgiveness of sins. Whenever you drink from the Passover cup, do this in remembrance of me, for I am the Passover lamb, given for the world."

After supper, Jesus withdrew from the others to be alone with God. He was filled with anxiety over what was to come. When he had gone a distance away, he fell to the ground on his knees, and prayed, "Heavenly Father, my life is in your hands, and I submit myself to your will. If it is possible, let this cup pass from me, but if it must be, then give me courage to endure it." After he had said this, an angel appeared to him to comfort him and give him strength, but when the angel departed, his anguish rose again, and he prayed more earnestly. He was interrupted by Peter's call.

"Master, come quickly. There are torches approaching."

Jesus stood and walked back to where the others were waiting. He could see the string of torch lights bobbing and weaving their way up the narrow trail toward the camp. "Father, the hour has come," he said softly. "Glorify your Son, so that the Son may glorify you."

When the detachment of guards became visible in the glow of the campfire, Peter unsheathed his knife and stepped in front of Jesus. "Who goes there?" he shouted. "What do you want?"

Judas turned to the captain of the guards. "The one I will kiss is Jesus. Take him, but leave the others alone."

"Identify yourself!" Peter reiterated, taking another step forward and brandishing the knife in his outstretched hand.

"It is I, Peter," Judas said. "Let me pass."

Peter lowered his arm slightly and motioned for Judas to move around him, all the while keeping his eyes fixed on the armed guards.

Judas approached Jesus and kissed him on the cheek. "Master," he said.

"Have you come to betray me with a kiss, Judas?" Jesus asked.

"I had no choice, Master," Judas said.

"You did have a choice, Judas, and you chose wrongly. You should have chosen to trust me."

The guards were not moving. They stood, seemingly mesmerized by the sight of Jesus.

"T-t-take him," the captain whimpered.

No one moved.

"Who are you looking for?" Jesus asked.

"J-J-Jesus of Galilee," the captain managed to say.

"I am he," Jesus said.

The guards actually took a step backward.

"I am the one you seek. If you've come to arrest me, do it. I will not resist."

"No! We will fight for you, master!" Peter said. He moved threateningly toward the guards.

Two of the other disciples drew their knives and lined up beside Peter.

"Put your knives away," Jesus said, "for those who live by the sword will die by the sword. Stand aside now, and let them pass. Is it not the Father's will that these things take place? Is it not my purpose to complete this mission?"

Peter slowly and reluctantly allowed his arm to fall to his side. He released the knife from the grip of his hand, and it fell to the ground. The other two disciples sheathed their knives and backed away.

"Take him," the captain said, with a stronger but unenthusiastic voice. One of the guards stepped forward and tied Jesus' hands with one end of a long rope, then, holding on to the other end, he led him away. Some of the guards went in front of Jesus; the rest followed behind him.

When they had gone, Peter stared at Judas for a long minute, trying to process what had just happened. Then he charged into him, taking them both to the ground. He landed on top of Judas and began to pummel his face and chest. "You're a traitor to our Lord! I'll kill you for this!" He stopped punching his victim and started choking him instead. When it appeared that he really was going to kill Judas, the other disciples pulled him off.

"Stop it, Peter! He isn't worth it!" Philip said, putting his face directly in front of Peter's to try and calm him down. "Let Judas go. We need to follow the guards to see where they're taking Jesus."

"They're taking him to Caiaphas's house," said Judas, picking himself up off the ground and straightening his tunic. "If you'll listen to me, I have a plan."

Peter broke away from the disciples holding him and tackled Judas again. "I have a plan for you!" Peter shouted. He had his hands around Judas's neck again.

"Peter, we don't have time for this! We have to go!" Philip said, as he and Thomas separated the two a second time.

"Wait, please!" Judas said, getting on his feet and dusting himself off. "We can turn this to our advantage! We can turn it to Jesus' advantage. We'll rally the people around him. Once Jesus is in prison, he'll realize the time has come to call for revolution. We'll free him, and he'll call us to fight."

Philip and Thomas held on to Peter's arms as they led him away. Peter looked over his shoulder. "Don't be here when we get back, Judas. If I see you again, I swear, I *will* kill you!"

Judas watched as his erstwhile friends disappeared into the darkness. He sat down by the fire to consider the situation—how it had all gone wrong. He realized there was no hope of his plans for a revolution under the leadership of Jesus. He had made an incredible miscalculation—an unforgivable mistake. The betrayal of his master weighed heavy on him, and he began to weep. After a time, he walked alone into the night, broken-hearted and ashamed.

Chapter 7
Jesus' Trial

Peter and the other disciples followed the lights of the guards' torches as they made their way down the hill along the garden trail and into the city. They were careful to keep their distance and avoid detection. They weren't certain why they weren't taken into custody along with Jesus, but if they were caught following him, they surely would be arrested—or worse.

By the time they reached Caiaphas's house, Jesus had already been taken inside. A small crowd was gathered in the courtyard, mostly the servant or slave escorts of the council members who were questioning Jesus.

"We'll be too conspicuous if we all enter together," Philip said. "The rest of you stay here at the gate. Peter and I will go inside to see if we can find out what's happening." The two men entered the courtyard and began questioning servants.

"Are you the only ones in Jerusalem who haven't heard of Jesus?" replied one of the servants to their inquiry. "He's subverting the nation and, just now, has been arrested by the Temple guards. The high priest and the council are examining him in preparation to charge him before Herod."

"I've seen this one before," a servant girl said, pointing at Peter. "I've seen him with Jesus. He's one of his disciples."

"I am not!" protested Peter. "I don't know the man."

"No, I'm sure of it. I remember you. You were with him."

"Woman, you are mistaken! I don't know him!"

"We should go," Philip whispered into Peter's ear, and they quickly left the courtyard.

"They have him," Philip explained to the others, "and they're trying him for subversion. We're too late to save him. The best we can do now is save ourselves."

"We're not too late!" Peter pleaded. "They'll be taking him from here to Herod's palace. We can attack the guards on their way and rescue him. Then we'll all escape to Galilee together."

"That's a suicide mission, Peter!" Nathaniel said. "They are soldiers and too heavily armed. And what are we? Fishermen and farmers with a few knives and clubs between us. We won't save Jesus. We'll get him killed and us with him."

"Didn't we say, on the road to Jerusalem, that we would die with him here, if necessary?" Thomas asked. "Didn't we commit to him completely as our Lord? I agree with Peter. We should fight."

"I agree," said James. "We can lie in ambush for them. Perhaps the element of surprise will give us the advantage we need."

"And where would we set an ambush in the city?" John said. "This is madness! Even if we were successful in overtaking the guards, we have no chance of escaping Herod's soldiers or the Roman Army. They would have us before we made it outside the city gate."

"Have any of you considered that, maybe, Jesus doesn't want to escape?" Andrew asked sadly. "Didn't he tell us time and time again, that this would take place? That he would die and then rise up to victory?"

"And haven't we said time and time again that he couldn't be speaking of his literal death, Andrew? Jesus teaches us truth through mysterious parables. We don't yet understand this truth. But how can a dead man rise to lead us to victory? How can a dead man save us?"

"I have seen the dead rise to life by his hand. So have you."

"And whose hand will raise Jesus, if he dies?" Philip asked.

"I believe in him," Andrew said.

"We believe in him too, Andrew," said James. "That's why we must rescue him. Then he'll teach us the meaning of this saying. We'll know the truth."

"This is over," Bartholomew said. "Whatever Jesus' plans were, Judas's betrayal put an end to them. We're no match for the guards alone, and the people won't follow us. Jesus will be either imprisoned or executed, and us along with him if we interfere. We can't save him. We can only save ourselves. We should go home to our families."

"That's it, then?" Peter asked. "We're going to desert Jesus?"

"No, no one is deserting Jesus," Thomas said. "It's true we're no match for the guards, and the people won't follow us with Jesus under arrest. But we're all staying in Jerusalem. Jesus has been in tight situations before. He may yet have a move to make, and we need to be here to support him if he does. We're all staying to see how this plays out."

The guards brought Jesus bound before the council. They were seated in two rows in a semicircle pattern at the front of the room. Caiaphas sat in the center chair, which was slightly elevated by a platform. Jesus was placed directly in front of Caiaphas, who eyed him with both pleasure and contempt. Using his left thumb and index finger, the high priest slowly twirled a giant jeweled ring around the middle finger of his right hand. Finally, he said, "You are charged with blasphemy against God and plotting to overthrow the king and the emperor. What do you have to say for yourself?"

"Why do you ask me this?" Jesus questioned. "I have spoken openly among the people in the synagogues and the Temple. Ask them if I have spoken anything but the word of God. You yourselves heard me speak, yet you did not arrest me for any crime."

"Because we were biding our time, gathering evidence against you."

"You have no evidence against me. Otherwise, you would have arrested me in the daylight, while the people were with me, instead of at night, in secret."

One of the guards standing beside Jesus struck him across the face. "Is that how you answer the high priest? Watch your tongue, prisoner!"

"If I have spoken falsely, then testify to the wrong. Who is bringing this evidence against me?"

"The council brings the evidence against you. But we have witnesses to your sins, and we will hear them again in your presence. Bring the witnesses forward!" Caiaphas ordered.

Three men were escorted by the guards from the back of the room. They stood before Caiaphas.

"Speak your testimony," the high priest said.

"This man said that he would destroy the Temple of God, taking it down stone by stone," said one of the men, pointing at Jesus.

"And," lied another, "he said he would overthrow Herod and become Israel's next king!"

"Is this true?" Caiaphas asked, with rehearsed concern. "Did you say these things?"

"These men have said so," Jesus replied.

Caiaphas turned his jeweled ring to the inside of his hand and slapped Jesus across the face. Blood trickled from the wound on his cheek.

"I ask *you*!" Caiaphas shouted, rising to his feet. "I want to hear it from *you*! Tell us the truth!"

"I have told you the truth, but you will not listen," Jesus replied. "Why should I tell you again?"

Caiaphas sat back down and pointed to the third witness. "You," he said. "What is your testimony?"

"Uh..." the man said, caught off guard.

The witness next to him quickly whispered something in his ear.

"Oh, yeah. This man said to us that he was God's Son."

Caiaphas shot back in his chair, again in apparent shock at hearing what he had paid the witnesses to say.

"Is this true? Are you claiming to be the Son of God?"

"I am," Jesus said.

"Ohhh!" Caiaphas cried out in exaggerated despair, closing his eyes and tearing his tunic as a sign of lament and grief. "Must we hear any more of this?" he asked, as if another word would break his heart in two. "What further testimony do we need? It is blasphemy, and you have heard it from his lips! Guards! Take this man away while we consider his fate."

The now-emboldened guards were rough with Jesus as they pushed him from the room. One of them kicked him hard on the back of his thigh, almost causing him to fall. Another stuck the point of his spear an inch into Jesus' back, and he winced in pain.

When they were gone, Caiaphas addressed the council. "I ask you again: What more testimony do we need? The man is a blasphemer and an insurrectionist. He is a danger to our nation and our faith. Will you condemn him and send him to Herod?"

"Maybe we should leave him alone," one council member whispered to another in jest. "He could be no worse a king than Herod."

Caiaphas saw the two men chuckling. "This is no laughing matter, brothers. This man is a serious threat to our authority. He must be dealt with expediently and harshly."

"I am not so sure he is a threat to us, or that he is a bad man at all," said Nicodemus. "We know these witnesses are liars. They have twisted his words to make him guilty of things he has not said or done. If he is dangerous, we should not have to trump up charges against him. Bring forward real evidence of his crimes. Which one of us can speak a truth against him?"

"Dear Nicodemus," Caiaphas said gently, with a sneer. "We know that you are one of his misguided disciples. We know that you have eaten with him and have sat at his feet, listening to his false teachings. You have been blinded, as the people have been blinded, by this devil's deceptions, but I say to you again, be careful, my friend. Do not defend him too adamantly, or you may find yourself beside him before Herod."

"Do not threaten me, Caiaphas. I have as much voice and authority on this council as you."

"Indeed," Caiaphas said, "but we each have only one voice. It is the council's majority voice that carries the ultimate authority and will render a decision on Jesus."

"Fine. Then if you have firsthand evidence condemning Jesus, speak of his offenses."

"I can speak of his offenses. He heals on the Sabbath. He disregards our purity laws. He encourages the people to insurrection. He speaks against our Temple authority, and not just ours, but Herod and Caesar's as well."

"Since when have you come to love Herod or Caesar?" Nicodemus asked.

Caiaphas ignored the question and continued. "But I do not have to speak against him. He has spoken against himself. Did he not say that he was the Son of God? Did you not hear this from his mouth?" Caiaphas waited to let his question sink in and allow the council members to recall Jesus' unexpected but fortuitous words. Then, for emphasis, Caiaphas recalled the exchange for them. "I asked him if he were the Son of God. I gave him the opportunity to deny this, to say no, but he said, 'I am.' He has condemned himself with this blasphemy."

All the council members, including Nicodemus, dropped their heads to consider Caiaphas's words.

"I believe he is an innocent man," Nicodemus said, defeated.

"He is not innocent, Nicodemus," Caiaphas said. "He challenges Temple authority—*our* authority. He is leading the people astray from the ways of Israel. He is calling for a new kingdom and a revolt against the emperor. If he is not stopped, the Romans will destroy us."

"You say this," Nicodemus argued, "but is the messiah not to deliver us from the hands of the Romans and restore the kingdom of Israel? Do the scriptures not teach this? How can a man say the things he has said and do the things he has done apart from God? Will we condemn another of God's prophets?"

"He is no prophet, Nicodemus. Your fears cloud your thinking. But prophet or not, is it not better for one man to die for the sake of a whole nation?"

"I cannot condemn him," Nicodemus said.

"Nor I," said another council member named Joseph.

"Then that is your vote," Caiaphas replied. "And the rest of you? What do you say about the crimes of blasphemy and insurrection brought against Jesus? How do you vote?"

One by one, each of the other council members voiced a vote of guilty against Jesus.

"Good," said Caiaphas. "It is done." He called the chief of the Temple guards before him. "Take Jesus to Herod and tell him the council has found him guilty of his crimes."

Judas rose from his knees after asking God, again, to forgive him for the thing he had done, and for the thing he was about to do. Earlier, he had made his way through the valley and up to the Mount of Olives where he had been with Jesus so many times. He remembered it as a peaceful place, and he desperately needed peace, but this time he found none. Instead, anguish filled his broken heart, and tears filled his eyes, as he considered his great sin, his shame, and his friend. Not only had he failed his master, he had betrayed him. He looked out over the valley toward Jerusalem, imagining what could be happening to Jesus at this hour. He carefully tied one end of the rope to the trunk of the tree and then threw the other end over a limb that protruded out over a ledge. He used his staff to fish the rope back to him, made a noose, and tightened it around his neck. After one last prayer for forgiveness, he closed his eyes and launched himself over the edge of the cliff. He felt a jolt as the rope went taut, then searing pain. The last thing he heard was the crack of his neck as the noose's knot struck against the side of his face. There was blackness…and then nothingness.

Herod had been quite agitated by Caiaphas's delay in delivering Jesus, but now that the man was finally standing before him, he was both pleased and disappointed. He'd heard of all the signs Jesus had done and for a long time had wanted to meet him, to test him and see if all he'd heard was true. Instead, what he saw in Jesus was a defeated man, bound and bleeding and weak. He was smaller than Herod imagined. "So you are the one who would have my kingdom."

"I have no desire for your kingdom or any earthly kingdom. I seek only the kingdom of God."

"You would usurp even the kingship of God?"

"Not usurp it, but I have been appointed by God to bring his kingdom to fulfillment."

"Israel *is* God's kingdom!" Herod replied defensively. "And *I* have been appointed by God as its king!"

"Caesar has appointed you king. Not God." When Jesus said this, the guard standing next to him knocked him to the ground.

"Stop!" Herod shouted. "Stand him up and unbind him."

The guard helped Jesus to his feet and used his sword to cut the ropes from Jesus' hands.

"Look at yourself," Herod continued, "and look at me. It is *you* who stand before *me*. It is *I* who occupies a palace and dresses in royal robes. It is *I* with soldiers at my command and the riches of the nation at my disposal. You live in the desert with wild animals and wear the dirty and tattered clothes of a peasant. You have no money and no army, except the misguided weaklings that follow you. And where are they now? They have deserted you. So speak to me, O King. Where is your kingdom? Where are your subjects? Who bows before you and fears you?"

Jesus did not speak.

"I am intrigued, though," Herod said, with an amused grin. "I have heard of the many miracles you have performed, the signs you have done. Do something here in my presence to convince me you are from God, and I will let you live. Call down fire from heaven and strike down the guards beside you."

The guards winced and took a step away from Jesus.

"Show me a sign from God that you are his king, and I will bow before you."

Jesus said nothing and kept his eyes pointed at the floor.

"You are a disappointment," Herod said, almost sadly. "And you are a charlatan, but you are no threat to my kingship and hardly worth my executioner's sword.

"Send him back to Caiaphas," he instructed the guards. "Tell him to send Jesus to Pilate if he wishes to charge him with insurrection."

The guards bound Jesus' hands again and led him away.

Caiaphas was angered by Herod's message, but he was not about to let Jesus escape the judgment of the council. He ordered the guards to chain Jesus and place him in a cellar room of the house, reserved for prisoners.

Peter and Philip had followed Jesus and the guards to Herod's palace and back to Caiaphas's house. They entered the courtyard again and began to question the people there to see if they could learn anything more concerning the fate of Jesus.

"We saw the guards take him to the prison cellar," one of the servants said. "The man is doomed. The council has condemned him, and they will deal with him as soon as Passover has ended. Herod probably sent him back here to await execution. Why do you care so much about him, anyway?"

"I'll tell you why," interrupted the same servant girl who had recognized them earlier. "These are two of his disciples. Can't you hear this one's Galilean accent?" She pointed at Peter.

"You are out of your mind, woman!" Peter said, almost shouting. "I have told you, I don't know the man!" It was almost dawn, and when he said this, Peter heard a rooster crowing at the sky's breaking light. Then he remembered Jesus' words. *Before the cock crows at the next dawn, you will deny me three times.* Twice earlier, and now a third time, he had denied knowing Jesus. His teacher's prediction about him had come true. Peter's heart dropped into his stomach, and he began to weep. He had forsaken his Lord. He was no better than Judas. He ran from the courtyard, guilty and ashamed.

Caiaphas awoke after a short and fitful sleep. He ate breakfast and then called for the guards to ready Jesus for the trip to Pilate's palace.

When Pilate heard that the high priest was asking to see him, he sighed in disgust. He didn't like Caiaphas. He thought him to be a self-righteous and arrogant bore, constantly demanding his time and energy over silly matters he couldn't care less about. What was it this time? Some complaint about a violation of "Jewish rights" or disrespect for their religious laws? He bent over backward trying to appease these stubborn and superstitious people, but they seemed forever discontented. As far as he was concerned, they had no rights, except what the emperor allowed them, and, for some inexplicable reason, Caesar allowed them much. Pilate longed for the day when he would be called back to Rome or, at least, to some more civilized post in the empire.

"Send him in," Pilate said, hoping to deal with Caiaphas quickly and then move on to a better rest of the day. He was surprised when Caiaphas entered the room with a man stumbling behind him and flanked by four Temple guards. It was obvious the man had been beaten. He had dried blood on his face and clothes. "What is the meaning of this, Caiaphas? Who is this man, and why has he been beaten?"

"He is a criminal, sir, and he threatens the peace of Rome. He was injured by the guards when he resisted arrest."

"And how does this man threaten the peace of Rome?" Pilate asked, thinking the biggest threat to *his* peace was Caiaphas himself.

"He is an enemy of Caesar. That is why we have brought him to you."

"I ask you again," Pilate said, aggravated. "What is his crime?"

"We found this man perverting our nation, forbidding us to pay taxes to the emperor, and saying that he was the King of Israel."

"You have a king, don't you?" Pilate asked, referring to Herod, whom he also disliked.

"We have no king," Caiaphas said sharply. "Herod is the emperor's appointed prelate, who fancies himself a king. We have no ruler, except Caesar."

Pilate felt a bit of vomit rise in his throat. He knew the Jews despised Caesar. Caiaphas's false show of allegiance and respect toward the emperor sickened him. "State your business, Caiaphas. What do you want of me?"

"Sir!" Caiaphas exclaimed in disbelief. "I have just told you this man is an enemy of Caesar. He is leading the people to insurrection against Rome!"

Pilate looked at the disheveled man standing before him. He seemed disoriented and completely unaware of the conversation taking place. "Well?" he asked Jesus. "Are you an enemy of Rome? Are you the King of the Jews?"

Jesus lifted his head and looked at Pilate. "They say so. You say so."

"I have said nothing!" Pilate demanded. "I am asking you a question!"

Jesus lowered his head again and did not speak.

Pilate studied Jesus for a moment. "Leave him with me," he said.

"But, sir," Caiaphas pleaded, "we have brought you this man and our accusations against him. We demand that you judge him!"

"You do not make demands of me, Caiaphas!" Pilate shouted. "Wait outside. I will question the prisoner privately."

Caiaphas stared at Pilate angrily, then turned in a huff and left the room, the guards following.

When they were gone, Pilate called for a chair for Jesus, who sat down, wearily. He ordered that Jesus' hands be untied, then he poured a cup of water and handed it to him. Jesus drank.

"I do not wish to harm you," Pilate said. "You do not look like a revolutionary to me, and I have heard of no riots or uprisings among the people, at least, not lately. I know Caiaphas. He is an over-pious pig. You have probably threatened his authority in some way, and he has hatched a scheme to be rid of you. But you must talk to me if you want me to help you. Now, tell me, are you calling Israel to revolt against Rome? Do you aspire to be king and overthrow Herod, Caesar's choice for prelate?"

"Are you saying these things about me?" Jesus asked.

"Goddammit! I am not saying anything! I am asking! Just tell me the charges against you are false, and I will release you! Do you not know that I have the power of life and death over you?"

"You have no power over me except that which my heavenly Father gives you. What has come to pass has come because it is God's will.

What will be will be. And this is the will of the One who sent me: that the Son of Man be delivered up to death and rise again."

"I do not understand," Pilate said. "Are you a king, or do you claim to be a god?"

"My kingdom is not of this world. If it was, my followers would fight to rescue me, but I will tell you this: I am a king, but not of this earth. It is a heavenly kingdom."

Pilate was confused. "Speak to me plainly. Are you a threat to the kingdom and peace of Rome?"

"Do you not think if I ask it of my Father, he would send angels to protect and deliver me from my enemies?"

"Am I your enemy?"

"I say this to you: I have come into the world to testify to the truth. Everyone who belongs to the truth listens to my voice and believes my words."

"Truth?" Pilate asked, almost dismissively. "Tell me, what is truth, really?"

Jesus said no more and Pilate asked no more questions of him, but, in thoughtful silence, he studied the man. After a moment, he rose and ordered the guards to bring Jesus something to eat, while he retired to his quarters for his own meal.

As he ate, he told his wife about the strange interrogation. "There is something about him," he said. "There is something about this whole episode that intrigues me and causes me great concern."

"I, too, have concerns about this man," Pilate's wife said. "I had a worrisome dream about him last night. I believe he is innocent of the charges they bring against him. Do not be complicit in their plot to kill him. Do not condemn him."

"I do not wish to condemn him," Pilate said, "but he will not talk to me. He speaks in riddles I do not understand. He says what is to be is to be. That it is his god's will."

"Nevertheless, do not convict him of these crimes. They are false. I have a bad feeling about this day. I fear for you if this man dies."

"Am I a Jew?" Pilate asked. "I am the Roman governor of this land. My fate is not determined by the superstitions of these stiff-necked people or their god. Jesus is right about one thing: What will be, will be. And I will decide what will be in this matter. I will have Jesus whipped to placate his accusers. Then I will release him."

When Pilate returned to where Jesus was, he brought him out on the palace steps to render his judgment. He was surprised to see such a large crowd gathered, no doubt, summoned there by Caiaphas and the other priests and Temple leaders to show solidarity against Jesus. The Jewish people were a genuine thorn in his side. He wished again for the day when he would be reassigned to some other territory and rid of them forever.

He shouted out to the crowd. "Your leaders brought me this man as one who was perverting your people and a threat to Rome. I have examined him, and I have not found him guilty of any of the charges brought against him. I will therefore have him flogged, and release him."

The crowd, who had already been prepared by the authorities, in case Pilate reached such a verdict, began to jeer and protest the sentence.

"He must be crucified!" Caiaphas shouted.

"Crucify! Crucify him!" responded the coached crowd.

"But he has done nothing to deserve death," Pilate replied.

The crowd began to chant in unison, "Crucify! Crucify! Crucify!"

This was not going as Pilate had planned. Concerned, he raised his hands to quiet the crowd. "Your leaders deceive you," he shouted. "I am telling you that I have questioned the prisoner, and he has committed no crime deserving death."

"No?" shouted Caiaphas. "We have a law against blasphemy! And according to that law, he should die because he claims to be the Son of God."

The crowd erupted with disdain against Jesus and began repeating their chant. "Crucify! Crucify! Crucify!"

When Pilate heard this, he became afraid, sensing a riot. Hundreds more, upon hearing the commotion at the palace courtyard, had swelled the crowd and were joining in the call for Jesus' execution. Pilate finally raised his arms again to calm the people so he could speak. "If you want Jesus crucified, then take him and crucify him yourselves!"

"We cannot put anyone to death during Passover," Caiaphas shouted, as the designated spokesman for the crowd.

"And Passover ends at dusk. You can come for him tomorrow." As Pilate said this, he was thinking he might seize the opportunity to have his soldiers whisk Jesus out of Jerusalem and away during the dark of night, putting an end to the madness.

"He must die today! You are no friend of Caesar if you do not condemn this insurrectionist!"

The crowd cheered Caiaphas's demand.

Pilate was already less than a favorite among Caesar's governors, partly due to the continual unrest in Judea. If word of another riot got back to the emperor—a riot caused by Pilate's defense of a criminal—there would be hell to pay. His wife's prophecy was proving true. This day was not going well for him. And he was done with it. He called for one of the servants to bring a bowl of water. Again, he raised his arms to quiet the crowd.

"Very well," he shouted. "You want this man condemned? He is condemned, but, see, I am washing my hands of this. I am innocent of this man's blood!" He dipped his hands in the water, wiped them with a towel and tossed it to the floor.

"His blood be upon us and upon our children!" Caiaphas shouted.

The crowd erupted again.

"Take him," Pilate said to the soldiers. He briefly made eye contact with Jesus. He saw both pity and forgiveness. He remembered Jesus' words—*What will be will be*—and he walked back into the palace, ashamed.

Chapter 8
Jesus' Crucifixion

The soldiers took Jesus to the prison yard and stripped him naked, except for his undergarment. They tied him to a post and flogged his back and legs with a cat-o-nine-tails (a leather whip with shards of metal attached to its nine ends). With each lash, the sharp metal tore into Jesus' flesh, causing him to cry out in pain. When they had finished, he was a bloody mess. They made a crown of caper vines and pressed it down on his head. The fishhook briers bit into his scalp like serpent's teeth, and every movement caused the thorns to dig deeper into the skin. The soldiers threw a dirty blanket over his shoulders and put a stick in his hand.

"There is your robe, O King, and there is your scepter. All hail, Jesus, King of the Jews!"

They all laughed at him and mocked him. They kicked and hit him and spat on his face.

"Prophesy to us, O King. Who is it that hit you this time?" they would ask, as they took turns striking him.

Finally, they brought a cross and threw it on top of him, almost knocking him unconscious.

"Get up!" one of them demanded, kicking at his legs. "You are late for your appointment on the hill, and your guests are waiting."

Jesus struggled to his feet and began to limp toward the gate.

"Wait!" said the soldier. "You are forgetting your cross. Do you expect someone to carry it for you?"

Jesus stumbled back and tried to pick up the cross, but, in his weakened state, it was too heavy for him.

"Your Majesty, allow us to help you," the chief soldier said, with a sarcastic smirk. He motioned to two other soldiers, who lifted the cross and dropped it onto Jesus' shoulders.

Jesus' knees almost buckled under the weight, but he managed to keep his feet beneath him. He balanced himself and winced with pain as he shifted the cross on his shredded back and shoulders. He shuffled his feet forward, dragging the cross along with him. He staggered along the cobblestone streets, lined with people—some of them crying, others laughing and insulting him—until all his strength left him. Then he crashed down hard with the cross landing on top of him, pushing his face into the pavement. His mouth and nose were bloodied. Despite the stinging whips of the soldiers and their commands for him to get up, he couldn't move. Finally, impatiently wanting to get on with the task at hand, they lifted the cross off of Jesus and raised him to his feet. They conscripted a couple of men from the crowd to carry Jesus' cross for him. When they reached the base of the hill, Jesus collapsed again. They kicked and whipped him, but he couldn't stand. Then, at the leader's command, two of the soldiers grabbed Jesus by his arms and dragged him the rest of the way to the place of execution.

At the top of the hill, they laid Jesus on the cross. Some of the soldiers stretched his arms out over the cross bar while another nailed his hands to the wood. Then they placed his feet, one on top of the other, and nailed them to the cross as well. They lifted the cross up and let it drop into a pre-dug hole. It landed with a thud, causing Jesus' flesh to tear against the nails. He screamed in pain. One of the soldiers placed a ladder against Jesus' cross and, climbing it, nailed a sign above his head that said, JESUS, KING OF THE JEWS. The soldiers laughed at this, but the priests and Temple leaders who were with them were indignant.

"Take the sign down!" one of them insisted. "It is an insult to us. It should not say he *is* King of the Jews but that he claimed to be King of the Jews."

"It says what it says," the chief soldier replied rudely. "Take the ladder down. The sign will stay."

It was about ten o'clock in the morning when Jesus was crucified. Two others were crucified with him, both guilty of robbery and other violent crimes. There were many from Jerusalem who had come to witness the crucifixions, and the Temple leaders decided to take the opportunity to decry Jesus a final time, exposing him as a charlatan and fraud. They had been right about him all along, and the people needed to know it.

"There he is!" said one of the priests smugly. "This is the ultimate end for all who would blaspheme the faith of Israel. You, who would destroy the Temple and its leadership, save yourself!"

"Yes," said a Pharisee, "you say you can save others; then save yourself! Come down from the cross, if you are the Son of God!"

"Yes, King Jesus," mocked another. "Come down now, and we will believe in you!"

They all shook their heads and laughed. They picked up dirt and gravel from the ground and threw it at Jesus.

Some who were his followers, including Mary, his mother, and Mary Magdalene and John, his disciple, were sitting at the foot of the cross, weeping. Jesus looked down at them.

"Where are the others?" he asked, between anguished breaths.

"I sat watch with them all night outside Caiaphas' house," John said. "When the guards moved you from there to Pilate's palace, we were all following, but later, when I turned to look for them, they were gone. They must have fallen behind. I haven't seen them since."

"They didn't fall behind," Jesus said, grimacing. "They ran away. You are brave, John. The others have faltered during the time of trial. They are afraid, but they will find their courage."

Jesus looked at his mother lovingly and then nodded toward John. "Woman, this is now your son."

Then he said to John, "Behold, this is now your mother."

Mary and John embraced and wept in each other's arms.

"Mary," he said to Mary Magdalene, "do you love me?"

"I do love you. I have always loved you. I *will* always love you."

"Do you believe and understand who I am?"

"I do," she said through her tears.

Jesus smiled. "You will be the first to see me when I return. You will be the first disciple and witness of the resurrected Lord."

"You are dying," said one of the men hanging next to him. "We are all dying! A man cannot return from the dead. But, if you are the messiah, then save us all, while we are still in this life."

"Shut your mouth!" scolded the man on the other side of Jesus. "Have you no fear of God? We're here as just desserts for our sins, and our condemnation is righteous for the deeds we've done. But this man has done nothing wrong. His condemnation is the sin."

Then he said to Jesus, "Lord, remember me and forgive me when you come into your kingdom."

Jesus looked at him. "I promise you that this very day, you will be with me in paradise."

It was about noon when a strong wind began to blow, kicking up dust from the ground. Suddenly, the sky was filled with clouds, and the day turned dark as night. The people, expecting a storm, scurried away toward the city for shelter.

The chief soldier, a centurion of the Roman guard, ordered his men to gather their equipment and return to the palace. "You and you, stay with me," he said to the two soldiers closest to him. "We will remain until these men are dead."

The women and John also remained there, grieving at the foot of Jesus' cross. They huddled together, covering their eyes with their garments to protect them from the dust and sand in the air.

From another hill, a distance away, ten frightened and heartbroken men had watched all these things take place. The original disciples of Jesus had returned to their Garden of Gethsemane camp, and from a vantage point at the edge of that hill, they could see Golgotha, the place of execution. Even, now, in the darkness, they could see the silhouette of the three crosses, Jesus' in the middle. They wanted to go to him. They wanted to be with him and the others there, but they were afraid. Peter had already been recognized as one of Jesus' disciples and, now, they feared being arrested themselves as accomplices and co-conspirators of Jesus. Only John and the women had remained faithful to Jesus. They had all deserted him, just as Jesus had predicted they would. The *women* had remained faithful—the *women*—and they had run. What cowards they all were.

Suddenly, they heard Jesus cry out. It was faint from where they were standing but clear and blood-curdling just the same. Peter repeated the words as they echoed in his head. *My God! My God! Why have you forsaken me?* He covered his face with his hands and wept.

At three in the afternoon, the wind ceased. It was still dark, and there were rumblings of thunder in the clouds.

The centurion suddenly became quite anxious. "Check the bodies," he said to his soldiers. "See if they are still breathing."

The soldiers rose and checked the men on either side of Jesus. "These two are dead," one of them said.

"And the one in the middle?" the centurion asked.

One of the soldiers picked up a stick and prodded Jesus' leg. Jesus stirred slightly. "Good as dead," the soldier said, "but, still, he seems to have breath in him."

The centurion sighed, as he looked up at the dark sky. The churning and angry clouds appeared to be descending upon them, readying to swallow them up. "Finish him!" he ordered fearfully.

The soldier took his spear and shoved it through Jesus' side into his lung. A short hiss of air came from the wound. Jesus didn't move. "If he wasn't already dead, he is now," the soldier reported.

A lump grew in the centurion's throat as he looked up at Jesus. Despair filled his soul. He fell to his knees.

"Sir?" the soldier asked. "Are you all right?"

The centurion shook his head. "We blew it," he muttered.

"Sir?" the soldier repeated.

"We have sinned against the God of the Jews," the centurion said. "For, truly, this was his son."

At that moment, the clouds engulfed them. Blinding lightning bolts and deafening thunderclaps filled the air. An earthquake shook all of Israel, and many of the buildings in Jerusalem collapsed. Huge chunks of the Temple walls fell in on themselves, and the curtain of the sanctuary was torn in two. When it was over, the frightened soldiers hurried back to the palace, but John and the women remained there with Jesus, wailing and beating their chests in lament for their dead master.

There was a man named Joseph, from Arimathea, who was a member of the Temple council. Like Nicodemus, he believed in Jesus and had argued on Jesus' behalf that he was an innocent man. Joseph was also a rich man and had influence with the Roman court. He went to Pilate and asked if he might take the body of Jesus and have it buried before dusk, the start of the Sabbath. Pilate granted his request, and so he and Nicodemus went to the hill, and, along with the others there, they lowered Jesus from the cross and wrapped him in a clean linen cloth. They carried him to a nearby cemetery, where Joseph had a new tomb hewn out of rock for his own burial place, and there they laid Jesus.

Together, they rolled the huge capstone in place to seal the tomb's entrance. It was almost dusk when they finished their work, so they all went home to observe the ritual of Sabbath rest.

Chapter 4
Jesus' Resurrection

Early, before sunrise on Sunday, Mary Magdalene awoke, dressed in her black mourning tunic and veil, and went to the tomb to be with Jesus. This was the third and last day that his spirit would linger nearby before giving up hope of reuniting with the body and going on to heaven, or to God, or to wherever it is that spirits go when their earthly unions with the flesh are done. She knew others would come to mourn with her, but she wanted this early morning time to be alone with her beloved Jesus.

The cemetery where Jesus was laid was part of a beautiful garden, filled with olive and sycamore trees, and blooming shrubs and flowers. Mary stopped along the way, picking some of the flowers as a bouquet for Jesus' tomb. When she finally arrived at the tomb, she was startled to see that the stone placed to seal its entrance had been rolled away. Someone had arrived before her. But why were they inside? She went closer to the entrance and called out, but no one answered her. With some fear, she held her lamp in front of her and slowly made her way inside. The lamplight filled the interior of the small crypt, and her heart sank in despair. The tomb was empty. Not only was no one there attending to Jesus, but his body was gone! There was nothing, except the perfumed spices they had left beside the body and the neatly folded linen shroud in which Jesus had been wrapped.

Mary ran from the tomb, her head spinning. What had happened to him? Had robbers broken into the tomb and stolen his body away? And, if so, why had they left the valuable spices behind? It was almost dawn, and the new light was beginning to make the garden visible. She strained her eyes, scanning the landscape, looking for anyone or anything that might help her unravel this mystery and locate the body of her Lord. Suddenly, she saw a shadow of movement. It was a man moving through the early morning fog in front of her.

"Sir!" she called out, as she ran toward the darkish figure. "Please, sir," she said when she came to him. "They've taken my master's body away from his tomb. Can you tell me where I can find him?"

"Mary," he said kindly.

It was still too dark to recognize his face, but when she heard his voice she knew him. "My Lord!" she exclaimed, as she fell at his feet and wrapped her arms around him.

"Do not hold on to me, Mary," Jesus said, "for I have not yet been made whole, but go and tell the others that I have risen, and am ascending to my Father and your God. Tell them to go back to Galilee, and I will meet them there."

When he had said this, he disappeared before her eyes, and she was astonished and afraid. She walked back toward the tomb, weeping, believing she had seen a ghost.

Just then, an angel appeared above the entrance to the tomb and said to her, "Woman, why are you weeping, and why do you tarry at this empty tomb? Jesus is not here. He is risen. Now go and do as he has told you, and announce the good news to the disciples."

Mary ran all the way back to the house where the disciples were staying and told them all that she had seen and heard, but the men were incredulous and supposed that Mary was mad with grief.

"Go and see for yourselves, then," Mary said.

Peter and John looked at each other. "Didn't he say this very thing?" asked John, excitedly. "Didn't he tell us that he would rise from the dead?" John leapt up and ran for the door with Peter close on his heels. They didn't stop running until they reached the tomb. They went inside and found it just as Mary had said.

"It's true!" John said excitedly. "The Lord has risen, just as Mary told us!"

"It's true that the tomb is empty," Peter said skeptically, "but I'm not sure we can make anything more of it than that. I want to believe. I want Jesus to be alive, but we saw him die. How do we know this isn't some cruel joke perpetrated by the Romans? How do we know that this isn't the work of grave robbers or even some of his own followers to strike fear in the hearts of Jesus' enemies?"

"Have you forgotten Lazarus?" asked John. "And the man in Nain? If he can raise others, surely, he can raise himself!"

"I don't know those men were dead. Perhaps they were only sleeping—sick and unconscious."

"Come on, Peter! Seriously? You do know! Are you suddenly a doubter of Jesus as the messiah?"

"I don't know what I believe anymore!" Peter shouted in desperation, "Except that Jesus wasn't supposed to die. And, yes, I am a doubter that the dead can raise the dead! I will not let a grief-stricken heart overrule a rational mind! I'm going home!"

They went back to the place where they were staying, but they didn't go home. They decided it best to stay in hiding for a week or so, and then to sneak out of Jerusalem, unnoticed, and return to Galilee.

A few days later, the disciples were gathered together. The doors of the place where they were staying were locked, for fear of the authorities, who were searching for them. The Temple leaders had been informed of the empty tomb and rumors were rampant in Jerusalem that Jesus had been raised from the dead. They had sent their guards throughout the city to find the disciples and bring them in for questioning. They believed Jesus' disciples had stolen his body away in an effort to incite the people against them. If this was so, then the disciples were guilty of collusion and perpetuating the blasphemy of Jesus. They would need to be tried and punished, as an example to the people of the consequences for such actions.

The eleven disciples and Mary Magdalene and Mary, the mother of Jesus, were in hiding together. They were running low on food and supplies, so Thomas had volunteered to go out of the house and buy what was needed to get them through the next couple of days until they could make their escape out of the city.

Suddenly, though the doors and windows were locked, Jesus stood among them, and said, "Peace be with you."

They were all shocked and afraid and fell to their knees.

Peter said to him, "Forgive me, Lord, for deserting you! Forgive my faithlessness!"

Jesus reached out and placed his hand on Peter's head. "You are faithful now, Peter. And, I tell you, I will build my kingdom on such faith."

He lifted Peter to his feet, and the others slowly stood as well and gathered around him, weeping for joy. He spoke to them for a while, reminding them of all he had said to them and how all that he had told them, and all that the scriptures had predicted, had taken place. "But why are you still in Jerusalem?" Jesus asked. "Why didn't you go on to Galilee as I instructed you?"

No one spoke for a moment. Then Peter said, "We were afraid... and we doubted. We didn't believe."

"Believe in me, now," Jesus said, "From now on, you need fear nothing, not even death, for in my rising to life, I have defeated death and destroyed it forever.

"Stay here for one more day," Jesus said, "and then return to Galilee. I will meet you there." After he said this, he disappeared as suddenly as he had appeared. And the disciples were amazed.

When Thomas returned, the others told him about Jesus and all he had said to them. But Thomas didn't believe them.

"You are as crazy as Mary," Thomas said to Peter incredulously. "Look, I know you want to hope that what Mary said is true—that she saw Jesus alive. I understand what grief can do to people. It makes us see what we want to see, believe what we want to believe, but we all witnessed his crucifixion. So don't try and placate me with some tale of a ghost or a come-back-to-life, good-as-new Jesus. Until I see the mark of the nails in his hands and place my hand in the spear wound in his side, I won't believe any of this! Please, let me grieve the death of my master and friend, without these stupid stories of a risen Jesus."

That evening, as they were having supper, with the doors and windows shut and locked, Jesus appeared to them again.

"Thomas...do you doubt?" asked Jesus. "Come. Place your fingers in the holes of my hands. Put your hand in the wound in my side. Do not doubt but believe. I am he, who was crucified and has risen."

Thomas stood, then fell to his knees at the feet of Jesus. "My Lord and my God!" he cried.

"Thomas, you finally believe because you have seen me, but blessed are those who have not seen and, yet, have come to believe."

Jesus sat at the table and ate with them, and all their hearts were filled with joy as he spoke to them. When supper was over, he instructed them, again, to rise in the morning and leave Jerusalem for the Sea of Galilee. "I will find you there," he told them. After he had said this, he disappeared before their eyes.

When morning came, the disciples left the city and began their journey back to Galilee.

The disciples and Mary Magdalene and Mary, the mother of Jesus, had been back in Capernaum for almost a week. Those who had homes there returned to them. The others stayed as their guests. Every day, they would gather at the house of Mary, Jesus' mother. They would walk together along the shore of the lake, and along the streets and in the surrounding hills, looking for Jesus, but he did not come to them.

Finally, after several days of waiting, Peter said to the others, "I'm going fishing."

"Why not?" Andrew agreed. "We might as well do something useful."

"We'll go too," the others said, and all of the men went to the dock and took one of the boats belonging to Peter and Andrew's father.

While they were fishing, a good way off shore, a man on the beach called out to them. "Children, have you any fish?"

"No," Peter called back. "The fishing isn't good today."

"Cast your net on the other side of the boat, and you will find some."

They hauled in the empty net and cast it on the opposite side of the boat. Suddenly, the net was so of full of fish they could hardly pull it in. Peter looked back at the man on the shore, and his heart soared.

"It is the Lord!" he said to the others. He dove into the water and began swimming toward Jesus.

The others managed to haul in the net and followed him in the boat. When they reached the shore, they saw that Jesus had started a charcoal fire and was cooking a few fish on it.

"Bring some of the fish you've caught, so we'll have enough to eat."

They did as they were told and placed some extra fish on the fire. Then they sat down. Jesus took a loaf of bread, broke it, and gave each of them a piece. When the fish were ready, they ate and talked for a long time about all the things that had happened to them during their time together.

Then Jesus told them about all the things that were to come—how they would each go their own way, taking the good news of the risen Christ to the people. He explained to them that they would be persecuted by nonbelievers and that many of them would die for the sake of the gospel and his name. "Do not be afraid, for the Spirit of God will be with you to guide you and give you strength in the days ahead."

After he had spoken all these words to them, he stood and said, "Follow me." He led them to the top of a hill, and there he instructed them a final time. "Begin in Jerusalem and go from there, preaching repentance and the forgiveness of sins to all nations. All authority on Earth and in heaven has been given to me, and I impart it to you. Go, therefore, into all the world, baptizing in the Name of the Father, and of the Son, and of the Holy Spirit. Teach the people everything that I have taught you, and to obey God's commandments. Remember I am with you always, even to the end of the ages."

When he had finished speaking, he raised his hands and blessed them, and, as he was blessing them, he began to rise up into the heavens.

The disciples watched him rise into the sky, growing smaller and smaller, until he ascended into the clouds and was gone.

"Holy crap!" whispered Peter.

"Holy crap!" the others repeated together.

One by one, the disciples wandered back down the trail toward Capernaum, none of them speaking a word. Finally, only Peter remained, staring up at the sky where he had last seen Jesus. The sun was sinking below the hills, and the day was at its end. Peter thought about Jesus, and the life of Jesus, and all of its meaning. He thought about his own life up to this moment and of all that might lie ahead. He wasn't afraid. He didn't feel alone. "Holy crap!" he said again, and he smiled and joyfully danced his way down the hill toward home.

Acknowledgements

Acknowledgement is given to *Traveling the Silk Road: Ancient Pathway to the Modern World*. (Sterling Signature, New York. 2011.) for information about camels as well as descriptions of the ancient trade routes and some of its cities. It should be noted, however, that while the qualities and attributes of places mentioned in this book are similar to real places (past or present) along the Silk Road, many of the cities named are purely fictitious.

My sincere thanks to my editor, Susan Giffin, for her patience, guidance, and good ideas, and for not flunking me in grammar and punctuation (or not telling me if she did).

To Robyn Lipscomb, Karel Ramsey and Cyndi Sheppeard, my advance readers, for their thoughts and suggestions.

To George Pejakovich, my geography guru; and to Connie Vosburgh and Kent Wingerson for answering evening calls to tell me which keys to push to make my computer behave.

To my family for allowing me a year's worth of holidays, off days, and our vacation time to virtually disappear into the private recesses of my basement office to complete this project. It's good to be back!

And, finally, to YOU for buying this book. I am grateful!

www.ingramcontent.com/pod-product-compliance
Lightning Source LLC
Chambersburg PA
CBHW030548260626
47157CB00006B/2224